BLACKWOOD MANOR

By:

Tina Cooke

Dedication

To my husband, whose unwavering support and love inspire me in every endeavor, and to all who believe that magic and mystery surround us—you only need to open your eyes to see.

TABLE OF CONTENTS

Chapter 1 1

    Ring, Ring ....

Chapter 2 11

    Memories Await ....

Chapter 3 20

    Ghostly Encounter ....

Chapter 4 26

    Fire in the Boathouse ....

Chapter 5 29

    Morning Deliveries ....

Chapter 6 32

    Email Horror ....

Chapter 7 36

    Road Trip ....

Chapter 8 42

    Dock Work ....

Chapter 9 46

    Gravely Suspicious ....

Chapter 10 49

    Mollys Find ....

Chapter 11 51

    Small Town Authority ....

Chapter 12 54

    For the Sake of Finger Prints ....

Chapter 13 66

    It was just a dream, or was it.....................................

Chapter 14 68

    Dinner is Served...

Chapter 15 73

    A Quiet Evening ....

Chapter 16 76

    The Key to More Mystery...

Chapter 17 86

   A Glimpse into The Past ....

Chapter 18 100

   A Day on The Beach ....

Chapter 19 129

   Thunder, Lightning, Shadows and Surprises ....

CHAPTER 20 142

   Clues in the Cabin ....

Chapter 21 144

   Sleepless Vigil ....

Chapter 22 145

   Morning Revelations ....

Chapter 23 150

   Hidden Clues ....

Chapter 24 154

   Awakening Rituals ....

Chapter 25 160

   The Mysterious Email ....

Chapter 26 166

   Lunch Time ....

Chapter 27 168

   Unexpected Guests ....

Chapter 28 177

   Ritual of Light ....

Chapter 29 179

   The Charged Circle ....

Chapter 30 187

   In the Bedroom ....

Chapter 31 191

   Discussion About Someone in the Basement ....

Chapter 32 194

   No Safe Haven ....

Chapter 33 197

   Morning Calm ....

Chapter 34 200

    Through the Looking Glass ....

Chapter 35 201

    Lost and Found ....

Chapter 36 205

    Pop In Visit ....

Chapter 37 211

    Experiments with a Portal ....

Chapter 38 214

    Secret Meeting ....

Chapter 39 223

    Closed case revisited...

Chapter 40 226

    Vigil for Ryan ....

Chapter 41 241

    Fear of the unknown ....

Chapter 42 244

    Bugs, bugs and more bugs ....

Chapter 43 253

    Echoes of an Argument..

Chapter 44 263

    Message from Mr. Davies....................................

Chapter 45 272

    Grandmother's Spell..

Chapter 46 279

    Night to Resolve ....

Chapter 47 288

    White-Eyed Woman...

Chapter 48 291

    Homecoming...

Chapter 49 293

    Mysterious Old Lady's Warning ....

Chapter 50 299

    Secrets in the Attic...

Chapter 51 304

    Sister's Power ....

Chapter 52 314

    Hair's Mystery ....

Chapter 53 321

    White eyes, screaming ....

Chapter: 54 327

    Doctor's Double ....

Chapter 55 351

    Noon Strike ....

Chapter 56 369

    Davies' Legacy ....

Chapter 57 374

    Blessed Be ....

Acknowledgment

My deepest gratitude goes to my family and friends for their unwavering belief in my talents and for their patience as they waited—sometimes for years—for this project to come to life. To my co-worker who gently nudged me to see it through to completion, you know who you are—thank you for the encouragement.

A heartfelt thanks as well to the incredible team at Callaghan Publications for their dedication, guidance, and hard work in helping me navigate this journey. I couldn't have done it without you all.

Chapter 1

Ring, Ring

Ring, Ring

"Hello?" A sleepy voice answered. Tara was still half asleep.

"Good morning. This is the front desk calling about your wake-up call." The too chipper of a voice was offensive to Tara's ears so early in the morning. How long had this person been awake? It just wasn't right that someone was that happy first thing in the morning. She looked at the clock on the bedside table that read 7:30 am. This was just cruel and torturous. She thought to herself.

"Thank you, I am up," Tara replied.

"Wonderful, Ms. Ward. Your breakfast will be served at 8:30," the front desk's voice said.

The receiver in her ear clicked and then buzzed. Tara lied there for a few minutes, listening to the buzz of the receiver in her ear, trying to muster the energy to keep her eyes open. She finally reached over and hung up the phone. She lied under the covers for a short while, looking at the sun, trying desperately to peak through the crack in the curtains. She wondered what today had in store for her and her sister.

Slowly, she climbed out of bed, opened the curtains to a bright cloudless sky, she stretched to the warmth of the sun that was beaming in through the window. She thought it best to get her sister up.

Carla was always a hard one to wake up. She seemed to need more time than most to get moving in the morning. Carla and Tara had adjoining rooms on the third floor of the Holiday Inn. Tara slipped her robe on and put her feet into her slippers. She shuffled over to the door and gave it a knock. The door opened immediately. To Tara's surprise, Carla was awake and wide awake.

"Why don't you shower and get yourself presentable while I pack my things, then I will come to your room, and we will have breakfast together," Carla suggested.

"Okay, sis," Tara responded.

Tara agreed through a couple of yawns and was still stunned that her sister was so wide awake and ready for the day. *"Who lit a fire under her this morning?"* She queried to herself.

Tara had just stepped out of the shower, and the phone was ringing. She ran to answer it.

"Hello? Ms. Ward" Front desk's phone.

"Yes," Tara replied.

"This is the front desk. We were just wondering if we could send up your breakfast now and if there was anything you might want to add to your menu before we did?" They read what was on the menu for that morning's breakfast.

- *Two plates of eggs, ham, home fries, rye toast buttered, jam on the side.*

- *A plate of mixed fruit, whipped cream*

- *Two glasses of orange juice*

- *One pot of coffee.*

"That sounds great, just the way it is, thank you," Tara replied.

"Wonderful, we will send it right up," the front desk's receptionist chimed.

Tara quickly got dressed and told Carla the breakfast was on its way. A few minutes later, Carla came in with her suitcase in tow. She had finished packing and placed both their bags next to the door.

"I am starving," Carla said as she rubbed her belly and then flopped on the bed. "You know, I just don't understand all this," she continued. "Everything has been shrouded in mystery ever since we received the news of Mom and Dad's plane going down." Carla stared at the ceiling.

"I feel the same way," Tara said, sharing her feelings.

Tara knew exactly what she meant. She didn't understand it either, and to be perfectly honest, she was a little uneasy about all this secrecy. Tara sat down on the bed beside her sister and told her how she felt. Carla seemed to relax some, knowing that she wasn't alone in her worries.

The two sisters sat in silence while eating their breakfast. Two papers came with their meal, and they were both reading the daily news. The silence was broken by a knock at the door. Tara wiped her mouth and went to answer it. Carla never budged or even looked up from her paper. On the other side of the door was a bellhop.

The bellhop said, "I have come to retrieve your bags, Ms. Ward. Your limo is here and waiting for you whenever you are ready." He politely reached for the bags and placed them on the golden trolley he had with him.

"Please tell the limo driver we will be down shortly," Tara said.
The bellhop nodded and left. Tara closed the door and went back to finish her breakfast.

"Gee, do you get the feeling we are being rushed?" Carla said sarcastically.

"I find this all so curious, don't you, Tara?" Carla asked, folding up her paper and placing it on the tray.

"Yes, but I'm sure all will be revealed soon enough. I hope." Tara was getting tired of all this secrecy. She figured if her parents were dead, why couldn't they tell us so we could mourn them properly, have a funeral then figure out how to move forward? Instead, they were rushed to the hotel the very next day. No one would answer any of their questions. All they kept saying was, "You will understand everything in a short time." Well, as far as she was concerned, time was up. She was really starting to get annoyed with all of this, but she didn't want her sister to know how she was feeling. It didn't take much to fuel Carla's fire, and with all the latest events, she didn't want to upset her any more than she could help.

The girls finished their breakfast, checked their rooms to make sure they didn't leave anything behind, and both headed out the door. Tara stopped at the front desk to hand in the keys. Sure enough, the limo was sitting right outside, waiting for them. It was the same driver who had brought them here two days ago. Mr. Davies, a man in his forties, was well-groomed, with dark hair cut short, casual clothes, bright teeth, and green eyes. He was a rather handsome man and looked nothing like a lawyer. He was also a family friend who had arranged everything for them according to their parents' wishes. He had been the one to tell them about their parents and to say it was important that they follow his rules and accept the oncoming changes and plans that had been made for them. He also mentioned that it was their parents' wish, and that he would explain what he could at a later date.

Mr. Davies greeted them as they stepped into the limo. It was a fair-sized limo, a little larger than the one they arrived at the hotel in.

Mr. Davies gave the driver instructions. Tara and Carla couldn't hear what he said. As Mr. Davies was talking to the driver, Tara thought to herself that she couldn't get over the fact that both she and her sister were adults, all of 20, and they were still being treated as if they were children who needed a glass house around them. "A glass house with tinted windows to protect them from onlookers." She remembered her mother saying that, as their parents, they had to protect them from the outside world, and one day, they would understand why. Tara figured it was because both she and her sister, being twins, had a gift that was unique to them. They could see the past, present, and future; they were psychics, and their parents didn't want people to abuse them for their gifts. Their mother was psychic as well and had worked with the police on many occasions to help find missing persons. Their father was a private eye, and the two often worked alongside each other.

Mr. Davies offered the girls some coffee. He poured while the girls fixed their own. The limo was really decked out in nice, soft black leather with curtains on the side windows. There was a TV and a bar in the back with a small fridge. The coffee was from a thermos that Mr. Davies had brought himself.

"Okay, now that we are on our way," Mr. Davies started but was interrupted by Carla. All of a sudden, her attitude changed. She was frowning, looking out the window with her arms crossed. She then looked—or shall I say, scowled—at Mr. Davies.

"Just where are we going anyway?" she demanded.

"You are going to stay at your grandparents' estate, Blackwood Manor, for a while," Mr. Davies continued. Trying not to show his impatience with Carla, he spoke in the same even tone he had started with.

"Then could you please tell me what is going on and why so much secrecy?" Carla asked.

"That is what I am trying to tell you. Now, if you will please let me explain," he said and reached into his briefcase. Carla crossed her legs and gave a big, exasperated sigh. Mr. Davies pulled out a report on the accident.

"You are going to tell us that we are in danger and that our parents' bodies were not found in the plane wreck." Tara was staring off into space as if she was reading something from outside the car.

"You also have proof that you know who may be behind this and that they may be after us," Tara continued, rubbing her temples. Carla knew by the look on her face that she was getting a vision. Tara always rubbed her temples when this happened. Tara once told her that they throbbed and pained. Carla herself never experienced such a physical aspect to her visions; however, when she experienced them, she blacked out. Mr. Davies just looked at Tara and then back to the papers in his hand. He then put them back in his briefcase.

"That's pretty much it," Mr. Davies said, bewildered.

"Your parents were right. You do have an outstanding gift," Mr. Davies said.

"Unfortunately, my gift is only good if I am in close proximity to the event," Tara said.

Tara looked down at her fingers in her lap and said nothing, but she couldn't help but think: if they had such a wonderful gift, then how come they couldn't see or even contact their parents? Both Carla and Tara had tried a few times the night before in the hotel room, but both came up with nothing. Tara's greatest fear, although she said nothing to her sister, was that their parents had crossed over, and it might be too soon to contact them in the spirit realm. Tara had never had any trouble contacting spirits before, and neither had Carla, as far as she knew. She was aware there was a waiting period, but how long it took for each person could vary, and she wasn't sure.

"Yeah, so we've been told," Carla replied curtly. Tara believed her sister's frustration stemmed from their failed attempts to contact their parents the night before.

"So, answer me some more questions," Carla said, sitting forward.

"What proof do you have? Did you catch the person responsible?" Carla shot a glance at Mr. Davies as she took a sip of her coffee.

Mr. Davies began to explain. He told them that their mother had been helping the police with an investigation into the disappearance of a famous writer, Anthony Keenan. He had gone out for his usual walk-through town, making all his regular stops except his last one—stopping for coffee at a local diner on the outskirts of town. He went there every morning before heading up the highway for his 2 km walk back to his house.

None of the townspeople saw anything; it was as if he just disappeared between stops. The waitress at the diner called his house to check if he was okay. It was unlike him to miss his daily walk. His wife answered and explained he was out walking and hadn't returned home yet. She was already getting ready to go look for him, as it was unusual for him to be so late.

His wife was worried. This wasn't like him at all; he was a very punctual man, and everyone in town knew you could set a clock by him. His wife thanked the waitress for calling and letting her know that he hadn't made his regular stop. The waitress felt bad for worrying Mrs. Keenan. Mrs. Keenan then contacted the local sheriff, who, after a lengthy search, contacted the police. Mr. Keenan was still missing.

"Your mother is a very reputable psychic," Mr. Davies said.

The police believed she was getting close to finding Mr. Keenan and that he had been taken to Maine, which was the last clue they received about his whereabouts. Your parents were on their way there to meet with the local police when their plane went down.

"Before your parents left, they gave me strict instructions regarding what should be done in the event of their demise." Mr. Davies hung his head.

He continued, "I didn't believe they were in danger. I thought they were just being cautious and putting their affairs in order, something they hadn't yet finalized."

Tara, now feeling anxious, asked, "What kind of danger do you think we are in?"

"I don't exactly know. We have investigators looking into it right now, but unfortunately, your parents weren't clear on the specifics," he said.

"Well, I don't feel warm and fuzzy about the information you've given us so far," Carla stated.

Mr. Davies tried to reassure the girls. "Look, I've known you and your parents since you were born. I am just as concerned about their whereabouts as you are and equally concerned about your safety. I'm following your parents' instructions to the letter. There's enough money to support you both for the rest of your lives and much more. They asked me to make sure you were well protected, and they felt your safety would be best secured at the estate."

Mr. Davies was clearly anxious. You could see he was upset by the whole situation, and it seemed he wasn't expecting the attitude from Carla. Carla just turned to stare out the window. Mr. Davies looked at Tara, who shrugged and said, "I think we're all under a lot of stress right now," as if she were apologizing for her sister's behavior. They sat in silence for a while. Mr. Davies thought to himself how hard this must be for them. The girls were very close to their parents growing up, unlike most teenagers. He decided to give them some space and was content with the quiet.

The driver's voice came over the PA system.

"We are fifteen minutes away now, sir." The voice had a distinct Australian accent, which was a pleasant surprise to hear, thought Tara.

Mr. Davies pressed a button on the console beside him. "Right, thank you, Paul." He then remembered Molly's request for eggs and milk. "Could you please stop at the town grocer?" Mr. Davies asked. "Sure thing," the Australian voice shot back.

Tara's curiosity got the better of her. "The store?" she asked.

"Yes, Molly asked me to pick up a couple of items on the way," Mr. Davies explained with a grin. "Twenty years old, and still full of questions and curiosity," he thought to himself, appreciating the trait.

"They arrived yesterday and have been getting things in order for your arrival," Mr. Davies explained.

"I'll be back in a moment. Is there anything I can get for you while I'm inside?" Mr. Davies asked.

Both girls shook their heads and said, "No thanks."

Mr. Davies wasn't long. The driver popped the trunk, and Mr. Davies placed the bag inside before getting back in. The car drove off.

Carla sat up straight, looking around. Her mood had clearly shifted, and she seemed excited.

"I feel like a kid again," she said.

"It's been years since we've been here," Tara commented.

"Apparently, your parents kept up with the property's maintenance after your grandmother's passing," Mr. Davies said as he rummaged through his briefcase. This time, he pulled out two brown manila envelopes and handed one to each of them.

"I was going to wait until lunch to give you these, but go ahead and open them now," he said, smiling.

The girls exchanged curious looks before opening the envelopes. Inside were legal documents, but the first one said it all: the deed to Blackwood Manor, with both their names on it. Carla was ecstatic, as was Tara. They had always loved the house and cherished their summer vacations there when they were younger. They both had great childhood memories. Their grandmother had taught them how to dowse with a pendulum when they were about ten. They would play hide and seek and use the pendulums to find each other. Tara remembered trying to confuse the pendulum by leaving it in a spot, hoping Carla's pendulum would pick up its vibrations instead of her own. It didn't work, of course, and as sisters do, Carla and Tara would bicker, accusing each other of cheating. The mood lightened, and Mr. Davies could tell that things didn't seem as bleak anymore.

The limo pulled into the long circular driveway, and Molly and James were waiting for them on the front porch.

Molly and James had been around since the girls were born. Their parents met Molly and James in Mexico during a vacation when the couple were young lovers without jobs or a place to live. The girls' parents offered them a job and a place to stay, and they ended up becoming part of the family. Molly and James were like second parents to the girls, and they loved them as if they were their own. Molly and James thought of the girls as the children they couldn't have themselves.

"What will happen to Molly and James?" Carla asked before getting out of the car.

"Your parents provided them with enough money to live comfortably for the rest of their lives. They were also offered the choice to stay on and watch over you girls, and they accepted," Mr. Davies said.

"And what did they say?" Tara asked.

"They said they wouldn't have it any other way," Mr. Davies replied with a smile, knowing this was the reassurance they needed.

Paul, the limo driver, opened the door for the girls. Mr. Davies followed behind. Tara and Carla ran to Molly and James, greeting them with warm hugs as they all walked inside.

Chapter 2

Memories Await

Tara was putting her things in her room, thinking about how the place looked almost the same as she remembered. It was a comforting feeling. The walls appeared freshly painted; her dresser looked refinished and shone like it was brand new. She plopped herself down on the bed, which was the same—a four-poster bed with a pink comforter and a pink canopy with lace trim all around, just like she remembered. The mattress still sunk in the middle and wrapped itself around you as you lay in it. She remembered how much she loved that bed, especially on stormy nights. Tara explored her bathroom, and everything was the same: a pedestal sink, a tub on legs, and a toilet with a pull chain.

She thought they would have upgraded but hadn't. It really did add character to the place. There was floral wallpaper and a plush pink rug to go with the décor. Tara laughed to herself, thinking, "It's a good thing I still really like the color pink."

She then went to her closet and immediately noticed the smell of cedar. Taking a deep breath, she thought about how smells can really bring you home to a place you haven't been in a while. Tara put away the clothes she had with her, but before leaving to meet everyone downstairs, she stopped and looked at the desk by the window. The desk was new and all set up, and she was waiting for her computer to arrive. It hadn't been there when she was little, but somehow, it seemed to fit into the scheme of things.

Carla was in her room checking everything out as well. It was the same as Tara's, but Carla didn't like the color pink. Her favorite color was green, and her canopy bed was green with white lace all around. Her rug matched, as did Tara's, and their bathrooms were the same, with green and pink shower curtains. Carla left her suitcase on the bed and figured she would put her stuff away later. She wanted to go downstairs and see Molly and James, hoping there might be food around; she was hungry again. Carla wasn't usually this hungry but figured it was due to all the excitement and the fresh country air. She opened the door and stepped into the hallway at the same time as Tara, and they both laughed. They had been doing that for as long as they could remember. The fascinating similarities between twins even threw them for a loop sometimes.

Tara and Carla linked arms as they skipped down the hallway, just like they used to when they were little.

They arrived in the dining room just as James was telling Mr. Davies how much he and Molly loved it up here. Molly chimed in, saying she wasn't sure she could get used to being up here without Mr. and Mrs. Wood. The girls entered the room, and the conversation stopped. Tara was glad; she didn't want to talk about it. If her parents were truly dead, she would mourn them when she knew for sure. The girls took their seats beside James and Molly. Mr. Davies noisily rummaged through his briefcase. He pulled out two small boxes and handed them to the girls. They opened them, finding necklaces with large stones hanging from them. Carla's was a large serpentine stone delicately wrapped in gold and hanging from an equally dainty gold necklace. Tara's necklace was just as daintily wrapped but had a large rose quartz. Both stones were flat and oval in shape. Inside the box was a small note that read, "Keep these close to your heart where they can be kept warm. They are sure to protect you and keep you from harm. Grandma."

"Where did you get these?" Carla asked, intrigued by the mystery surrounding the necklaces and mentally noting to find out their origin.

Tara looked on eagerly for the answer as well.

"They were given to your mother, to be passed on to you the next time you came to the house. The whole thing was shrouded in mystery, and I'm not sure your mother even knew what the note meant," Mr. Davies explained.

Mr. Davies then wanted to talk to the girls about the deed. He wanted to explain everything about the property and what was expected of them. One stipulation of the deed was that the house could never be sold and must only be passed down to the next generation. The house had been in the family for over a hundred years, and it was to stay within the family. Both girls agreed it wasn't even an issue; there was no way they would ever sell the house. They had too many cherished memories of the place, and they made it clear they would uphold their family's legacy.

Mr. Davies went on to explain there was a small clause they should know about, which stated that if there was no one to pass the house to, it would be turned over to the Town of Good Bay, Ontario.

Molly put some food out while they were talking: egg salad sandwiches, tuna sandwiches, and a garden salad with some juice. Carla fiddled with her necklace while listening. She couldn't get over the fact that the necklaces were so large yet so light. Stones were generally heavy in nature. On the back of the necklace was a symbol of some sort; she recognized it but couldn't quite place where she had seen it before. She made a mental note to look it up once her computer arrived.

James and Mr. Davies were starting to talk about fishing, and they were setting up a fishing date for when Mr. Davies was on holiday. James then offered to take him to the boathouse and show him the boat. Both men excused themselves and headed for the dock. Carla and Tara helped Molly clean up the dining room and prepare the tea and cakes for the patio out back.

"How are you girls doing?" Molly asked, concerned for them. It had only been two days since they received the news, and she was worried about the twins' emotional well-being.

"We're okay. How about you?" Tara replied. Molly told them she was still in shock and couldn't believe that their parents were gone.

Tara corrected her. "They are not gone. We do not know what happened to them, and it's still possible they are alive and well somewhere." Tara was trying to stay strong and optimistic.

Molly looked really concerned at the girls, who were nodding in assurance of what Tara had said.

"Well, I sure hope that you're right," Molly said.

"Now help me get these teacups together," she added, changing the subject.

The girls put all the cups, spoons, napkins, plates, and saucers on the trolley to go outside. Molly finished pouring the tea, then placed the pot on the trolley.

Just then, there was a knock on the front door.

"That must be Ryan. Mr. Davies is expecting him," Molly said as she ran for the door.

"Another surprise, surprised?" Carla asked Tara, shaking her head. "I wonder who this guy is and why Mr. Davies asked him here."

"Like I said before, I'm sure it will all be revealed in due time." Tara took the trolley and pushed it outside. Carla followed. The two girls set up the table when Tara realized they were short a cup and plate. She ran back inside to gather the missing items. Carla went down to join the men at the dock to let Mr. Davies know that Ryan had arrived.

James and Mr. Davies were so involved in talking about the fish in the lake that there were, of course, a few stories about the one that got away. Mr. Davies told Carla to send Ryan down to the dock.

Carla returned to the patio just as Molly was introducing Ryan to Tara. Carla watched from a distance as she walked back. She couldn't help thinking what a good-looking man Ryan was. He had shoulder-length dark hair, a mustache, and was neatly groomed. He wore a red t-shirt that clung to his body, showing off his muscles and washboard stomach. Carla figured she had best stop drooling and act properly in front of their guest.

"Carla, come and meet Ryan," Molly urged, pushing her forward.

"Nice to meet you, Carla," Ryan said, holding out his hand.

"Nice to meet you, Ryan," Carla replied as she shook his hand, feeling like she was blushing from the guilt of checking him out.

"Mr. Davies asked me to tell you to meet them down at the dock," Carla said, trying hard to act uninterested.

"Ryan, would you please tell them to come and have their tea and cakes before the tea gets cold?" Molly prompted.

"Yes, ma'am," Ryan said as he walked away toward the dock.

"Carla, you really must work a little harder not to be so obvious," Tara teased.

"You just be quiet. I was not obvious at all," Carla snapped.

Tara laughed as if to disagree. The men headed back for their tea, and Tara poured it as they neared.

"Well, I suppose you've all met Ryan," Mr. Davies said. "He is going to stay here, help out around the place, and keep an eye on the property," Mr. Davies continued. "He'll be staying in the guest house. Is everyone okay with that?"

"I suppose so," James said. "There's a lot of work that needs to be done around here. Do you think you can keep up?" he asked Ryan.

"I'll certainly do my best," Ryan replied.

"Now, James, don't start in on him already," Molly warned.

"Hush, woman. I need to know these things," James said.

Molly and James always bickered this way, and the girls thought it was funny. The two deeply respected each other and were very much in love.

Everyone enjoyed the afternoon, chatting about the things to do in town and engaging in regular chit-chat. Around five in the afternoon, Mr. Davies announced he was heading back and that his limo driver should be arriving anytime now to pick him up. Everyone walked Mr. Davies to the front and waited with him for his ride.

"Now, remember, you have my number, so if you need me for anything, and I do mean anything, just give me a call. Otherwise, I'll be back in a week," Mr. Davies assured. He shook James's hand and gave Molly and the girls a peck on the cheek as his limo pulled up.

"Ryan, take good care of this family," Mr. Davies said. "They mean the world to me."

"I will, sir. You can count on me," Ryan said, shaking his hand.

Mr. Davies got into the limo, and they drove away with him waving as they went down the driveway.

Everyone returned to the patio to help clear the tea.

"Why don't you make yourself at home, put your stuff in the guest house, and familiarize yourself with the grounds? We'll start fresh tomorrow morning at seven sharp," James said.

"Dinner is at six-thirty. I'll send one of the girls over to fetch you," Molly added.

"Sounds great," Ryan said, excusing himself.

Carla and Tara helped Molly clean up the dishes. Tara then decided to finish putting her things away in her room. She saw boxes in the hall from her room in the city and knew she had quite a bit to sort through. It was really nice of Molly and James to gather their stuff for them. Carla said she was going to do the same.

They both agreed to be down for dinner and headed to their rooms.

Tara was so intent on putting her clothes away that she became lost in her memories of childhood spent here on the estate. She remembered sitting down at the dock with her towel and a Nancy Drew book. The sound of the waves lightly splashing onto the shore was so clear in her mind. She loved the Nancy Drew mysteries and always wanted to be like her. She remembered sitting there for a long time reading, and when it got too hot, she would just jump into the lake. As an adult, she longed for those simpler, carefree days spent doing whatever intrigued her at the time. The memories of her childhood were comforting nonetheless.

Tara was putting away her shoes in her closet, which had shelves designed just for her shoes. Little cubbies were stacked three rows high from the floor, with each cubby housing two pairs of shoes. Tara suddenly stopped, feeling pain in her temples; she was getting a vision. She remembered hiding in her closet—it was a scary, not fun, feeling. The vision wasn't clear; all she knew was that it wasn't a memory—it was the future. And it was definitely her hiding, wishing she were small enough to fit in the shoe cubbies. The vision lasted only a couple of seconds.

"What was that all about?" she thought. Tara considered it for a moment, then wrote it off as stress, deciding that it wasn't actually a vision but a fear of what they knew and what they still didn't know. She dismissed it and went back to putting her shoes in order.

The last thing to do was put her purses in order. She loved purses and shoes. Tara knew she had more than she needed, but she could never pass up buying them. She would even buy hats to match; she also loved wearing hats, especially when she was younger.

Tara finished putting her things away and felt great, as if she was finally home again. She went to the window to look out over the lake and the property. The computer desk was situated in front of the window, and she thought how great it was that she would be able to see outside while working on her computer.

She could hardly wait for the computer to arrive so she could get back to work. She needed to be kept busy—an idle mind just brought back hurtful memories of her parents' disappearance. She started to feel depressed again, so she shook it off and was going to head downstairs to the dock when she noticed her sister, Carla, walking towards the dock with Ryan.

Tara watched them for a moment. Carla and Ryan went to the end of the dock, talking. Carla was pointing out towards the lake. Tara figured she was telling him about their adventures in the boat when they were young. Tara went downstairs, and due to the grumble in her stomach, it must be close to suppertime. She checked her watch as she left her room, and sure enough, it was six-fifteen.

Before entering the living room, she heard Molly and James arguing. She waited out of sight to hear what they were arguing about. James seemed very upset, while Molly was trying to calm him.

"I just don't like it. There is something not right about him," James was saying. He wasn't going to let Molly change his mind. "We don't need help. We've never had help. There is just something not right, and I'll need proof before I change my mind."

"Just don't make the boy feel unwelcome, James. I trust Mr. Davies, and I believe he wouldn't have done this if he didn't feel it was necessary," Molly said as she got up and walked into the kitchen.

"James, call the girls; dinner is ready," Molly politely ordered. She knew how to stop James' ego from getting too hyped up. She understood how he felt—there was too much secrecy and too many unanswered questions, and she was sure it was leaving them all with fear.

James got up from his chair. Tara came around the stairs to meet him.

"Tara, could you please call your sister? Dinner is ready, and Molly needs help setting the table," James requested. He always knew how to maintain order in the family and reinforced the importance of family teamwork.

"Sure," Tara said and went outside to get Carla. She called to Ryan and Carla to let them know dinner was ready, then went into the kitchen to help Molly get dinner on the table.

When everyone was there, they all sat down for supper. Molly had prepared a wonderful chicken casserole with a salad and fresh buns with butter. Everyone dug in, passing the food to the right. The silence was deafening. Molly couldn't stand it anymore. "What exactly do you do working for Mr. Davies?"

"I do a lot of things, and one of them is investigation and protection. That's why I'm here," Ryan replied.

"Yes, I was curious as to why Mr. Davies brought you here," James said.

"I realize you're probably unnerved by my presence, and I promise I won't get in your way. I'll help out as best I can around here," Ryan said.

James gave Ryan a hard stare, wondering. He couldn't help thinking that what Ryan said seemed rehearsed and not from the heart. "Huh, well, I hope you turn out to be an asset, but don't mind if I see for myself," James snarled.

Ryan was taken aback by James's comment. Molly was disgusted by James's attitude. "James, he's a guest in this house. Please treat him as one."

The girls were used to James being overprotective but still felt bad for Ryan having to endure such scrutiny.

After dinner, the girls helped Molly clear the table and do the dishes. Ryan excused himself, saying he still had some unpacking to do. James went out to the back, to the boathouse. He was always working on some project there. James was quite handy with his hands and liked making things.

"What is James working on now?" Tara asked Molly.

"I don't know for sure, but he mentioned the dock needed support." Molly just shook her head. "I can finish up here. Why don't you both go relax?" Molly urged.

Chapter 3

Ghostly Encounter

The night was warm and still. There was a full moon in the sky. It was beautiful, large, and seemed so close to the earth that you could see the craters clearly. The sky was clear, with all but one cloud in the shape of a snake draped across the moon. It was a sure sign of a storm coming.

As Tara sat on the front porch, taking in all the events of the last few days and gazing up at the moon, she became very calm and at ease. This place was home, and all its surroundings felt right. Tara could hear the waves gently coming ashore and the bats flying from tree to tree, catching their daily protein. It was nice to finally feel relaxed after everything they had been through in the past week, not to mention the unknown that lay ahead. But for now, she was just happy to be at peace in the country.

Thinking of this made her feel a bit hungry, so she decided to make some tea and sandwiches to take to her room. She would have that on her balcony and turn in for the night; it had been a long day. Comfort food and hot tea were always best to end a very long and busy day.

Tara couldn't believe she was hungry again, but then again, she hadn't eaten much at supper. She wondered if lunch and supper were too close together, along with all the events of the day. It was an eventful, long day, and as much as she tried to reduce her stress, it sometimes got the better of her, which affected her eating, she had noticed. But right now, she was feeling very good and hungry. She smiled to herself.

Tara had walked around the grounds and went to the water for a while before going inside to get something to eat. It could be the fresh air, she figured—being unused to it could make her hungrier than usual.

She came in through the front again after making a lap around the house. She saw Carla watching TV with Molly and James in the den as she walked by, heading for the kitchen. She put the kettle on and then prepared the teapot.

She chose a two-cup teapot, then looked over her choice of teas: peppermint, raspberry, pumpkin spice, chamomile, and of course, regular pekoe tea. She decided on chamomile. Then she stood staring into the fridge to see what struck her fancy for a sandwich. She could hear her mother's voice, the memory of her chastising her about keeping the fridge door open too long. Her mother would say, "That is not the way to cool the house down or warm up your food." She smiled as she thought back to those times.

She saw that there was cream cheese and cucumbers; she hadn't had that in a long time. The last time she remembered having that was when she was young, and her grandmother would make them for her and her sister to have a royal tea party. She couldn't help but smile at the memory of happy times with the whole family. Tara loved to reminisce about childhood times at Blackwood Manor.

Carla and Tara loved to have tea parties on the patio and pretend they were royalty, entertaining guests from around the world. She remembered the vivid imaginations she and her sister had. She thought back to those tea parties and could see the guests they made up as if they were real people. "Such fun we had hosting tea parties for our elite guests," Tara thought, and she couldn't help but smile. The more she thought about it, the happier she felt.

The kettle started to boil, so she grabbed it before it started to whistle. She then made the tea and placed the sandwiches on the tray with a napkin and a small jar of honey to sweeten the tea.

Just as she was ready to pick up the tray, she could hear her name being whispered from behind her. "Tara, Tara?" She figured it was Carla. Carla had an incredible knack for showing up when Tara was preparing food and asking her to make the same for her. Tara didn't know if it was a twin thing or if Carla had planned it that way, she thought a little skeptically.

Tara turned around, ready to give her heck, but it was not Carla. It was a smoky figure, but clear enough to see that it seemed to be the ghost of her grandmother. She was standing behind Tara, motioning for her to follow her. Tara was stunned and didn't move right away. She put the tray down and looked back at her grandmother, who seemed to be getting impatient. Tara gestured for her to go first. The figure floated by her and went to the cellar door off the kitchen. She stood by it until Tara got there, then went through the door as if it wasn't even there. Tara opened the door, but her grandmother wasn't anywhere she could see. It was very dark down there, so she started looking for a light on the walls but couldn't find one. Tara was shaking, and she couldn't believe this was happening. "I suppose I have to go down." She couldn't believe her grandmother's spirit was actually here. She was excited and a little unnerved—it was her first encounter with a spirit she could see. She figured it must be important for her grandmother to come to her, Tara thought to herself, so on she went.

She started to descend the stairs. With each step, the stairs creaked. It was really kind of creepy. She reached the bottom, and when she stepped forward, something brushed her face. She started panicking and flailing her arms, wondering what could have hit her. All she could think of was a bat. Tara liked bats, but not when they were that close. Her hand grabbed what it was, and she realized it wasn't a bat at all but a string hanging from the ceiling. She pulled it, and the cellar lights came on. The cellar was full of cobwebs and boxes piled to the ceiling. This room looked as if it had been forgotten. The apparition of her grandmother was back; she was bending over an old trunk. Tara whispered, "Do you want me to open the trunk?" Tara asked. She waited, watching her grandmother, for a sign.

She shook her head no and pointed behind the trunk. Tara moved the trunk away from the wall. There seemed to be nothing there except more cobwebs and a few spiders.

She looked at her grandmother, puzzled. Her grandmother then bent over and pointed to a certain brick in the wall. Upon closer inspection, Tara could see a faded symbol drawn on one of the bricks close to the floor. As she looked at her, she whispered again, "Shall I pull the brick out?"

Grandmother's spirit nodded her head to agree, Tara swore she could hear her saying "yes, yes," but it was faint.

Tara tried to pull it out, finding that it wasn't as easy to grip on to the brick, but she did finally work it free. She then looked at her grandmother again and she saw that she was nodding in excitement for her. Tara reluctantly put her hand in the hole to reach to see what exactly could be in there. She had to surpass her fears of creepy crawlies in order to do this. She could feel a small wooden box inside the hole and pulled it out as quickly as possible. As she blew the dust and webs off the box, she heard her grandmother say, "Hurry, please hurry." Tara grabbed the box and stood up, putting the brick back in its place and the trunk the way it was found.

"Keep the box to yourself and do not show it to anyone other than your sister," she whispered, disappearing. Tara looked at the box and wondered what was in it that was such a secret. She couldn't wait to see what was inside.

Tara felt all alone for a moment and sad that she didn't have time to talk to her. Then, she decided to quickly take the box with her tea up to her room to have a look. She wanted to see what this was before anyone else.

Tara put it on the tray and covered it with her napkin. She then quietly went past the den where they were watching TV. She peered in the den as she went by and noticed that they were all asleep.

Once in her room, she turned on the light at her desk to give her some light on the balcony off her room. She set herself up outside. She poured herself a cup of tea and sat staring at the box, thinking, *"Why was it hidden in the wall?"* it frightened her to think of what kind of a secret needed to be hidden in the cellar wall. Tara sat for a minute, trying to muster the courage to open the box. She lifted the latch on the outside of the box and pried open the lid. Inside was a letter folded in four and an old-fashioned skeleton key.

Tara placed the key on her necklace along with the pendant of the stone that they received from Mr. Davies. Tara then opened the paper to reveal that it was a letter to her grandmother her name was Elsa Wood.

Tara's grandmother's hidden letter says:

Dear Elsa,

You may have won this battle, but I will get you no matter what it takes. Be assured that even after we are both gone from this plain, I will seek my revenge and find what is rightfully mine. Your family will pay for your wrongdoings. I will see to that, so mark my words, I will never rest until justice has been served my way, and your family will pay for as long as your blood runs through their veins.
Sarah

After reading the letter, Tara tried to make sense of it all. There were so many questions, the mystery of the letter and key hidden so well away from prying eyes, but why, what did the key conceal? Tara was determined to find out but wished her grandmother would just come and tell her and explain who this Sarah person was.

Tara was shocked by the threatening tone of the letter. *"Why was it hidden away, though?"* she thought.

"Who was this, Sarah? What was her grandmother keeping that was hers? Why did she take it from her, to begin with? What did the key belong to?" Whatever her grandmother did, Tara felt she had a good reason, and this woman, whoever she was to her grandmother, sounded right out of her mind. This was all so confusing for Tara, and she really wanted to know more about her grandmother's past. "So much mystery these days". Tara thought

Tara looked at the paper on which the letter was written; it was old and yellowed with age, and the print was starting to fade. She thought she needed to preserve this letter for further information. Tomorrow, she would go to the library, have it photocopied, and place both in a plastic cover for protection against continual aging. There were so many questions that needed to be answered.

Tara's head started reeling with all the unanswered questions, and the more she thought, the more questions presented themselves.

She poured herself another cup of tea and finished her sandwiches. She decided to call it a night and figure out how to answer the questions in the morning. As her mother always said,

"Everything looks better in the morning." She knew her mother was right and tucked herself in for a long, comfortable sleep. Tara could hear her mother's voice calming her, and soon, she was asleep.

Chapter 4

Fire in the Boathouse

Tara could hear yelling coming from outside. She jumped from her bed to look out the window. There was a light on in the boathouse, and this was where the yelling was coming from. Tara ran down the stairs to the door and opened it. She heard a horrible explosion, and then the boathouse was on fire. Tara started yelling and screaming for help. It was then she realized that things were different as she looked upstairs, waiting for someone to come down. There was a rug that used to go up the stairs, but it had been removed and left as bare hardwood after they refinished the place. There was a light fixture on the ceiling where there was now a chandelier.

The place was the way it had been when she was a little girl. Tara then looked down at her nightclothes and realized she had never owned a nightgown like this. Tara started to scream and scream as she watched the fire engulf the boathouse. Then she saw a man come from the fire and flop out on the dock. Then there was nothing, just blackness, which scared her even more. She heard her name being called, quietly at first, then louder, and then she felt herself being shaken awake. When she opened her eyes, Molly was standing over her. Tara jumped to a sitting position, feeling disoriented. "The boathouse is on fire, we have to do something," Tara said, panicked.

"No, no, it's okay, you were dreaming, Tara," Molly tried to reassure her. Tara looked at her pajamas, but they weren't the same as what she had been wearing a minute before. Tara then told Molly about what she saw. Molly seemed to be listening eagerly. She then stroked her hair and said that it was just a dream. She looked at the desk with the tea and sandwiches and said, "It's no wonder you were having a nightmare. You know that happens if you eat before going to bed." Molly smiled and helped Tara get tucked back into bed. Tara apologized for waking her. "Never you mind that. You get a good night's sleep now," Molly said as she left the room, closing the door gently after her.

Tara looked at the clock on her nightstand, which read twelve-thirty. She had not been sleeping for long. As she looked out the window, she could see the brightness of the moon but could not see the moon itself. She took great comfort in the moon and its phases. You could tell a lot from the moon, she had learned from her grandmother's teachings. She then started thinking about her grandmother and the letter. When was that letter written, she wondered? Her computer was supposed to be arriving tomorrow, and she found herself even more anxious for its arrival. Tara wished her sister was awake; she wanted to talk to her, but she found it very hard to get back to sleep. To be quite honest with herself, she was actually afraid to go back to sleep.

Even though she realized that it was not her she was dreaming about, she remembered feeling close to the people who were in the boathouse and the man who was on fire on the dock. Well, she thought to herself, here is a new mystery to solve, not that she was short on mysteries that needed solving. She loved solving mysteries and figured she got that from her mother. Tara lay there, looking out her window at the blue glow the moon cast over the earth, thinking about her parents. Did they survive the crash and were hurt somewhere? Were they even on the plane at the time of the crash, and if they weren't, where were they, and why didn't they try to get in touch with them?

"More questions," Tara thought in anger. "So many questions; how can they be answered?"

Tara decided that she was going to have to try to get a vision or do a tarot reading to see if she could find out the circumstances behind her parents' disappearance. She was actually excited about that and couldn't believe that she hadn't thought about it before. After all, that was what she and Carla did for a living. They were paid professionals who helped people learn things about themselves and their lives. They had always been known for their psychic abilities.

That was the answer, and she knew it. But she couldn't understand why she and Carla hadn't thought of this already. They had been so focused on contacting their parents that they never thought of using the tarot to find out what had happened or what was going to happen. The more she thought about it, the more awake she became. Tara thought they must have been so distraught over the news that it didn't even cross their minds. After all, everything moved so fast after they found out, and they really didn't have time to think about it much.

Tara climbed out of bed and went searching for her tarot deck. They were her best tools to help get herself into an altered state of consciousness. Tara found the cards and laid them out on her bed. She then went to her dresser and took the picture of her parents to the bed with her. There she sat, looking at the picture, and picked a few cards. She sat there, looking at the cards she laid out. The first card was the Ten of Cups, which was a family setting with many people, lots of food and drink, smiling faces, and an abundance all around. The second card was The Devil, which was a dark room with high ceilings and a large stone in the center of the room, with a man and a woman chained to the stone by their feet and hands with shackles. The chains were long, but not long enough for them to reach the door or the window that was positioned so high on the wall that they could not reach it.

Tara saw clearly that her parents went on this mission but never made it to the plane and that they were being held prisoner somewhere. Tara kept pulling cards but found that she wasn't getting any further or more information. She put the cards away, the picture back on her dresser, and then got back into bed. She knew that she needed tomorrow to come quickly, and the only way that would happen was if she went to sleep. She closed her curtains and jumped back into bed. Clearing her mind, she fell right to sleep.

Chapter 5

Morning Deliveries

The next morning, Tara awoke early. The sun was just peaking over the horizon. She could see it was still dark in her room but could see the glow of the orange through the small opening in her curtains. Her clock read six o'clock, and she stretched as she realized that she hadn't gotten that much sleep, but her mind was so full of questions. Tara still couldn't shake the memory of her dream. She lay in bed for a few minutes longer, listening to the birds chirping their morning song. The chirps were soft, and she wished that she had heard them the night before; the soft lullaby they sang would have put her to sleep for sure. She could picture the mother bird singing softly to her children to wake them up. "What a wonderful idea." Tara thought she would do that when she had children of her own. Tara lay there listening and thinking about the events from the day before. The flooding of questions came back to her. The thought of how real the dream felt. Where to begin, she wondered. Tara's brain took over, and her thoughts drowned out the birds' songs. She realized it was time to get up. Lying there was now just making her restless.

Tara showered and got dressed for the day. She went downstairs and quietly made herself some tea, careful not to wake anyone else. She sat out on the patio, sipped her tea, and watched the stillness of the lake. The more the day grew, the rougher the waters became. She sat staring at the boathouse, which was the same boathouse that had always been there. Why did she dream of a fire that never happened? This puzzled her. As she sat thinking and replaying her dream, she heard a car pull up in front of the house. Tara quickly ran through the house to the front door to see who it was. There was a van out front. Two men got out. They went to the back of the van and pulled boxes out of the van. Tara became excited; she knew it was her computer. She looked at her watch, but it was still really early, only seven o'clock. Tara went out to meet them.

"Good morning," Tara said, feeling chipper and friendly as she met the delivery men who had brought their new computer equipment.

The delivery man replied, "Good morning; I hope we didn't wake you with our arrival?"

"Not at all; I have been up for a while," Tara said as she watched the dark-haired one close the van.

Tara asked the delivery man, "Do you set them up for us, too?" Tara was hoping that they would; she hated setting up computers. There were so many wires and connections, even though everything came color-coated.

The blonde delivery driver smiled and said, "No, I am afraid we just deliver. " He handed Tara a clipboard for her to sign for the delivery and continued, "I don't think you will have trouble setting these up."

Tara couldn't help staring at him. He seemed really familiar, but she couldn't place where she may have met him. She signed the clipboard.

Tara asked, "Do you have a business card in case we notice something missing and need to contact your company?"

"We are making the delivery for a..." he hesitated while rifling through some paperwork, "...Mr. Davies. You should probably contact him."

Tara figured that Mr. Davies seemed to have everything under control.

"Thank you for the delivery," Tara said as she watched the men climb into their van and drive away.

Tara checked out the boxes and went to pick one up, expecting it to be heavy. To her surprise, the boxes were quite light. She opened one of them and saw inside that they were laptops. She opened the rest of the boxes and saw that there were two printers, two mice, two mouse pads, and two keyboards to attach to them.

Tara carted them up to her room; she left Carla's equipment outside her door.

Within minutes, Tara set up her laptop and turned it on. She saw all her files were transferred onto this computer, which was good; she wouldn't have to figure that out. She had nothing to hide, but it still upset her that someone must have seen the details on her old computer. She made a mental note to speak with Mr. Davies about that later.

Tara noticed on the toolbar that her email count was two hundred and thirty emails.

"They had only been offline for 3 days. How could she have gotten so many emails?" Tara thought. Figuring it was a glitch or something, she took a deep breath and hit the open button.

Chapter 6

Email Horror

Carla was awake and listening to the rustling in her sister's room. "Tara was not usually an early riser, what could she possibly be doing?" Carla thought to herself as she listened to her sister move things about.

As she lay there for a few minutes more, she remembered her dream that kept waking her up in the middle of the night. It was she and her sister with their parents at the estate with their grandmother. They were laughing and joking and having a wonderful time playing on the beach. Then, out of nowhere, a dark figure appeared and started to kill everyone in her family, and just before the dark figure could turn on her, she woke up. She would wake up, and again, when she fell back to sleep, the dream would repeat itself.

Carla got up, threw her robe on, and headed for her sister's room. She opened the door and almost tripped over the boxes outside her door, not expecting them to be there. She dragged them into her room, opened them up, and was just as excited as Tara was that she had her computer back. She was even more delighted to see that it was a laptop with connections for printer and mouse etc. She immediately put her computer together and got it turned on. She noticed that her stuff was already uploaded to the computer and thought it was cool; it saved her a lot of extra work. She looked at her email icon and couldn't believe her eyes. "Two hundred and thirty emails?" she questioned, thinking that she really had her work cut out for her.

She aimed the mouse pointer at the icon, closed her eyes, and pressed the mouse button. She quickly opened her eyes, hoping that she was still dreaming.

The inbox was full, but all the subjects were the same. "You can't stop me" is what they read. The repetitive subject line sends a chill down her spine, making her nervous to open them and yet at the same time, curious to see what it was about. To calm her nerves, she told herself it was probably just spam.

When she opened them, she saw a picture of a dark figure in the distance, and in front were gravestones with each family member's name on them, including Carla's.

She searched the picture, staring harder and harder at the dark figure in the background. The graves looked so real. Carla choked back a scream; the figure was the same as in her dream from the night before.

Carla was beside herself. She started to cry. *"What did it all mean?"* she thought. Overwhelmed by fear and confusion, Carla feels helpless and desperate for answers. She didn't know what it was all about; she found herself pacing back and forth in front of the computer. She couldn't think straight.

Carla recognized that panicking wouldn't help, and she needed to regain control of her emotions to figure things out, "I have to calm down and reason," she thought to herself. She then decided to have a shower and ready herself for the day. While in the shower, she wondered if her sister had the same thing on her computer. She probably didn't have them because she knew she was awake and most likely had her computer together. She would come to her room and wake her, wouldn't she? Carla thought. She would go and talk to her as soon as she got dressed.

Before Carla went to her sister, she hit the print button and took it with her in case this wasn't on Tara's computer. When she grabbed the picture from the printer, she looked at it again. It was much larger than on the computer screen. She noticed that the tombstones only had dates on the family members that had already passed. Even her parents had a date, but it was the date of the plane crash. This was a clue, she figured. Whoever did this knew they were supposed to be on the plane that day, but who could it have been?

This person must also believe that her parents perished in the crash and didn't know that their bodies were never found. "Or did they?" Carla started to have some doubts creep into her mind. She started to get confused. What were the answers? Everything just started to feel more complicated now and she wished she could just get a good understanding of the situation and what was really happening.

"Did they know something we didn't know?" The thought upset her greatly, and she chose to believe that this person didn't know. The other stones had the names but just "R.I.P." and no dates. This was on the stones of people who were still alive. "Should I be taking this as a threat?" She thought. "Well, whatever it is, this person knows the family well and possibly has been keeping tabs on us, but for how long?" that thought gave Carla the creeps and sent shivers through her body.

As she looked at the picture some more while sitting on her bed, she realized that this grave was the one where her grandparents were buried.

Many photographic tricks could be done with computers and technology these days, but this seemed superimposed and not real at all. "Who would do such a thing and why?" she continued to wonder. She was starting to feel angry and frustrated. "Well, we are going to get to the bottom of this and make this person regret what they are doing." She thought confidently.

She then focused her attention on the figure; the only details she could make out were that it seemed to be a real person, but she couldn't determine whether it was male or female. It then dawned on her that if she saved the picture to another file, she would be able to enlarge it even more. She hoped this would work, but the chances were slim, depending on the pixels in the picture.

The same results came. The picture was too distorted to see any real details; the only thing she accomplished by this was she would see that the figure was wearing a full-length cloak; the hood was pulled down well over the forehead, shading any features of the face. She noticed the head was tilted downward as if in prayer or shame. She sat back in her chair, disappointed. As she sat there wondering what to do about this, she noticed that the figure was standing beside the tree and that the hood of the figure was touching the lowest branch of the tree. "This person was really tall." She thought she would have to go to the graveyard and see for herself how tall this figure was. Rage started to take over where despair had been settling.

She had a computer friend who could find the email's ISP number. She emailed her friend, sending the original along with it. Asking him for his assistance in finding this horrible person. Carla hit the send button and found that she was feeling a little better, more confident, and in control.

Chapter 7

Road Trip

Tara sat staring at the inbox; all the emails read the same thing: "Your troubles have just begun."

"What is this," she thought. *"This must be a joke. Two hundred and thirty emails with all the same subject line."*

That was crazy; Tara decided she needed something to eat before getting involved in anything. Her stomach was growling; the tea was not enough; she would have some toast, she thought to herself. She pushed herself away from the computer and headed for the kitchen. As she walked into the hall, she noticed the computer boxes that she put in front of Carla's door were gone. She knew Carla had woken up, had seen the boxes, and was probably setting it up right now. She then continued down to the kitchen. She felt she couldn't get there fast enough because her stomach was talking to her. Molly was already flipping pancakes as Tara walked into the kitchen.

"Good morning, sleepy head," Molly said.

Tara just laughed, "I have been up since six this morning. The computers were delivered, and I have already set them up, and it seems that Carla is setting hers up as well."

"You're kidding," Molly couldn't believe she never heard a sound. "You must have been awfully quiet."

"I was trying, I didn't want to disturb you again after last night's screaming fit." Tara cares about her sister and wants to keep things peaceful at home.

"Oh, you never mind that, dear. Sometimes these things happen," Molly went back to making her pancakes.

"Are you hungry?" she asked.

Tara hadn't eaten anything yet and was feeling very hungry after being focused on setting up the computers, "I am starving."

"Good, then you just sit down there and dig in," Molly said as she put a plate of pancakes on the table in front of Tara. Tara dug right in. She wolfed her pancakes down so fast she couldn't remember tasting them.

"Wow, you were really hungry. Would you like some more?" Molly said, amused at the speed at which Tara ate them.

"No thanks, I am full. For now, at least." Tara picked up her plate, took it to the sink, poured herself a glass of juice, and went out to the patio.

Carla came into the kitchen, and Molly set her up with her own plate of pancakes.

"You can't be as hungry as your sister," Molly observed.

"Tara's up?" Carla asked.

"She sure is. She ate her pancakes and is sitting on the patio with her juice as we speak." Molly pointed out the window to Tara. Carla told Molly that she would be taking her pancakes outside to eat and talk to Tara. Tara was glad to see her sister and helped her with her plate and juice.

"Did you get a chance to set up your computer?" Carla asked as she continued to eat the pancakes before they got too cold. That was the problem with pancakes; they seemed to get cold really fast.

Tara shook her head in discussion and said, "Yes, I set it up and couldn't believe that there were so many emails, all with the same subject line."

"Same here," Carla managed with a mouth full of pancake. "Did you open them"?
"No, I was too hungry to be bothered with Spam mail, I will look later," Tara said.

Carla wiped her mouth with her napkin and then drank some of her juice. "I will go with you, you will not like what you see, I am sure of it."

"What do you mean by that?" Tara asked.

Carla then started to tell her. She could tell Tara was horrified by the look on her face.

"My subject line was not the same thing," Tara explained.

"I can't wait, let's go now," Tara rose from her seat and headed for her room.

Carla grabbed her empty plate and glass, took it to the sink, and followed her sister to her room.

Tara sat down in her chair with her finger on the mouse, ready to open the first mail.

She opened the first one, and sure enough, it was the same picture as on Carla's computer.

She then frantically clicked on the next one, then the next, and the next. They were all the same. She looked at her sister. "What does this mean?"

"I don't know." She then showed her the picture she got from her computer.

She told Tara about the nightmare. Tara then told her sister about the visit from her grandmother as she retrieved the box and its contents. Carla pointed out the height of the figure and told her about the email she sent to her friend. They both decided that they needed to make a visit to the cemetery where their grandparents were buried.

They immediately got ready to go.

"Shouldn't we let Ryan know where we are going?" Carla asked.

"No, let's not. He doesn't need to know everything we do," Tara replied.

"Oh, for Pete's sake, you sound just like James," Carla said disgusted.

"Just trust me, we can handle this one on our own, just the thought of him having to go everywhere we go doesn't sit well with me," Tara reassured Carla that they don't need anyone's help.

"Fine, fine, we will go on our own." Carla wasn't happy about it, but she trusted her sister's feelings and intuitions. However, she would never give her the satisfaction of knowing that; therefore, she would always challenge her opinion.

The girls went downstairs and told Molly they were taking the van to go into town for a while. They explained they just wanted some sister time alone. Molly thought that was a great idea and that they needed it.

Tara drove, and when they arrived, Tara drove as close as they could get.

They walked over to the grave and positioned themselves as if they were the cameramen taking the picture. That's when it hit them.

Tara, as she wanted answers, said, "If the figure is in the background, then who took the picture? Were there two people involved? Or was there just one person, the cloaked figure with a tripod?"

They studied the picture of the surroundings. There were her grandparents' headstones, and along the same row, there were other headstones just like the picture, but they belonged to people buried there. They did not have the R.I.P. or any family member's name that they recognized. Carla and Tara figured that whoever did this must have put false fronts on these headstones just for the picture. They then took their attention to the tree at the back of the picture; sure enough, it was the same tree that was behind their grandparent's tombstones. They went to the tree to figure out how tall this person actually was.

"If you look at the picture, you can see the figure's head is about two inches below this branch," Carla said, pointing to the branch from the picture.

As she touched the tree, a flash of light blinded her, and then all she could see was everyone dressed in black, crying over a grave as if a priest had said some words to help the soul pass. Carla saw herself standing beside her sister and Molly. Then the vision changed, and Tara, Molly, and herself were visiting a gravesite. She tried to focus her view so she could see who it was. The scenery changed, and now she was standing behind them. Carla looked around them and she could read the carvings, it was James.

She could see his birth date but couldn't make out the full date of his death. She saw the month of May, she thought that is what it said but it was fussy at best. Then the vision focus changed and she could see the dark figure and again she was so startled at what she saw it broke the vision. Carla felt weak and sat down. Tara knew she was having one of her visions and waited patiently, then went to her side when she saw her sit down.

Tara was worried about Carla; she had lost all the color in her face.

"Are you okay?' She noticed Carla was weakened after her vision.

Carla nodded. She put her head between her knees to stop the feeling of nausea. After a few minutes, Carla told her sister what she had seen. "What did you see?" Tara asked her.

"It wasn't clear," Carla said. She didn't want to tell her sister just yet what she saw.

"It was along the same lines." She lied.

"Oh, okay." Tara didn't push the issue.

"What does this figure want?" Tara asked, frustrated and confused. Who is this figure, and why would they want to hurt us?"

"Do you think it has anything to do with the letter Grandma showed you?" Carla asked.

Tara thought about it for a few minutes and said that they would have to figure that one out and that it was most likely the reason.

Tara reached into her purse and pulled out a measuring tape. Carla held it at the bottom, and then Tara brought the other end up in the same spot as in the picture. "Six feet five inches," Tara said, "if we are correct in what we are seeing in the picture, then this person is very tall."

"Must be a man. Not too many women are of that height," Carla stated.

The girls decided to sit on a bench for a few minutes. These visions that Carla gets take a lot out of her.

The cemetery was quiet. There didn't seem to be anyone but them. All the flowers were in bloom and the trees were bright colors and shades of green and red. There seemed to be a lot of catalpa trees throughout the place. The leaves were very large and they seemed to accentuate the beauty of the flowers. Tara looked at her watch. It was already eleven o'clock.

"How about we check with the curator to see if he saw anything strange lately?" Tara suggested.

The curator's office was on the other side of the cemetery, so Carla and Tara decided to drive the car closer rather than walk, as Carla was still feeling weak. Tara thought once they spoke to the curator, they would go into town and get her something to eat and drink to bring back her strength.

Chapter 8

Dock Work

Molly decided to prepare for lunch, but she figured the girls would be back for lunch and quite hungry after their shopping spree. Even though they didn't say they were shopping, she just figured that was what the girls would do, and they would end up coming home with armfuls of new purchases.

Molly was thinking how good this would be for the girls to get their minds off their parent's disappearance and also from being shipped to the country, still not really knowing why. The girls were always strong when it came to stuff like this. She herself wished she had half their strength at dealing with tragedy. However, she did worry; there had to be despair on some level, and she knew it. The girls had always confided within themselves they rarely went to their parents or Molly and James for guidance and support. Molly just figured out who would know them better than each other. After all, they were twins.

Even though she knew the girls would be well taken care of for the rest of their lives, she couldn't help thinking about how they would manage if anything happened to her and James.

The girls were like their own children. Even though they spent lots of time with their parents, Molly and James were always there. James used to love taking the girls fishing in the boat. James was the only one who would go on the rides at the CNE when they needed an adult with them. Molly could remember countless days of sitting and playing tea party and hairdresser, even the dentist. Molly could remember many times being a student in their class when they played teacher.

Molly started to feel sad, thinking about days gone by, and decided to stop. She looked up from the sink where she was peeling the shells off eggs for the egg salad sandwiches. She looked out the window to see James strolling toward the house. "He must have smelled the eggs," she thought. Egg salad was his favorite, and he figured he could smell out the eggs from miles away.

James took his shoes off on the sun porch that was off the kitchen and came in, gave Molly a peck on the cheek, and washed his hands. "You should tell the girls to come downstairs. It's a lovely day for a boat ride," James said.

"The girls are already up and out early this morning; they decided to spend some quality sister time in town," Molly told James.

James gave Molly a strange look of worry, she then told him to have a seat and she would make him a sandwich. James poured himself a glass of milk and sat at the table like an obedient child waiting for his lunch.

The doorbell rang.

"That must be Ryan," Molly said as she wiped her hands on her apron and raced by James.

"Something not right about that boy," James snarled
"Oh nonsense, you just don't like strangers," Molly retorted.

Molly greeted Ryan at the door and ushered him into the kitchen.

"Have a seat and I will give you and James a sandwich, I hope you like egg salad; its James' favorite," Molly said as she put the sandwiches together.

"James, get Ryan something to drink," Molly ordered.

James rose and went to the fridge. "Milk, okay?" he snarled.

"Milk is fine, thank you," Ryan said, not letting on, he heard the snarl in James's voice.

Molly gave James and Ryan their sandwiches and sat down with her own.

"The girls not joining us?" Ryan asked.

"They've gone to town," Molly replied, kicking James under the table.

James didn't even flinch; he just kept on eating, staring straight down at his plate.

"Isn't that right, James?" Molly asked

"Uh-huh," was all he said.

Ryan expressed concern, "Shouldn't they have waited for me?"

"Oh, I am sure they will be fine, they need some sister time, they are very close you know more so than most sisters and twins," Molly explained that they relied on each other all the time.

When lunch was over, James rose, gathered the plates, and took them to the sink. Molly had brewed the tea and brought it to the table with some homemade tarts.

"Let's have tea and dessert outside. It's a beautiful day," Ryan suggested.

"Good idea, don't you think James?" Molly asked him, trying to get him to say something.
James just nodded and went to hold the door for Ryan and Molly. They carried everything out to the patio. They all seemed to sit there in an awkward silence, sipping their tea and eating their tarts.

James piped up and said, "How's about you giving me a hand repairing the dock after tea?"

"Sure, I would be glad to help," Ryan said.

They finished their tea, and the two men headed down to the dock. Molly sat and had another tea while looking after them. Molly felt the same thing about Ryan but didn't tell James. There really was no explanation for why she felt that way, so she figured she wouldn't let on. She didn't want to raise James's internal alarms any more than they already were.

James briefed Ryan on what needed to be done on the dock. The ladder leading into the water was getting all rotted out and very slippery. He asked Ryan to take the steps out of the water and handed Ryan the tools he needed. He told Ryan that he had made new steps for the dock and that he was just finishing the last part while Ryan removed the original. Ryan went right to work. Even though James was working hard on what he was doing, he was keeping a watchful eye on Ryan. James thought that he seemed to be a fairly well-built man; he showed no signs of not wanting to be there. James started to relax a bit, but he was still leery about him. "Just a gut feeling," James thought to himself.

"Not that he is a bad guy or anything, but he's hiding something that I know for sure.

Chapter 9

Gravely Suspicious

Carla and Tara approached the office, noticing that it looked closed. As they got closer to the door, they realized that it was dark inside, but the door was slightly open. Both girls cautiously opened the door wide and hollered in, "Hello, is anyone there?' Tara said as she and Carla stood still, waiting for a reply.

There was no answer, so they walked inside. There was a desk straight ahead. Filing cabinets lined the wall behind the desk. The office was paneled all around; there was a table and four chairs on the right side of the room. Books were on the table. Tara walked over and saw it was a catalogue for caskets and tombstones. She noticed a door and tried it. It was open as well. She pushed the door open and peered inside. It was a washroom. Carla was busy looking at papers on the desk, taking care not to disturb anything.

"There is no one around," Tara said.

"He must be in the cemetery working," Carla said.

Tara went to help her sister look through the papers on the desk. As she leaned over, she whacked her knee hard on the draw of the desk that was partly open. The jarring caused the mouse to move on the mouse pad enough to remove the screen saver. Tara gasped as she looked at the computer screen. Carla came around to see what she was looking at. Tara was pointing but couldn't get any words to come out. Carla couldn't believe her eyes either. It was an open grave in this cemetery with a man lying dead with an axe embedded in his head, and if that wasn't bad enough, the tall hooded figure was standing over the grave looking in at him. The figure's head was down, but his hands were clasped in front of him. They noticed a ring but couldn't make out what the insignia was or if it was a symbol. Carla told Tara to print the picture. Carla realized that this picture was part of an email as well. Carla printed the picture and then forwarded the email to her computer and to her friend, asking if he would trace this one as well and explaining that it was sent to a different computer.

The girls then left the office to see if they could find the grave, hoping that they would find nothing and the curator was okay. They walked to the section that could clearly see on the computer picture; it was section 'L'. They could see a grave as they approached that was open with mounds of dirt sitting on either side. They carefully walked up to it uncertain that they wanted to look in. Both girls held hands, took a deep breath, and peered over the side. Sure enough, there in the deep grave was a man face down with an axe embedded in his head. Tara and Carla both gasped in shock. Carla started to cry and panic. "Oh my god, oh my god." Tara took her and turned her away from the grave.

"What are we going to do?" Carla said, all panicky.

"Go over by the car and wait for me," Tara demanded. Tara went back to the grave and looked in. She could see that blood was still dripping from the crack in his skull. This must have happened not long before they got there. Tara looked around the graveyard as far as she could see. She scoured with her eyes the tree line of the forest that surrounded the cemetery. There was no one there, but she couldn't shake the feeling that the killer wasn't far away. She walked back to Carla, who was standing by the car.

"What, what did you see?" Carla asked.

"Nothing, but I think we should leave right away," Tara said, helping her sister get into the passenger side of the car.

Tara took one more look around, screamed, and ran off. "Tara, where are you going?" Carla yelled after her and then took off after her sister. As she was running to catch up with Tara, she saw what Tara was running after. It was the figure in the pictures. He was quite a ways ahead, dodging in between the trees. Tara yelled after the figure to stop, but the figure just kept running. He leaped over the fence that separated the forest from the cemetery and took off into the forest.

Tara stopped at the fence, slumped over, and gasped for breath. Carla was right behind her doing the same.

"Are…you trying… (Pant, pant) to kill me?" Carla asked.

"No… What are we…going to do?" Tara asked.

Carla just shook her head. When they caught their breath enough to start walking, they walked back to the car.

"I want to have a look inside the office quickly before we leave," Tara said.

"I don't know, Tara; what if the figure comes back, or worse yet, what if the killer never left and is still around? We could be next." Carla made a good point, but she just had to go back in. She couldn't help wondering where the curator was.

Tara looked all around the desk and on the cabinets for a clue. Nothing. She opened up the desk drawer, and inside was a closed picture frame. The picture was of a man, a woman, and two small girls. It was hard for her to tell, but she had a hunch that the man in the grave was the curator. Tara could feel the panic rising in her stomach.

"We have to get out of here and fast," Carla said, feeling the panic rising in her stomach as well. Both ran to the car. Tara jumped into the driver's side, took the keys from her purse, started it up, and sped away.

Chapter 10

Mollys Find

Molly cleaned up after lunch, and then went to clean up the girl's rooms, make the beds and what not. She had the clean sheets from the closet and was headed for Carla's room when she passed the window, something caught her eye. The sun was gleaming off of something shiny coming from the tree house. Molly wondered what it could possibly be. She personally cleaned it out; she knew there was nothing left inside it.

"It has been a few years since then," she thought. "Maybe there were some children playing in there at one time and left something." Molly figured that once she was finished making the beds, she would go have a look.

Molly carefully climbed the ladder leading up through the trap door on the floor. She pushed the door open and climbed in. Molly looked around and noticed the only thing in there was a pair of binoculars lying on a wooden crate.

She looked out the window in front of the crate; from this angle, she could see if she was sitting on the crate, and there was a great view of the girls' bedrooms. There was nothing else on that side of the house to see. They were the only two windows directly in front of the tree house. Molly was not impressed. She ripped a piece of her t-shirt off and held the binoculars with it, hoping she didn't smear any prints; she had watched enough CSI shows to know never to touch it without gloves, and seeing how she didn't have any gloves, she figured the t-shirt would be good enough.

Molly took them into the kitchen, placed them into a large paper bag, and then placed the bag on the table. There is something strange going on here, she was thinking to herself. She stared at the phone, deciding whether or not to call the police. She then decided she would talk to James first before phoning. The men were so into their work that she figured she would wait for them to come in. Molly started getting things ready for supper but couldn't take her attention off the paper bag sitting on the table. She was going to have to go tell them to come in. She couldn't wait any longer. "After I get the potatoes done," she thought. This would give them a little more time to come in on their own.

The potatoes were finished; they still were working on the deck. "They must almost be finished by now," she thought, James had told her that there wasn't much more to do and promised he wouldn't be working on it for the rest of the day. Molly went to the back door and called to them. They looked up at her. "Could you both come here for a second?" Molly hollered. The men both looked at each other and started to head for the house. As James got closer, he could see the worried look on Molly's face, he picked up his pace a bit to get to her sooner. Ryan noticed that James was now in a hurry and hurried along with him. "What is it? What's the matter," James said, grabbing Molly by the shoulders.

Molly ushered them inside and explained what was in the paper bag on the table.

"You must call the police," James said. Ryan agreed. Molly picked up the phone and dialed. When Molly got off the phone, she told the man that someone would be by soon.

They all breathed a sigh of relief. Ryan sat thinking for a moment, then turned to James and asked him if he would give him a hand setting up a video camera that might catch the person coming back. The owner, he explained, didn't know that the binoculars had been taken, so the chances were good they could catch the person when they came back for them. James agreed, and they both went to Ryan's cabin to get the equipment.

Chapter 11

Small Town Authority

Carla suddenly realized it was wrong running away from a crime scene without notifying the police. "Stop, stop the car," Tara jumped from Carla's sudden outburst. She pulled the car to the side of the road.

Carla looked all upset, understandably of course, she was upset as well after what they saw.

"We have to tell the police," Carla said. 'Christ, we can't just leave him and go home," she continued.

Carla was near tears. Tara thought about it for a second, then turned the car around and headed into town.

"I believe there is more to this than just random murders or stalking of one family," Tara said.

"What do you mean?" Carla asked.

Tara's gut feelings were strong, "Well, I have a hunch this has something to do with magic."

"Magic, why do you say that?" Carla questioned.

"Well, think about grandma's letter and who we are; we come from along the line of witches, the Black-Wood witches, right?" Tara looked at her sister, waiting for it to sink in.

"Whatever grandma did to this person they must have been involved with the witches in town," Tara explained.

"But you have no proof of that, we have nothing to go on," Carla said.

"I know. It is just a hunch, and we will figure it out when we get back home, but first, we need to inform the police about the man in the cemetery," Tara said.

"We will tell the police everything we know up until now. Although…" Tara paused.

"We won't tell them about the emails or that we know anything about the email at the curator's office." this person, I believe, is dealing with magic and only magic will catch him. She thought. Carla agreed.

Tara parked the car in front of the police station. The sheriff was on the phone when they walked in. He gestured for them to take a seat. Then, he stuck his index finger up as if to say he would be with them in just a minute.

"Yes, mam, I will have someone look into it right away. I am sure it was nothing more than teenagers getting a cheap thrill, but we will come to check it out." The sheriff ended and stood up.

"Okay, bye." The sheriff hung up the phone.

He looked over at Tara and Carla sitting on the bench. Carla was looking at her fingers as if to groom her nails. Tara was staring down the hall at some kind of ruckus going on down there.

"Well, ladies, what can I do for you?" he asked, not knowing how serious the answer was going to be.

The girls approached his desk and told him all about their visit to their grandmother's grave. They went to talk to the curator about putting flowers on the gravesite when they noticed an open grave and out of curiosity, they went to have a look, not expecting what they were going to find. They lied, but they didn't want the police involved in this case without Mr. Davies knowing first. The Officer took their statement and then their names. He stopped and looked up at them. "Do you reside at the Blackwood manor?" he asked.

Both girls nodded, "Yes." Tara asked, "But… how do you know?"

The sheriff chuckled and said, "It's a small town, ladies. Everyone knows about the Blackwood twins." He then continued

"I just got off the phone from your aunt, is it Molly? It seems she found some binoculars in the old tree house." The Officer said, "These binoculars wouldn't be yours, would they?" he asked.

Both girls shook their heads and explained that they hadn't been in the tree house since they were young girls.

"Well, I was going to send a car out to your home but now I think I will go out there personally." The Officer dispatched a car to the cemetery, then grabbed his keys and said to the girls let's go. The girls got in their car and followed the Officer to their home.

Chapter 12

For the Sake of Finger Prints

Ryan and James were setting up the equipment just behind a bush that was at the corner of the house. James ran the cord along the side of the house, hiding it in the grass. He then fed it through a window in the basement then went inside to plug it in.

As they watched the video feed, they made sure that the angle of the camera would allow for a good view of the person going up and coming back down. Hopefully, they would get a good frontal shot of the person's face. Ryan turned to James. "I know you don't know me very well, but I promise you that I am here to help the girls and protect you and them from harm."

"I'm sorry, but what is a boy of your status going to do? Don't get me wrong, your sentiments are noble and duly noted," James said.

Molly heard James as she walked over to see how they were making out.

Ryan, looking a bit stung by James's words he didn't know what to say except, "I believe we need to call Mr. Davies." Ryan then excused himself and went in to the house to make the call.

"James, you have hurt his feelings," Molly said, disgusted with him.

"Well, his wounds will heal, it just goes to show you the boy is too soft to be a big protector," James replied with a smirk, "Let's go back to the house and put a pot of tea on,"

James showed no remorse for his words. Molly walking back with him was thinking about what James said. She knew he was right but he didn't have to be so curt. She really was surprised at James's blatant boldness towards Ryan. James put the kettle on as Molly gathered the teacups and saucers.

James listened to the conversation that Mark was having with Mr. Davies. He couldn't hear everything but what he could hear, he just knew there was more to this situation than they were letting on. James could feel his defenses rising higher in him. His protection shield was wrapping around him as he was headed for warrior mode and preparing for battle.

James brought out the pot of tea and poured them each a cup. Ryan said that he had called Mr. Davies and he would be coming right away.

"And Molly," Ryan said, "Mr. Davies told you not to worry about dinner and that he would bring it with him."

Molly was going to answer when she heard a car pull up. "Oh I hope that's the girls," she said and rose from her chair and went to meet them at the door.

Molly was happy to see them and wanted to catch them up on the day's events since they have been gone. The car was a police car, she had forgotten about calling them for a moment when she noticed that the car behind him was the girl's car. Molly stayed on the porch, watching the girls pull into the driveway.

The Officer greeted Molly on the porch. She waited for the girls with the Officer to join them. The Officer had explained to Molly that the girls knew about the binoculars and her phone call and that he would explain further inside. She gave the girls a hug. "Are you both okay?" she asked them.

"We are just fine, let's go inside and talk," Carla said.

James poured them each a cup of tea as the girls started to explain about the computers arriving and the emails that they both had on their computers. They continued to tell them the reason they went to the cemetery and what they had found while they were there. Then they told them about going to the police station and that she was on the phone at the time with the Officer who was there. Now that they had explained everything to that point they now wanted an explanation as to why Molly called the police. The Officer then explained that to the girls. The girls were shocked. Molly showed the Officer the bag with the binoculars in it.

The Officer took a glove out of his back pocket and put it on his right hand. He opened the paper bag and peered in. He just stood there looking inside at the binoculars, not doing anything. He then closed the bag back up. "Have you touched these at all with your bare hands?" He asked, looking straight at Molly.

Molly showed him her shirt where she ripped a piece off of it to grab the binoculars. She told him how she learned not to touch it from watching CSI shows.

He just laughed at her. "May I use your phone?" he asked.

"Sure, it's right there," Molly said, pointing to the wall beside the fridge.

The Officer used the phone, it was a brief conversation and none of them could pick up what he was saying. He came back to them. They were all eagerly waiting to hear their next instructions.

"I have an Officer coming out with a finger printing kit, he will dust the tree house and put in a report," he said.

"What about the binoculars?" James asked him.

"I will be taking them with me, I will drop them at the lab on my way back." He explained.

"When will you know anything?' Tara asked.

Officer Thompson said, "Probably tomorrow afternoon at the latest, I will see to it there is a rush put on it."

"In the meantime, try and relax, after the Officer dusts the tree house he will bring his results back to the station, fill out his report and then he will be surveying the property this evening." He continued

James then told the Officer that he and Ryan put up a camera to catch anyone if they came back. The Officer thought that was a good idea and instructed him to tell the Officer of its location when he got there so as not to disturb it while patrolling the grounds.

They all agreed. The Officer then handed James his card. Officer Thompson was his name. James was taking every inch of him into his memory.

Molly could tell by watching how observant James was being. Officer Thompson was a man in his fifties, slightly balding on top, he was dressed in casual clothes dress clothes but not a uniform. He wore glasses that he looked over the top of most of the time.

James deduced him to be a lazy man by not wanting to take his glasses on and off at the appropriate times. He just left them on the bridge of his nose. The man seemed to be well-educated and had been in the business for some time. His hair was graying but not entirely. He was sporting the salt-and-pepper look. The one thing that seemed to stand out the most was his eyes. They were a bright green. James didn't know why, but they seemed to be piercing, and unusual. As they were seeing Officer Thompson to his car, another car pulled up.

Officer Thompson waited for the other car. Another Officer climbed out of the car and came over to greet him. They exchanged a few words, and then Officer Thompson got in his car and pulled away.

"Hi there," the Officer said as he reached for James's hand.

"I'm Officer Jenkins, here to do the dusting," he said with a smile. The girls and Molly chuckled and led him into the house. James didn't even notice until he got back inside to see that Ryan was on the phone. The Officer didn't want a seat; he just wanted to get right to work.

"Could you please show me to the tree house?" he asked.

James took him right away, and Tara followed.

"This was our tree house. James and my dad built it for us when we were little." Tara felt like she needed to explain.

The Officer turned to James and said, "Job well done, sir."

James just nodded, all proud.

"There isn't much to see up there. According to my wife, she would know she was the one who cleaned it out several years ago," James said.

"That's fine. I will just have a look and see if there are any prints I can get at all, " he said and went right to work. He opened his kit and started with the ladder that led up to the tree house.

He noticed that James and Tara were still standing there watching him, so he told him that he would be there for a while before he was done and that he would come in to let them know when he was finished. They agreed and went back to the house.

Ryan was telling Molly and Carla that he could have a look at the computer files and that maybe he could find something out. He gave Carla his email address and then asked her to go upstairs and send the emails over to his computer. Carla did, and Ryan headed over to the house where his laptop computer was set up. James said that he was going to put the tools away from this morning's work at the dock and headed towards the water.

"Can I help you get dinner ready, Molly?" Tara asked, wanting to help take some of the burden off Molly.

Molly smiled at Tara and answered, "That's okay, dear; Mr. Davies is bringing dinner with him."

Molly sat herself down at the kitchen nook. Sitting in the kitchen was always Tara's favorite place to sit and think, so she joined Molly. The window was a bay window with light yellow curtains that went halfway up the window. The window faced east, and it caught the first sunlight of the day. It was a cozy spot with a plush cushion bench that fit snuggly into the window.

"Mr. Davies is coming, why?" Tara asked, puzzled as she joined

Molly at the table.

"Ryan thought it best that he come out." Molly was not saying everything, and Tara knew by the look on her face that there was more to that than she was willing to let on. She wondered what had happened while she was gone. She also knew that Molly would not say anything if she asked. She figures that James was being his usual overprotective self, and that really got on Molly's nerves. Molly was the kind of person who, even if she had her reservations about you, would still be sweet as pie until you did something to prove her suspicions were correct.

"What time do you expect him here?" Tara asked.

"He should be here within the hour." Molly's hands were in front of her on the table; her fingers were intertwined together, and she was moving them nervously as she stared at them.

"Molly, something is troubling you. What is it?" Tara asked.

"Oh, I'm sure it's nothing, but I can't help thinking that you girls are in grave danger," Molly said.

"Nice choice of words," Tara said, and they both broke into laughter.
"Oh my," Molly said, putting her hand over her mouth, then said, "Pardon the Pun," and they both broke out laughing again.
When they stopped laughing so hard, Tara could see how the toll of the day had tired Molly out.

"You look tired. Why don't you go take a nap? I will wake you when Mr. Davies arrives," Tara encouraged Molly.

"That's a good idea. I suppose a half hour or so would do me good." Molly rose from the nook and went upstairs.

Tara sat there thinking about Molly and how she didn't like to see her worry so much. It wasn't good for her. However, she had to admit that if she were in her position, she would probably be just as worried. Tara's mind was going through the day's events, trying to find something in her memories that she may have overlooked, anything, even a small clue as to where to go from here. Tara was lost in her thoughts as she replayed the day's events in slow motion. She didn't even hear the kitchen door open. It was Officer Jenkins with his kit in hand.

"Excuse me, miss, I am finished dusting the tree house," he said.

Tara jumped; his voice had startled her back to the present.

"Oh, great, that's great." She was at a loss for words.

"I am going to take this back to the lab, head back to the office, fill out a report, then after supper, I will be here surveying the property for intruders." He was looking right at her but wasn't sure by the look in her eyes that she was hearing him.

"Okay, that's fine; I will walk you to the door." Tara rose from her seat and headed to the front of the house.

"There is one other thing I will need from everyone here, and that is all your fingerprints, just so we can eliminate you as a suspect." He said with reservation in his voice.

"Suspects? Of what?" Tara asked.

Feeling a bit embarrassed to say so, Officer Jenkins hung his head down and looked at the floor, unable to look her in the eyes.

"Of both the murder in the cemetery and the tree house intrusion." He was waiting for her to blast him and then kick up a fuss.

Tara understood the need for fingerprints to help illuminate them as suspects, "Oh, that, of course we did touch stuff, I suppose the stress of it all I was just not thinking clearly."

Tara offered up her hands to the Officer, "Well, you can have mine now if you like, then I will call Carla from upstairs to come."

Tara continued, "Molly, however, just went to lie down for a bit, and James is at the boathouse."

Officer Jenkins shared his interaction, "Yes, I saw James and asked him first, he didn't like it much but he agreed."

"So, if you could just hold your hands out in front of you palms up then," he said while opening up the kit. He pulled out a piece of cardboard-looking paper, only white, and it had a clear sticky film over it. He peeled back the film and asked Tara to place her right hand on the paper and press down as firmly as she could. Tara did as he asked, and when she did, she saw the blank paper transform; right before her eyes, a black figure of her hand appeared. The details of her hand were so clear. She then turned her hand to look at it, but there was no ink on it whatsoever.

"It's a new technology. You don't have to get your hand all inked up," Officer Jenkins said as he saw Tara checking out her hand.

"Well, what will they think of next?" Tara was being sarcastic, but Officer Jenkins took her seriously and said, "Actually, they are coming out with a laser printer that will copy your handprint right onto a disc." He placed the clear paper over the handprint, labeled it with her name, and then placed it in his kit.

"I will go get Carla," she said to the Officer, and she ran up the stairs. The Officer stayed exactly where he was. He looked around, taking in all the décor of the hallway and the pictures that surrounded him. These pictures were old, he noted, and the two girls in the picture were with an older lady in one, then an older man; these were all their family photos, he supposed. Tara came down with her sister. The Officer repeated the procedure with Carla.

"I would really rather not disturb Molly if you don't mind getting her prints at a later time," Tara asked.

"No problem. I will get them later tonight when I come back; that way, I can drop them off at the lab tomorrow morning when my shift ends," he said.

They walked with the Officer to Ryan's cabin. Carla was talking to the officer about the recent incident in the cemetery and wanted to know if anything had happened before they arrived there. She was grilling him pretty good and surprisingly, he was being very forthcoming with information. Tara thought he was a very attractive man; there was something about this Officer that made her feel comfortable. Mostly, when she was around Officers, she was apprehensive, but not with this one. Even though she wanted all this to be over, she was hoping she would get to see a lot of him.

They knocked on Ryan's door. They could hear his footsteps approach on the hardwood floor of the cabin. He was a little stunned to see us all at his door but quickly asked us to come in. They explained why they were there and Ryan promptly put his hand out, ready to have it printed. Tara laughed, knowing Ryan was thinking he was going to get his whole palm inked.

Tara couldn't contain her excitement about this technology and blurted, "They have a new way of doing it now," she told him.

"Less messy," Carla added. Officer Jenkins showed the paper to Ryan and explained how it worked. When Ryan was done, he, too, inspected his hand for ink and was impressed.

Tara told him about the laser printer they were coming out with.

"Well, I will be going then; I will see you all later." Officer Jenkins picked up his gear and headed out the door.

"I'm going to stay here and talk to Ryan for a while if you don't mind, Tara?" Carla asked.

"And if that is okay with you, Ryan?" she chuckled as she asked him.

"That's fine by me," he said with a delighted smirk on his face.

Tara, noticing the secret passion behind his eyes, decided to walk the Officer back to his car.

Tara offered her kindness to Officer Jenkins, "I will walk with you."
"Glad for the company, Ms. Wood," he said, holding the door for her. She looked back at Carla and saw Carla giving her a wink.

"What a girl always thinks about guys," Tara thought. She walked the first few paces with the Officer in silence and then she said, "You can call me Tara." trying to establish a more personal connection between her and Officer Jenkins.

He looked at her, puzzled for a moment, then said, "That would be fine, Tara."

"My name is Dave." He smiled as he watched her reaction, she seemed pleased. He thought to himself that there has not been a prettier girl in these parts for a long time. Most of the girls he grew up with were from this town and they were all married or spoken for.

"Have you lived here all your life?" Tara asked.

Officer Jenkins proudly answered, "You bet, born and raised here."

"How about you?" he asked, "Where did you grow up?"

"I am from Toronto, and my grandparents owned this estate," Tara said.

Officer Jenkins thought in silence for a moment.
"Your family owns the lumber yard, right," he asked.

"Yes, that's right." Tara could see he was trying to put things together.

"We spent a lot of time up here when my grandparents were alive..." Tara's thoughts veered off into Nostalgic memories, and she was wondering about the connection, if any way back then, and secretly hoping for one.

"That's right, I remember you now, the twins. You girls always won the races at the annual picnic." He was smiling as he accessed his memory.

"I always wanted to be able to run as fast as you." He started to laugh. Intended to make Tara smile and ease the emotional weight of their conversation.

Tara remembered the picnics and was reminiscing about the fun times when she was a girl and carefree. Tears started streaming down her face. She was so embarrassed but couldn't stop them from flowing. Officer Jenkins saw her tears and took her gently by the shoulders. "Its okay, we will find this person and get to the bottom of it, I promise."

"I am so sorry; I don't know what has come over me," Tara said, wiping her eyes.

He understood her emotional turmoil, "I do, you have been under a lot of pressure and it has finally come to a head."

She just nodded and agreed, and that was right. It was finally hitting her. She couldn't help thinking she wished she were a little girl again with nothing to worry about.

She acknowledged his comfort and expressed her need to shift her focus, "Well, thank you for your understanding; I am not normally so emotional," she chuckled, wiping her tears away as they reached his police cruiser. "I should be getting the dinner table set for Mr. Davies's arrival."

"That's okay. I will leave you to get to it and will see you later this evening. You take care." Officer Jenkins then got in his car and looked sincerely at her.

Tara knew that he really meant what he said and that he wasn't just saying it. Tara saw him off down the driveway and then went into the house.

Mr. Davies was bringing dinner, and then she thought the least she could do for Molly was to set the table. Tara put the cutlery out, plates, napkins, and glasses for drinks, salt and pepper as well. She didn't know what kind of food he was bringing, so she didn't know what kind of condiments to put on the table. She figured that it was okay to leave until he arrived.

Tara poured herself a glass of juice and then went outside to sit on the front porch in the shade. She could hear laughter coming from

Ryan's cabin. She knew that her sister was taking a liking to him and hoped that her sister wouldn't let herself fall for him too quickly. Her concern was that we didn't know him all that well and that his job may take him farther away after he was finished here, and she really didn't want to see her sister's heart broken.

Tara closed her eyes and settled back in the rocking chair. She was listening to all the sounds of the countryside, the birds, the leaves rustling together as the wind pushed them around. She could hear the waves splashing up on shore and the boats going by on the lake. What a peaceful place to be, she thought as she drifted off into sleep.

Chapter 13

It was just a dream, or was it

The thunder clapped, the lightning was bright and one fork after the other hit the ground in the distance. The winds were severe, howling through every little crack they could find. Outside the window, the tree branches were banging up against her window. She was so afraid they would break the window that she got on the floor with her blankets and pillow away from the window. She was telling herself that she wasn't afraid of the storm, that it was nothing that would hurt her, and that it wouldn't last long. She tried and tried to convince herself of that repeating over and over it won't hurt me, it won't hurt me. Just at that moment she could hear some yelling coming from downstairs. She wanted to go see what it was all about but was afraid to move. The yelling got louder and things were banging around. She knew she had to go see what was happening. She grabbed her blanket and wrapped it around her as she snuck out of her room and down the dark hallway to the top of the stairs. There, she crouched down in the dark. She could see two people standing in the hallway arguing back and forth and yelling over the claps of thunder that were almost constant. She could see that it was her grandmother and another woman. Her grandfather wasn't around anywhere. She then realized that she didn't recognize this other woman and that her grandmother was very young, not at all like she remembered. Even as far back as her childhood memories, her grandmother always had gray hair. For some reason, her grandmother was young, with long dark hair down her back and in a braid. Tara then came to the realization that she was dreaming and then tried desperately to wake herself up but couldn't. She took a look at herself and didn't recognize the nightdress either, and her hair color was different not to mention the fact that she herself was very young.

As she listened to the argument that took place, she heard them talking about a boy. It sounded to her that she was accusing her grandmother of taking him from her. The woman was completely distraught. As she watched her grandmother, she could see she was upset as well, but she was telling the woman that it wasn't her fault and that this would be good for the boy in the long run. The woman didn't want to hear that; she then said that she would be back and that she would seek her revenge upon her and her family.

The woman stormed out the door as her grandmother tried to keep her in the house. She begged the woman not to venture out in the storm, to stay the night and leave in the morning. That it was too dangerous. The woman didn't listen and as she went for the door handle that was when she saw a little girl who seemed to be hiding behind her mother. The little girl looked at the top of the stairs where she was sitting crouched behind the railing and gave a tiny wave to her. When the lady shut the door behind them, her grandmother looked up at the stairs as well. Tara felt fear that she was in trouble for spying, but then her grandmother gave her a wink, then everything went black.

She couldn't see a thing. The thunder was still persistent and she made her way back to her room with the light from the lightning strikes. As she climbed into bed, she heard a door slam. It startled her so much that she froze on the spot. She then started to come out of her dream; the dream world was fading away as she opened her eyes to see Mr. Davies coming up the steps to the house.

Chapter 14

Dinner is Served

Tara greeted Mr. Davies as he approached the porch. Carla and Ryan were coming out of the cabin. Tara thought they must have seen him pull in. They went inside. Tara took the parcels from Mr. Davies and headed for the kitchen. He brought Swish Chalet for everyone. Tara could smell it and was getting hungry. She glanced at the clock; the time on the clock read five fifty-eight, almost six o'clock. She thought to herself that she was asleep for a while. The dream was so real that she knew that she wouldn't forget it.

She put the dream aside for now and turned to her sister to ask her to wake Molly up.

"I will let James know Mr. Davies is here," Ryan said, then headed for the boathouse.

Tara looked out the window to see James sitting in one of the dock chairs, fishing off the end.

"Well, you girls have had quite the eventful day, I hear." Mr. Davies was trying to make conversation. Tara started to tell him all about the day's events when he noticed Molly coming into the kitchen. He interrupted Tara to say hello to Molly.

"You look well rested," he told her as he took her hand and gave the back of it a kiss.

She blushed and said, "You are too kind." For some reason, this time, when he did this, it made Tara want to gag. She was shocked at herself for having that reaction, but nonetheless, she still wanted to gag.

"I have set the table so we can sit down and eat before it gets cold," Tara said, taking the platters of food to the table.

Carla gave her a hand; shortly everyone was sitting at the table.

Dinner was dished out and it was very silent as everyone started to eat.

"This just hits the spot, Mr. Davies; thank you," James said.

Everyone from there thanked Mr. Davies for the meal.

"No problem, it was the least I could do intruding on you like this." Mr. Davies took a sip of the lemonade that was in front of his plate. Mr. Davies addressed everyone now that his stomach was partially full.

"I have to tell you that in light of the events that have happened in this short period of time, the Royal Mounted Police are stepping up their investigation. They have been involved since the beginning because of your parent's disappearance." He said, looking at the girls. Mr. Davies was very good at balancing hospitality with duty and did it so seamlessly that you would hardly notice.

He was easing the conversation into more serious matters so as not to alarm everyone too quickly. "They believe because of the emails, the binoculars etc., in only a short period of time that this person behind all this has inside information as to your whereabouts."

"They also have come to believe, due to their extensive investigation, that they, for some reason, thought you girls to be on that plane as well."

Carla and Tara looked at each other. "That's funny because in the beginning, we were going to be going with them but canceled our tickets," Tara said.

"It was supposed to be a mini vacation for us while they did their searching," Carla added.

"Who but your parents, James and Molly, would have known about this trip?" Mr. Davies asked. The girls sat and thought about it for some time. Then, coming up with nothing, they both shook their heads.

"That's okay. The local police will be working alongside the RCMP in this investigation and hopefully, we will have a lead tomorrow when the results come back from the lab." He said.

"Well, for now, just relax, finish your dinner, and I will be sticking around for a while just to be on the safe side if that's okay with everyone. I will see if the B&B down the road has any vacancies," Mr. Davies took another mouthful of food.

Molly glanced at James, who knew exactly what she was thinking. He nodded, giving her the go-ahead to say so.

Molly was extending hospitality and kindness, "Mr. Davies, there is no need to rent a room when we have a perfectly good guest room sitting empty."

"Well, if you're sure you don't mind, I would love to stay here." He said.

"Great, then after dinner, I will make up the bed for you," Molly said as she went back to eating.

"Ryan, you are awfully quiet," James said, trying not to sound suspicious but concerned.

"Just enjoying the meal, James. I think Mr. Davies has covered everything." Ryan replied.

As dinner was finished and Molly and the girls were cleaning up, Mr. Davies asked Ryan why he was not with the girls when they went to the graveyard.

Ryan told them how they had left early and told Molly that they wanted sister time. Mr. Davies nodded his head. "You must, from now on, be sure to go after them if they do not want you with them."

"Yes sir," Ryan replied, feeling chastised for not doing his job.

"No offense, but what is Ryan here going to do for the girls if they do get into trouble?" He looked at Ryan, then continued, "He is just a young man."

Mr. Davies then could see the picture here and this explained the tension that he felt from the table.

"I assure you that Ryan here can handle himself. He is a private investigator working for the RCMP he was assigned to this case for the protection of you and the girls. He is highly trained in martial arts; he is a sharpshooter and has served on the swat team." Mr. Davies explained.

Ryan just hung his head. James, not knowing what to say, opened his mouth and said the only thing he could think of. "Well then, boy why didn't you say something from the beginning? I knew you were hiding something." James whacked him on the shoulder in a friendly manner and they all had a good chuckle about it.

"So, James? Maybe we can get some fishing in while I am up here, that is if things settle down some." Mr. Davies suggested.

James perked up right away; he loved fishing and even more, loved to fish with people.
"Most definitely," James said, rising from his seat.

"What about you, Ryan? Do you fish?" James asked him.

"Yes sir, I like to fish, but we will see when the time comes, I think at least one of us men should be here with the woman at all times," Ryan replied.

"That's Ryan for you, always working." Mr. Davies said.

"Let's step outside onto the patio and talk about the types of fish I can look forward to catching, then shall we." Mr. Davies suggested. The men then all rose to their feet and followed James out to the patio.

The evening was cooling off some, not a lot, but enough to sit comfortably outside. The sun had made its way across to the other side of the lake now and shade was coming in from the trees that were in the west direction of the sun. There were still a few hours of daylight left and the sun was still shining on the beach. Mr. Davies took in the sites of the water. A few water skiers on the lake and a couple of sea dos went speeding by.

"I am going to have to purchase me some property up here, I think, it's so peaceful and relaxed in the country." Mr. Davies noted.

"Yes, that it is," James agreed, underscoring his appreciation for the area.

The men started talking about the one subject that James loved best, fishing. James was an expert on the fish and how to catch them. He told some of his great tales about fishing up here with Mr. Wood when the girls were younger. He told Mr. Davies that Mr. Wood, the girl's grandfather, was the one to teach James everything he knew about fishing. He even left James in his will and all his fishing gear. You could tell by James' face how he missed and admired the girl's grandfather. Mr. Davies and Ryan sat there taking in every word James said. He was good at keeping people captivated by his stories.

Chapter 15

A Quiet Evening

Molly and the girls were in the kitchen cleaning up and making tea to take outside.

Tara and Carla were drying the dishes while Molly washed them. There weren't many because the meal was taken out and came with its own plates. There was just cutlery and glasses that needed to be washed.

When Molly was finished washing, she went and put the kettle on and set up the tray for the tea. She placed the cups, saucers, sugar, and milk on the tray and waited for the water to boil for the tea.

"Molly, I forgot to mention that the Officer that was here earlier dusting for prints will be back this evening and he wants to get your prints as well, I told him that you were resting earlier and that I didn't want to disturb you," Tara said.

That's fine, and then she looked at the palms of her hands. Tara just smiled and then explained the new procedure they had and how her hands would not get dirty.

"Good, I can imagine how hard it would be to get that ink off," Molly said.

The kettle was whistling away and Molly hustled to the stove to get it. She poured the tea and placed the pot on the tray.

"You girls take that out and I will be along with the sweets," Molly said as she went to the fridge. The girls went outside and set up the tea for everyone. Carla poured it.

"Molly is bringing out the desert in just a moment," Tara advised.

"Oh, I don't know if I could eat another bite." Mr. Davies sat back in his chair, pulling at his pants waste.

"Molly makes great deserts and I bet you will change your mind once you see what it is," James said.

"I could go for something sweet," Ryan licked his lips in anticipation.

Carla just smiled at him. Molly came out carrying a pie and some plates, napkins and forks. 'Anyone up for strawberry rhubarb pie?" she asked. Everyone said, "YES".

They were all enjoying their pie and tea as Officer Thompson came around the corner of the house. "Pardon my intrusion, but I rang the bell and there was no answer, so I took it upon myself to see if you were out back." James stood up to greet the Officer.

He put another chair on the table and asked him to have a seat.

"Please join us for some pie and tea," Molly insisted.

"Don't mind if I do, thank you," The Officer said.

Molly then went into the kitchen to get another plate, teacup, and saucer.

James introduced Officer Thompson to Mr. Davies.

"I suppose there is no new news as yet?" Mr. Davies asked him.

"Not yet, sir, but by noon tomorrow, we should have something on the prints, we have put a rush on them at the lab," He explained.

"Great, looking forward to seeing that." Mr. Davies said.

Molly returned and dished the Officer out a piece of pie, poured him some tea and sat down to finish her serving.

"Let's not have any more talk about these nasty things that are going on while we enjoy our desert." Molly requested.

"Here, here," said Mr. Davies, and they all dug into their desert in silence.

James started talking to the Officer about fishing and if he liked to fish. The Officer told him about the fish that he has caught on his past vacations and how he was looking forward to fishing again on this vacation. Molly had made another pot of tea and cleared the desert away. They were all sitting enjoying the evening. Officer Thompson asked Molly if he could get her prints now and she agreed.

"Ryan, have you found anything out yet on the emails?" Mr. Davies asked.

Ryan said, "Not as yet, I have a scanner set up right now scanning the IP address as we speak."

"Great, then later we will go have a look." Mr. Davies said.

They all sat enjoying the evening and watching the sun go down. The sun was a bright orange as it descended down behind the horizon. The breeze that was there when they first came out was gone and everything was still. The boats have stopped on the water except for a few fishermen. James mentioned how this was the best time of night for fishing as the fish tend to come close to the surface to catch the flies above the water. The Officer excused himself, thanking them for their kind hospitality. He told them that he must get to work.

"Yes, I think we are going in as well, the mosquitos have started biting, I have noticed," Molly said.

They all grabbed something from the table and came inside. Molly and the girls tidied Up. Molly then joined the men in the living room and Carla and Tara excused themselves to work on their computers.

Chapter 16

The Key to More Mystery

Carla followed Tara into her room and closed the door.

"Tara, you said you saw grandma that she came to you?" Clara asked.

Tara flopped onto the bed, feeling exhausted. She then propped her head up with her hands and told Carla again what happened that night in the kitchen. She then showed her the key around her neck.

"Do you have any idea as to what that could open?" Carla asked her.

She just shook her head and gave a big yawn. "There must be magic behind all of this; we haven't done any magic since Grandma died," Carla said.

Tara expressed her belief that their current struggles were separate from their past. "I also feel that whatever happened to Mom and Dad had nothing to do with what they were working on at the time."

"Well, what do you think it could be?" Tara said, sitting up against the pillows on the headboard.

"I don't know, but I think we have to figure out what the secret is that grandma was hiding and hopefully that will lead us to who is behind this," Carla said as she stared out into the darkness of the night.

The moon was almost full and not a cloud in the sky.
She remembered back when they were young, going to her grandmother's rituals with her mother and dancing in the moonlight, singing songs to the goddess, drinking apple juice, and eating moon cakes. Sometimes, on a warm night, after everyone had left, the four of them would go skinny-dipping in the lake. Those were fun days.

"I think grandma would be disappointed with us if we just neglected our Wicca background," Tara said

"I agree, so why don't we make tonight our first night back into the magic realm," Carla said excitedly.

"What did you have in mind?" Tara asked.

Carla suggested casting a circle to see if they could invoke their grandmother's spirit to come forth. Tara thought it was a wonderful idea. They started getting things ready right away. Tara grabbed a pad of paper and pen off the desk and then sat down to think of how they were going to construct it. Carla joined her. As they were making notes, they both fell asleep. Both were so tired from such a trying day.

They were so tired that they didn't hear Molly and James go up to bed. Mr. Davies said his goodnight and went to his room. All this conversation was just outside Tara's room. They didn't hear a thing.

Tara was entering her dream state, and she found herself standing in the doorway to her room. She was young again. Dressed in a nightgown unfamiliar to her. As she stood there, she could hear voices coming from the attic. Curious, she tiptoed down the hall to the door that opened up to the staircase to the attic. She carefully opened the door as not to make a sound, and then quietly ascended the staircase. Once at the top, she stood on the other side of the door, which was left open a crack, to listen. She didn't recognize the voice at first. She quickly took a peek into the room.

She could see the silhouette of her grandmother; it was dark all but a couple of candles that were on a table in front of her. She looked as if she was wearing a black robe or cloak with a hood. She was pretty sure it was her grandmother. She was chanting something over and over and swaying back and forth. Tara tried to hear what the words were but couldn't quite make it out. Tara just sat quietly, listening and watching everything that she did. She took something from one bowl and when she put it in another bowl, there were sparks and sizzles, and then a flame rose really high and quickly went back down to nothing. Her grandmother then put her hands up to the ceiling and asked Hecate if she could see it in her heart to let her husband live. There was a big gust of wind that started blowing everything around, the wind blew the pages in the book that her grandmother had in front of her, the windows started to rattle, everything was shaking then a flash of light came from nowhere and fell down into a bottle that was on the table where her grandmother was.

Her grandmother then took a cork that was sitting beside it and corked the bottle. She then thanked the goddess Hecate for her assistance; she chanted praise and thanks to her. Then a slight breeze rose and the candles went out. There was complete darkness, Tara just sat there watching and waiting. A small shimmer of light appeared again in front of her grandmother. She was picking everything up off the table and putting it into a chest. All accept the bottle with the cork in it, which she placed in the pocket of her apron, which she was wearing under her cloak. She placed everything, including the cloak into the chest. She then took a key from around her neck and locked the chest then put it back around her neck. Tara looked closely at the key; it was the same key she was wearing. As Tara stumbled to find the key beneath her nightgown, she panicked because it wasn't there. Her foot slipped off the stairs that it was resting on. It was a small thud but enough to make her grandmother turn around to look. She quickly slunk down the stairs and out into the hallway and back to her room. When she hopped into bed, she pulled the covers over her head. There was complete darkness. She lay there, scared she was going to get caught.

Tara jolted away, seeing herself beside Carla just as if nothing happened. Carla was sound asleep. She thought about her dream for a moment. Who was the little girl in her dream? And why do I keep dreaming that I am she? She was asking herself. She remembered watching her grandmother in the attic and then it dawned on her. The key, the key was for the chest in the attic. Excited now, she woke Carla up and told her about her dream and that she knew what the key opened.

Carla, not awake yet, was having a bit of trouble taking this all in.

"Carla come on, we fell asleep, we need to get to the attic and see if the chest is still there," Tara said, tugging at Carla's feet.

"Okay, okay, give me a minute," she said, sitting up.

"What time is it?' Carla asked.

"Twelve o'clock," Tara answered, looking at her digital alarm on the nightstand.

Carla and Tara grabbed everything they thought they would need, including some candles, some matches, an incense burner, and incense, and then headed up to the attic.

Quietly going by everyone's rooms so as not to wake them.

The attic door creaked when they opened it.

"It didn't creek in my dream," Tara whispered.

"Shhh," Carla said.

They went up the stairs to the attic; it was dark and lots of cobwebs. It didn't seem that anyone had been up there in quite a while.

They brushed the webs away and opened the door. There were more cobwebs with lots of dust. At every step, the dust just flew up around them. The attic was over the garage, and once they got in there, they realized they didn't have to be as quiet. They were far enough away from the rooms that they could move around and not disturb anyone. They kept everything to a whisper, though, just in case.

"I hope we remember how to do this, it's been a while, and actually, come to think of it, we never did this before," Carla said.

"No, we haven't, but if my hunch is right, we won't have to guess at it because Grandma's book of shadows should be in the chest," Tara said.

Carla looked around the room, "what chest?"

Tara couldn't see a chest either. It was dark and there was a lot of stuff up here. There was an old dressmaker's mannequin, boxes galore, and an old wardrobe with a mirror on the front of the doors. Old pictures, Tara recognized a couple of them before they redecorated the living room that they used to be hanging on the wall. There were two large portraits of her grandmother and grandfather that used to hang in the hallway going up the stairs to the second floor.

"It has to be here; it just has to be," Tara said with desperation and disappointment in her voice; Tara was anxious to find the chest. She believed it held the answers they were looking for.

"If it's here, we will find it. Relax and help get this wardrobe open," Carla said as she struggled to open the doors.

Tara and Carla both pulled on the doors. They were jammed shut, it seemed. They tried again and again when finally, one gave way, sending Carla backward and landing on her, but with a thump. Tara started to laugh, covering her mouth to muffle the sound that she could not restrain from making.

"Are you okay?' She asked Carla as she started to get her composer.
"Yes, I am fine, just my dignity is bruised," She said. That's when Tara noticed that Carla had been laughing too.

Carla stood up with the help of her sister. They went to the cupboard, moved the clothes around, and then they saw it. The chest was set at the back of the wardrobe. It was a fair-sized chest that would take both of them to get it out. They each took an end that had small handles for them to grip. They pulled it out of the wardrobe and placed it by the window. The window wasn't very big, but enough of the moon's light could get through so they could see what they were doing.
Tara took the key from around her neck crossed her fingers showing Carla and Carla did the same, then she took the key and placed it in the keyhole. Two clicks and the lid popped open.

Tara was struggling to see and realized they needed more light she turned to Carla and asked.

"Carla, can you light one of the candles in the bag so we can see better."

Carla lit the candle and held it up over the chest. Tara pulled out a large black cloak, just like in her dream. There were bowls, herb bottles, candles, crystals, Athame, a wand, a chalice, and a cast iron bowl, which she remembers was where the fire came from.

"Wow, it's all here just like in my dream," Tara said as she reached to the bottom of the chest and found the book. A thick book, leather bound with iron bandings on the front and back. It was heavy. It had to weigh at least 8 pounds. The book was about six to eight inches thick. Every page was written except a few at the back, which were left blank.

Tara placed it on the floor, and the girls looked through the book to find a ritual that they needed. They didn't have a clue what it would be called, but they figured they would know it if they saw it. That is, if there was anything like that in there. They flipped page after page praying that they would come across something they could use to help guide them at least. Tara stopped turning the pages.

"That is the one she used in my dream. Tara exclaimed.

Carla thought about the word dream and believed it was more than just a dream, "I don't think you can call these dreams, I believe you are having visions or are being guided by grandma somehow through a dream," Carla said.

Tara thought about it and realized her sister was right
"It's true they say that spirits contact us through our dreams more easily because that is when our minds are most open to anything," Tara said.

Carla nodded and Tara went back to looking for the right spell. There were a lot of pages to look through and they didn't want to spend all night looking. Carla took the athame out of the chest and pointed it at the book.

"Show me the page that will bring our grandma to us this night.'

Carla said.

A soft breeze picked up in the room, and Tara immediately took her hands off the book.

The pages started flipping by them as the breeze blew. Then it all stopped like it was never there to begin with. The book was now open to a page with the title "Veil Crossings." Tara read what was on the page, and sure enough, this was what they were looking for.

"Ah ha, do you believe it, I did that," Carla said, all excited.

Tara figured that she would jump up and down if she could without waking anyone. Tara smiled and said, "Way to go sis, I didn't know you had it in you."

Carla was proud of herself and decided there and then to be more committed to their heritage,
       "Well, I made up my mind that if we were born with it, we might as well use it." She commented

"I agree," Tara said. They picked up the book and made an altar out of the top of a box that they found to be sturdy enough.

They set up the altar according to the diagram in the book and then they took the crystals and placed them in a circle around them. The book called for something to be placed in the spot where you wanted the person to come. It had to be something of theirs for them to connect to. Carla thought right away and put her grandmother's cloak on the other side of the box. They ensured the crystals were placed accordingly to encompass the box, the cloak, and them.

They then were instructed to put certain ingredients into the glass bowl; there were some herbs, vervain, oak moss, patchouli and lavender if it was female, and hops if male. They placed this in the bowl. Then they were told to place some of the graveyard dirt in the other glass bowl, but never mix the two ahead of time, was the warning. They both looked at one another in question.

"I don't think I want to find out why, do you?' Tara asked.

Carla just shook her head. Carla silently agreed with Tara's hesitation.

They had to light the charcoal and place it in the cast iron bowl. They were all set.

They held hands and read the next part. They would need a pin. Tara rooted around for a pin. Sure enough, there was a pin in the small box where they found the charcoal. They then started to chant the words from the book as they pricked their fingers, putting a drop of blood each into the cast iron bowl.

"We call to you, Grandma Wood, from far to near, we call you here." They chanted confidently, determined to trust in the ritual despite any lingering doubts or fears.

They then placed the herbs into the bowl, it spattered and flared up in flames, and then they added a pinch of the dirt. They put their hands over the bowl as it smoldered; they moved their hands in a circular motion, the contents of the bowl started to stir along with them.

They continued the chant. "Our blood to your blood we do summon, stir, and call you forth, Grandmother Wood, come to us, come to us!" They then took the contents of the bowl and dumped it onto the cloak as instructed.

All but the burning charcoal, they wouldn't want a fire to start. The ashes on the cloak started to swirl in a circle, a spiral shape was forming from the ashes. The ashes then rose off the cloak higher and higher they stopped rising at about four feet off the ground but still swirling in the spiral pattern. Tara and Carla just watched in amazement then the ashes stood still. Slowly they trickled down to the cloak. As the ashes dissipated a form was taking shape in the ashes place. Before long the girls were staring at a figure that looked like their grandmother. The form was very still, and then when the last ash dropped, their grandmother's eyes opened. She looked around the room and smiled when she looked at the girls.

"Girls, you look wonderful. You're all grown up now, and might I say, what a great job you did in summoning me across the veil."

Grandmother was proud and impressed with her granddaughters for successfully performing the ritual and summoning her.

Tara and Carla gave her a hug; Tara didn't want to let go.

"I won't be able to hold this form long, so we best have our talk," she said to the girls.

"We've missed you so much," Carla said.

"I know you have, but I have been with you the whole time and that is why I have appeared to Tara that night." Grandmother reassured them with a hug that her spirit has always been near.

She looked at Carla and said, "Unfortunately… you, my dear, have put up some sort of barrier that I could not penetrate. You really must not hold so much hostility it's not good for you physically." Carla knew exactly what her grandmother was referring to and promised her that she would try and let it go.

They sat and talked for a while, catching up. Their grandmother said that she was aware of most things in their lives. She explained that she every now and then would peek in on them and see what was going on.

Tara was frightened but knew she needed to know about her parents good or bad.

"Is our mother and father up there with you?" Tara mustered the courage to ask about their parents.

"I was going to tell you that, but no, they are not here with me. I have not been able to focus on them since the accident. But believe me, I have not stopped trying to find them." The grandmother responded, clearly saddened by the whole thing.

"However, I believe that your parents are still alive somewhere, and I have a feeling I know who is behind this whole thing, " she continued.

"Does it have anything to do with the person who wrote you that letter?" Tara connected this clue, indicating she has some knowledge of her grandmother's past conflicts.

The grandmother confirmed the connection, "Yes, she was, and my cousin who turned into a nemesis of mine."

"What did you have of hers that she wants, we could get it and give it back." Tara felt the best way to resolve the conflict was to help return whatever her grandmother's nemesis wanted.

"It's not that easy. Let me explain." Their grandmother then explained the history behind the letter.

Chapter 17

A Glimpse into The Past

It was the summer of nineteen sixty when Elsa Wood and Walter Black had married and bought the estate. They decided to give the estate a name, so they called it Black-Wood, using a combination of their sir names. They couldn't wait to start a family, and within a few years, they had a baby girl named Margaret, who was the girl's mother. After Margaret was a year old, they tried for another but were never successful. They never gave up hope that she would have a brother or sister one day, but as they soon realized that it was never meant to be. Margaret was an only child.

Elsa had a cousin Sarah, whom she was really close to all her life. They grew up together as good friends. Sarah spent most of her life with Elsa and her family. Sarah wasn't as lucky as Elsa and didn't have the stable home life that Elsa had. She came from two parents who were alcoholics. Her father spent most of his time in prison on DUIs or from getting into fights with people at his local bar. They never had much money to speak of and what they did have, they drank. Sarah went hungry a lot of times and would always miss school because her mother never got up in time to get her ready for the bus.

One day, Elsa visited Sarah with her family and Elsa's mother talked her into letting Sarah stay with them until they got on their feet. Sarah lived with them most of the time, and the two girls got along great, better than their sisters. Sarah would go and stay with her parents once in a while on weekends when they were sober. Sarah stopped visiting her parents when she got older; she found that she had nothing to say to them, and her eyes were open to the situation. She was never comfortable around them. When Sarah was about fifteen, her parents were in a car accident in which they both perished. Sarah grew up with Elsa and her family. She grew up and finished school. Sarah married and moved two years before Elsa and Walter. They had a nice home in town. Her husband worked for the mining commission that Walter and his family-owned. Elsa's family came from old money and owned a lot of the town's businesses.

Sarah and her husband, Carl, didn't have a lot of money to speak of, but they were comfortable. They had a boy, William, within the first year of their marriage and then they had a little girl Mary, the same year Margaret was born.

Sarah, Carl and the kids would often come and stay with them for a weekend in the summer. One summer, the men went fishing while the woman stayed back with the kids to let them swim and play on the beach. It was the same as most weekends except for the tragedy that was going to take place that afternoon.

The day was going well; everyone was full from lunch and Elsa and Sarah were reading their books while keeping an eye on the kids. A police boat approached the dock with the men's boat in tow. Their men were not in sight. The Officer told them there was an accident and that Carl didn't make it, but Walter was in rough shape and currently in a coma at the hospital. Just then, two more Officers came to the backyard. The kids were crying, and the lady Officer said that she would stay with the children if they wished to go to the hospital and that her partner would take them. Elsa and Sarah agreed and quickly left with the Officer. The children struggled with the Officer wanting to go with their mothers. Sara and Elsa promised them they could come the next time, then told them to be good and that they would be back soon. The lady Officer looked at William as he just stood there with a blank face, no tears but a hint of anger in his eyes. He never said a word or even tried to comfort his sister.

The Officer had taken them inside and given them something to eat as she tried to explain the particulars of the accident to the children in a manner that they would be able to understand. She told them that sometimes it was better to draw a picture when they were feeling bad, that it helped to take the pain away for a while. The girls went to Margaret's room and brought down some paper and crayons. William just sat there staring out the window.

Sarah and Elsa were met at the hospital by the doctor, who explained that the boat capsized near the damn and that the undertow was strong, which pulled Carla to the bottom; he was trapped in some weeds. Walter, it seemed, fell from the boat but far enough away from the damn that the undertow didn't take him. It seemed that he must have hit his head on something and was knocked unconscious and floated up on the beach beside the damn. Apparently, there was a couple of kids fishing not far away from the damn and saw the accident. They quickly ran for help.

Sarah was devastated, shaking uncontrollably. The doctor insisted on giving her something to calm her down. Elsa told the doctor that she would be staying with her at the estate until she was on her feet again. The doctor stayed with her while Elsa went to see her husband. She, too, was in deep shock but couldn't help thinking how lucky she was to have her husband. She felt guilty for feeling relieved that he was going to be okay while her cousin's husband was dead. She gathered herself and went back to Sarah and they went with the Officers to take them home. On the ride home, Sarah calmed down and told Elsa that she appreciated keeping them there until they could get back on their feet. She knew she didn't want to be left alone right now and she wasn't even sure she would be able to deal with the kids. Elsa understood and comforted her the best she could.

When they arrived home, it was around eight o'clock that evening. The Officer had managed to put the girls to bed with a promise that their mothers would come and see them when they got home. William however, insisted that he stay up to see them when they arrived. Sarah took William up to his room and spoke with him up there. She thought she had him all tucked in for the night when she came downstairs to talk with the Officers, but she was wrong. He snuck out behind her and watched from the top of the staircase. He couldn't see much but could hear everything. The Officers were telling Sarah and Elsa the whole story from the boys that were fishing nearby. The ones that called for help. They said they saw the two men in a fistfight standing in the boat. Both Sarah and Elsa looked at each other, puzzled. They have never fought before or even shown any hostility towards each other. This behavior had to be wrong; the boys had to be mistaken. The Officer then told them that the boys saw one man, Carl, take the paddle and whack the other man on the head. The man went flying over the front of the boat. They figured that the commotion of the man falling out caused the boat to jerk, throwing the other man out; unfortunately, when he fell out, the boat had already drifted too close to the damn. They never saw him come up out of the water, but while one boy ran for help, the other saw the first man floating near shore and he went to pull him up out of the water. This puzzled them both, but Elsa said that when Walter was well enough to talk, they would straighten this all out.

When Walter was released from the hospital both Sarah and Elsa questioned him as to what happened on the boat that day. He had already given his statement to the police, but Sarah and Elsa wanted to hear it from him. They were sitting outside on the back patio at the time, having tea after supper; the girls were playing on the beach. William was supposed to be in his room. He had been misbehaving at supper and Sarah sent him to his room for a while. Walter told them both that when they were out fishing, everything was going well until Walter had a big fish on his line. Carl got upset that he didn't catch anything that day and was acting very odd. Walter asked him for his help to bring the fish in; Carl insisted that he could do it himself. Walter said that he kept saying things like it's my fish anyway. They got into an argument about the fish and Walter said he remembered telling him that he was being silly and acting like a child. That is when Carl took a swing at him. Walter said that he didn't fight back but was trying to get Carl to stop swinging punches at him and calm him down. Walter then explained he turned to save his rod from going in the water and losing the fish, and then that was all he remembered.

A few weeks went by, Sarah seemed to be getting better but was on medication from the doctor to combat depression. She knew that she needed to get back on her feet to take care of the children, and they had a home to go to, so she would soon have to face that.

It was nearing Lammas, and Sarah and Elsa were preparing for the festival to come. Elsa's parents were Wiccan, so raising her children with the traditions of Wicca, Sarah included. They were raised with spirituality and practiced as they got older.

They were always included in the family rituals on the Sabbats. Lammas was Sarah's favorite, normally. Elsa knew this and tried to make it fun for her. They spent the day baking bread and cakes. They made a special evening feast after the ritual. The children were helping, as was tradition on Sabbats. The girls were having fun mixing the nuts in a bowl with the spices of the season. William just sat on the back patio, watching Walter prepare for the fire that evening. Walter had asked him to help with the firewood, but

William just ignored him. He was really taking his father's death hard. Sarah had taken him to the doctor for a check-up. The doctor said he was fine and that this was his way of dealing with the accident and his father's death. He reassured them that he would soon snap out of it and all would be good, but to be aware of any mood swings or possible breakdown.

William was angry, and his anger grew as the days passed. His anger was mostly directed at Walter.

Around three that afternoon, they decided to have a small meal to hold them over until the feast later that night. Walter tried to strike up a conversation with William. He said that if he liked, he would take him fishing the next day. William blows up at Walter and accuses him of wanting to take him out on the boat to kill him like he killed his father. Everyone was shocked at what they heard. Sarah slapped William across the face; her reflexes got the better of her. William then turned on her and told her that she was blind and that Walter never wanted his father around. Sarah sent him to his room. He pushed his chair out so hard that it fell to the floor, and then ran to his room. They all realized now why William was behaving the way he was. He blamed Walter for his father's death; he must have heard the conversations the adults had. Walter went up to William's room right after they finished eating to have a talk with him. Walter tried to tell him that he loved his father and would never want to hurt him. William didn't believe him. William said that if he had given his father the fish his father would have been alive today. Walter explained that he felt that Carl must have been ill because it was not like Carl would behave like that. Walter said that there was an autopsy performed on his father before he was buried and that he would see if the doctors found anything during it that would have caused him to behave in that matter. William told him to go ahead; it didn't matter; he was still dead, and it was still Walter's fault.

Walter returned downstairs and told Elsa and Sarah what the boy had said. Sarah then told Walter that the doctor said that Carl had a tumor, but it was not life-threatening and could have been operated on with ultimate success. She said that she didn't think that it was important to share that information under the circumstances. This could very well have been the cause of his behavior. Walter said that he would see the coroner after the next week to verify if it could have caused him to act like that. They all agreed and continued with the preparations for that evening.

Sarah and Elsa had invited a few people they knew to celebrate Lammas with them. They started the celebration, dancing and singing and having a great evening. William sat on the sidelines, not wanting to participate. He just watched. When the ritual was over, everyone gathered for the feasting, and William took part in the feasting. He actually seemed to be more sociable. When the feasting was over, Sarah and Elsa put the kids to bed, including William. It was late and they were all tired; it didn't take them long to fall asleep. The adults all sat by the bonfire for a while longer, enjoying each other's company. When everyone went home, Walter put the patio chairs away in the boathouse and then disposed of the fire. Sarah and Elsa went in to tidy up the kitchen from this evening's event. They were putting food away and doing dishes when Sarah looked up and saw flames coming from the boathouse. Elsa ran right away while Sarah called the fire department. She was worried about Walter, she couldn't see him in her sight, she grabbed the garden hose, turned on the water and ran with it. It didn't stretch that far, but she tried to put the fire out with what water would reach.

Elsa panicked and kept yelling for Walter, but no one answered. Sarah came running with a couple of buckets. They couldn't get close to the heat from the fire, which was too much for them. Mary came running out yelling for her mother but Sarah kept saying telling her to stay back. Mary yelled that William wasn't in the house and they couldn't find him. Elsa knew right away that he must be in the boathouse too. Sarah and Elsa soaked themselves in water and were to go into the boathouse. We could hear the fire trucks pull up. Before we knew it, the pump trucks were pumping water from the lake. They had the fire out before we could even get through the door. The captain had a flashlight; he went in with two other men behind him. They emerged within minutes with Sarah's son and Walter. William just had smoke inhalation, and he would be fine; they administered some oxygen to him. Walter was unconscious and would have to go to the hospital.

The fire chief decided that both could use a good look-over and insisted they both go when the ambulance arrived. The ambulance was there within minutes; Sarah went to get the girls quickly dressed so that we could follow them to the hospital. Margaret was standing at the door, looking out at everything going on. She was traumatized and hasn't liked fire since.

We met up with the doctor in the hospital and he informed Elsa that Walter had a slight concussion and minor burns to his hands and legs. The best thing for him was rest. He then turned to Sarah and told her that her son would be fine and that he was resting with a sedative and getting plenty of oxygen. He said that he wanted to keep him overnight, but she could see him now if she liked. Elsa told her to go ahead and she would come to get her after she saw Walter. Sarah went and took Mary with her. The nurse stopped Elsa before she went in and told her that she had given him something for the pain and that he might not be with it, so not to be alarmed.

Elsa went in and saw that Walter was resting comfortably. His hand was wrapped in gauze bandages and he looked like he was getting ready to put boxing gloves on. He had a special lightweight blanket over him so it wouldn't bother his legs. He opened his eyes and smiled up at her. Elsa could see he was tired and drugged up. She kissed him and told him she would be back for breakfast. As she was walking down the corridor to Sarah, she thought that Walter probably wouldn't even remember she was there.

Elsa noticed two policemen sitting on the bench outside of Williams's room. They stood and tipped their hat to her as she approached. She asked why they were there and they explained that they were called in by the fire department. The fire department found that the fire was started on purpose. An investigation was always warranted when arson was involved. Elsa was puzzled; she couldn't believe that it was arson. She asked how they knew. They told her that they found a box of matches and gas was strewn all over everything in the boathouse. Elsa took a seat on the bench and the Officers stood in front of her. This was too much for her to handle. The one Officer pulled out his notepad and pen and then asked her what took place that evening. She explained about the company she had around the fire that night. They then wanted to know why the boy was in the boathouse that late at night and not in bed. She told them that he was in bed as far as his mother and she knew. They both put the kids to bed before they went out to join the rest of them at the fire. That was about eleven o'clock. It wasn't the first time they had put the children to bed and went outside for a fire. The Officer assured her there was nothing wrong with that but asked again why he was there. Elsa said she had no idea, and nobody had even heard or seen him come out. She then informed the Officers that they were going to have to ask William those questions because he was the only one who could answer. Margaret was so traumatized that she never let go of Elsa's dress for a minute and hid behind her every time they spoke to someone. No one paid her any mind. She was just five years old. They went into the room where Sarah and William were. Mary was sitting on the end of Williams's bed. William was dopey from the relaxants the nurse had given him. Sarah was talking to another Officer. She told the same story that Elsa said but added that her boy must have been trying to help Walter when he saw the fire. She was then stumped when the Officer asked why he didn't let anyone know that there was a fire. Elsa then stepped in and took Sarah by the elbow and pulled her away. Then Elsa informed the Officer to direct those questions to William when he woke up and if there were any more questions for them, they were going to have to wait until morning. She then led Sarah and Mary out to the hall, continuing to the car without looking back. Elsa knew in her gut that William had something to do with the fire. She didn't want to blame him, but after his behavior over the past couple of weeks, she wouldn't have put it past him.

The next morning the investigator was knocking on the door with a couple of policemen and what seemed like the whole fire department. Elsa told them they could go ahead and investigate the boathouse, then asked the investigator to join them for breakfast on the back patio. They all sat down to eat toasted buns with jam and tea. Sarah and the girls were very quiet. The investigator thanked her for the food and tea, informing her that he hadn't have breakfast yet and that it hit the spot. He then took out his notebook and read what he already had. He told them he hadn't gone back to the hospital as yet and thought he would wait for them and they could all talk about what happened. One of the Officers came up with a burnt baseball glove and bat. He asked if this belonged to anyone here. Elsa looked at Sarah, but she didn't say anything. She could see that the evidence was getting stronger against her son. Elsa then said that it looked like Williams. Sarah shot her a dirty look. The inspector was writing all this down. Elsa knew that he didn't miss the dirty look she gave her either. He put his notepad away and asked if he could help them clear up breakfast. Sarah and Elsa said that they were fine doing it. They told the girls to get ready to go to the hospital. They went upstairs to get dressed and clean their teeth. Sarah followed Elsa into the kitchen, putting the cups in the sink. She turned to Elsa and told her to please not incriminate her boy for this. Elsa just told her that she would tell the truth, then took her hands and told her if it was her son, then he needed help in getting by this, that even she should see how angry he has become and that she couldn't deny that William blamed Walter for his father's death. Sarah shook her head no, then pulled her hands away in anger and told Elsa that there was nothing wrong with her boy and that he didn't need help, maybe Walter was the cause of Carl's death. Elsa couldn't believe what she was hearing.

The drive to the hospital was a quiet one; no one seemed to be talking. Sarah now had a very scorned look on her face and Elsa could see that she was now thinking along the same lines as her son. The investigator met them in Williams's room; Sarah turned to Elsa and told her to stay outside with Margaret. Elsa and Margaret went to Walters's room. He seemed to be in better form today and the nurse was feeding him his oatmeal. She told Elsa that he didn't need anything for the pain today that was as strong, so he should be able to answer any questions the investigator had. Walter, between mouthfuls, said that they had taken his clothes and bagged them. That the investigator wanted them. I told him I would come back with more clothes for him this afternoon.

When the nurse left, I sat down and asked him what had happened that night. He shook his head in disbelief. He told Elsa that he was putting the chairs away, and when he turned around, William was there with his bat in his hand and the glove on the dock beside him. He then took a swing before he could stand up straight and stop him. He said that he wasn't knocked unconscious yet but couldn't move for the stars in front of his eyes. His vision was blurry, but he could see and smell gasoline being poured all over him and the things around him. Then, the whole place went up in flames. He said that was when he must have passed out.

The inspector came into the room and Walter told him the whole story again. The inspector asked why we thought that William would want to hurt him. Elsa explained about the accident, which the inspector remembered and told him that William, on more than one occasion, had blamed Walter for his father's death. He was very angry that Walter was alive and his father was dead. The boy was eight years old and things like this were very confusing for children. Elsa turned and saw Sarah standing in the door way. She knew she had heard everything that she said to the investigator. She could just imagine how angry she was with her now by the look on her face. Elsa added to her statement saying that he was a good boy and was just confused with everything he was feeling, that it hadn't been easy, Mary had Margaret to help her, but William had no one his age to help him.

Sarah brushed pass me and handed the inspector the cloths he wanted of Williams. The inspector looked through the back and found his shirt, there was a hole in the shirt. The inspector then explained that the shirt matched a piece of material that was found caught on a nail that was sticking out from the bench table that was in there. Elsa remembered that Walter was going to fix that because he was always scrapping his side on it. The inspector looked at William, who was standing in front of Sarah. She had her hands resting on his shoulders as if to assure him that she was there to protect him. The inspector looked right at the boy and asked him to point blank why he wanted to hurt Mr. Wood. William looked down at his feet, then looked up at the investigator and said that he had to because that was the way his father would have wanted it. It wasn't fair that his father had to leave and if Walter left, his father could come back. The investigator looked at Sarah in question. What he said made no sense to the investigator. Sarah asked him why he thought that. William turned and looked at his mother and said that he had seen this man at his father's funeral, and that was what he had told him. Walter had to die for his dad to be happy. He told William that his father may even come back. When asked who this person was and what he looked like, William told the investigator that he was a tall man dressed in a black cloak, he couldn't see his face, but he seemed like a nice man. The inspector closed his book and told the ladies that was all for today. Sarah was puzzled; she didn't know who to be mad at Elsa or William. The investigator said he would be around later this evening to check in on us. Elsa told him that wasn't necessary, but he insisted anyway. Sarah, Mary and William waited for Elsa and Margaret out in the hall. Elsa told Walter that she would be back with some cloths for him shortly. She kissed him goodbye and lifted the Margaret up to give her dad a kiss.

When they got home, Sarah asked the kids to go outside and play for a while but to stay away from the boat house and the Officers. The children complied and played on the beach instead. Elsa looked out the window to see them and noticed William was playing with the girls. That was the first sign of him being normal in weeks. Sarah then jumped down Elsa's throat. Yelling at her, asking her how she could be so insensitive, and accusing her of hating her and her kids. Then she broke down and cried, asking why would he think that there was a man; he was just making it up so he didn't look so bad. Elsa tried to comfort her, she put her arms around her, but all she could think of was that William needed help. Sarah heard screaming coming from outside and stood up to see they both went to find out what was the matter. William had ahold of both their hair and was pulling them along the beach. Sarah promptly grabbed William by the arm, gave him a spank on the bottom and told him to go to his room. She then stayed to see if the girls were okay and then went up to see him.

Elsa got the girls some ice for their heads to take the sting away, then gave them some juice and asked them what happened. Mary said that they were playing nicely together when he started talking to nothing and saying that he couldn't do something like that; when we asked to do what, he laughed and said that this man was telling him to do something to us. We laughed at him, there was no one standing there, the girls said and then he got angry, grabbed our hair and started pulling us. Elsa said that was fine, told them to finish their juice and go back outside to play. The girls gulped their juice and ran outside. Elsa went up to see if everything was okay with Sarah and William when she heard them yelling at each other. She listened to what they were saying and heard William yelling at Sarah, saying that Walter had to die and that he wanted him to die.

There was pure silence after that. So silent you could hear a pin drop. Elsa stood still afraid that the floor would creek if she moved. Just then, the door opened, startling her and Sarah by the look on her face, which quickly turned to anger. Elsa purposely stood in her way, blocking her from leaving the room; she told her that she was coming up to see if everything was okay but over heard what William had said. She then told Sarah that he needed professional help. She had better come to her senses and stop protecting him that protecting him wasn't going to do him any good in the long run. Sarah pushed Elsa out of her way and told her that she should mind her own business.

Sarah and William spent all their time in Sarah's room. The next couple of days were spent in silence when Elsa was around Sarah, and William spent their time in her room. Sarah seemed to leave Mary in Elsa's care all the time and it seemed to Elsa that the only child that mattered to Sarah was William.

It was seven o'clock one evening and we were all sitting in silence at the dinner table as usual. Every night, like clockwork, the inspector came by to check on how we were all doing. And sure enough, the knock on the door was right on schedule. Elsa answered the door and this time, he had an Officer with him. We invited them in, and they promptly took a seat at the table.

The inspector immediately started telling us what they had found out about the case. They took the blood samples from the bat and matched them to Walter's blood. William was going to get up from the table when the Officer stood up and asked him to please stay seated. William looked scared and so did Sarah. Elsa felt badly for Sarah. The Officer told Sarah that the boy was going to have to go with them and that they would be taking him to a detention center. Someone would call her the next day to give her details of his court date and visiting privileges etc. Sarah flipped, grabbed at her son, and refused to let go. The inspector and the Officer had to pry her away from the boy. The girls started to cry; they were scared, and Elsa took them and held them. The Officer escorted William to the police car by the elbow. Sarah followed him out and gave William a hug and told him to be good.

She spent the next two weeks visiting him, when she wasn't there, she was in her room. She dragged poor Mary everywhere with her, even to her room with her. She wouldn't let her play with Margaret anymore. Walter was heartbroken when he found out the news and told Elsa to tell Sarah that we would do everything we can to help. When Elsa told Sarah this one day at breakfast Sarah told her not to bother that they would be moving out by the end of the week. The day they left Sarah turned to Elsa and said that she wanted what was rightfully hers to have and that she will see to it that she gets it. She told Elsa the family heritage is hers to have and Elsa wasn't strong enough to have it. Elsa knew exactly what she was talking about, one it was the Book of shadows and the secret spell to retrieve another's power. This was a forbidden ritual that was to never be used.

Sarah and Mary got a house in town and wouldn't take any phone calls from Elsa or Walter. Elsa and Walter kept up with the news on William and it turned out that he was found guilty and would have to serve time in juvenile detention.

Sarah ended up having a nervous breakdown that she never recovered from, and Mary was sent off to an aunt's to live in the States. Walter and Elsa tried to get custody of Mary, but the courts said that it was in her will that the child goes with this aunt.

When William finally was released, he was sent to his aunts as well, when he was old enough, he came to the house, he stood at the door and promptly told us what had happened to his mother and that one day he would seek his revenge on Walter and Elsa.

"So, you see, girls, there are a lot of things conspiring against you right now, and your mother and father have been caught up in this ordeal." Grandmother shared the complicated history which helped put a lot of pieces of the puzzle together for Tara and Carla.

And explained the limitations of her spirit, "I so wish I had confronted this situation long ago, and maybe this would never have happened." She hung her head and played with her fingers frantically. "I wish there was more that I could tell you or do for you, but my hands are tied here on this plane of existence. I know we all think that when you die, your spirit can then see what they want and go where they wish, but it's not quite like that. We don't get to see everything we want to, but we can check in from time to time to see how our loved ones are doing. It's not like you would imagine at all, we don't have the free rein that we think we would have. It's like a graduation experience that you work toward, hard to explain. There are limits on what we can do and where we can go, and that can be upgraded. I will try and explain better later; however, for now, I need you girls to know after William was released from his custody and into his aunt's custody, there was a dark presence that seemed to come over the house. I, unfortunately, was not able to figure out what it was, and when I passed, I was getting close; I didn't leave a record because I didn't want anyone or anything to have a hold on me. Girls please be aware and be careful."

Carla and Tara were amazed that they were even getting to speak with their grandmother. As they sat listening to her, she started to fade.

"Grandma, you are starting to fade in and out, what's wrong?" Tara asked.

"I have been here too long already and they are calling me back, I will leave you with this information for now, we will talk again soon," she promised the girls and blew them both kisses before she vanished.

Carla's eyes started to well up and she reached for the end of her shirt to wipe her eyes.

"I know how you feel. I miss her so much, but at least we know we can have some contact with the ones we love who have passed over." Tara said as she started to pack up the stuff on the altar.

"Well, look at it this way: we still have what it takes," Tara tried to lift Carla's spirits. Tara smiled at Carla and gave her a pat on the back. "Yeah, it is getting late and I don't know about you, but I am tired." Carla stood up and helped Tara put all the stuff back in the chest.

Chapter 18

A Day on The Beach

Tara was woken up the next morning by many voices that seemed to be coming from down stairs. She lied in her bed, taking her time to wake up. She glanced over at the clock on her nightstand. It was 10:15 in the morning. The last thing she remembers from last night was looking at the clock before she closed her eyes it read 1:40 a.m. She remembers thinking that it seemed like they were only up in the attic for a short time, she could hardly believe that much time had passed. As she lied in bed thinking about seeing her grandmother again and the story, she told her and her sister about their mother, more questions arose.

Tara thought, "Where was William today and where was his sister Mary?" these were things she was going to see if she could find out somehow. Tara was thinking to herself, wondering about William and Mary's whereabouts after hearing her grandmother's story.

She knew she needed a game plan. But where to begin? It was such a long time ago, she thought. The voices downstairs seemed to get louder, "what is going on?" she asked herself as she got out of bed and dressed.

She looked out the window to see what kind of a day it was. She was amazed at the beautiful weather they were having this year. The sky was a clear as could be, not a cloud in it. The blue seemed to be radiant as it met the lake on the horizon; you would have sworn the sky was coloring the lake to match it. There wasn't much of a breeze up either and that would explain why there were no parasailers on the water. The waves were small, almost not visible and they were far apart, so in between the waves, the water shone like glass. She turned her attention to the thermometer that was just outside her window. It was eighty outside in the sun already and it was still morning. Tara then knew it was going to be a hot day, so she dressed appropriately. She put on a nice halter top that was knitted with fine wool, it was short and showed off her belly, which she had pierced.

Then she put on a pair of low riding shorts to show off the tattoo of a Celtic design and woven into the design was a dragon fly. Her hair she decided to put up in a ponytail for the day. She figured that later today, she would go swimming.

"That's it," she thought to herself, "I am going to get back to work answering my emails and helping my customers. I am going to take my laptop to the beach and work there, get a suntan while I am working" pleased with her idea she tucked her laptop under her arm and went downstairs.

The noise of voices seemed to have moved outside to the patio because the house was now quiet. She peered out the kitchen window to see who was there. Molly, James, Ryan, Mr. Davies, the detective, the Officer, and two other men she had never seen before. They were all sitting on the patio. Tara decided to make a plate of fruit and cheese and some crackers for breakfast. She noticed they had a pot of tea in front of them on the table and decided to put the kettle on in case anyone wanted more tea. Tara arranged her plate of food along with a cup and saucer of her own. She left her laptop on the kitchen table until she found out who and why these people were here.

"Good morning, sleepy head," Molly addressed Tara the minute she came out the door.

All the men rose from their seats in a polite gesture to acknowledge her presence, then sat themselves down again.

"What's going on this morning?" Tara asked. Are we having an Officer's convention? "

Tara saw that the two Officers were wearing uniforms but had never seen them before. As she looked at their crest, she realized they were detectives from the RCMP. They weren't in the full uniform that you see them wear, just a shirt, tie, and dress pants. Their shirts were decorated with the crest and their status within the organization. The detective from town and his Officer were dressed in nice clothes as well, but not the uniforms of the police station. Mr. Davies was sporting a blue tank top and black shorts, the khaki kind. Ryan also wore a green golf shirt and some white shorts.

James had gone to get Tara a chair and was placing it beside Molly.

"We were just saying that the prints came back negative; there is no record of those prints on file. That is the bad news." The detective said. Officer Thompson continued, "But we have a lead on the emails that Ryan had scanned. They led to an account held by a Mr. W. Jackson; however, we are still trying to locate him. There seems to be no address on file for Mr. Jackson, and we are not sure how he was able to establish an account without any information. But be assured we are doing everything we can to find out where this person is."

"That's great. Will you let us know as soon as you find something out?" Tara asked.

"Of course, we will keep you posted immediately upon anything that arises. We expect you to do the same, please." Officer Thompson said.

Just then, Mr. Davies stood up and addressed the other two gentlemen. "This is Officer Mackenzie and Officer Jones. They are the gentlemen looking into your parents' disappearance."

Tara stood, shook both their hands, and sat down again.

"How is that going? Have you found them yet?" Tara asked, almost afraid of the answer.

"No, I am sorry to say we have not found out anything as yet. We have men at the sight and at the place of destination that was intended. We also have men searching in-between. There have been a few small leads but so far, they have not panned out into anything substantial." Mr. Mackenzie told Tara in the most apologetic way he could.

Tara shifted her gaze back to Officer Thompson and noticed that he was staring at her off in a daze. She gave a smile in his direction when he noticed he quickly turned his eyes to his teacup. "Mr. Thompson, what is the next course of action then, with no fingerprints to go on?" she asked.

"We are going to do everything we can to find this Mr. W. Jackson." He assured her.

"Speaking of which, I believe the day is getting away from us as it is, so we will be on our way, any questions just give me or Officer Thompson a ring. We have left our cell phone numbers with Molly." The detective said as he stood to leave.

The RCMP Officers also said their goodbyes, and James saw them all in their cars at the front of the house, leaving Molly and Tara sitting alone.

"Did you get a good sleep?" Molly asked.

"Yes, it was very sound this time," Tara replied. The two sat and talked about the weather for a while.

Molly then told Tara how worried she was. She said that the Officer they had stationed on the property last night said there was no commotion whatsoever. She told Tara that it seemed very strange that no one came back for the binoculars. Tara thought about it for a minute. She knew they were an expensive pair too, she had to agree with Molly that it was really strange.

"Do you think we are being watched that carefully? Someone saw me take them out of the tree house and knew not to bother coming for them." Molly questioned.

Tara acknowledged Molly's suspicion, "I hate to say it, but it sure seems that way, doesn't it, but who and where would they be watching from?" Tara said as she looked around. They were not close to any of their neighbors, and at least two acres on either side of the house were full of dense forest.

There was an island not too far out into the lake but far enough that not even a high-powered set of binoculars or telescope was going to allow you to see the happenings of the estate.

"Did you mention this to the detectives while they were here?"

Tara asked Molly.

Molly explained that she only just had that realization, "No, I didn't, it just came to me now as I sat here talking to you. I was thinking about what they had said and it came to me that we must be being watched all the time."

"I have to agree with you, Molly and we need to find out who. I will give Officer Thompson a call later and see what he says." Tara agreed.

Molly stood and gave Tara a big hug, then gathered up the dishes to carry them in. Tara went with her, holding the door. She was going to make herself some tea to take down to the beach with her. Molly gave her a hand, setting it up. Tara decided that she was going to get her bathing suit on now so she could plop herself down on the beach and not move for the day. Molly thought her plan was a great one and that she needed to have a day of relaxation.

Tara was changed into her suit with a towel in hand and headed back down to the kitchen. Carla was standing in the kitchen telling Molly about this weird dream she had that there was a box she was in and the box had speakers in it, but all that came out of the speakers was a bunch of voices, mostly men talking, but what they were talking about she said she couldn't make out. She said that these voices wouldn't shut up and they were driving her crazy; just when she thought she couldn't take it anymore, the voices stopped following a couple of bangs, and that was when she woke up. Tara started to laugh and proceeded to tell her that the voices were a bunch of men, that they were here in the house and outside, and that the banging noises were probably their car doors as they were leaving. Tara and Molly told Carla all about their visitors this morning and Tara told her of her plan to work and relax on the beach. Carla thought that was a great way to spend the day. She told her sister that she was going to change into her suit, grab her laptop, and meet her on the beach. Molly then took another mug out of the cupboard and placed it on the tray for Carla to share in the tea as well.

James and Ryan came through the kitchen door and saw Tara dressed in her bathing suit and holding her laptop.

"Where do you think you're going?" James asked, smiling at her.
"To work." Tara laughed. "It's not many people who can go to work in their bikini," she said.

"That's for sure, spoiled, spoiled." James joked with her. James continued teasing, calling Tara spoiled.

Wanting to make Tara and Carla comfortable while they work on the beach. "Ryan and I will get you a couple of lounge chairs and a table to put your tea and treats on." He said, and the two of them headed for the boathouse.

When Carla came down, Tara was waiting for her to help with the door. She was balancing the tea tray on her laptop to take down to the beach. She had her towel draped around her neck and was all set. Molly offered to help, but Tara said that she could manage it just fine.

When Carla and Tara got to the beach, the chairs and table were all set up for them, but no men were in sight. They got themselves settled with their tea, which was all made. Tara sat back with her eyes closed for a few minutes, feeling the sun beating down on her face. She thought about how glorious it was and how lucky she felt to be so well off. She just wished her parents were here to thank them for ensuring a good life for her. Her thoughts were interrupted by Carla's yawning. She could never yawn quietly. Carla, for as long as she could remember, yawned making the sound of a roaring lion. Besides Carla's yawning and the odd boat going by it was pretty peaceful. Tara turned her computer on and noticed that Carla was already into her work. Reading her emails.

"You know what we forgot, tarot cards," she said.

"I'll go get them, where are yours?" she said.

"They're in the top drawer of my desk, the Robin Wood deck, thanks." Carla was gone like a shot.

Tara opened her email to see twenty-four new emails. She was afraid to open them because of the last time. She looked to see who they were from first, realizing that most of them were from her clients. The ones that weren't she didn't bother to open. Today she didn't really want to know. Carla was back in a flash with the cards and a bit out of breath. "What did you do run the whole way?" Tara laughed. "Yes, I don't want to waste a minute of this gorgeous day," she said, opening her computer again.

Tara told her how many emails she had and then asked what her emails were. Carla stated that she had about the same, and only a handful were not from her clients. "Are you going to open the other ones?" Tara asked Carla.

She just stared at her for a moment then said, "No, I don't want to know."

They both agreed and then went to work doing their readings for their clients.

Carla and Tara have been reading the tarot cards since they were about 12 years old. Their mother taught them how to read the tarot to hone their psychic skills. They showed psychic potential at a very young age. One day, the girls were playing, and their mother had a lady come in for a reading. This day for some reason, they were more interested in what their mother was doing than any other day before. They sat quietly while their mother read the cards. Later, when the lady left, they asked her to teach them to do the same. They were so interested that their mother bought them their own cards, and from there, they started reading for their friends when they came to play. They weren't getting any real information but their mother knew the day would come when they hit on a real reading. It was a matter of patience and practice. Sure enough, one day when, as they were playing up in their room with a friend, Tara hit it on the nose. Later that night, at supper, she was telling her mother about the reading but mostly about how she felt during the reading. It was as if she was not really there, that she was floating while her body was doing all the work. But the part she couldn't get over was that all this information was just flooding into her brain, so fast that she wasn't sure she could keep up. She was afraid that her tongue was going to trip over her words. A few days later, the parents of the girls that Tara did the reading for were at their front door. Tara and Carla's mother answered with hesitation, not knowing if she was going to get screamed at or not.

The girl's parents immediately started saying "thank you" over and over that if it wasn't for Tara's reading, the father would never have bought a lottery ticket, and they won one hundred thousand dollars. These people were ecstatic.

A short while later, Carla experienced the same thing and from then on, they knew that they couldn't read just for fun anymore and that the messages they were receiving were for real. When the girls were fourteen, they offered to do a reading for their school to help raise some money. One of the parents that Carla had read recognized her talent and knew that Tara was her twin. She went over to Tara's table and had her do a reading for her as well. She couldn't believe the similarities of both readings. She went to the girl's parents when they came to pick them up and asked if she could have a word with them. She told Carla and Tara's parents that these girls were extremely talented, that they should be reading for money, and that she had just the right connections. This lady hooked the girls up for a party reading for a very famous couple for their anniversary.

They were such a hit at the party that many people started calling them to set up a reading. Tara and Carla's mother set up a website for them. She even set up an account with PayPal for those who wish to have their readings done over the internet. They have become renowned psychics, with most of their clients being stars and many famous people, including a few top executives. Both Tara and Carla have degrees from the University of Toronto, both majoring in psychology.

Tara finally finished the first email and began reading the second one. It was from a lady whose grandmother had just passed away, and she was clearing out some of her things. She mentioned that they were all each other had. Now that she is gone, she feels so alone. But however, the only thing consoling her was that she was looking for her grandmother's prize possession. It was a mirror that she had acquired in Egypt when she was on her last dig. She was an archeologist all her life and worked for the British Museum of Antiquities. They displayed the mirror in an exhibit until her grandmother was retiring, and then they gave her this mirror as a gift. They had many Egyptian mirrors throughout the museum and they all agreed they could part with this one. She went on to explain that when she was a little girl and was sad, her grandmother would get the mirror out and tell her to look into the mirror and the mirror would show her how beautiful she was, but only if her heart was true to herself. She said that when she was done, she would hide the mirror in a secret place, but she never told her where that place was, and now she has taken that with her to the next life. Could you please see if you could locate it for me? She asked, then signed it.

Grandmother's beautiful little girl.

Tara tossed the cards and drew out one card at a time. The first card she pulled was the ace of swords, a single sword lying on the bed. Right away, Tara got the vision as to where the mirror was. She wrote back immediately:

"Dear GLG;
Your grandmother kept her prized possession close to her heart at all times. There is a slit in the mattress where she sleeps. There you will find the mirror."
Tara.

She sat there for a moment, thinking how easy that was. She also was thinking that the email had an air of familiarity, but what? Tara sat staring at the computer, searching her brain for what was it that made it seem familiar. From out of nowhere, it seemed she realized it was her grandmother's crystal ball that she used to hide away from her and her sister to make sure that we didn't play with it either. The memories started to flood back now faster than she could keep up. Her grandmother used the crystal ball to see people and what they were doing. She used it to find people who were missing and to check up on those she needed to keep an eye on. Tara felt a surge of excitement start to build within her. She knew they had to find that crystal ball.

She quickly told Carla what she was thinking about and how the email reminded her of the crystal ball.

"Yes, yes, I remember that," Carla said, sitting up and closing her computer.

"I haven't seen that since we were twelve, at least." Tara nodded and shuffled her deck of cards, Carla watched.

The first card she pulled was the ace of shields. She realized that this card meant that it was shielded from prying eyes. The card gave her the impression of comfort and privacy, but other than that, she wasn't getting any more. Carla pulled the next card, and it was the moon. Suggesting her reflection, deep secrets, and an open mind. But she wasn't getting anything more than that from the card either.

"Oh sure, we can see clearly when it's to help someone else, but when it comes to us, it then chooses to be cryptic," Carla says, annoyed.

"The first card suggests comfort and privacy, so what better place than her old room?" Tara suggests.

"Well, it's a start, but James and Molly sleep there, and we can't just go snooping into their room," Carla said.

"No, you're right. That is why we are going to tell Molly what we need to do. Then she can come with us, and if she doesn't like us going into something, she can look at it herself." Tara explained.

"Good idea," Carla said.

They closed up their notebooks and went into the house. They told Molly all about the email that led Tara to think about the crystal ball. When they were done, Molly agreed to go with them. Molly unlocked the bedroom door and let the girls in. She sat herself down on the bed while the girls looked around, getting the feel of the room. It was a lot different from when her grandmother stayed here. The one thing Tara noticed that didn't change was the curtains on the window. Tara walked over to the curtains and felt them, she saw that they were drawn back with fancy rope ties just like the tarot card. There was no shield, of course, but the open window.

"Have you washed these curtains since grandma died? Carla asked.

"Yes, a couple of times," Molly answered.

The girls pulled the curtains this way and that, looking for something strange or unusual. They saw nothing. They started feeling the walls with their hands for loose spots in the walls or the window sill. Still nothing. The girls were discouraged.

"The other card was a reflection, open mind, right?" Carla asked but was stating a fact at the same time.

"It's funny, you would say, because there is a certain time of day when you can't see your reflection in the dresser mirror because of the sun shining so brightly on it," Molly said.

"These dressers belonged to your grandparents," Molly added.

The girls looked at each other, and both asked at the same time. "When is that?"

"Around four o'clock when I come up here to get washed for dinner," Molly answered, her statement was a clue to help solve the mystery.

"Do you notice anything else?" Tara asked anxiously.

"Not really," Molly replied. "I don't even bother with the dresser mirror now; I just use the one in the bathroom."
Tara looked at her watch they had an hour and a half before four o'clock.

"We have a bit of a wait before then," Tara told them.

"Well, let's go downstairs and have a cup of tea and some scones while we wait," Molly suggested.

"Good idea," Carla said.

Tara just sighed, she wanted to find it now, "Come on Tara, we have waited this long, what's another hour and a half." Tara was saying to herself here, trying to calm her impatience.

"Exactly," said Molly, holding the door open for the girls.

Tara noticed that Molly checked the door handle after the door closed.

"Why do you keep the door locked?" Tara asked Molly.

"I don't, the door locks itself always has, it seems no matter what I do, the door locks on its own," Molly explained.

"I just check it out of habit now," Molly explained the door mystery.

Tara and Carla looked at each other.

"It's in there, that's for sure. Why else would grandma want the door locked all the time," Tara said, her suspicion deepening.

"Well, that was what I was thinking, that it was the spirit of your grandmother because I have had James look at it, and he can't seem to stop it from locking either," Molly said thinking to herself that their grandmother probably put a spell on the door to ensure to keep people out especially curious little girls.

The girls put the kettle on while Molly collected the cups and saucers, some napkins, and the scones that she had made fresh that morning. When the kettle boiled, Carla poured the tea and brought it to the table.

"Oh, we forgot the butter for the scones, I'll get it," Carla said.

As she was rooting in the cupboard for the butter, she glanced out the window at the boat house. She saw that there was no one down there and it made her realize that she hasn't seen Ryan all day or James, for that matter.

"Where is James?" she asked as she sat down at the table with the butter. It seemed strange not seeing James and Ryan all day.

"He and Ryan went into town for a while to get some supplies," Molly said. There was a slight tinge of concern on her face. The girls noticed.

"What is it Molly," Tara asked, she noticed Molly's concern and directly asked her about it.

"Oh, it's nothing. They probably are just having fun buying the supplies for…," she stopped dead in mid-sentence. Carla and Tara looked at each other and then back at Molly.

"What?", continued Carla, sensing something was off, she pressed Molly to finish her thought, eager to know what she almost revealed.

"I was not supposed to say what it was for, James made me promise," Molly admitted her hesitation, explained.

"Okay, don't tell us that's alright, but why are you concerned?" Carla respected Molly's promise but still tried to understand why she seemed worried.

"I didn't even know they left," Carla said.

Molly reassured Carla, "No, they didn't want to bother you, you both looked like you were hard at work."

Carla expressed mild concern, "Just they have been gone for most of the day."

Carla laughed, "Oh, poor Ryan, he is probably getting lectured to death."

"Now, now be nice. James just worries about you girls, is all, besides any man who can endure James' suspicious nature and still stick around has to be a pretty good guy." Molly defended James, reinforcing his suspicious yet protective nature for the girls as well as letting them know of her approval of Ryan. Molly said with a snicker. They all started laughing. It was no secret of James' suspicious nature. Their laughter was interrupted abruptly by the phone ringing. Tara got up to answer it.

"Hello?" Tara answered the phone politely.

"Yes, this is Tara Ward speaking."

Carla and Molly were reminiscing about James and Carla's first date. They didn't notice that Tara turned white and took the phone around the corner.

Tara, shocked and disbelieving, asked, "Are you sure its their car, Officer?"

"Yes, ma'am, we received a call about a car swerving on the road and getting dangerously close to the cliff edge on highway 28, I dispatched a car immediately but when the Officer arrived, he saw the car over the edge. The car was banged up quite bad but there was no one in the vehicle when the Officer climbed down." The Officer explained the situation.

"Where could they have gone? They could have been hurt, delirious even." Tara said near tears.

"Yes, ma'am, we have Officers on foot and in the car looking for them now, we will notify you if we find anything, and ma'am, could you please do the same if they show up at home." The Officer tried to reassure Tara.

"Yes, of course, I will phone right away," Tara promised to keep in touch.

"Thank you, ma'am," the Officer said and hung up.
Tara hung up the phone and then sat down at the table, she didn't know how to tell Molly.

"You're as white as a ghost, what's wrong?" Carla asked.

"It's Ryan and James, they had an accident," Tara began breaking the news gently, not revealing everything at once.

Molly's eyes welled with tears as she covered her mouth with her hand.

Tara rubbed her shoulder and continued, she explained the situation in more detail, "The Officers that went to the accident couldn't find them, they have Officers looking for them now on foot and by car."

Molly, distressed, asked, "Where did it happen?"

"Hwy twenty-eight," Tara gave the location, providing Molly with all the information she had.

"Oh, I bet they're okay and decided to walk to the nearest place to get help, that's along a stretch of road with no one around for miles," Carla said, trying to reassure Molly, but it wasn't working, she could see that.

"I just knew there was something wrong, I could feel it in my bones," Molly said, wiping her eyes with her napkin.

"Are they sure it was their car?" Carla asked.

"Yes, the ownership was still in the car registered to Ryan and for some reason, James' wallet was still in the car, sitting on the passenger's seat." Tara was relaying information from the police about the accident.

"That's odd, don't you think?" Carla asked.
"Well, that's what I thought but I guess anything can happen. If you were in an accident, you probably wouldn't even notice that it was missing for some time." Tara was trying to rationalize the oddity Carla pointed out.

Carla emphasized, "Yeah, I suppose but you know James, he protects that wallet like it holds the holy grail."

Tara felt urgency, "We need to find that crystal ball more than ever now so we can see if they are alright." Tara said.

Carla agreed and they both looked at Molly. Molly swallowed the lump in her throat and sat up straight, sticking her chin up, being as brave as she could be, then said.

"I agree, let's go find that crystal." Despite her distress, Molly decided to join.

It was still too early, but they would just look for it anyway. Once inside the room, Tara tried to imagine the angle of the light on the mirror and where it would reflect. It was a large area to cover if they had it right. They started looking and feeling the wall behind the bed where they thought the light would shine, but they felt and saw nothing out of the ordinary. They started looking at the floor around the window and behind the curtains, but still no loose floorboards.

"Would she have hidden it that well?" Tara asked.

"I have washed and cleaned every inch of this room and have never seen anything, so if there is something in here, it must be hidden well," Molly said.

"Okay, keep looking, we only have fifteen more minutes left," Carla said, getting back on her hands and knees. Molly excused herself.

Carla sympathized with Molly, "Poor Molly, James and her have never been apart, what would she do without him?" Carla asked.

Tara reassured Carla, "Oh, I bet she would surprise you, she is a pretty tough cookie, you know." Tara said.

Molly went to the hall window and looked out, praying that she would see the men come walking up the drive. But there was no sign of them at all. The sun has gone around the back of the house now and it made the front look rather eerie to her. She stood and watched for them for a few minutes, she noticed the sky was darkening to the north and it looked as if they may be in for a storm later. She really hoped they made it back before they got caught in the storm. They don't need to add pneumonia to their injuries, she thought to herself. Just as she was going to turn to go back to the room, she noticed a figure at the end of the driveway, half concealed by the bush. Molly watched for a moment, thinking it was them, but for some reason, she restrained herself from running to them. This figure didn't move any closer but just stood there looking at the house.

"Girls, girls, come quick," Molly called urgently, having spotted a mysterious figure. Molly shouted in panic.

They both heard the panic in Molly's voice and quickly ran to her. They stopped where she was noticing she was staring out the window, and they looked.

"Do you see him?" Molly asked,

"Where am I looking?" Tara asked her.

"By the end of the driveway to the left by the bush."
both their eyes went right to him as she gave them directions.

"Do you see him?" she asked again.

"Yes!" "Yes!" They shouted at the same time.

"What is he doing there?" Tara asked, but no one answered.

"Okay, Molly, you stay here and keep an eye on him at all times, Tara and I are going to go lock up the house to make sure he can't get in," Carla said.

Molly nodded, and then the girls took off down the stairs to lock the doors and windows. Carla took the back of the house and Tara took the front. They didn't draw the curtains closed because they didn't want to make him think they saw him. As the girls snuck around the house, trying not to be seen from outside. They heard Molly call to them.

Molly called out to the girls, "Girls, he's moving closer to the house around the bushes to the left, where they lead around the back."

Carla hurried to get everything locked up, even the old storm cellar hatch in the basement. Both Carla and Tara were done at the same time they met each other in the front hall by the stairs.

"Did we forget anywhere?" Tara asked.

"No, I don't think so. We should be locked up tighter than a drum," Carla replied.

They both went back upstairs to meet Molly. Molly had moved now and was back in her room looking out the window. Carla and Tara went to see what she was looking at but saw nothing.

"Where did he go?" Tara asked.

"I don't know, I have been watching to see him when he comes round the back, but he hasn't appeared yet." Carla realized the time and asked Molly to move away from the window so as not to shade the light coming in from outside. Sure enough, they saw the mirror was covered in light. There was a tiny fissure in the mirror that created a small beam of light to bounce off in a completely different direction. It pointed to a floorboard near the wall on the right side of the bed by the closet. Tara went right over to it, Carla following. They felt around but saw nothing. Then, Carla leaned on the floor with her left hand to reach for her right to open the closet door when she heard the board creek. The board went into the closet. Both girls emptied the closet out and then started to pry the board up. It was easy as they saw this board had been cut and a small hole was drilled in the board that would fit a finger. Sure enough, it was like a box lid. They pulled it up and underneath, they found a small stand and beside it, wrapped in a black silk cloth, was the crystal ball they were looking for.

"There he is, he is around the back now," Molly said.

"Molly, come away from the window. You don't want him to see you. We want to let him think he has gone unnoticed." Tara said.

Molly backed away from the window. Out of sight, she looked at the girls and noticed that they found it. They showed Molly the ball.

"Okay, now I think we better go downstairs and call the police to let them know he is around the house," Carla said.

They all rushed down to the dining room. Molly said that she still wanted to watch him and see what he was up to. This way, she said she could avoid any more surprises.

Molly made herself comfortable just out of sight in the living room that overlooked the lake. She saw that he was standing beside the tree house, trying to conceal himself.

She wished she had the binoculars, but the police haven't given them back yet. She found that strange, seeing how they didn't find anything on them.

Tara picked up the phone and started dialing the police. The phone rang and rang, but no one ever picked up.

After repeatedly calling the police station with no success, Tara felt worried, "That's strange, there is no answer at the station."

"That is strange, you probably dialed the wrong number try again," Clara suggested.

Tara dialed again, but still no answer. "I will try again in a minute, maybe they have too many calls at once and are just having trouble answering them," Tara said.

She was trying to console herself, but a police station that can't handle all the calls was strange, especially in such a small town. She then thought that maybe all of them were out looking for James and Ryan, but even that didn't make sense, and there should still be a dispatch lady there.

Carla was setting up the ball, she polished it up and was sitting in front of it. "Do you remember how to make it work?" she asked Tara.

"Wow that was so long ago, I'm not sure," Tara responded.

"Is he still there, Molly?" Carla asked.

"Yes, he is standing by the tree," Molly said.

"Girls? I was just wondering why he would be here in broad daylight like this. Why is he not scared of one of the men seeing him?" Molly asked.

They both sat staring at each other, realizing they were thinking the same thing. *He knows that James and Ryan aren't here. Did he have something to do with their accident?"*

Carla grabbed the ball and shook it, "Work, damn it work," She was panicking and Tara could see it.

She placed her hands on Carla's and said its okay, we will be fine, but you can't shake the ball and make it work, well at least I never saw grandma do that. She tried to add some humor. Carla didn't laugh, but she knew her sister was right.

"You keep trying and I will try calling again," Tara said.

Still, there was no answer on the other end. Tara was starting to believe that either he did something to everyone at the station or he had rigged their phone so that we still got a dial tone, but it called no one. She decided that she was going to try another number. The grocery store was only a block away from the station and if she could get through to them, they may be able to tell the police for her. She dialed the grocer's number and waited. …three…four….five….they could be busy serving customers…nine…ten…eleven…twelve. Tara hung up; it was definitely the phone he had rigged somehow. Tara was more concerned than ever. If he went through all that trouble, then he is planning on doing something other than spying on us this time.

"Carla, could you please go upstairs and check the emails that you didn't want to check earlier today?" Tara had a bad feeling and wanted to find out

"What, what for?" Carla was surprised.

"I have a hunch and it's not a good one, please." Carla agreed and went upstairs right away.

"How is it going in there, Molly?" she asked.

"Okay, it doesn't seem like he is moving, he's just standing there." Molly was observing the figure outside.

Tara gazed into the ball and asked quietly if it would show her where James and Ryan were. She sat and stared at the ball, which was changing color, Tara started to get excited.

"Show me, James and Ryan," she asked again.

The colors were changing faster and faster this time, and then they stopped on black with a shimmer of light in the distance. She looked closely and saw that it was a light shining through a crack that looked like a wooden door or wall. But it was too hard to see anything else.

"Show me the police station," she commanded.

The ball changed colors again, getting progressively faster. Then it was clear and she could see people working away on phones and computers. There had to be, from what she could see, at least three Officers and the dispatch lady. Just as she thought, they were cut off from the world, locked in their home with this crazy figure lurking about the house. She could feel herself starting to panic and wanted to run to the car and try to get away. She stopped herself, realizing that he had probably booby trapped the car as well. Then she had a horrible thought, *"What if he knew that they knew he was out there."* Her thoughts were interrupted by the pounding footsteps of her sister running down the stairs. Something was definitely wrong.

Carla didn't say anything. She just shoved the papers that she printed in front of Tara.

Tara gasped. The pictures were of James and Ryan tied to each other back-to-back in a small boxlike structure, blindfolded.

"These emails were from earlier, but I don't think they had left yet, how could this be true," Tara asked, puzzled.

"I don't know," Was all Carla could say.

"How could he have known that they were going out today?" Tara asked aloud, not really directing it at her sister. Carla just shook her head.

"We can't show these to Molly," Tara said. Carla agreed as she took the paper, folded it up and tucked them in her back pocket. Tara then told her she was able to get the ball working, and she explained what she had seen. Wherever they are, Tara thought, it is really dark there. The girls just sat there for a few minutes, thinking to themselves.

"Girls this figure has been standing in this same position now for a long time. I am beginning to think it's a decoy and not really him." Molly said.

Both sisters jumped from their seats and went to Molly. They stood there looking out at the figure, and sure enough, he had never moved a muscle.

"Molly, you stay here and still watch him while Carla and I check out other windows, just holler if something happens or he moves okay?" Tara said.

Molly nodded, never taking her eyes off the figure. Carla was already at the front door window looking out down the driveway. Tara remembered that there were two windows, one on either side of the attic, giving two different views of the yard, so she headed up there. As she was going up the stairs, she passed Carla and gave her a pat on the back. She quickly ran to the attic and looked out the west window. She scanned the yard carefully, checking out all the trees and bushes, but she didn't see anything that looked like this dark figure.

The sky was growing darker and even though the sun wasn't due to set, it looked outside as if it was nightfall. They were in for a real doozy of a storm, and that was for sure. She thought as she headed for the east window that they had better prepare the candles and lanterns in case the power went out. That would just make it even scarier than it already was.

Tara was questioning, "Was that what this person was waiting for, nightfall?"

Well, based on the way the sky was looking, he might just be ahead of schedule. She looked out the window; there were a lot of trees on this side and it was hard to see through them in this dimming light. She was straining her eyes to see and she caught something moving alongside the house. She couldn't see it clearly because of the angle, but she saw that it was moving around the front of the house towards the other side. She quickly went back to the west window and waited to see. Sure enough, she saw the figurehead over toward Ryan's cabin. He slunk around the back of the cabin and was out of sight. Tara ran down the stairs to see Carla was now with Molly.

Tara informed Carla about how close the figure had gotten to her, "Carla, if you had of been at the front a minute ago, I believe you would have seen him go right by you."

"No way?" she said "where did he go now?" Carla asked.

"He went around the back of Ryan's cabin and then out of sight," Tara informed about the figure's movements.

"Do you think he went into Ryan's cabin?" Molly asked.

"I don't know it's getting harder to see clearly with the darkening of the sky," Tara said.

Just then in the distance, they heard thunder rumbling
"I think what we should focus on doing right now is preparing for the storm and getting candles and lanterns ready in case the power goes out," Tara suggested.

"I don't know if you remember or not, but the power always goes out up here in a storm," Molly said with a sigh.

"But that's okay because of that, I have a stash of candles in the basement for just these occasions," Molly said with a grin.

"I'll get them," Carla said.

Molly told Carla where they were and she told Tara where the lanterns and oil were downstairs as well.
Both girls left Molly upstairs, and as they rummaged through the debris, they didn't take long because they were afraid of leaving Molly upstairs alone. They knew they should stay as close to each other as possible from now on.

As Carla reached the top of the stairs, the kitchen was lit brightly by a flash of lightning. It startled her so much that she almost sent the box of candles flying across the kitchen.

Carla set up the candles in the living room and dining room while Tara filled the lanterns with fresh oil and wick. They were set. So they thought.

"What about weapons? Shouldn't we have some close by?" Carla asked.

"If we have weapons close by, then if an intruder comes in, they will also be handy for them," Molly said.

"Right, I see your point," Carla said. "We will just outsmart him."

"That a girl." Tara encouraged Molly's calmness and strategic approach.

Molly seemed awfully calm for some reason. Tara knew this should make her feel better, but it didn't. Now that everything was set up, they all sat around the dining room table looking at the crystal ball.

"I've gone blank, what should we look for or ask it to show us," Tara asked.

They sat in silence for a few minutes, thinking.

Molly suggested using the crystal ball to observe the figure, "Hey, if he can watch us from outside, why don't we try and watch him from here?"

"Great idea," Tara said as she stared into the ball and asked it to show her the dark figure. The ball changed colors again, increasing in speed as before, then stopped; the scene was dark, but they could make the figure out it was the figure beside the tree house tree.

"It's not showing me the true one," Tara said.

"Try again." Molly urged.

Tara tried again, asking for it to show her the true figure this time, "Again, it stopped on the man by the tree," she said, expressing frustration.

Tara was confused, "I don't get it. Why does it keep showing me this figure, he is obviously not the right one, or at least he wasn't unless he has switched himself for the fake." Tara said he is using magic to throw us off. He must realize that we have magic in our blood as well, either that or he thinks we will just be fooled by the image of the tree, but we saw him and we know he is at Ryan's cabin.

Molly jumped from her chair and went to the living room window to see. It was getting darker now and it was harder to focus on anything, but she could still make out the figure, which seemed to be in the same position as before.

"You girls, keep trying, I am going to watch and see if this one moves." Molly decided to monitor the figure from the window.

Tara decided that she was going to ask another question. "Show me the face of the figure," She commanded the ball. She wanted a closer look at the figure's face, hoping to gain new insights.
This time, it showed many faces blending in together instead of swirling colors. They were all faces that she knew well, at least the ones she could see in the beginning, but then they just became a blur after a while, going so fast. Then it stopped; it showed a woman's face, one that the girls had never seen before.

"Molly, come in here for a second, please," Tara called Molly to look at the new face that appeared.

Molly came in, looking over Tara's shoulder. "Do you recognize this face at all?"

Molly thought for a moment, then said, "Yes, it looks a lot like your grandmother's cousin, the one whose husband died in the fire." She said, examining the face closely.

"She has aged quite a bit since I remember her, but it sure looks like it could be her." Molly was examining the face.

"Wasn't she put in a mental institute?" Tara was puzzled by the appearance.

"Yes, that's right, she never got over her husband's death properly," Molly said.

"How could it be her then?" Carla asked

"Oh, I don't think that figure out there is her, the figure is way too tall. She was never more than five, one or two in height." Molly remembered, "She was shorter than your grandmother."

"Have you tried finding the men yet?" Molly asked.

"Yes, it showed us them, but wherever they are, it is so dark I couldn't make out anything," Tara answered, choosing not to tell Molly the pictures from Carla's email.

Molly continued her vigil at the window, watching for any signs that he may leave or maybe she would be able to find out what he was up to.

Tara and Carla sat at the table, trying desperately to get the ball to work right.

"Here, let me have a go at it," Carla said. Carla and Tara traded places in front of the boll.

Carla concentrated on the figure in Ryan's cabin; she was unconsciously rubbing the ball with her left hand, putting herself into a trance. Tara watched her closely and noticed her eyes go out of focus. Then she saw the ball swirl with white clouds and then have black clouds mingling with it until the ball went completely black. Tara looked at Carla, and at this point, Carla's left hand stopped moving and relaxed itself on the table. Carla was seeing something she could tell. She watched her sister closely in case she had to pull her out of it if she saw things getting too much for her.

Carla felt herself slipping away as if she was falling into the ball itself. She saw the cabin and felt herself moving closer to it. Then everything went black; there was a small light up ahead and she went closer to it. She then realized as her eyes came into focus that she was in Ryan's cabin. How did she get there? She was frightened but knew there was no going back now. She walked into the back of the cabin where he kept his computer. She could hear something rustling in the room. It was the black figure she knew it was. Carla could feel panic start to rise in her, but she knew she had no choice but to get it under control and move forward. She quietly entered the room, seeing the figure bent over the desk. He seemed to be looking for something. Carla just wanted to get a look at the person and maybe ask what he wanted with them. Carla also knew that she was risking her life but came to the understanding that if it had to be her life to save her family, then so be it. She moved forward and decided to jump the figure, tackle him to the ground and…well, she wasn't sure what to do next, but that was her plan. She readied herself to pounce when the figure whipped around to face her. She stopped in her tracks and found herself staring into eyes like lightbulbs. The light kept getting brighter, and she tried to back away, but she couldn't move. She couldn't move anything, and the panic started to rise in her again. Her head was hurting from the light being so bright. Whatever he was doing to her, she couldn't even blink or move her hand to cover her face.

Tara saw her sister's eyes widen and panic on her face. Then, in her eyes, she could see a growing light taking over her pupils. Tara panicked and immediately pulled Carla away from the ball. It seemed to work; the light disappeared and Carla's head fell backwards.

Carla? Carla? Tara shouted and shook her.

Carla lifted her head and her hands went straight to her eyes. "Are you okay?" Tara asked her.

Carla reassured Tara, "Yes, I think so, but I can't see very well and my head is killing me." She said as she rubbed her temples. Tara went into the kitchen, grabbed a couple of aspirin from the cupboard, poured a glass of water from the tap, and gave it to Carla, helping her hold it in her shaking hands.

"What happened and what was that light? Tara asked.

"You saw that too?' Carla said in surprise.

"Yes, I saw that in your eyes and pulled you away from the ball," Tara said.

"It really frightened me. Are you sure you're, okay?" Tara asked.

Carla nodded her head and took a big gulp of water, then she told Tara what had happened. "it was like I was there." She said.
"I wonder if you left your body? I have seen you trance out before, but never like that." Tara commented.

"Well, whatever happened, he knew I was there. He looked me right in the eyes with lights instead of eyes that froze me every part of my body. Thank goodness you pulled me away from it, who knows what would have happened." Carla recounted the terrifying encounter she had in her vision with the figure as she rubbed her eyes to help them focus.

"Girls, come quickly. I see a car coming in the driveway, it must be James and Ryan?" Molly said running to the front door.

"Wait, don't open the door, what if he is there?" Tara said.

"I never saw him leave, but I did see a bright light go on in the cabin for a bit," Molly said, not knowing what Carla had seen. Carla and Tara just looked at each other.

"It is Ryan and James, they are getting out of the car," Molly said.

"Okay, wait until they are right here, then open the door and tell them to hurry," Tara advised Molly to wait.

Molly was getting excited watching in anticipation for them to come in.

"Why is the house so dark?" James asked no one in particular.

"Looks as though the power may have gone out but, they have

the candles lit though, maybe the power went out prematurely with this storm coming." Ryan replied.

James just grunted in agreement and then got the stuff out of the trunk.

"I will run over to the cabin and get the generator and meet you inside," Ryan said.

"Good idea," James said.

Ryan started for the cabin when the front door flew open. Molly stepped out and yelled at Ryan, "No, no you mustn't go there; both of you get inside now, hurry." James heard the panic in her voice and quickly shut the trunk and headed for the house. "Ryan, never mind that there is something wrong inside," James yelled at Ryan.

Thunder started roaring loudly overhead so loud that Ryan just barely heard Molly and James. James looked at Molly on the porch her face full of worry, he hoped the girls were okay.

As soon as they reached the porch, Molly started jumping up and down telling them to hurry, hurry. Then, they shut the door and locked it behind them. The men entered the hallway, seeing the two girls, Tara and Carla, standing there looking unscathed. James turned to Molly, who was looking out the window of the door. "What the hell is going on that is such a panic?" James said being a little worried and put out.

Molly answered him, not even turning around. "Oh, James, you have no idea," was all Molly could say.

The girls took the men into the dining room and sat them down. Tara told Molly to forget the window and come sit with them. Molly refused, saying someone had to watch for him. "Watch for who? would someone please like to tell me what was going on?" James said angrily. Ryan went over to Carla, and seeing that she was pale, he sat down beside her and held his arm around her. She caved in and rested her head on his shoulders, trying to hold back the tears that insisted on trickling down her cheek. Ryan held her hands in his other hand, hoping that he could stop them from shaking. Tara started to tell them from the beginning what had happened.

Chapter 19

Thunder, Lightning, Shadows and Surprises

Molly never moved from the window the whole time, watching for any movement from Ryan's cabin. Molly piped up and told James to look at the tree house and see the figure standing beside it. James got up, went over to the window and peered out at the tree at first he didn't see anything, then as his eyes focused in the dark, he could make out a figure standing just behind the trunk to one side as if it was looking around the trunk trying not to be seen.

"I am going to check the phone for a line out," James said.

"There is no phone line; they seem to be down, I think he cut the lines," Tara said.

"And no power either and I believe he had something to do with that as well. The lights and the phone went out at the same time before the thunderstorm even got close." Carla told James, noticing that she had finally stopped shaking and that her vision was coming back.

Ryan let go of her hand and gave her a one arm squeeze, then rose.

"My cell phone is in my cabin or I would go get it." Ryan said.

"We really need to go for help, we can't just sit here waiting for him to make his next move, can we? Especially now that he knows we know where he is." Carla said.

"Which reminds me, what happened to you guys this afternoon? Tara asked.

James then left the window where he was watching the decoy figure by the tree and sat down on the stool. He told them they left the house and went into town to get some lumber for the dock. They ordered the lumber and decided to pick up a few things in town. They weren't long, really, maybe a half hour to forty-five minutes in town. They started to head home along highway 121 when the car hit something in the road. It blew both tires on the passenger side. James lost control of the car, which then decided to head over the side of the road along the embankment and then it went down into the field where they came to a stop. James went on to say that when they figured out that they were unhurt, they went to the road to see what it was, but neither one of them saw anything suspicious. They assessed the damage to the car and found both tires were blown. They figured that their location was halfway to nowhere. That is the section of the road between town and Blackwood Manor that has no houses, no gas station, no nothing for a half hour. You can't even get a signal in that area on your cell phone. Not that Ryan had his phone on him, which he promptly apologized for. He meant to bring it, but he just forgot. They decided that they would walk back into town, hoping that someone would come along and give them a lift. Not a soul went by it was a long, hot walk. When they reached town, they went straight to the gas station to enlist a service truck to get their car on the road again. In a short time, they were on the road with the truck; he brought two tires, which James had bought before they left. It was a while before the serviceman could get the tires on the car. The ground was so soft that it was hard to get a jack under the frame, so he had to use the wench on the tow part of the truck. He kept the car lifted and towed it up the embankment back onto the road. They thanked the guy and he was on his way to another call not far from Blackwood Manor. James and Ryan got themselves back on track and started to head home. About ten minutes down the highway, they saw an overturned truck on the road; as they neared, they saw that it was the service truck from town that helped them out. They pulled the car over and went to see if the driver was alright. He wasn't anywhere around the vehicle. They panned out and looked for him, but no sign at all.

Ryan used the truck's radio to contact his headquarters to tell them of the accident. Ryan was kind of surprised that they didn't know about it, he figured that the driver would have radioed for help right away. Ryan informed them that the driver was missing and that it wouldn't be a bad idea for them to send the police and ambulance just in case he was injured and wandered off in shock. They said they would send someone right away and Ryan told them they would wait for the police to show up. Ryan asked the dispatch if she would do them a favour and call the house for them and tell them they would be home soon. The lady on dispatch said she would. Ryan and James decided to wander around a bit more to see if they could find the driver, if he was in shock, he wouldn't have gotten too far. The radio sounded in the truck and Ryan ran back to the radio. The lady came over the air saying that she tried that number, but the service was out. Ryan thanked her and told James. They both figured that the storm that was looming ahead must have been what took out the service. When the police arrived, they stayed to help them look for the driver. The ambulance just sat waiting for a signal. One police Officer yelled from the bushes a few yards away that he found the driver. The ambulance attendants started running toward him with their gear. The driver was sitting up against the tree shaking and half unconscious; they started working on him right away. Then got him to the ambulance and drove off. A tow truck pulled up, spoke to the Officers. The Officers then came over to James and Ryan to get a statement. As James and Ryan were giving their statement, the tow truck driver came over and told the Officers that there are massive puncture holes in all his tires. James and Ryan had just finished telling the Officers how that happened to them, but when they checked the road out, there was nothing to be seen. The Officers let them go because the sun was going down and they wanted to get this cleaned up before it got dark.

"That's when we came home," Ryan said.

"I have something to show you both, but it's on the computer and we have no power for me to even print it out with," Tara said.

"What is it?" Ryan asked.

Tara sat close beside Ryan and James moved over, knowing that she was going to whisper.

Tara told them about the picture they saw of the two of them. "What was the darkness that we saw," Carla asked.

James and Ryan thought back to the events of the day. James piped up and said it must have been when the two of us were trying to look under the car to see if we could get it jacked. It was really dark at that time, he remembered mentioning it to Ryan. The storm clouds were coming overhead and it made it really dark, so dark that they couldn't see anything under the car.

There was silence, and no talking was to be had by anyone. James wandered over to Molly and told her to have a seat and that he would take watch. The storm had gotten bad now and the lightning was lighting up the yard as if it were day. Molly didn't take a seat she just stood with James at the window.

James could see the light on in the cabin and wondered what exactly this person was looking for. He looked down at Molly and at the time, she was staring up into the night, watching the lightening in the sky. She didn't see what James saw, the person coming out of the cabin now and working his way towards the house. James didn't know what to do this was the first time in his life that he was feeling helpless and scared that he may not be able to protect the family.

"Molly, take the girls with you and make a pitcher of iced tea for us, would you and maybe some snacks, no need for us to go hungry while we wait for this to be over." James stroked Molly's hair. Molly just nodded and went and gathered the girls into the kitchen to make some food for the men and themselves. Molly knew James too well and knew that he wanted to talk to Ryan alone, he must be up to something. Molly was worried. She tried hard to keep it from the girls, but she knew the girls were clever and would sense it anyway.

James called Ryan over toward the window and Ryan then saw this person carefully working his way towards the house. "What do you think we should do?" James asked Ryan.

"Well, I think we should be ready for him, arm ourselves and hide the woman." James nodded, thinking that was a good idea.

The girls had made the snacks and the iced tea and were now sitting quietly in the living room. James told Ryan that where they were was the safest place for them.

Tara was watching her sister. She could see that she was scheming something. She knew that look better than anyone. She used to get that look whenever she was planning something that would inevitably get them into trouble. Tara was also trying to hear the conversation between James and Ryan but wasn't having much luck with that either. She felt restless and bored.

Carla's eyes shifted from staring at the men to the dining room table and back again. Tara noticed this, knowing she was going to execute some sort of plan. Sure enough, Carla rose from her seat, walked over to the dining room, and sat down in front of the crystal ball. She looked up and called to Ryan, "Ryan, can I see you for a second please?" Ryan gave James an inquisitive look, shrugged his shoulders, and then went to see Carla. Carla was now standing in the doorway of the dining room and positioned herself in such a way that Tara couldn't see what Carla was saying, she was at least hoping to read her lips.

"What's up?" Ryan asked.

"Well, I have been thinking and wondering why the hooded figure would close off the power and the phone lines to the house just to snoop around your cabin." Ryan shrugged.

"It just seems odd to me that the hooded being would find or think they could find something of interest within your cabin." Carla paused, watching Ryan's facial expression. Just as Ryan was going to reply, Carla stopped him with her hand signal, just suggesting not to speak. "None of the emails we have received ever included you suggesting one of two things. You were of no interest to him, and he didn't even know about you or your position here at the manor. But in either case, then why would he be in your cabin, and what exactly do you think he could find of any importance. Ryan could see through Carla's facial expression that she was not just being inquisitive. She was suspicious and her body language suggested hurt and anger. Ryan told Carla that he had wondered the same thing but didn't mention it, probably for the same reason that she felt the need to keep it from James. Carla scowled but knew he was correct; if James knew, he would be upset and angry, who knows to what extent. But who knows, maybe he had thought of it and was biding his time.

Carla started to relax as she watched Ryan and how calm he was. Ryan reached out to grab her shoulders, holding her gently but firmly, and said, "I would never do anything to harm you or your family. I would do everything in my power to see that you were all safe, not only because I was hired to do so but because I have become fond of you all." He winked at Carla, "and especially you." Ryan pulled her close to him and wrapped his arms around her. He could feel Carla relax even more into his embrace.

"Okay, you two," James said from the doorway.
Ryan went back to stand beside James, giving Carla another wink.

Carla sat down in front of the crystal ball. She stared into it with apprehension. She was afraid of getting stuck in his gaze like the last time, but she knew she had to do something. She needed to know where and what he was doing. She decided that she was going to give it another shot.

The ball turned completely black as she stared into it. As it started to clear, she could see the hooded figure. He was still inside the cabin at the computer. She allowed herself to move closer to get a better look, but she could only get so far as if there was a barrier blocking her way. She tried a different angle, and still, she was blocked. Then, it dawned on her what he must have done. He has put a charm up so that if she attempted this again, it would draw her right here and not to his actual location. Just then, she heard James tell Ryan that they should go out and see if they could find him. Carla ran over to them and told them that they couldn't go out there, then she explained that. "He's not in the cabin anymore, he could be anywhere, just waiting for you to go looking for him."

"I think everyone should pick a different spot in the house and watch out the window to see if we can spot him, maybe then we will be able to see what he is up to next," Ryan said.

James agreed. Molly took the attack, Carla went to the kitchen to watch out the back by the water, and Tara went up to her room to look out on the balcony. James and Ryan kept vigil at the front of the house. Twenty minutes went by and nobody reported anything unusual. James called everyone back to the living room. When everyone was sitting, he said that him and Ryan were going to go see if the coast was clear. Molly jumped up and grabbed James' arm. "Please don't. You must stay here where you're the safest." She was shaking and tears were streaming down her face.

Just then, the lights came on. Ryan ran to the phone. "It's working again," he shouted as he started dialing the sheriff's office.

James calmed Molly down, hugging her and telling her that whatever he was up to, he was done. "It was over for now. I think he just wanted to put a big scare into us, is all." James was trying to reassure her. "However, I still think that Ryan and I should go to the cabin and see what this person was up to." Molly squeezed him tighter; she was determined not to let him go.

"Actually, we can't go over there yet," Ryan said. "The sheriff was sending Officers over and told us to stay away from the cabin until they could complete an investigation of it."

Molly released her hold on James. She looked better and calmer. Everyone relaxed, just knowing that the Officers were on their way here.

"Girls? Let's make some tea, shall we?" Molly asked as she headed for the kitchen.

The girls followed. Molly filled the kettle and placed it on the stove. Carla gathered the cups and saucers while Tara placed some cookies on a plate.

"Could you watch the kettle for me, I'll be right back." Molly headed for the cellar stairs.

"What is she doing?" Carla asked.

"I don't know but I'm sure we will find out soon," Tara replied.

The girls made the tea and placed everything on the tea trolly to wheel out to the living room.

Molly came up the stairs panting, carrying a heavy wooden box. Carla ran to her side to take the box from her. "Why did you do that? You should have asked one of us to help you with this?" Carla scolded. She took the box from Molly, and it was pretty heavy.

"What in this thing anyway?" Carla asked.

"You will see when you open it in the living room," Molly replied.

"Your grandmother left strict instructions not to give it to you until you showed some signs of interest in your gifts. I was going to give it to you this afternoon, but then all this happened." Molly explained.

Once they were all settled back with their tea, Molly told them to open the box. Carla put it on the couch between her and Tara. She opened it up to find a large book. Its cover was made of wood, which was intricately carved with a beautiful Celtic braid around the edges. A pentagram carved in the center entwined with a leafy vine. There was an indent in the center of the pentagram, and it was as if something was missing from there. You could see in the indent that there was a type of crystal embedded in the wood. Did a crystal peace break off? They wondered. They opened the book up, and on the inside was a poem of protection for the book.

"In the realm of magic, this book shall reside.
Only the chosen shall see what's inside, the secrets which trusted be,
may no unprepared eyes see.
Guardians from the four directions hear me and lend thy protection.
May these truths of Earth and skies shaded be from prying eye,
but to the witches whose map this be,
may the way be plain to see. And through all the coming ages,
may we find home in these pages.
So mote it be!"

The rest of the pages were blank.

"What is this?" Carla asked. Tara looked inside the box and there was an envelope at the bottom. She opened it. It was written by her grandmother.

"Dear girls, if you are reading this note than you have found your way to your gifts. I am so happy that you have embraced what has been passed down to you from many generations. You girls are truly blessed I knew it from the day you were born. This book will assist you in all that you need and whatever trouble you may encounter. I hope. This is my grimoire, and the information on these pages has been passed down through the generations as well. They are tried, tested and true to work or they would not be in the book. Please feel free to add any that you may find helpful and most of all, don't forget to pass this along to your children as well. There is a special crystal key that had to be divided in half because your mother was the first to have more than one child in a long lineage. Your mother has this crystal put away for you so if you don't have it, you better ask her for it. Do not let anyone have access to the book when you are not using it. Make sure that the crystals are separated. This will prevent it from being used or stolen. Once you start reading it, you will understand why it is for your eyes only. Tell Molly thank you for keeping it safe all these years. She is blessed with gifts of her own, ask her about them sometime. Wink, wink.

Tara and Carla looked at Molly, who at this point, was blushing; she turned her head away from the girls. "Molly, is there something you would like to share with us?" Tara teased.

"Another time maybe," she said.

So, take care, my darlings, know that I love you.
Blessed be, Gran

"There are many things that you girls don't know about just yet and maybe when this is all over, we will sit down and talk," James said.

"I knew the girls were psychic, that they took after their mother, but I would never have guessed to what extent … I mean, I have never met…. I really don't know what I am trying to say." Ryan stumbled over his words.

"Does this upset you?" Carla asked him.
"No, I don't think so, I don't really know much about it. Maybe as you discover who you are, I will learn more and we will see from

there." Ryan replied.

"Yeah, maybe," Carla answered. This disturbed her, she really liked Ryan and she didn't want this to be a problem, but she also needed to know who she was and what kind of gifts she had. She hoped that he would not be frightened away by this.

James could see the tension in Carla and knew exactly how Ryan was feeling. He had been there as well.

"Ryan, it's not as bad as you think," James said "I have been in this family for a long time and have seen many things, all good, you get used to it. It just becomes a way of life."

James gave Ryan a couple of manly pats on the back, then laughed.

Molly spoke up to change the subject. "I don't mean to be negative but I can't help wondering why this figure didn't try to break in or hurt one of us. Why did he spend all his time in the cabin?"

James glared at Ryan briefly, then said. "You know that crossed my mind as well, what do you think he was looking for, Ryan?" Ryan knew this was coming, James was no fool. It was just a matter of time before he started to question Ryan's part in this.

"James, I am as perplexed as you are," Ryan said sincerely. James made a huffing sound and took a sip of tea.

"I realize it was hard for you to trust me with the girls' safety, not knowing who I was or my background. I see how much you love them and how protective of your family that you are. I understood where you were coming from and as you know, I have grown quite fond of Carla, so please believe me when I say I would never do anything to put any of you in harm's way. I don't know who this is and I don't know why he is doing what he is doing. As far as my cabin goes, there really isn't anything in there that you don't know about anyway." Ryan explained that, as best he could, he was hoping that James would see that he was telling the truth. Ryan also knew that he only had it in him to make that speech once, so if James didn't believe him, he would just have to live with it.

Everyone went silent. Carla was looking at Ryan with fondness. "Ryan is not involved in any of this, but you can be sure I trust him fully." Carla broke the silence

"I too believe Ryan is being sincere when he says he doesn't know anything," Tara said.

Molly had these questions as well, but hearing Ryan explain she too believed him.

The doorbell rang, everyone stood up. "Just stay there I will see who it is," Ryan waved his hands for everyone to sit down.

"Who is it?" he asked.

"Sheriff's men." The voice replied.

Ryan then peered out the side window and sure enough, it was an Officer. He also noticed that, as he looked past him, there were four police cars in the driveway. Ryan gave James a nod that all was okay, then opened the door.

Officer Thompson stepped through the door. "Evening, everyone," he greeted, "You folks have had quite a scare I hear."

"That's for sure!" Molly piped up.

"The Officers outside will be scouring the outside looking for any trace of this person, they will be checking the hydro box and the phone lines. They will be going over the cabin as well. We could be here for a while, but there will be lots of movement outside, but we will keep you posted at all times. I will be taking the statements to everybody here." Officer Thompson explained.

Molly escorted him to the living room and then scooted off to the kitchen for another cup and saucer. She poured the Officer a cup and handed it to him.

"Thank you, Molly." He said. Molly just nodded and sat down.

Officer Thompson took down their statements of what took place that day right from the beginning. James and Ryan told him about their trip to town and the events that took place on the way back.

They all made sure to leave the part out about Carla and the crystal ball. After most of the statement was taken down, he got up and checked the phone by lifting the receiver and listening for a second before hanging up.

"Well, everything seems okay now." He said. Then asked, "he never once tried to get in?"

"No, not once; we held vigil at all the windows to be sure we saw him coming if he decided to," James explained that they saw him leave the cabin about an hour before the lights came back on. They saw him go to the west side of the house and then they never saw him again. Officer Thompson got on his radio and relayed what James just said.

Tara got up and followed him into the dining room. She wanted to move the crystal ball before she noticed it. It was too late; he saw Tara pick it up and move it to the cabinet with other crystal items. "What that?" he asked.

"This? Oh, it's just an antique that I found at the flea market the other day. We were checking it out earlier." Tara lied.

Officer Thompson walked back into the living room, Tara followed.

"Well, I am going to head out and see what's up, I'll keep you posted," he told them. James and Ryan went out on the porch with him.

Molly looked at her watch. "Wow can you believe it's already after one in the morning?"

"No wonder I am so tired," Carla yawned.

"Yeah, me too," Tara said.

Molly got up, went to see James. "Do you mind if we go to bed now?" Molly yawned, then continued.

"The girls are exhausted." Molly said.

"No of course not, I am sure you must be tired as well," James told Molly. He gave her a big hug, kissed her on the forehead.

"Good night, Ryan," Molly said.

"Good night, Molly," He replied.

Molly opened the door to go back in, then turned to the men and asked, "If they find anything, James, you will tell me right away, right?"

"Of course, honey, right away," he promised.

Molly told the girls that there was no need for them to stay up any longer. The Officers are taking care of everything and James and Ryan will be waiting up until they are done. Tara and Carla went to the porch to say their goodnights. Molly waited for them at the bottom of the stairs. She saw them to their rooms and then headed for her own.

CHAPTER 20

Clues in the Cabin

Mark and James were sitting comfortably on the front porch, watching the bustling of Officers on the lawn and in the cabin. Officer Thompson was standing on the lawn talking with another Officer, about what in particular they didn't know. Other Officers were scouring the grounds with their flashlights and then there was the Officers in the cabin. Ryan figured that they were probably looking for fingerprints, hair sample or clothing sample etc.

The storm had passed now and Ryan could see the moon peeping out from behind a lonely gray cloud. He realized that it was a full moon as he watched the cloud clear away. The moon was very prominent in the sky, mesmerizing if you stared too long. The air was humid for the hour but he figured it was due to the weather.

James knocked Ryan's arm to get his attention. Ryan looked in the direction that James was looking in. he noticed that Officers were coming out of the cabin now. One was calling Officer Thompson to go to the cabin. The Officer hurried over.

"I wonder what they found?" Ryan said.

"I don't know, but it seems that there is something of interest over there," James replied.

The two of them watched intently. James moved closer to the edge of his seat. Anxious to know what was going on, he then turned to Ryan and said.

James felt uneasy about the situation, "I need to know something."

"Go ahead, ask me what you want." Ryan sighed knowing that it was about him and his involvement in all this. James was a smart man. It was only a matter of time before he turned to Ryan about this.

"We are going to be called over, I think, and before we do, I need to know if they are going to find something that will incriminate you in all this somehow?" James asked reluctantly.

"No, James, I told you I was hired as a detective to help keep you all safe; you did a check on my credentials, so you know I am on the up and up," Ryan announced easily.

James blushed he didn't think Ryan knew about that. Ryan could see his embarrassment.

"Every time someone does a check on us; we get a call letting us know. They don't tell us who it was, but generally, it is the people we are working with directly. I knew it was you, and I didn't blame you for doing it. Frankly, if the tables were turned, I would have done the same." Ryan said hoping to put James at ease.

James smiled at Ryan. They went back to watching the Officers talking just outside the cabin. Finally, Officer Thompson went into the cabin with the other Officers. He emerged again within about ten minutes. He waved to James and Ryan to join him. They quickly went out to meet him.
"Come inside, I have something to show you." Officer Thompson announced.

"Did you find a lead?" James inquired excitedly.

"Well, I am not sure it's a lead; you may be able to answer that better." Officer Thompson held the door for them to enter.

Chapter 21

Sleepless Vigil

Tara couldn't wait to get to sleep, she changed into her nightclothes as quickly as she could and then jumped into bed. She thought she would be asleep before her head hit the pillow.

Unfortunately, Tara couldn't sleep after hearing all the Officers bustling about on the property. Her mind started to swim with the thoughts of the day. Then she started thinking about everything that has transpired since her parents went missing. Still, the same questions keep arising.

"What did this person want? Who was it? Why? And what about the strange things that have transpired here in the house? The crystal ball. The book."

The book, Tara thought they didn't even look at it closely. She thought. She told herself that her and Carla would have a better look at it tomorrow.

She now heard the police pulling away, and then she heard the front door close and James coming up the stairs. She got out of bed to have a look outside. She saw the cars pulling away but Officer Thompsons was still there. He looked as if he was filling out a report while he sat in his car with his legs outside. Unable to sleep, she watched him from the window until he left. Tara crawled back into bed, closed her eyes and cleared her mind.

Chapter 22

Morning Revelations

When she opened her eyes the next morning, the sun shone into her room, warming her face. She could smell food cooking. It seemed to her as if she had just closed her eyes to go to sleep.

She wished it wasn't real but recognized she had to face the truth. *"Yesterday's events felt like a dream, a bad one at that."* She lay in her bed, enjoying the comfort and peace of the day that was beginning. She didn't want to get out of bed, knowing the events of last night were real. She knew that once she put her feet on the floor, she would have to deal with the reality and the big question…. *"What next?"* So far there are no leads. This person was really covering his tracks.

Tara's frustration grew as she realized they were still in the dark, *"What about my parents? They haven't heard anything about the investigation; how come? Where are the two connected? If so, how?"* Tara's head started spinning again with the questions from the previous night and some new ones. Tara could feel her temper starting to rage. She knew today would be the day that she would get some answers; there would be no more mysteries, just answers. She was angry now, feeling like they were all just sitting ducks waiting for the next strike. This angered her. She prided herself on being independent, but with each passing day, she felt more and more helpless. She was now determined that she would succeed in finding the answers to her questions. Tara's bed was no longer a source of comfort; it had become her think tank. She pulled the covers back and then sat on the side of her bed. The breeze coming in the window felt very humid already. She looked at the clock. It read eight-thirty. It would be a scorcher of a day if the humidity was already in the air. There may even be another possible storm coming.

Tara showered in a cool shower, flung her long blond hair up in a high ponytail, applied some mascara, and then went to her dresser to pick out today's clothes. She chose a light cotton pair of shorts in blue with a matching short spaghetti strap top. She shuffled her feet into a pair of blue sandals by her bedroom door and headed downstairs.

The smell of home fries wafted up the stairs. Her stomach was growling with hunger.

"Good morning, Tara; I hope you had a restful sleep," Molly asked.

"Very restful but way too short," Tara proclaimed.

Molly chuckled; she knew exactly how that felt. She was up early herself. James was up even earlier. His rising from the bed is what woke Molly. She asked him what he was doing up so early when he told her to go back to sleep. He and Ryan were anxious to look in the cabin. He explained that he told Ryan to sleep on the couch for the night until his cabin could be cleaned of the mess the police left it in. They didn't miss a thing, that's for sure. There was powder everywhere. James told Molly that a burglar wouldn't have left it in such rough shape. That's when Molly got up to make breakfast to give herself some energy if she had that much cleaning to do.

Molly dished out a plate of home fries, bacon and eggs for Tara as she retrieved a glass of orange juice from the fridge.

"Is Carla up yet?" Tara checked on her sister because she wanted to discuss the mysterious events or tackle the day together.

"No, not yet," Molly said as he joined Tara with her plate.
A pot of tea was already brewing on the table. Molly poured them both a cup.

"So, we're the only ones up then?" Tara asked.

"No, the men were up a while ago and are now over at Ryan's cabin," Molly explained about the mess James said the cabin was in and how she had her day marked out for her with all the cleaning.

"Don't you worry about the cleaning, Carla and I will do the cabin," Tara said.

Molly started to protest, but Tara wouldn't let her; she insisted that she and her sister were going to do the cleaning.

Molly and Tara finished their breakfast. Molly collected the plates to take them to the sink. She looked out the window scowling in the direction of the cabin.

"Is something wrong, Molly?" Tara asked noticing the look on her face.

"Not really, dear. it's just…well its…" Molly hesitated, unsure how to express herself.

"Spit it out, Molly. What's on your mind?" Tara pushed.

"Well, I am beginning to wonder if Ryan is reliable. He seems nice enough, and he has been extremely helpful around here, especially with James…but" Molly paused with a great sigh as she stirred her tea nervously. Tara had a hunch she knew where she was going with this because it had already crossed her mind. She went on to tell Molly that she had concerns as well.

"But," Tara continued for her, "If he meant us any danger, he would have had ample opportunity since he had arrived," Tara assured her. "Besides, we would have detected it a long time ago. It just wasn't in the cards," she said jokingly.

Molly laughed. "Yes, I suppose you're right." She said, smiling at Tara.

Molly poured them another cup of tea and as Tara was stirring in her sugar when Molly asked her this time what was on her mind. Tara stared into Molly's eyes for a few seconds thinking that other than her parents Molly knew all there was to know about her and her sister.

"Is it true that Carla and I have more to discover about our talents?" she was almost embarrassed to ask.

"Yes, it's true," Molly nodded her head.

"So besides tarot reading and the odd visions, there's actually more that we can do?" Tara's curiosity was peaked. Things were starting to change so fast. Tara's internal thoughts were, "Carla with the crystal ball, her with her dreams, and seeing her grandmother. Where were these other talents before?"

"I suppose now is as good a time as any to tell you something your mother was going to tell you girls on your next birthday; which I don't think she will be back in time to do so herself, considering it is next month," Molly said.

"I have already broken the rules by giving you girls the book, but I think it has something inside that will help you with our situation," Molly said.

"Yes, the book, we didn't really get a chance to look at it last night. But it was odd the books pages were blank," Tara queried.

"The poem described how we could reveal the page content by using the crystals…" Molly reminded Tara.

"Yes, that's exactly it, are you wearing your crystal pendant still?" Carla asked. She surprised them both as she walked into the kitchen with the book in hand.

"I was thinking about the book all night long, well most of the night anyway. So shall we see what's inside the book?" Carla placed the book on the table and then took a seat beside Tara.

She placed her crystal inside the spot on the front cover then Tara did the same. "I imagine Gran enchanted these crystals and gave them to our mother to go with the book and she must have given them to Mr. Davies just in case." Carla noted. Both crystals seemed to wedge themselves in just nicely like they were magnets that clung to the book and each other.

Carla looked at Tara, "Well, let's see if it works." She said as she opened up the book.

She flipped the pages and sure enough the pages were filled with writing. "Wow," was all they could say. Molly took a look at the book as well. "I suppose you girls have a bit of reading to do, eh? I will get you some breakfast Carla, you should eat before you two get started." Molly acknowledged that Tara and Carla now have a major task ahead.

"Yes, I suppose you're right." She said, rubbing her stomach to say she was hungry.

Chapter 23

Hidden Clues

James and Ryan went into the cabin. They saw that everything was turned upside down. The cushions were pulled off the couch, the rug was rolled up. Even the ashes from the fireplace looked as if they were sifted into a bucket. There were ashes all around the fireplace and on the floor. There was fingerprint powder everywhere.

"You weren't kidding when you said this place was a mess," Ryan stated in disbelief.

Even the bedroom had a good going over. James put the cushions back on the couch. Then fixed the rug in the room. He then took the ashes out to the garbage and brought back a broom to sweep up the mess around the fireplace. He then took the ashes to the garbage, tied it up and placed it outside in the wooden bin.

"What exactly are we looking for?" James asked.

"I don't know, but I thought maybe if we could see where he was looking, we may be able to see what he was after, but judging by the mess in here I don't think that is possible. I will check the computer files, though; that's where Carla said she saw him the most," Ryan replied.

James just took a seat on the couch for the time being while Ryan went through the computer.

Ryan started opening the files one at a time. There was a program on the computer that he could see the last time that the files were accessed. He never actually thought that would come in handy until today. Each file seemed to be opened at the same time that the hooded figure was in his cabin. So Ryan knew he went through every file on his computer. This wasn't much help to him, he was hoping that it was only one or two of the files but now he would have to open every file to look at it for himself.

Most of the files seemed to be in order and the information was nothing that Ryan could see being of any importance to him. Finally, he clicked on one file marked BWM. This was the file that he kept copies of reports that he sent to Mr. Davies on the girls, police reports etc. There were also the copies of reports the Mr. Davies sent him in regards to the investigation of their parents. When Ryan opened it up there was nothing there. Everything was missing. All the reports were gone, he had deleted everything from the file. Ryan thought to himself that this was strange, why didn't he just copy them or print them, it was as if he wanted us to see that this file was most important to him. He told James what he found. James went over to have a look.

"What was in there that would be so important to him," James asked.

Ryan told him that it was just updated from the investigation on both ends, the girl's parent's disappearance and the trouble the girls have been having with the hooded figure. Nothing of any importance at all," Ryan said.

"I can get the files back. All I have to do is talk to Mr. Davies and ask him to send me a copy of all the files, which I will do right now; I was going to call him this morning anyway in regards to last night's events," Ryan said picking up the phone.

James sat back down in the chair while Ryan made his call. James started looking around the cabin. He thought to himself how it hadn't changed at all since him and Molly occupied it many years ago. James looked at the fire place remembering many a night how they used to sit cuddled together watching the fire, listening to the sounds of the wild out the window. Wolves howling, owls hooting. His eyes dropped down to the floor where he then was thinking about the rug. It looked worn but not in too bad of condition considering how old it was. It was a Persian rug, antique now for sure. It was given to the girl's grandmother when she was just a young girl herself. It was always on the floor of her room, and then she took it with her when she got married and brought the rug here. This is where they lived until the estate was built. James then looked around the cabin to the bedroom. It was tiny but cozy, with a high four-poster bed and netting hooked to the ceiling so you could keep the mosquitos off of you during the night. This was also an antique as well as the quilt that was usually on it. The quilt was on the quilt rack at the end of the bed. The quilt was hand made by the girl's great grandmother and it has been passed down from generation to generation. James's heart started to melt as he thought about all the work Molly has done over the years to preserve everything so nicely. She took great care and pride in her duties. He loved her more today and with every passing day.

"Yes, okay that's great we'll see you then," Ryan said.

James was jolted from his trance state of reminiscing by Ryan's voice. Ryan turned to James as he hung up the phone.

"Mr. Davies will be here this afternoon and he's now sending me the files again, plus bringing a hard copy, which he will mail out as well from now on." Ryan was watching the computer screen, waiting patiently for the documents to come through.

"If there was nothing of importance in those documents, then why did he take them?" James asked.

"I figure he took them because he wanted to show us exactly what information he was after. Or maybe to try and halt our investigation" Ryan said the computer made a light dinging noise which drew Ryan's attention back to his computer.

"Yes! All the files are back now, I am just going to password protect my files and computer. Something I should have done but didn't figure it would be a problem up here." Ryan said as his fingers flew around the keyboard.

"Ding, ding-a-ding," The computer called out again. Ryan clicked it.

"It's an email from Mr. Davies. He says to tell Molly not to worry about lunch and that he will bring it. he says he has something for each of us when he arrives." Ryan read.

"Wonderful. We can relax for a while; maybe we can see if we can get some work done on the dock. Are you up for that?" James asked, rising from his seat, ready to get going.

"I would like to make a phone call to the sheriff about what he found last night, and I still have to pick up the report from the sheriff's office," Ryan stated.

"Well, I'll tell you what, then let's go get a cup of tea; we can get the boards out of the van, haul them down to the dock so they're there and then we can take a ride into town," James suggested.

"Let me just make a call to the sheriff's office to see what would be a good time to come down," Ryan picked the phone back up and dialed the number. He was really curious to find out what the item was that they found.

They wouldn't tell them last night because they wanted to test it for fingerprints. Officer Thompson didn't want him getting their hopes up.

Chapter 24

Awakening Rituals

"Look at all the pages, where do we begin?" Carla said as she ate her breakfast watching Tara flip the pages.

"Yeah, too bad there wasn't an index," Tara replied.

She leafed through the pages taking note of the titles but none seemed to click with what they were going through. There had to be over three hundred pages in this book. Some of the pages looked so old and most of the pages were on parchment paper. The oldest ones had fancy writing and some designs around the pages. A lot of them had symbols such as pentagrams, moons and suns, runes, astrology signs.

"Here it is, I think I found what we are looking for," Tara pointed out.

"It says to enhance or awaken your abilities." Carla read aloud the heading.

"Yeah, that's the one we need, what does it say?" Carla asked.

Tara read the page; when she was done, she said. "Sounds easy enough."

"Yeah, well look at the list of items we need, I hope we have everything," Carla said.

"Read them off to me. I may know where some of the stuff is," Molly said.

"Okay, matches..." Tara began listing.

"In the drawer," Molly went to get them.

"...black thread, red thread, yellow thread." Tara continued reading.

"In my sewing kit." Molly went to the fridge, sitting on top was her sewing kit. She pulled it down then picked out three spools of thread: red, black and yellow. She put them on the table beside the matches. She then went over to the cupboard and pulled out a serving tray. She set it on the table then placed the items on it.

"A white candle…three quartz crystals…. paper and red inked pen…and a heatproof bowl," Tara ensured everything was accounted for.

"I have the red inked pen and paper in the draw with the pads of paper for shopping and a white candle in the emergency box of candles" Molly said as she went from place to place collecting the items for the girls.

"The crystals I saw were in the chest along with the cauldron in the attic," Carla remembered.

"Okay great, we're all set then, I will get the crystals." Carla took off for the attic.

When she got back, she placed the cauldron with the crystals inside it on the tray with everything else.

"What else does it say?" Molly asked

"Well, according to this, we have to wait for a full moon and to perform it outside when the moon is at its peak," Tara read.

"So I suppose that means when it's at the highest, it's going to go for the night and if it's like the sun, it will be right overhead." Carla thought aloud.

Molly looked at the calendar, "It's a full moon tonight girls."

"Well, what luck is that," Carla said

"I somehow don't think luck had anything to do with it. I believe we are being guided by an unknown force." Tara smiled at Molly.

"I had nothing to do with the circumstances, you know that it's just plain coincidence," Molly smirked.

"And you know as well as we do there are no such things as coincidences," Carla piped up.

"What does it say we need to do with all this stuff?" Carla asked.

"Well, first we have to make a braid of the three colours together, tie them in a knot at the ends, then we write on the red paper something like this...*I Tara Ward, dedicate myself to the divine Feminine and her consort. That she may guide me, awaken and enhance the gifts that have been bestowed upon me as my birthright.*" Tara carefully read the instructions from the book and guided Carla and Molly through the ritual's purpose and steps.

"Then we tie the braids around the candle, light the candle and read aloud what we have written. Then we burn the paper in the flame, when it has turned to ash, we then release the ashes to the wind." She continued.

"Then it says we are to chant ...*I am her, she is me*...three times, then we sit silently and await messages that will come." Sounds intriguing, Tara said as she finished reading the first half of the instructions.

Molly's face turned grim all of a sudden.

"What's the matter Molly?' Carla asked.

"I don't think I like the idea of you girls being alone in the dark outside, not after what happened last night." Molly voiced her concern.

"We have to do this though," Carla said.

"Yeah, we have to, "Tara agreed.

"Well, let's talk to James and Ryan. Maybe we can all stand vigil while you perform this ritual," Molly said.

"Don't you girls worry about it. If I have to stand out there with you and carry the shotgun, I will do it," Molly said jokingly.

They all laughed at what a visual that gave off. Molly patrolling back and forth with a gun over her shoulder.

"Yeah, you laugh but I will if I have to." She said seriously this time.

"That's what's so funny, we know you would." The girls said.

They were laughing in hysterics this time; even Molly couldn't help herself and started to laugh in spite of herself.

The front door opened, James and Ryan came through the door. "Molly?' James inquired.

"We're in the kitchen," Molly yelled back.

"What are you girls up to?" Ryan asked.

"Sit down and we'll pour you some tea and tell you all about it." Molly said as she got up to put more tea on.
Carla and Tara started to tell them about the book and the ritual they needed to do.
Ryan had a funny look on his face as the girls explained all this to them.

"What's the matter, Ryan?" Carla asked.

"Well, it all sounds so strange to me; I guess I never thought this stuff was true; psychics, yes, but witchcraft?" Ryan voiced his skepticism about the mystical elements.

"We will have to tell you all about the family history, but it isn't as bad as you think," Molly said.

"Please just try to keep an open mind?" Carla pleaded.

Ryan nodded and agreed not to pass judgment. He promised

Carla he would keep an open mind.

They sat and talked about how they were going to keep the girls safe while they drank their tea.

"Oh, we better get going if we are to meet Officer Thompson at the station," Ryan said, noticing the time on his watch.

"Why are you meeting up with him?" Tara asked.

"He found something last night in the cabin, and he wanted to take it for fingerprints, very curious actually; he wouldn't tell us what the item was; he just asked if we kept sticks around the cabin for any reason; we don't of course, well I never noticed any sticks lying around the cabin," Ryan said.

"No, there wouldn't be any sticks in the cabin; all the kindling is in the bin out back," Molly said.

"That's what I told Officer Thompson last night so he took it to analyze it," James said.

"Yeah, so we are off to find out the results and to see just what kind of a stick he found," Ryan explained.

They both rose from the table. James kissed Molly goodbye, Ryan gave Carla a wink, and then they left.

"I have a few things I would like to do today myself Tara mentioned. For starters, I want to talk to Mr. Davies and find out what is happening with the investigation. I feel the more information on our parents' disappearance, the more we will be able to put together about this strange person here if the two are connected," Tara said. Just then, the door opened, and Ryan came running through to the kitchen.

"I forgot to tell you that Mr. Davies is coming this afternoon, and he's bringing lunch with him. We'll be back as soon as we can start without us if he shows up before we do," Ryan said quickly, then ran back out the front door.

"Well, I guess my phone call can wait until he arrives then," Tara said.

"Well, I have a lot of work for me this day. What about the apparent mess at the cabin?" Molly sighed.

"We'll help you with that, right Tara?" Carla offers their assistance.

"Right," Molly agreed.

They all cleaned up the dishes then grabbed some cleaning supplies and headed over to the cabin.

Chapter 25

The Mysterious Email

"Doug, could you come here for a moment?" Officer Drake asked. Officer Drake was the head of the police department in Cedar Falls. He mainly stayed behind the scenes, making sure everything ran smoothly from the office. He keeps his Officers in line. If it were the big city, he would be the captain.

"The results are on your desk from the stick, and I would like you to look at a message that I received this morning over email." Drake emphasized.

Officer Thompson (Doug) went over to his desk. He picked up the folder and read the results of the test. They found a fingerprint on the stick but couldn't get a match.

"Damn!" He said, disappointed. He then went to Officer Drake's desk, where he was waiting for him with the email pulled up on his computer.

"Well, what do you make of this?" he asked.

The picture was a dark room with no windows, and he could barely make out the figures in the middle. There seemed to be light but very dim coming from the top of the picture permeating downwards, but it was not enough to illuminate the subjects.

"I'm not sure, it looks like two people back-to-back." He said.

"Do you have a magnifying glass there?" Doug asked.

Officer Drake riffled through his desk drawers and finally came up with one, "Here you go." Drake provided the magnifying glass.

Officer Thompson scanned the picture on the screen up close with the magnifier. All he could make out was two people back-to-back, one looked male the other female.

"Can you print this out for me?" Doug requested.

"Sure." Drake agreed without hesitation.

Officer Thompson went to the printer grabbed the print then scanned it again.

"Here, look at this piece down by their hands. It looks as if it's a rope; maybe they are tied together, " he said.

Officer Drake took the magnifier and had a look for himself.
"Yeah, it sure looks that way to me, also if you look up it seems that they have something tied around their neck that's attached to the ceiling." He confirmed.

"I saw that too, but I wasn't sure if it was that or if it was a shadow of something." Officer Thompson said.

"Who are these people?" he asked.

"I don't know, we haven't gotten any reports of missing people yet. The only people we know that are missing is the Wards. Could it be them, you think? His country drawl is coming out. I did a check on the IP address but it seems that whoever did this did it from a library computer not far from here." Officer Drake speculated about the identity of the figures in the mysterious image.

"Where exactly?" Doug asked.

"Just over the town of Cavan. When you're done with James and Ryan, maybe you can take Bill with you and head over to Cavan and see if we can't find out who did this." Officer Drake said.

"Sure, I will call ahead and let them know we are coming." He said and headed for the phone on his desk.

The office was small but still roomy enough to fit eight desks comfortably. Officer was at the back by the door to the holding cells.

Ryan and James arrived right on time for their appointment.

Officer Drake showed them over to Doug's desk. Doug finished up the phone call.

"James, Ryan, glad you could come." He said as he shook each of their hands.

He reached into his desk drawer and pulled out a zip lock bag containing a stick.

He took it out of the bag and handed it to James. "Well, does it ring any bells for you?" he asked.

"Not a one." He said, passing it to Ryan.

Ryan examined it. The stick was about twelve inches in length at the most. It was polished smooth with some wood stain; it looked like lacquer. There were symbols carved in it that were very tiny around what seemed to be the base. It looked very well worn, as if it were used quite often, for what he couldn't begin to imagine.

"If it is the hooded figures, then I suppose he will be wanting it back; by the looks of it, he uses it a lot," Ryan stated.

"Yeah, we thought the same thing, so we are going to post some units around the clock at your place for a bit, maybe we'll get lucky and catch ourselves a hooded figure." Officer Thompson made a fishing pun.

"Seriously though, he may come back this time we want to be ready for him." He said.

"I hope he does come back looking for this thing. I have certainly had enough of this character, I want him behind bars just for being the nuisance that he is." James said.

Ryan and Doug looked at James and laughed.

"No disrespect meant, James, but I think we all feel the same way." Officer Thompson smiled at James. "We'll get him, you can bet on it."

"Oh, did you find any prints or anything that could help you find him?" Ryan asked.

"As a matter of fact, we were able to pull a print from it but the bad news is there was no print to match it." This guy is not in the system so it seems he has never committed a crime as yet." Doug said.

"That's not very helpful," James stated.

"No, it's not, but let's hope we have something he really wants bad enough to come and get it, and because this may warrant another visit from him. I want you all to be indoors after dark for the next few days. Doors and windows lock, okay." Officer Thompson asked them.

"There's just one more thing," Doug said as he pulled the print from under a folder on his desk.

"This just came through, do they look familiar to you?" Doug presented a mysterious photo to James and Ryan.

James and Ryan studied the picture.

"It's really hard to make anything out of this," James said.

Ryan agreed, "All you can really make out is the silhouette of the people. Whoever did this, seems to know exactly what they are doing, meaning they must have great knowledge of photography to be able to achieve these results."

"Very good. I didn't think of that, but I bet you're right." Officer Thompson looked at the picture again, this time with new insight.

"So, we are looking for someone possibly with a photography background. Excellent, this gives us two possible clues. Not much, but it's better than what we had to go on." He turned to James.

"What's your other clue?" James asked.

"Well, we know the computer he used to send the picture came from a library computer at Cavan Library. I am heading over there now with Officer Mathews, we will keep you up to date if we find anything else out." Doug outlined the next steps.

"Thank you," James and Ryan said in unison, then shook his hand, took the stick with them and left.

James was quiet on the drive back; he hadn't said a word for over half the ride.

"What's on your mind?" Ryan inquired.

James just looked at him and then went back to staring out the window.

"I can't help thinking that these people in the picture might be Mr. And Mrs. Ward." James voiced his fear.

"Yes, but it may also not be them." Ryan tried to reassure him but knew he didn't do a very good job.

"What are we going to tell the girls and Molly?" Ryan asked.

"Well, I don't think we should tell them about the picture, however as far as the wand is concerned, that new book they have may have something in it about that wand or even the symbols that are on it." James decided to withhold potentially alarming information. "They are not like anything I have ever seen."

"No, me either." Ryan agreed with James.

They both went quiet again. The car rolled into the driveway after twenty minutes of silence. James grabbed Ryan`s arm before he got out of the car.

"They are not going to be happy with the lockdown after dark, so we will have to keep and extra eye on them. I know these girls, they want to do something. There is no stopping them. They will find a way to sneak around you to get what they want." James knew their determined personalities and how difficult it would be to keep them from taking risks.

"I understand, so we have to be the last to go to bed then. Oh yeah," Ryan said as he yawned a fake yawn.

James smiled then let go of Ryan's arm.

Chapter 26

Lunch Time

Ryan and James were getting out of the car when another car rolled up behind them. It was Mr. Davies's car. They waited on the porch for him before they went into the house.

"Ryan, could you give me a hand, please." Mr. Davies yelled to Ryan.

Ryan went over to his car; he loaded his arms with parcels from the grocery store. Then he went to his trunk, and from there he retrieved five boxes all wrapped up with brown paper and hemp like string. It looked as if all parcels had a small white tag attached to the string.

James opened the door for the men and yelled through the house, "Molly, Mr. Davies is here with lunch." There was no answer. "Molly, did you hear me? Mr. Davies is here." Still no reply.

Ryan and Mr. Davies went inside, with James following. Mr. Davies went through to the kitchen and placed the food on the counter. "I will set the table," Ryan said as he started getting the plates and cutlery out of the cupboard.

"I am going to see if I can find the girls," James said, leaving through the back door.

"Are the girls okay, Ryan?" Mr. Davies asked.

Ryan reassured Mr. Davies that the girls were fine earlier, "Yeah, they were okay when James and I left."

"They are tough girls, but how is Molly holding up?" Ryan shifts focus to Molly.

Ryan commented on Molly's composure, "She seems to be a rock through this hole thing. Did you bring the paper copies?"

Mr. Davies patted his briefcase, which was sitting on the kitchen chair. "Yes, sir right here."

"What are all these parcels?" Ryan shifted the conversation to the parcels.

"Well, you're just going to have to wait and find out. It's a little something for everyone." Mr. Davies added a touch of mystery.

Ryan finished setting the table. "What exactly did you bring with you for lunch?"

"Well, I stopped at this little diner on the way up, you know, the little one just on this side of town." Mr. Davies explains where he got the food.

"Yeah, I know the one," Ryan said.

"Well, I picked up their special, ribs, corn on the cob, and mashed potatoes."
"Wow, that sounds more like dinner than lunch," Ryan said.
As he reached into the fridge for the butter and then went for the salt and pepper.

"Well, by the time we finish eating, it will probably be closer to two o'clock anyway, then Molly will only have to make something light for supper."

"You're always thinking." Ryan laughed.

Chapter 27

Unexpected Guests

James walked around the house looking for the girls but didn't see anything. He had checked the boathouse, thinking they may have gone for a boat ride. But the boat was still there. James started toward the front of the house when he looked at Ryan's cabin. He saw someone move by the window. He went over to see if the girls were there. James knocked lightly on the screen door. He couldn't see anyone through the kitchen, and no one came running to the door. He started to feel a little panicky. James went around the wood shed and grabbed a plank of wood to use if needed. He went back to the door, opened it quietly, and snuck in. he heard rustling coming from the bedroom. He couldn't help but think to himself that the cloaked figure was back already for that stupid wand. James put his back to the wall and moved quietly over to the doorway. He could now hear music coming from the bedroom. The radio was on low. He raised the plank of wood over his shoulder, ready to strike, then moved into the doorway. There, he saw Tara and Carla making the bed. They didn't even notice him standing there. Molly came around the corner from the ensuite bathroom.

Molly was surprised, "James, what are you doing," She asked. Staring at the plank held above his shoulder. He must have looked like a fright to Molly, he thought.

"I... I knocked, but no one answered, and I thought, well..." James was explaining why he entered.

Molly started to laugh, and the girls looked at James with a smirk on their faces, trying to hold back the laughing at how silly James looked. Molly put her cleaning bucket down and came over to James, who still had the board over his shoulder, ready to strike. She grabbed the plank from him and then kissed him on the cheek. "We're okay, James." She said he gave her a hug.

James was still concerned about potential danger, "You really shouldn't leave the door open like that; I could have been the cloaked figure."

"Oh, James, we were okay," Molly was trying to downplay James' concerns, reassuring him that everything was under control.

"Yes, you are, but I am just saying that it could have been different. It could as easily have been the cloaked figure instead of me." James emphasized dangerous situations.

"Yes, dear, you are absolutely right; we will be more careful from now on," Molly reassured James, then turned to wink at the girls.

"Mr. Davies is here with lunch; that is why I was out looking for you," James said as he looked around.

"You girls have done a wonderful job in cleaning this place up. It was a real mess, wasn't it?" James stated.
"Yes, it was, but we all worked together and finally got it cleaned up. I was just finishing up the bathroom when you came in." Molly said.

"Well, let's all go get lunch before it gets cold," James said as he led the way, grabbing the cleaning supplies for the girls.

Molly made the tea and brought it out on the tray to steep while they ate their lunch. Mr. Davies was, as usual, calm and charismatic toward Molly.

"This looks wonderful, Mr. Davies. Thank you for bringing it out." Molly said.

"My pleasure; I know how hard you work to keep things running smoothly around here, so anything I can do to elevate some work when I come over is my pleasure." Mr. Davies said.

James rolled his eyes, looking at Ryan, then stuck his finger into his open mouth to make the gagging gesture. Ryan chuckled, and Mr. Davies looked at him. Ryan just bowed his head to look at his watch, pretending he didn't do anything. Mr. Davies scowled, then turned back to Molly. "I brought you all a gift he said as he grabbed the small boxes wrapped in brown paper. He started handing them out to everybody.

"Go on, open them up," he said anxiously everyone put their forks down and opened their gift. It was quiet. James and Molly just looked at each other quietly in confusion.

"Well? What do you think?" Mr. Davies asked.

Tara and Carla looked happy as they pulled out their gifts. "I love it; how did you get it in this colour? Purple is my favorite colour," Tara said.

"Yes, and mine too, it's burgundy," Carla stated.

Mollys was red as she turned it over and over in her hand. "I haven't got the foggiest idea on how to use these things," She said.

Mr. Davies just laughed and said, "I am sure the girls will help you with that."

"Why?" was all James could say.

Mr. Davies, turning a little more somber, said to James. "These are for you to use if the power ever goes out and if you have an emergency. After the last incident, I figured these would be your best defence; this way, you can get a hold of the police if anything happens. I am sure he can't cut the power on these cell phones." He continued. "I am actually surprised that you never had one to begin with, especially up here when there is nothing around for miles." He said.

"Yeah, well, I don't know how to work these things either," James said, scowling at the phone he held in his hand.

"Ryan, I know you must have lost yours somewhere, so this is why I got you another one," he said disappointedly.

"I didn't lose mine; I left it in the office back in Toronto," He said.

"Why would you do that?" Mr. Davies said disgusted.

"I didn't do it on purpose," he said defensively.

"I just didn't remember to bring it. It's probably still sitting on my desk back at the office." Ryan continued explaining.

"Huh." That was all Mr. Davies could say.

Ryan was taken aback by Mr. Davies's attitude towards him. He was never like that with him or anyone else. Ryan was suspicious about him and his attitude but couldn't put his finger on what was wrong. "Besides, how did he know that he LOST his phone or he just left it in the cabin." He thought to himself. It just seemed odd.

"The phones are already activated; you can use them anytime, anywhere, and the bills will be paid through my office. So, you don't have to worry about that. Just do me one favor: please carry them with you at all times. What with this creep around you just never know. I don't want any of you to be harmed unnecessarily." They all nodded in agreement.
Everyone had finished eating, and Molly started to clean up the plates.

"It's such a lovely afternoon; why don't we have tea and cakes out on the patio," Tara suggested.

"That's a great idea," James said as he rose.

Mr. Davies noticed that everyone left their phones on the table. He stopped everyone, then pointed to their phones. "Get into the habit of taking them with you everywhere you go." They all came back and grabbed their phones from the table. Molly set up the patio table with the tea, and Tara followed with the cakes.

Tara and Carla sat their listening to the conversations and played with their phones. Little did anyone else know that Carla and Tara were testing each other back and forth, making plans for this night's ritual from the book. When they heard Ryan and James speak of the conversation, they had with Officer Thompson. It immediately got their attention. James looked at the girls as they looked up from their phones. "I know you had something planned for this evening, but you will either have to postpone it or do it during the day," James said.

"We can't. The book clearly states we need to do this outside under the full moon," Tara pleaded.

"I know you were looking forward to this, but we can't have you alone outside at night with that person lurking about," James demanded.

Mr. Davies looked at them all with great confusion. He had no idea what they were talking about. Ryan saw the confusion on his face and started to explain. His expression immediately changed as he nodded his head to what Ryan was telling him. "I am sure there's a way we can let the girls do what they need to do if we are all watching out for them," Molly suggested.

"Well, we'll see," James said. He went on to explain what Officer Thompson's men found in Ryan's cabin. James rose from his chair and went to the front hall, where he left the wand. He showed it to everyone at the table and told them that Officer Thompson feels this may be a prized possession of the cloaked figure and that he is pretty certain he will return to get it. "Tara? Carla? If you could look in the book of yours and see if anything is describing this thing, maybe we can figure out what it is used for and maybe you can find out what the tiny symbols mean on it as well." James suggested.

"I will go get the book," Tara said as she ran from the table, leaving her phone there.

"Uh, uh, uh. Your phone," Mr. Davies reminded.

"Oh yeah, this could end up being a pain in the ass." She replied as he came back for it.

"There is a carrier in each of your boxes that you can put your phone in and clip it to your pants, so it won't be a problem." He said.

"Boy, you thought of everything, didn't you," Carla said, amused.

Ryan was amused as well. There was being protective, and then there was being obsessed. Ryan still had a funny feeling but still could not put his finger on it. He has known Mr. Davies for 6 years and has worked alongside him for the past 4 years, and he has never seen him behave like this. Ryan made his mind up to watch him, hoping to find out what he was up to.

Tara came back with the book. Carla and Tara looked through it carefully. Mr. Davies was showing Ryan the papers and Molly and James the reports on the girl's parents.

"Have there not been any more clues as to where they are?" Molly asked.

"I am afraid not, but don't get discouraged. We are still hard at work trying to find out." Mr. Davies reassured her, patting her hand.

James just sat there and read the last report. "Was there no luggage found, clothing, hair samples, anything?" James asked.

"No, and that is the funny thing. It was as if they never boarded that flight at all." Mr. Davies highlighted.

"Maybe they didn't then. Maybe they are somewhere else, and we just jumped to conclusions." James said, hopeful.

"No, I'm sorry they were on that plane. We have eyewitness accounts of them boarding the plane." "The stewardess remembers serving them drinks when they got up in the air." Mr. Davies said.

Molly heard this and perked up right away. "I thought you said there were no survivors?" she asked.

"They were all killed but the pilot and the one stewardess. The pilot is still in a coma, but the stewardess is recovering from her injuries and making great progress." Mr. Davies said non-saliently.

Molly just shook her head. "It doesn't make sense."

"No, it doesn't make any sense; if they weren't on that plane when it crashed, then how did she identify them?" James said angrily.

"Please be assured I have the best men on the job, and we will find out what happened, and as soon as I know anything, you will know." Mr. Davies reassured again.

"I think we found something," Carla said.

"Yes, the symbols seem to be runic alphabet. And the stick seems to be wand used for magic purposes." Carla said.

"That's great, what can it do," Ryan asked.

"I think you can change things with it. I am not sure, but apparently, it was made by the magician himself, and it is attuned to his energy. So, if we used it, the magic may backfire," Tara said.

"I will go up get the laptop and we can look up the runes on it and see if we can find out the meaning of them. This book describes them but just says that it is a magical alphabet." Carla said.

"If we find out what they mean, we should write that in this book alongside the alphabet. It looks like that was the intention but was never finished." Tara said.

Carla went to get her laptop she grabbed her phone waved it at Mr. Davies boldly then left. Mr. Davies just smirked at her attitude.

When she came back, she had her phone clipped to her belt. Ryan watched Mr. Davies smile when he saw that she had it clipped to her. He also noticed that Mr. Davies couldn't seem to keep his eyes off the book the girls were looking at. Ryan knew he was an antique fanatic but he has never seen him look at something so hungrily. Ryan found this odd as well.

"How long are you staying with us this time?" James asked Mr. Davies.

"Well, seeing how it's Friday today if you don't mind, I would love to hang around for the weekend." He asked.

"Sure, that's no problem, maybe we can get in some fishing?"

James said, elated. He hadn't done any fishing yet and was itching to go.

"I'd love it if maybe we could make it a boy's day with just us three." He suggested.

Ryan nodded his head in agreement.

"That's a great idea. Let's do it tomorrow morning, then say early, around six a.m." James said.

Mr. Davies and Ryan agreed.

Carla turned the laptop around for everyone to see. She pointed out the three symbols that were on the wand.

"See these symbols here." She pointed.
"They are the ones on the wand. They each have a different meaning." She said,
"The first one is:

THURISAZ - The seeing of the future.

The second is :

KENAZ - Beacon or torch.

The third one is:

HAGALAZ - Destructive forces. "

"What does that all mean?" Molly asked.

"I am not sure but judging by the explanations I don't think he should have this back?" Tara said.

"Yes, but by judging by the explanations, this could be all the more reason he will want it back," Ryan said.

"See this makes it riskier for you to be out at night time alone," James said.

"I still don't see why we can't if you are watching while we do it?" Carla pleaded.

"Yes, I think they should do it because they need to bring forth the powers that are hidden within them." Molly added, "Their powers could really come in handy at this time."

"Well, you have a point, but still, you have to remember the chaos that could occur as well because they don't know how to use them and they don't even know what they are until it happens. You remember Molly." James said you could see he was trying to remind her of a time long ago. You could see in Molly's eyes that she understood what James was saying.

"I realize the risks, but we still have to let them do it." She insisted.

"What risks." Both girls said in unison.

Molly patted Carla's hand and winked but did not explain. Instead, she continued the conversation and planned how they were going to protect them when the moon came up.

Mr. Davies decided to stay with Ryan in the cabin for the weekend. He told Ryan he would sleep on the couch and not to worry; he would be completely fine on the couch. Ryan agreed. He actually liked this idea because, because of Mr. Davies's behaviour today, he would be able to watch him more closely.

Chapter 28

Ritual of Light

The rest of the day went rather fast. Dinner was over before they knew it, and the sun was going down. They actually had a wonderful day. They put aside all their worries. Mr. Davies went to the cabin to do a little light reading while Ryan and James continued the work on the dock, which they had finally completed. The twins went for a swim and did some sun tanning with Molly. Now it was evening and they were sitting having tea on the patio again. The evening was warm the sky was clear. In the west, you could see the sun taking its final journey for the day and leaving behind the beautiful pinks and gold. "Pink sky at night, sailors delight" was the phrase running through Tara's mind.

She had a great feeling about the ritual this evening and could hardly wait to see the results. She was baffled that this secret was kept from them for so long. She figured that they did it because they didn't want them to have a hard time growing up with their friends. It still wasn't easy because of the one gift they both had that was not kept from them. Now Carla was already showing signs of advancing. She was not adept with it yet, which was clear. She needed this ritual to help her better understand what it was. Tara also wondered what her gifts might be; nothing had really made it prevalent that she had any other gifts. She really wanted to be blessed with gifts, but she couldn't help but think she might regret them as well. But she told herself she couldn't think of these things and that they needed to do the ritual to be able to hopefully get this cloaked figure and save their parents.

James had put the wand in the safe that was behind the pictured rug hanging on the wall in the library. There was no way the cloaked figure could get it.

"The moon is starting to come up," Carla said excitedly.

"Why don't you girls go get the stuff we put together and bring it out," Molly suggested.

The girls left.

"Okay." James said, "We will be in the boat house watching, and you and Ryan can be in the kitchen watching from there," Ensured that everyone has their role.

Mr. Davies and Ryan agreed.

The girls started setting up their space. They chose a spot out by the lake beside a wooden tree. It was the most beautiful of all spots when there was a full moon. They have a picture in the estate on the library wall that shows the moon in its full glory shining on the lake and illuminating the branches of the Wood tree. It was always the girls' favorite picture. The girls had read the book and followed all the instructions on how to set up the altar and create their sacred space. They were told it wasn't always necessary to use salt to cast the sacred space, but they chose to use it this night because they felt they needed the extra protection. They cast the circle and called in the Goddess and her consort. They then sat on the grass with the thread and each braided their own. They then tied it to the candle. They took the pen and paper and wrote down the script from the book; when they were both ready, they started reading the script aloud. Each taking turns reading. They repeated it and repeated it faster and faster. Both of them were amazed that they were doing this. It was as if they were being guided by some unseen force. They started moving in a grapevine manner around in a circle their feet going faster and faster. The energy they were raising was strong both of them could feel it. They were getting tired but couldn't stop. All of a sudden, the entire circle was filled with a white light as if someone had put a big spotlight on them. The source of the light was hard to determine but they were all aglow.

Molly was jumping for joy, for this wasn't the first time she had seen this rite performed. Both Ryan and James were watching and saw the light. Ryan was taken aback by what he was witnessing. James just took it in stride. He had seen and taken part in many of things over the years with this family and his wife, and he was never really shocked anymore. He looked over at Ryan, who was somewhat dumb founded by the whole thing. His mouth was agape in awe. He looked at James but couldn't manage to utter any words. James just laughed and said, "You'll get used to it."

Chapter 29

The Charged Circle

Tara and Carla noticed they were starting to slow down, this not being of their own accord. Then the light stayed for a little bit longer then started to fade. The girls immediately came to a stop. They both fell to the ground. They looked at each other and started to laugh.

"I think the ritual went well." Carla laughed.

"Yes, sis, I do believe it did." Tara joined her. "What an amazing feeling that was, I had no control over what I was doing."

"I know what you mean, it was as if someone had taken over our bodies and were doing it for us." Carla painted.

"Yes, but if someone else was doing it, then why are we so tired and out of breath," Tara said.

Carla shrugged her shoulders and just laid back on the grass to catch her breath. Tara joined her. The kitchen door opened, Molly came out. She was wearing a large grin.

"Excellent, excellent girls, the ritual went well." She was bouncing her way over to the girls.

"Have a seat, Molly, and tell us about the first time you did this ritual," Tara said

Molly looked at her inquisitively. "Whatever do you mean?"

"You are just way to happy about how the ritual went that I know this isn't the first time you have seen this," Tara stated.

Molly smiled at the girls, "That's a story for a stormy night."

Ryan and James were headed over to the girls as well. Ryan went to step across the line of salt and was thrown back two feet, where he landed on his backside. "What the hell was that?" He was shocked. Neither one of the girls could figure out what had just happened.

"Ryan, are you okay?" Carla asked.

"I am fine; my ego is a little bruised," Ryan replied. Carla snickered.

"The girls have a protective circle of salt around them that has been charged by their energy and the moons energy. This circle will not allow anyone in that is not invited." Molly explained.

"I am sorry, I should have warned you about that but I was just so excited that the ritual went according to plan." Ryan stood up brushed off his pants.

Once he gathered himself together, he asked, "So it went well then? That is what was supposed to happen?"

They replied, nodding their heads, "Yes".

"Well, that's great I suppose, now what?" he asked.

"Now, the girls will have to take the circle down and clear the salt away. Then, they will leave the candle lit. When they go to bed this evening, their dreams will tell them the next step." Molly explained.

Both girls just looked at Molly and then said at the same time, "Really?"

They were just as lost as everyone else but Molly, who seemed to know everything. The girls took the circle down and swept away the salt. They gathered up the stuff they had and the paper ashes from burning them in the flame of the candle they released to the wind over the lake. They took the stuff into the house, where they all sat and had tea and cookies. The evening was beautiful. Tara noticed that everything seemed clearer and crisp. Sounds were sharper, and the colour was brighter, yet everything was the same. It was the strangest sensation; even her taste buds were heightened. She wondered if Carla was seeing the same thing. What did this mean? She wondered. She didn't really care about the answer; she was enjoying this new sensation of hers and didn't want it to go away.

"What was the bright light we saw surrounding the girls in the circle?" Ryan asked.

Molly smiled, "It was the divine light from the goddess of the moon and the divine light from the god here all around them. It was their blessing to the girls they were awakening their gifts with their divine light."

Ryan just shook his head and said, "Wow, this is all so new to me."

"How do you think I feel?" Carla said, "This stuff is so new to us, we didn't grow up seeing stuff like this, you know." Carla gave Ryan a friendly shove.

James got up and went to the front door. He looked through the window in the door. He could see the police car parked out front, but he couldn't see the Officers. James then stepped out onto the porch. He looked around but still didn't see anyone there. He wondered where they could be. He wasn't worried; they were probably doing their rounds of the house.

Molly snuck up behind him. "James, honey, I don't think we have anything   to   worry   about   this   evening."

He smiled at Molly as he put his arm around her and pulled her close. They both looked up at the full moon. "It is a beautifully peaceful night out, isn't it?" James said.

Molly just nodded, comforted by his arm around her. She hoped the night would remain peaceful. She looked around the grounds, noticing how bright the moon made everything. When she realized neither of the police were there. "Where are the Officers, James?" she asked.

"I don't know actually I was wondering the same thing," James admitted his uncertainty.

"Does it worry you?" Molly asked.

"Well, to be honest, it is a little unsettling." He said honestly. There was no point trying to cover up how he was feeling. Molly had the gift of seeing right through him.

"Maybe Ryan and I could look around the back while you distract the girls." He said.

Molly laughed, "You won't be able to get anything by these girls easily again."

"Right, you are right; we will just tell the girls our concerns. I am sure they won't panic, and besides, I don't think there is anything wrong anyway," James said.

Molly and James went inside and told the three of them about the Officers. Tara just looked at Carla and Carla looked at her. "I will make more tea." Carla said nonchalantly "I'll help" Tara said. Strange unspoken communication. That seemed to go unnoticed by everyone except Molly.

James and Ryan went outside while Moly watched the girls in the kitchen. They didn't speak but were busy getting a new pot of tea ready with new dish of cookies.

"Are you girls okay?" Molly asked.

They looked at Molly and said. "I think so, we are finding that we see things quite sharply; all our senses are heightened," Tara said, Carla nodded in agreement. Molly just nodded her head.

She knew exactly what the girls were talking about. "Well, that is part of the initiation and you will get used to it after a while," she said.

The other thing is that we seem to be able to read each others mind. We don't need to speak aloud to each other anymore." Tara said Carla again nodding in agreement. "That is something I was wondering about. It is most likely because you are twins." Molly stated.

Ryan and James came through the back door to the kitchen where the three girls were still standing and talking.

"Well, what did you find?" Molly asked

"Nothing, everything seems to be quiet out there," James reported their lack of findings.

"What about the Officers? Are they back in the car?" Molly asked.

"Well, not exactly…." James hesitated.

"What do you mean not exactly?" Molly demanded.

"…Well, we couldn't find them. They don't seem to be anywhere." James said.

Molly immediately looked terrified. James could see the stress in her eyes. "It's okay. That doesn't mean anything bad is going to happen." They may have seen him and followed on foot. Don't go worrying just yet." James said to her.

Ryan went over to the phone and picked it up. The line was working so he dialled the sheriff's office. Officer Thompson answered the phone.

"Sheriff's office Officer Thompson speaking," Thompson answered.

"Hi, this is Ryan from the Blackwood Manor." Ryan started

"Hi Ryan, how is everything? Are the girls, okay? He asked.

"Well, that's just it. We happened to notice that both the Officers were missing. Their car is here but they are nowhere to be found." Ryan stated.

"Well, they haven't checked in at all." The Officer said. "They were supposed to check in over an hour ago." "I will send a car over…no, actually I will come over myself. I will see you shortly." The line went dead.

Ryan hung up and then lifted the receiver again. Nothing dead silence. Mr. Davies came in to see what was keeping Ryan. Ryan was dialing a number on his cell phone. The phone then gave an excruciating beep in his ear. He looked at the phone only to see that it was registering no signal. He spotted Mr. Davies standing there. "Check your cell phone for a signal." Mr. Davies pulled his cell phone from its belt clip. He shook his head. "No signal."

"That's not right, when I bought these phones, they said they were the best and could get a signal in places where others couldn't and come to think of it, the phones have always worked up here, right?" He was puzzled. "You don't think something is going on, do you?" He asked Ryan.

"I don't know, but I think it would be best to lock the place up and take protective measures," Ryan said. Mr. Davies agreed. They went into the other room to notify the others.

"Oh great, that's just great; why the hell can't he leave us alone," Carla said angrily.

"Now, let's not jump the gun here; it could just be an electrical storm causing this somewhere in the vicinity," James tried to calm them with reason. But his gut was telling him something else.

Everyone went around locking up. "Shouldn't Officer Thompson be here by now?" Molly asked.

Just then, there was a knock on the door. James went to see who it was. Officer Thompson was standing outside. James opened the door and the Officer pushed his way in quickly then shut and locked the door behind him in a hurry.

"I am sorry James, but something is not right out there. I had to leave my car about half a mile down the road. It just gave out on me, but the lights and horn were flashing and beeping like crazy. It stopped and then there was no power at all. I hurried here on foot. Is everyone okay?” Thompson explained.

James guided him into the living room, where everyone was sitting. “We are all okay here, but there is no phone connection, even the cell phones have no signal,” James said.

Molly poured him a cup of tea. “Well, I don’t know what’s going on, but I had no radio either as soon as I drove up the hill.” He sipped his tea and thanked Molly.

Molly looked at the girls, who seemed to be staring off into space.

“Did anything happen tonight that was out of the ordinary?” he asked, looking at the girls. Ryan seemed to notice their strange behaviour as well and quickly tried to divert the Officer’s attention away from them.

“Actually.” Ryan started getting his attention. “We were outside for most of the evening and everything seemed peaceful. However, there was this bright light, but we didn’t see where it came from.” Ryan was successful in diverting his attention away from the girls.

“Were there any reports about an electrical storm in the area?” He asked.

“Not that I heard of everything seemed to be quiet today.” He pondered.

Molly noticed the girls look at each other then motioned to Molly to follow. “We are going to refresh the tea if you will excuse us.” Mr. Davies, and Officer Thompson were the only ones seated and they rose as the ladies left the room.

In the kitchen, Molly put the kettle on again. “What was that all about girls?” She asked.

“Well, Carla started. We both had this vision the Officers were lured away it was really dark out and they were radioed by another Officer of some trouble just over at the beach. They ended up all going there then the vision went black.” Carla said.

"Yes, but then I could hear a voice telling them they would be released in time if they cooperated. It looked as if they were put in a cell, and it seemed to have bars on it. There was only one candle lit, so I couldn't see much, and I am sure they couldn't see well either. It was as if I was seeing from a different view from them, meaning as if I was a bug on the wall or something," Tara explained.

"Do you think that this person is the cloaked figure?" Molly asked.

Both girls answered, "I don't know for sure."

"Well, do you think you could go back to where they are?" Molly asked.

"Maybe we could try," they said in unison.

Molly fixed the tea up then took it to the living room. The girls excused themselves for a moment to go to their room.

When they left, they could hear everyone discussing any new findings for this cloaked figure. They were getting into quite the debate as to weather the cloaked figure had anything to do with the missing policemen. Carla was thinking to herself about how they was going to tell Officer Thompson of their findings. Tara was thinking how odd it was that they still had power but no phones.

Chapter 30

In the Bedroom

Tara went right for the grimoire and opened it up to the first page. She started skimming through it. "I wish it were tomorrow already, maybe then we would know what we were doing." She said.

"Yes, but it doesn't seem to matter totally about tomorrow because we can already get visions, and both of us can speak to each other through thought," Carla added.

"I guess it will just increase as time goes on." She said.

"Yeah, I suppose you're right. If it hit us all at once, we might go out of our minds." Tara agreed.

"Found anything on this yet?" Tara asked.

"No, not yet. Here, you look while I try getting a vision," Tara pushed the book across the bed to Carla. She then sat with her legs crossed eyes closed. She tried to clear her mind. It wasn't working. She tried seeing the vision over again hoping it would take her to something new. Again, nothing. She got up from the bed and went out onto the balcony. She figured she was pretty safe up this high. She was staring off across the water, watching the moon's first quarter glistening off the water's ripples. Everything went black she felt as if she was going to fall over. She hung on tight to the railing. Then her vision cleared but she was looking at the Officers that were locked up in this cell. She heard footsteps approaching. The men all stood up. There was a figure that looked smaller in size and was carrying a tray. The tray had some food on it. But she couldn't make out what it was. It also had a pitcher of water and 4 glasses for them. The figure was covered up too well for her to get a glimpse of whom it may be. But she could definitely see the figure was smaller in comparison, maybe even female. She opened a small section of the cell and passed the tray through. The cloaked figure spoke and said, "It won't be long now just a couple more hours and you will be free" the voice Tara heard was not that of a man but then it was not that of a woman. The voice almost sounded garbled.

She has heard that sound before but couldn't remember where off hand. The other Officers took the food and drink then sat back down. They started talking to each other about where they were. They have not seen this place before. One said we can't be too far from town and thought that they may even be right in town somewhere. Nothing else was happening so Tara told herself that she wanted out. She then opened her eyes and could see clearly again the moons shimmering of the water. She blinked then noticed her sister was standing behind her. "How's your hands?" Carla asked her. She looked down at her hands tightly gripping the railing of the balcony.

"Now that you mention it. They are asleep." Tara wiggled her fingers free from the railing.

"What did you see?" Carla asked.

Tara told her what she saw and heard. "Yeah, I think I know what you mean by garbled. Hey, isn't that what you see on TV when the bad guy is trying to disguise their voice?"

Tara thought for a moment about it, then said, "You're absolutely right." "The most important thing here is that the cloaked figure is not working alone," Tara suggested.

Carla agreed. "What are we going to do now? Should we just sit on this information and wait and see?" Carla asked.

"I don't think we have much choice when you consider how it's going to sound if we tell Officer Thompson what we know and how we know it." Tara continued, "The figure I saw said it wouldn't be long before they were released, but a couple of hours before then, so I think we should just wait and see what happens next."

Downstairs, Officer Thompson was talking to them about the Officers and what their individual positions were while they were there.

"It seems to me that the cloaked figure is probably involved and wanted them out of the way in order to come onto the property." He stated.

"But where is he and what is it he would wants," James said, but as soon as it came out of his mouth, he figured he knew what it was. He looked behind him at the wall with the picture rug hanging. James jumped up, moved it aside, and then opened the safe. Sure enough, the wand was still there. He locked it up and then put the rug back in place.

"What was all that about?" The Officer asked.

James replied, "Nothing, I just have some personal papers and such I wanted to make sure they were still there." That seemed to suffice but Molly gave him a funny look and he was hoping that neither Molly nor Ryan would say anything about what was really in there. James didn't know why he was keeping this a secret from the Officer but he just felt that there were ears listening that shouldn't be.

The girls came back downstairs and rejoined everyone in the living room. Officer Thompson had suggested that the men take a walk around the house to make sure everything was ok. The ladies were instructed to stay in the living room, where they were safe and out of site.

"Just around the house and back in, I don't want him getting you like he got the other Officers." Molly voiced her concern.

James kissed her on the forehead, "Once around the house, we promise."

The men left and Molly locked the door behind them.

"So, did you get any visions while you were upstairs?" she turned to ask the girls.

Tara told her about her vision and Carla told her she didn't see anything in the grimoire about visions or anything of the like.

"Well, at least you got something," Molly said. Molly then told the girls what the Officer had said and how James had checked the safe and lied about what he was looking for. She then reassured the girls that neither Ryan nor herself ratted him out about his lie.

"Strange, I have had that same feeling; I shouldn't be speaking aloud of things I know all evening. I wonder if it is some kind of spell the cloaked figure has put on the house, almost like a listening spell." Carla said.

Tara was beginning to feel uneasy and didn't like the feeling, so she suggested they put the dishes away.

"No, we were instructed to stay in the living room until they got back," Molly said, taking the tray from Tara and putting it back on the coffee table. "Let's just sit and relax until they are back." She suggested.

With that, the girls sat down together on the sofa and Molly took her spot in the antique high back chair. They sat in silence for a few moments, looking at each other and listening for the men. "They're okay out there, aren't they?" Carla queried, breaking the silence.

"Officer Thompson is with them, and they are all walking together, so I am sure they are fine," Molly assured.

"I can't stand the suspense; it's driving me crazy, please Molly, I have to do something," Tara said.

Molly grimaced and against her better judgement, she let Tara take the tray to the kitchen.

"Just put the dishes in the dishwasher and come right back," she instructed Tara.

Tara nodded and was off with the tray.

Chapter 31

Discussion About Someone in the Basement

"We could have a game of cards," Molly suggested.

"It doesn't take that long to walk around the house that we would be able to get a card game in," Carla said.

Molly agreed. "Just a suggestion."

Tara came flying around the corner, out of breath and whispering to them both. "There is someone in the basement."

Molly and Carla jumped up, "What should we do?" Carla asked.

"The door to the basement has a lock on it," Tara said. "I latched it as quietly as possible, but it is only a chain latch, they are easily broken," She whispered.

"Yes, but maybe it is enough of a deterrent that they will leave." "Actually," Molly continued to whisper, "That person would have to know exactly what they were looking for because there are many large bushes growing over and around that cellar door on the outside." Molly pondered.

"Well, this person has been obviously lurking around for some time now. Maybe they just discovered it." Tara said.

With that the front door opened and the girls went running to the men whispering that there was someone in the basement.

Officer Thompson took the lead while the girls went back to their seats in the living room. James and Ryan followed while Mr. Davies stayed with the ladies. They all sat in silence listening to what the men may find in the basement.

It was quiet for some time, and then they heard all three of them come up into the kitchen laughing. "It was a bat flying around, I will see to it that I release it tomorrow," James said. "Then I will find out how it got in and fix it so it doesn't happen again," James reassured everyone.

Everyone gave a sigh of relief. "Did you find out anything on your walk?" Molly asked.

"No, I don't understand why there was a fuss for nothing," the Officer said. "Still, I think it's best we stay right where we are until we at least get our communication back." Officer Thompson suggested. Nobody argued with him they just settled back in their chairs. Molly was listening to the men talk about fishing and she started to doze off in her chair. The girls were doing the same as they were sitting on the floor Tara leaning on Molly's chair and Carla leaning on Ryan's leg. Just after 2 am there was a knock on the door. Officer Thompson jumped up with his gun drawn. He woke James who had dozed off as well. "Answer the door James and I will cover you."

James groggily went for the door. He looked out the window to see who it might be. There standing on his porch was the four Officers. James told Officer Thompson who it was then opened the door to let them in. Everyone was awake now seeing hearing the delight in James's voice and Officer Thompsons they came in to the living room. James and Ryan pulled some chairs over from the dining room for them to sit.

"What happened?" Officer Thompson asked.

The tall man with the mustache answered. "I got this call from Sam here." He pointed to the blond Officer sitting next to him. "that he was in trouble. I couldn't make out what he was saying, but I went to his assistance right away." He paused. "Then, when I got there, the other Officers were there as well." He pointed to all of them. "They all told the same story as to why they were there." he said.

The blond Officer, Sam, continued. "Yeah, we were talking about it when everything went black."

The other Officers nodded in agreement. "The next thing we

know, we wake up in a cell. It was underground, which was obvious by the smell of damp ground and the lack of windows. But it was a cell nonetheless," Sam was recounting.

A clean-shaven Officer with dark brown hair then said, "This cloaked figure came to see us but kept back in the shadows and all he said was that he would be letting us go shortly, to just cooperate not to cause a fuss and they would be released before they knew it."

Molly had gone to get them water in the meantime then was pouring them each a glass.

They all sipped the water, thanked Molly, and then the first Officer spoke again.

Chapter 32

No Safe Haven

This small cloaked figure, a few hours later, came in with some cereal bars and a pitcher of water. She told us we only had a couple of hours left. It was obvious that she was using a voice enhancer to change her voice so as not to be recognized as a woman. But I have heard enough of those before that you can pretty much tell if they are female or male. The next thing I know, a couple of hours later, this small figure comes back, throws hoods into our cell, and tells us to put it on. She then came and led us out one at a time. Tied the hood around our necks then led us to a vehicle like we were on a leash. The next thing we know we were stopped she booted us out then sped away. I had been counting since we pulled away from the cell to when we stopped. It works out to be about a twenty-minute drive.

When she sped away, she was headed west. "So, we must have come somewhere from the east twenty minutes down the road. There was one turn that I remember as well." He drank some more of his water.

"What happened here? Anything?" He asked Officer Thompson.

"Nothing, we lost all communication and my car broke down up the road. Cell phones won't even work". The other Officer reached into his pocket for his cell phone then remembered that they didn't have any of their equipment on them. Their two-way radio, their cell phones, their guns, their clubs, nothing.

Mr. Davies pulled out his cell phone, and there was a full bar. "Check your cell phone, Ryan." He said.

Ryan pulled his cell phone from his belt loop holder; sure enough, there was a signal again. James jumped up to check the landline, and sure enough, that one was working as well.

"Yep, this is working now, too." He said.

"Well, thank goodness, I will phone to get another patrol up here to relieve these men. So, they can get some sleep," Officer Thompson said.

"Yeah, so we can all get some sleep," James said.

"You best inform the relief team not to fall for that again." The Officer advised.

"All was well this time, but you don't know what might happen the next time." The first Officer said.

The Officers paired up and did a once around the premises. The second team checked out the cabin where Ryan was staying. When they came back to the main house, they noticed an envelope taped to the front door. The one Officer took it from the door and said "This guy even creeps me out, he stalks around unnoticed right under our noses."

"Yeah, it's creepy, alright." The other said.

The Officer gave the envelope to Officer Thompson. Everyone was watching him with suspense.

"You've noticed that your Officers have been unharmed. I will be blunt and tell you why I did this. Simply to show you that no protection can save the girls, and you would do your best to remember that." Officer Thompson read the note aloud.

He looked up at them all. He noticed their faces were bleak. "Don't worry, we will get this guy. The more he tells us, the better armed we can be." He tried to reassure them, but he knew that doubt was planted and that it was hard to prove otherwise.

Mr. Davies piped up and tried to help him reassure him. "The Officer is right, forearmed is for warned."

The other team of Officers arrived. Officer Thompson and the other Officers were on their way out again, and he tried to console them. Tara followed him to the door. "You lock this behind me and don't open it for anyone. Not even the Officers. Okay?" Officer Thompson emphasized security.

She nodded in reply; as she was just about to close the door, Officer Thompson turned back to her and said. "Listen, I know this is probably not the right time and you don't have to answer me, but." He paused.
Tara looked at him curiously, and then he continued. "When this is all over, would it be okay if I took you out to dinner?" Tara was taken aback. She was not expecting that at all. She didn't answer right away and the Officer looked a bit discouraged.

"I'm sorry I shouldn't have said that." He said in his difference.

"No, no that's quite alright, you just caught me off guard is all. I would love to have dinner with you when this is over and done with." Tara told him. The reality of what he said setting in made her heart skip a beat. She had been attracted to him from the first time he came to the house. Officer Thompson gave her a smile and told her to get some sleep. Tara smiled back, nodded and shut the door. She locked it up and returned to the living room.

"Woo, sis has a date." Carla teased Tara, ignored her comment and sat down beside Molly on the couch. Molly gave her a sympathetic pat on the knee.

"Well, we have had another long night and I think it's best we get some sleep," James said.

Tara looked at the clock, and it read 2:30 am. She wasn't even tired now. Over tired, she figured. Carla said that was a good idea, yawned, and said goodnight to herself. Ryan walked her to the stairs, kissed her goodnight and watched her ascend the stairs. "I will be heading over to my cabin now. Goodnight, all." Ryan said. Mr. Davies said goodnight and followed Ryan over to his cabin.

Molly and James said they were turning in as well. Tara followed them upstairs. The house was quiet once everyone was in bed. She could hear the crickets and that was all, but they were loud. Tara couldn't sleep, so she decided to read the grimoire.

Chapter 33

Morning Calm

The next morning, Molly awoke late. She was normally an early riser. The late nights were starting to take their toll on her. James was already up. Molly went to the window to open the drapes. She looked outside and saw James sitting on the dock in a lawn chair with a cup of tea. He loved his time alone in the morning to listen to nature wake up. It was the best time of the day, he always said. Even on late nights, he never missed getting up early. Molly went downstairs, put the kettle on, made herself a cup of tea and went to join him.

James was happy to see her. He got a chair for her to sit on right beside him.

"What a beautiful morning," Molly commented.

"It sure is. The girls are missing the best part of the day," he said.

"Yes, but they are exhausted, I think this takes more out of them than they let on." She said.

James just nodded in agreement. The two sat silently for awhile listening to nature. Loons were starting to call each other. The crickets were still chirping. You could hear the bubbles pop on the top of the water as the fish started to surface from the bottom of the lake, where they spent their nights in stillness. The sun was already quite always off the horizon, just enough to start feeling its heat. The orange glow on the water began turning yellow as the sun rose in the sky. Soon, it would be a bright white reflection.

Molly finished her tea and told James she would go start breakfast. He agreed that was a good idea and told her he was getting hungry.

"Would you like some help?" he asked.

"No, you just sit and enjoy. I will call you when it's ready." Molly said. She rose from her chair and headed back to the house.

The eggs were almost ready. The table was set for four. Molly went to the window and called James. He was in the kitchen in no time. "Wow, you really must be hungry." Molly smiled.

James rubbed his stomach in agreeance, then sat himself down at the head of the table. Molly served their breakfast with a fresh pot of tea. Halfway finished his breakfast, he said. "The girls should be up by now, with the smell of bacon and eggs wafting upstairs."

"They must really have been tired. I will go see them when we are done and keep their breakfast warm for them." Molly said.

Ryan came through the door, "Smells delicious did I miss out?" he asked.
"Not at all, have a seat and I will get you some breakfast." Molly served Ryan his breakfast and then started to tidy the kitchen.

"Will Mr. Davies be joining us for breakfast," James asked.

"No, he left early this morning with a note he left and said he got a message that he had to tend to something in the city but said he would call. James noticed that Ryan was not impressed by Mr. Davies behaviour but didn't comment.

Ryan and James talked about what was on the agenda for today. They both decided that they were going to just hang around the house and maybe do some fishing later in the afternoon. James said he was looking forward to it.

"I haven't gotten much fishing in this summer." He commented.

"You like fishing, don't you, Ryan?" He asked.

"Yes, actually I do, but I haven't fished for many years. Too busy with work in the city, I suppose." Ryan responded.

"Well, then it is settled. We will ask Molly nicely if she will pack us a lunch and we can spend the afternoon fishing." James said with renewed excitement for the day's events.

"I am just going to check up on the girls; why don't you boys take your tea and sit by the water for a while. You both deserve relaxation." Molly told them.

They thought that was a great idea. When Ryan finished his breakfast, they picked up their tea and headed down to the dock where Molly and James had sat that morning.

Chapter 34

Through the Looking Glass

Molly knocked lightly on Tara's room door. She waited for a minute, listening to a rustle or footsteps on the other side. She heard nothing. She then went to Carla's room as well, knocked on her door, listened, and again, there was nothing. Molly started to feel a pang of fear in her stomach. She opened Carla's door. No one was inside her room. Her bed was unmade and the usual sense of order was absent. She checked the bathroom and the balcony. No sign of Carla. Molly then went to Tara's room and found the same. Molly, in a panic turned to leave, but out of the corner of her eye, she caught a glimmer of light that came from the mirror attached to Tara's dresser. Molly stopped, looked back. She saw through the mirror a reflection of a portal that was on the wall by the closet. But when she looked at the wall it looked normal as ever. Molly then noticed the grimoire sitting on the bed open. She went over to take a look at it. Sure enough the grimoire was opened to a page that had instructions for a portal.

Molly on one had was excited for them that they found this but the feeling of excitement quickly vanished and was replaced with fear. "Where are they? Are they okay? Can they get back?" All these questions started rushing at Molly.

Molly decided she would phone them on their cell phones, but first she wanted to tell James and Ryan of her findings. She quickly scribbled on a piece of paper, "SEE ME THE MINUTE YOU GET BACK!" she signed it "Annoyed".

This was just in case they returned while she was talking to James and Ryan. Molly wondered if that might be too harsh, but she was annoyed that they should always let them know when they are going to try something like this. "What were they thinking?" Molly thought to herself.

Chapter 35

Lost and Found

"Wow, how cool is that," Tara said.

"Yeah, you just walk through, and you're in a completely different place. Who knew?" Carla agreed.

Carla and Tara found themselves standing in the alley just behind the town library. Only a few miles away from home. "Well, now that we know how to do it, we can go back and work on finding our parents," Tara said.

"Okay, let's go." Carla turned around, but there was nothing there. When they did it from the bedroom, they could actually see through the wall as if it were a movie screen." Where is it?" Carla said, starting to panic.

"Relax, we have the copy of the page from the grimoire. Don't forget we aren't far from home." Tara explained. Carla took the paper from her back pocket.

"Okay, okay, we're good," she said nervously.

"Remember, we just have to phone Ryan if we can't get it to work." Tara reminded.

With that, Carla's phone began to ring.

"They discovered we're missing. I told you we should have let them know." Carla scolded as she answered the phone.

"Hello"

"Where are you?" Ryan concerned.

"Nice to hear your voice too," Carla responded.

"Carla, do you have any idea how upset Molly is?" Ryan conveyed.

Carla paused.

"Well, do you?" Ryan asked again.

"We're sorry we thought we would have been back before anyone noticed." Carla responded.

"Well, you weren't and she is really worried, we all are." Ryan expressed.

Carla could hear Molly in the background talking to Ryan.

"Yes, they are fine." She could hear Ryan tell her.

"You are fine, aren't you." He asked them in after thought

"Yes." Carla responded succinctly to reassure Ryan that they are okay.

"Where are you?" Ryan tried to locate them
"We are at the library in town, but we can't figure out how to get back. We were just going to give it a try when you called." Carla explained.

She could hear a sigh of relief come from Ryan when he found out they were just a five-minute drive away.

Ryan told them to hang on for a moment, and Carla could hear him explaining it to Molly.

"Molly says she thinks she knows how to get you back, hold on I will let you talk to her." Ryan passed the phone over to Molly.

"Carla?" she asked

"Yes, Molly, its me. I am so sorry." Carla apologized.

"You girls gave me such a fright. Don't ever do that again."

Molly expressed her fear and frustration.

"We promise." Carla said, feeling like a puppy being scolded.

"Okay, never mind, your safe and that is what matters." She softened.

Molly then explained to her what she saw in the mirror in Tara's room.

"Maybe if you had something with a reflective surface you would see where the portal is like I did here in Tara's room. I think when you go through it closes behind you like a safety feature so no one else can see it." Molly explained.

Carla relayed this to Tara, who immediately started looking for something reflective. Tara found something shiny in a garbage can. It was a pie plate. She cleaned it up and saw that she could see her own reflection. It was not clear, but it was there. She showed Carla.

"If I can see myself, then it should work." She said. Tara held it up towards the wall where they had come through. Sure, enough she could see a shimmering reflecting back at her.

"I think we found it," Carla told Molly.

"Tara is coming through now," Carla said to Molly on the other end of the phone, who was sitting on Tara's bed.
Carla heard Tara's voice through the phone.

"She made it okay. Now I will come through," Carla informed me.

Molly then screamed through the phone, "No, stop!"

Carla did as she was told. "What's the matter?" she asked Molly.

"The glimmer in the mirror is gone from this side. Check your side." Molly explained.

Carla picked up the pie plate and looked in it and saw nothing. "I don't see the shimmer either anymore, what happened." Carla observed.

"The door must disappear when you come back through." Molly deduced.

"I am not sure you will have to find out about that before you go trying this again," Molly said.

"Yeah, I think we need to do some more trial runs," Carla noted.

"Wise idea, but this time, include us so we can help." Molly encouraged.

"Okay, we promise," Carla said.

"Now, how do I get back?' Carla asked.

"I think it's best I send Ryan to come and get you. We shouldn't play with this in a public place until we figure out how it works inside and out." Molly said,

"Good idea, I'll wait right here." Carla said.

Ryan was out the door before they even hung up the phone.

Chapter 36

Pop in visit

Molly had fixed an early lunch, seeing how the girls hadn't eaten yet. While at the table, they discussed that morning's events. Tara had brought to the table the grimoire. They needed to figure out how this portal worked and the book didn't seem to be very helpful. "We will have to make a note in here of the things we discover along the way," Carla said. "You know, for our future kids."

"Good idea," Tara agreed.
"In the meantime, until we figure this out, we are going to have to stay here on the property. There is lots of room to test it out." Tara said.
She was fixing her hardboiled egg and needed the salt. Without thinking, she asked Carla with her mind, not her mouth, if she would pass the salt. Carla nodded, then passed the shaker to Tara. The girls didn't even notice what they did, but everyone else at the table did.

"Well, I am glad to see that you are utilizing your gifts," Molly said.

"What else have you discovered?" She asked.

Carla looked at her and shyly said, "Well, lying in bed this morning, I was thinking of writing something down in my journal. I had the book, but I didn't have the pen." I saw the pen on the desk, and all I thought was that I wanted that pen." The next thing I knew, the pen came flying over to me. Something like this. She then thought of the salt she had just given Tara. The salt lifted up and came right to her, hovering there until she grabbed it. She quickly looked at Ryan. His jaw dropped.

"You're scaring poor Ryan," Tara said.

"Actually, I find that quite amazing. I am glad you girls have these special gifts." Ryan defended.

Carla could never be more relieved; she thought for sure he was going to tuck his tail between his legs and run for the hills.

After they were finished eating, the girls said they wanted to get started right away if anyone was up to help them out. James and Ryan just looked at each other.

"Well, I guess fishing can wait until tomorrow," James said, slightly disappointed. Ryan agreed with James they would both help out. Molly said she would help out as soon as she put the laundry on. That was a cue for everyone to gather their laundry if they wanted it washed. Ryan excused himself while he went to his cabin to retrieve his laundry. The girls left to get theirs as well. Molly had already brought James and her laundry downstairs.

Within no time, Molly had quite a few baskets to wash. "I can take my laundry to the laundromat in town, Molly if you like. You don't need the extra work." Ryan told her.

"Nonsense, you're the one person who doesn't make extra work," Molly said, taking the basket from Ryan.
"Well, if you're sure." He said.

She smiled and gave him a nod to get going with the girls. Molly new they were in good hands with James and Ryan, so she went about her business getting the laundry downstairs. While she was sorting the clothes, she started to daydream about the girls finding their parents and bringing them home. Once the first load was in the wash, she decided that she was going to contact the girls' grandmother. She went over to a wooden shelf that held all her preserves. Behind a case of pickled beets, she pulled out a book and a candle. Molly took it over to a folding table and lit the candle with matches she had kept with the book. She opened the book and chanted a spell. Within seconds, the girl's grandmother appeared.

"Hi Molly how are the girls?" Grandmother was checking in on the girls.

"Good, they found a portal spell in your grimoire." Molly said.

"Excellent, then their moving right along." Grandmother was pleased to hear this.

"Yeah, I suppose so, but it concerns me that you didn't leave any instructions about the portal." Molly expressed her frustration.

"I know. I used to keep saying that I would, but I never got around to it. Are they managing, okay?" Grandmother said.

"Well, they are upstairs working on it now, testing out all the possibilities," Molly reassured the grandmother.

"Excellent, it's good for them to discover these things on their own." Grandmother expressed approval of the girls' self-reliance.

Molly started to get frustrated with her nonchalance, "I worry about this person stalking them."

"Yes, the dark force that is around is getting stronger. I can feel it. But I am sure the girls will be fine." She believed the girls would be fine despite the danger.

"Well, I hope you're right. Are there any tips that I can give them?" Molly was looking for concrete advice.

"Well, as a matter of fact, I do recall one tip that would help greatly." Grandmother finally offered valuable advice.

"What's that?" She asked.

"To ensure passage back to where they came from, they are to put a personal item in the portal once it is opened. This way, if it closes, they will be able to open another in the exact spot." Grandmother shared critical information.

Molly, frustrated, said, "Well, seeing information like that is helpful." Molly mocked.
"Yes, it is called an enchanted key. I believe I put it in the back of the grimoire."

"Molly, I have to go now, my time is limited on this side as you know.' Take care and call me again if you need me." Grandmother ended the conversation.

"Bye," Molly said.

Molly went upstairs, where everyone was gathered in Tara's room. She stood watching for a moment. Then she suggested that maybe there was a key in the book that told them how to hold the portal open. Carla looked at Molly with a questioning eye. Molly quickly averted her eyes to the book where Tara was looking frantically at each page. "I don't see anything in here," Tara said, frustrated.

"Let me have a look," Molly said. She started leafing through the book. She then went straight to the back of the book. Sure enough, there was a keynote called the *'Enchanted key.'* "Here, this here should help, maybe." Molly pointed out. Try that and see if it works.

Carla was stunned. It seemed that Molly knew a lot about this stuff. "Did she just get lucky or did she have inside information she wasn't letting on to the rest of us." Carla thought to herself.

"Well, let's get started testing out all the possibilities of this portal," Tara said excitedly.

"Good Idea," Molly said. "I have some housework to contend with anyway."

"We will help you, girls. If you need it, just holler." James said, volunteering Ryan and himself.

"Thanks," Tara said, "Don't be surprised if you see us pop up out of nowhere." She smiled.

Molly left to go clean up the kitchen, which was her first job of the day. Ryan and James went out to the boat house, and they decided that they were going to throw a couple of lines in the water from the dock. This summer didn't have to get away from them without some fishing done. James, though, was determined that they were going to have time to get out in the boat yet for their fishing trip. Molly saw the guys sitting in there lawn chairs with the rods in the water and thought they could use some lemonade. The day was quite hot and muggy. There was a storm brewing in the air, and she could feel it. But it was a ways away yet and could even dissipate before it reached them. She mixed up some lemonade with some real lemons in it. With two glasses set on the tray with the pitcher, she walked it out to the men.

James saw her coming and went into the boat house to get a small table to put it on. "Thank you, Molly," James said, taking the tray from her.

"You're welcome," Molly replied.

"Would you like to join us?" Ryan asked.

Molly thought for a moment, then said, "Sure, for a little while."

Ryan went to get her a chair and placed it beside James's chair. He then poured the lemonade into the glasses. "You don't have a glass, let me get you one." Ryan noticed.

"No, no, sit down. I will just share from James's glass." Molly reassured Ryan.

"Are you sure? It would be no bother," Ryan insisted on being helpful.

"Sit, I am good," Molly assured.

They sat staring at the lake. The fishing rods were idle. "Have you had any nibble yet?" Molly asked.

"Not yet, it's been really quiet," Ryan said.

"It's been really hot these past few days, so the fish will probably stay down deep where it's cooler until later this evening," James said.

Molly took up James's glass to have a sip when Tara said from behind them, "Hi guys." Tara greeted the group cheerfully.

Molly jumped and the glass went flying into the lake. Tara laughed.

"I am so sorry for startling you, Molly." She continued to laugh. Molly found it funny as well. James picked up the glass with the fishing net before it sunk to the bottom.

Carla came through at that moment. "What did I miss?" she asked.

"I startled Molly, and she threw her glass into the lake," Tara explained the incident to Carla.

"Sorry, I missed it, that would have been funny," Carla said.

"Yes, it was," Tara confirmed.

Regaining her composure, Molly asked, "How is the experimenting going?"

"Good, we think we have all the kinks worked out." We still want to test a few more things to ensure." Tara said.

"Okay, we will see you later." The girls walked back into the portal and were gone.

Molly and the guys went back to enjoying the view.

Chapter 37

Experiments with a Portal

Later that day, they all enjoyed a barbeque and an evening tea under the moonlight on the front porch. Ryan wasn't with them for the tea though. Molly didn't say anything, but she was thinking that it had been quiet all day and that made her uneasy. She knew that something was brewing; she could feel it in her bones and it wasn't the storm she was talking about. Molly could feel James's uneasiness as well but she knew it wasn't for the same reason. She knew that he was upset about Ryan's mysterious absence.

Carla was exhausted. She and Tara worked hard all day testing the portal, working out all the kinks. She was lying in bed feeling pretty good about their progress. They even discovered they could open more than one at a time and they could connect the two in a smaller proportion to speak and see each other. It was rather exhilarating when they discovered the things they could do with it, together and apart. They particularly liked the discovery of their stone pendants. Tara noticed it actually when they first started experimenting. They had gotten separated somehow. Tara had called Carla on the cell and was trying to find her through the porthole. When she got close her pendant started to glow through her shirt. She then asked Carla to look at her pendant and sure enough, it was glowing as well. The stone pendants that together opened their grimoire also served the purpose of a locator beacon for each other. She remembered Molly telling them that they should get into the habit of taking and wearing the stones when they weren't around using the book so that the information inside it stayed safe. It was a good thing she said that or they may not have discovered what the pendants could do. She couldn't help but wonder if Molly knew all along about the pendants and the book's power.

"Why wouldn't she just tell us if she knew?" Carla wondered.

As tired as she was, she couldn't sleep. Her mind was reeling about that day's events. When her memories turned from her and Tara to Ryan. Just after supper, they were sitting at the patio set with

Ryan, Molly, and James when Ryan's cell phone rang. He took the call out of earshot from the rest of them. He came back to the table and told us he had to leave and would be back by nightfall. Ryan said he would have an Officer come closer to the house to take his place and that he should return late not to wait up for him. James tried to get him to say where he was going, and all he would tell James was that he was doing a little investigation on his own. He told him not to worry and that he would let them know when he got back if it went as well as he thought. He didn't wait for a reply he kissed Carla goodbye and then quickly left.

She remembered the look on James's face. He wasn't happy that Ryan kept him out of the loop like that. All he said was, "Why all the secrecy, it's ridiculous."

James was pretty quiet for the remainder of the evening. Molly tried to reassure him that Ryan could be trusted and he wasn't telling them anything for their own protection. But it didn't help. James was still quiet. Carla figured she knew what James was going through. He had just let his guard down and trusted him, and he was even starting to bond with Ryan, and then this happened. James felt betrayed and hurt. It was not easy for him to let someone into his heart, especially as far as "his girls" were concerned.

Carla felt sad for him. She herself was having similar feelings around Ryan's secret getaway. It was eleven o'clock when she decided to turn in. James. Molly and Tara had already gone to bed a half hour earlier. The Officer was still on the porch when she went to bed. She offered him a washroom break before she locked the door, then gave him a glass of iced tea. He was so grateful for her hospitality.

Carla glanced at the clock on her bedside table. It read twelve thirty-three. She had been lying awake this whole time. She wondered if Ryan was back yet. As she lied there debating whether to get up and have a look or not. She started to get this uneasy feeling in the pit of her stomach. Something wasn't right. She got up from her bed in a hurry, threw on a robe then tip toed downstairs, careful not to wake anyone up. She moved the curtain aside that covered the window in the front door. The Officer was not sitting in his usual chair. She figured he was probably patrolling the house grounds, which he did every half hour or so. She then went to the dining room window to look out; from that window, she would be able to see if Ryan's car was in front of the cabin where he was staying. She was hoping and praying with all her might that the car would be there. She moved the curtain aside, it was dark, very dark and the light on the porch made it impossible to see past it into the darkness. She knew she couldn't turn the porch light off either because that was an agreed upon signal to the Officers outside to tell them something was wrong in the house.

She stood thinking for a moment. *"What to do?"* She knew she wanted to call Ryan on his cell. But something inside her was telling her not to disturb him unless it was a last resort.

"Was it the last resort?" She questioned.

She decided to go look out the kitchen window to see if she could see the Officer anywhere. She looked through the windows and saw the moon over the lake shining on the water. It was shimmering like little diamonds, and she had the help of the moonlight in the backyard. She scanned the yard of the beach, and then, out of the corner of her eye, she saw a movement. Her sight went directly to the dock and boathouse. She squinted her eyes closed halfway and she swore she could see a figure crouched down on the dock beside the boat. James didn't put it in the boat house because we weren't expecting any bad storms that could damage it. The weather channel actually forecasted a dry, hot and humid few days.

Carla watched, it was definitely a person on the dock. Maybe the Officer was doing something, like checking to see if the boat was tied okay. "Yeah, that was all it was." She told herself. At that moment, the figure stood up. Her heart went into her mouth. She covered her mouth with both her hands to stop her from screaming aloud.

Chapter 38

Secret Meeting

When the phone rang, Ryan was relieved he had put the call in to his brother, who had worked on the police force for fifteen years. Ryan had asked him to look into this case for him and to do a background check on Mr. Davies. Ryan didn't figure his brother would find anything there, but it made him feel good. Ryan knew it was his boss, but he hadn't been acting himself lately and this disturbed Ryan. Even though he didn't know why. Mr. Davies was supposed to keep Ryan abreast of everything, but he noticed that on his last visit to the house, he was hiding something from him. Ryan, one evening, went to Carla's room as a favor to Molly to bring the girls some tea and biscuits. They had been up there for hours and Molly thought it would be a nice gesture. Mr. Davies had the guest room next to James and Molly's room. Ryan heard Mr. Davies having a heated discussion with someone on the phone. He stood and listened for a moment. Ryan couldn't make everything out, but he was sure he had heard him mention Tara and Carla. Something about getting too close to the truth. All the alarms were going off in Ryan at that moment. He didn't want to think his boss was any part of it, but a good detective never rules anything out. I was surprised when he decided to call his brother.

Ryan answered the phone, excusing himself from the table, "Hello?"

"Hi Ryan, I haven't got long to talk, but I found something I don't want to say over the phone." His brother's voice came through, hushed and urgent.

Ryan was intrigued. "Okay, I will come to Toronto…" Ryan was cut off.

"No, just listen, okay Ryan?' Don't say anything."

Ryan stopped mid-sentence, sensing the tension, "Okay."

"Remember the pansies?" His brother asked him and waited before continuing

"Uh. I think so," Ryan hesitated, wracking his brain.

"Okay, remember how mom used to pick them…" Brian asked, pausing briefly.

The memory stirred faintly in Ryan's mind. "Yes, yes, I remember."

"Okay, do you remember where she picked them?"

The memory stirred faintly in Ryan's mind. "Yes, I do, I remember."

"Okay, meet me there at pirate tea time.

Ryan laughed despite the gravity of the call, "Okay, pirate tea time it is."

Ryan's brother Brian hung up. Ryan looked at his watch. He had to hurry, and he had a longer drive than his brother did.

He went back to the table where they were all sitting and said. "I am sorry I have to leave for the evening. I will have the Officer come closer to the house and I will be back as soon as I can, but don't wait up for me."

James just glared at him. "Please don't worry. I will tell you everything when I get back. Its best you don't know anything just yet until I come back with the whole story. I have been doing some investigating on my own."

Ryan could see they were all stunned and confused by his leaving. He never left unless it was with James to go to town. Carla felt uneasy about not having him around especially at night time. Ryan could see the concern in her eyes. He leaned over and kissed Carla on the forehead.

"Please don't worry," Ryan said, addressing that comment

directly to James.

    With that, he left. He was on the road in twenty minutes. James, Molly and the girls watched him leave. As he drove, he was thinking about the phone conversation that he had with his brother. He was overly secretive, he thought. "What did his brother find that made him feel this insecure." He was anxious to see his findings.

    He couldn't help chuckling to himself about the pirate tea time. They used to play a pirate game when they were young. They played the game when they were away on trips mainly because they only had each other for amusement, so they came up with the pirate game. This way, they could both be pirates, both bad guys. They were playing one night after supper. It was about seven o'clock when his mother came out with a pitcher of iced tea. She called the boys, but they said they were busy at war with each other and to straighten her out, they both said pirates don't drink tea. She finally convinced them they could call a truce surely long enough to have tea with the queen. They both liked the idea and sure enough, they had pirate tea time at seven every night after. Then Ryan remembered the pansies. Once they were on vacation in Peterborough, they were out shopping when his mother spotted a cemetery that had a field of pansies behind it. She pulled in tell the boys she just wanted to have a look. There was every different color of pansy in the field that you could imagine. She wanted to bring some with her for the dinner table. She didn't want them to get squashed and needed something to put them in. while she was rooting around in the trunk for something. Ryan decided to climb a tree. Their mother came back with a paper bag to put them in. She took some paper towel, wet it with some bottled water and put it damp in the bottom of the bag so the stems could stay moist. Brian was dodging the crab apples Ryan was throwing at him. His mother called them over. Brian went while Ryan stayed in the tree. She handed Brian the bag to hold open, as she picked up the flowers, she started to say, "One for you and one for me and one for the monkey in the tree."

    Ryan only remembered too well. It took him right up to tenth grade to get rid of the nickname 'Monkey' that his brother labeled him with since that day. After that day, every time they went on vacation, they stopped there to pick pansies to decorate the dining table.

Ryan was getting close to the meeting place and he knew he was going to be early, so he stopped at a chip truck just outside of Peterborough. Bought himself some fries and a hot dog. He took it to the cemetery, where he sat close to the entrance to watch for his brother.

The sun was just starting to get decent in the west. It was still quite hot out. Ryan liked the summer months and knew that it wouldn't be long before the days got cooler and shorter. He could see the field of pansies. They were as colorful as ever. He couldn't believe they were still there after all these years. Looking over the cemetery, he realized that it was pretty small. Something he never really noticed when he was a kid. He did, however remember the dates on the stones were of early eighteen hundreds. He figured it was probably a private cemetery.

He remembered that they stopped vacationing up here when his father passed away. Ryan quickly dismissed those memories. They were still too painful. He would never forget the call that his father was shot in the line of duty. Brian, from that day, said he was going to become a cop just like his dad. Ryan wanted to be a detective. He liked the behind-the-scenes stuff rather than being right in the heart of it. Puzzles and mysteries were always his specialty.
Brian pulled into the parking lot right beside him. They both got out of their vehicles and stood between them to talk. They gave each other a brotherly embrace.

"so, why all the secrecy?" Ryan asked anxiously
Brian reached into the open window on the passenger side and produced a file folder.

"I just want you to know that this stuff was locked up so tight that it was very hard to acquire a copy. I am risking a lot giving you this info." He handed the folder to Ryan.

"Much appreciated bro," Ryan said.

"Only because you're my brother. I figure there is more to this case than meets the eye, and I wanted you to see for yourself just how deep you were into all this." Brian put his hand on his brother's shoulder. "You are deep!" Brian said.

They both sat down on a bench. Ryan saw stuff he knew about at first, but then he noticed files to the FBI. They were letters to and from Mr. Davies's office to someone else whose name was blacked out.
"Who would this be?" Ryan questioned Brian.

"As far as I can tell you, you'll notice further in this letter that you should mention the 'sphynx'. A code name, of course, but there is no mention as to who it may be or where their location is." Brian said, handing over the document.

"You'll notice a lot has been blacked out. They have the original copies locked up on microfiche somewhere." Brian told

"You should also know that the letters back and forth were intercepted by an agent on your case," He continued.

"They state that someone in Mr. Davies's office was involved or at least that's how it looks."

Ryan went to comment but only got his mouth agape when Brian cut him off. "Now, don't go jumping to conclusions. You can't be sure it was Mr. Davies at all yet."

"I know, I know." Ryan agreed.

"How many people do you have working at the office?" Brian asked.

"Well, we have seven detectives, three lawyers and three secretaries, and one receptionist. Why?" Ryan asked.

"Who would have access to the files?" Brian said.

"Well, they aren't locked up, so I suppose anyone could have access."

"I told you what Mr. Davies said on the phone." Ryan thought back to the call he had overheard.

"My gut tells me he's involved somehow," Ryan said.

"Just don't do anything stupid without back up and proof." Brian's enfaces were on the word proof. I didn't get time to read it all, take it with you and look it over carefully. Maybe there is something you may see." Brian continued.

"Whatever it is, they feel it is important enough to have it under tight security," he added. "If you find anything, let me know and I will be keeping a watch on it from my end as well."

"Thanks, bro, I appreciate it," Ryan said.

"Well, I should get back. I don't like to leave Maggy too long, you know, puppies," Brian said.

"Well, I always hoped to be an uncle one day," Ryan laughed. "I should be getting back too, I can't leave them alone either," Ryan explained.

"Yeah, you never really told me all that has happened, I didn't get a chance myself to read the file. Call me once you've read it and you get a minute so you can explain everything to me, ok?" Brian said.

"I will, I promise, you better get back. You still have quite a ride ahead of you and I would hate to think you may have quite the mess to clean up because of me."

Brian got back in his car, started it up, but before leaving, he looked at Ryan with questioning and worry in his eyes. Ryan could see it.

"Don't you go worrying about me now, you have enough to worry about," Ryan said as he patted the roof of his car to signal him it was okay to go. Brian pulled out of the parking lot and waved his hand out the window as he drove down the highway.

Ryan watched his brother down the road. He was excited about reading the file. It was dark by the time he started down the highway himself.

Ryan knew that if anyone was up when he got home, there would be a hundred and one questions. He knew he needed some answers before he went back. He decided to stop at a diner just off the highway. It was a little hole in the wall with a gas station attached. Right out of the movies, he thought. A couple of rigs parked off to the side.

He found a corner table by the window and ordered a club sandwich. He wasn't really hungry, but he didn't feel right sitting there without ordering anything. Ryan looked around and saw only a few people were in the diner. A couple of guys, 30ish, are still in work duds, having a beer. A younger couple sharing a glass of pop, they seemed totally oblivious to everything around them. "Love truly is blind" he thought. Then there was a man well-dressed sitting by the window staring out into the darkness. He was about mid-fifties and deep in thought. The waitress came over with the sandwich and coke he ordered. "Anything else I can get you?" she asked, eyeing the folder on the table.

Ryan smiled politely, covering the folder with his sandwich plate. "That's all for now, thank you." She half smiled, then nodded, and then went back to busying herself behind the counter.

Ryan opened the folder; the first few reports were of the initial crash and disappearance. He had a copy of that. Ryan flipped the pages over, not reading them but just scanning the information. After the first few pages, he stopped, but there was something about the reports that caught his eye. Mr. Davies's name was in everyone. These were accident reports from the scene. They were in the file only because it had something to do with the wards. Disappearance. Ryan started from the beginning. He read through all the pages. Mr. Davies was first on the scene, *"Why was he there? Why didn't he tell him this?"* Ryan concluded that he may have lied or as hard as it was for Ryan to put his gut feelings away, he gave Mr. Davies the benefit of the doubt and thought maybe the wards asked him to see them off, but still, Ryan was puzzled that he would leave this information out on his initial report to Ryan before he took the case. It was mandatory for the whole story to be laid out in front of the investigator, Ryan, before taking on the job. Ryan's gut feelings just got worse. Ryan remembered distinctly being pulled off another case he was working on to work on this one. He said that it was important to have his best agent on this job. When he sat down with Mr. Davies to discuss the case Mr. Davies had said that Molly and James had called Mr. Davies as soon as the Officers on the plane crash investigation had notified them of the Ward's disappearance. So why was he on the scene when the plane crashed? Ryan sat and thought about it for some time, tossing the conversation around in his head over and over. He could only come up with one conclusion: Mr. Davies lied. It was right in this report that he was there. Come to think about it, Ryan thought, he never saw all the police reports and the ones he saw came from Mr. Davies, so he had the opportunity to change anything in the document. Ryan just sat and shook his head.

Ryan wanted to circle certain spots in the report but didn't have a pen, so he called the waitress over. "Could you lend me a pen, I promise to give it back before I leave." Ryan asked her. It was then that Ryan took notice of her. She was young, around twenty, slim with long blonde hair pulled back into a braid. Her eyes were green and her nails were well groomed. There were no rings on her fingers and she didn't seem to have any kind of jewelry on, no earrings or necklace even. She reached into her apron pocket and then explored the pocket for a moment before producing a pen.

"Looks important, are you a cop?" she asked.

"No, a detective." Ryan answered, "And this?" he pointed to the folder which he had closed before he called her over... is just some small misdemeanor."

The waitress smiled and then went back to her counter before opening the folder again. Ryan casually took another bite of his sandwich and then looked around at the people in the restaurant. They seemed to be paying more attention to him now. He realized they probably heard the conversation between him and the waitress. No one in small towns like a detective hanging around. He then knew his time was limited, so he thought he had better do what he wanted to circle the important facts that he had found so far as quickly as possible and then leave.

Ryan finished his coke and the last bite of his sandwich then left, leaving the pen alongside the generous tip for his waitress. Secretly he was hoping she would put it towards some nice accessories for herself. As he drove away, he realized he didn't even know the name of that town he was in. However, he dismissed it quickly just knowing that he had to get back as quickly as possible.

Chapter 39

Closed case revisited

Ryan was thinking about what he read in the report. He was really anxious to hear Mr. Davies's side of the story. *"How would he bring this up?"* Ryan knew that if he pushed the issue to hard he would end up fired, so he would have to be diplomatic in approaching him. He was hooked; he knew that he needed to see this to the end. It would not bother him to be pulled off a case but this one was different somehow, not to mention that he had feelings for Carla. He also was quite attached to the rest of the family. Ryan was thinking about the family, James, Molly, and Tara. He started feeling guilty, as if he had done something wrong. He knew he should have told them what he was up to and felt bad that he didn't but he also knew that if he told them he was questioning Mr. Davies, he would be criticized and told that he was wrong. He didn't want to hurt them without proof.

He glanced down at the time on the car stereo it was getting late and he still was a ways away from reaching the manor.

"Tomorrow" he thought, *"I will do some research on the family history."* maybe there was something or someone in their past that would lend some insight as to the problem at hand. Ryan had a gut feeling that this whole thing had nothing to do with the book the Wards were writing but something that went much deeper. *"What was the book about?"* he questioned. He didn't know that either.

"What did he know about the book?" He knew they were writing a book about a case that had been closed due to lack of evidence. He knew the Wards were hired on the case after they had started the book but were hired on unofficially by someone who's name was blocked out in the report. *"I need to find out what the case was?"* *"I need to find out more on their book"* *"And I need to find out who the person was that hired them."* He thought as he made his way back. Ryan realized that he was so deep in thought that he didn't even realize just how close he was to the manor. Half an hour and he was there.

Ryan stepped on the gas a little, hoping to cut the time to twenty minutes. He knew Carla would be worried about him and probably waiting up to see when he got back. His mind skipped back to the folder and the emails that he saw. These emails bothered him as well because they were written back and forth between Mr. Davies and someone going by the name of sphinx. The most important aspect of this was that the police were monitoring Mr. Davies's emails. "Why? What did they suspect of Mr. Davies and why?" So many questions that need to be answered.

Angry feelings started to erupt within Ryan. He felt duped, used, and that did not make him feel good at all. Ryan stepped on the gas a little more. He felt an urgency to get back. It was now fear that he was feeling. His gut feelings were telling him there was something wrong. "God, I should never have left; what was I thinking? If anything happens to them, I will never forgive myself." Ryan was beating himself up and becoming more anxious. "Relax, you don't know that anything is wrong." He said to himself he looked at the speedometer. "Wow, I won't be any good to them dead now, would I?" he thought as he checked his speed, which was one hundred and sixty-five km/hour.

So many questions were reeling around in his head. "What was this sphinx guy? Where was he getting his information? Was the manor bugged? Was it one of the cops in town?" Ryan was kicking himself now. He should have already done the check on the house but he didn't because he trusted Mr. Davies. He didn't know what he was going to say or how he was going to broach the subject but he grabbed his cell phone anyway. He dialed the number and then paused before pressing the send button. Ryan then thought better of the call and knew he needed to get all his eggs in a basket before calling. Without the proper information he would just end up looking like a fool. Usually, he is very good at staying calm and clear-headed in his job no matter how extreme it gets. But he knew there was more involved in this case than normal for one he was attached to the family and especially to Carla. He knew it was love but he was playing it slowly because he didn't want to lose her. He also knew he really needed to keep his thoughts and emotions apart if he wanted to do his best work at keeping them safe. He thought about calling Carla to make sure everything was ok. But it was getting late and he didn't want to wake her up if she was asleep. Not only that he wasn't prepared to answer any questions she may have. But he couldn't ignore his gut that was telling him that he should never have left them alone that something was wrong. He was just going to have to wait and waiting was not his strong suit. He decided to call the Cedar Falls police. He told them who he was and that he just wanted to check in with the Officer that was on duty just to relieve his mind that everything was okay. The Officer at the station said that he would patch him through. Ryan waited, and then the Officer came on the line. "I can't seem to reach him, he must have left his two way in the car while he made his rounds."

"Yeah, you're probably right, thanks for trying. "Ryan said.

"No problem, have a great night."

Ryan remembered that he gave the Officer stricken instructions to be on the porch not in his car. Ryan figured that he probably never thought about the radio. But his gut feelings were still telling him there was something not right. He was hoping it was his own guilty feelings for leaving them vulnerable and not telling them why.

Fifteen minutes later, he pulled into the driveway of the manor and put it in the park when his cell phone rang, it was Carla.

Chapter 40

Vigil for Ryan

Carla couldn't relax, she trusted Ryan but there was something needling her about him leaving so secretively. Why wouldn't he share it with her? Did he not trust her? She decided to go down stairs and make a warm milk to help settle her nerves. Everybody had gone to bed a little earlier than normal. She figured that it was because they all felt out of sorts without Ryan around. They had all gotten so attached to him being there, even James. She knew as far as it went with her, she really loved Ryan. She didn't want to push the issue she just wanted to go slow in fear of chasing him away, after all she thought he would have left as soon as he found out that they were witches. She felt all warm inside thinking about him and that her background and what she represented didn't bother him at all. She hoped he felt the same way about her. She grabbed a pot from the drawer by the stove and as she passed the window to do so, she noticed something moving in the corner of her eye. Her first thought was it was the Officer making his rounds. She looked anyway. The movement was coming from the dock. She could see someone crouched down but couldn't make out the person in the dark. The Officer probably found something interesting and was checking it out. The boat was out there; James didn't put it away, so maybe he was checking out the boat. She turned to take the pot and place it on the stove. She then went to the fridge to get the milk. While she waited for the stove to heat her milk, she went back to the window to see if the Officer was still there. Just then, the person stood up from the crouch. Carla's heart went into her throat. "Oh my god, oh my god, it's the hooded guy." Carla was dancing a panicked dance quietly around the kitchen; she was beside herself, not knowing what to do. All she could think about was that Ryan wasn't there. "Shit, shit, shit," was all she could say. Her brain was reeling "I am going to have to wake up James." She thought. She ran as fast as she could on her tiptoes so as not to make any vibrations or creeks that could be heard outside in the still of the night. She glanced at the window beside the front door and saw headlights coming in the driveway. She quickly looked and sure enough, it was Ryan. She never even thought to call the Officer and now she decided to look out on the veranda. The Officer wasn't there.

She dialed Ryan, "Hey Carla, what's up? Are you still awake?"

Carla was panting and whispering in a panic. "Listen the hooded figure is on the dock Ryan, be careful. He doesn't see you yet. What are we going to do? The Officer isn't at his post on the veranda."

"Okay Carla calm down. I will drive up without the lights, watch for me and let me in. In the meantime, call the station and tell them the Officer is missing and the hooded figure is there, got it?"

"Okay, I will." Carla hung up.

She did just what Ryan told her then she let Ryan in the door. He went right to the kitchen window. It seems he never noticed Ryan come home.

Carla ended the call then joined Ryan in the Kitchen. Ryan was crouched down peering over the windowsill frame at the back door. He grabbed Carla in his arms, trying to comfort her.

It did feel good to have his arms around her, "Look, he's still there." Ryan pointed out.

"What's he doing?" Carla asked.

"I don't know, but whatever it is, it's in or near the water," After he said that, Ryan had a horrible thought; neither of them had seen the Officer who was on duty. Ryan quickly dismissed it. He didn't want to think that who ever this was would actually to that far.

"Go wake up, James and Molly. Let them know what's going on, but don't put any lights on." Ryan told Carla

Carla did as he asked. She was so scared and relieved at the same time that Ryan was back.

Ryan was still watching the hooded figure. He stood up and then looked toward the house. He started for the house when the headlights showed down the driveway to the beach. The hooded figure then ran the other way along the beach past Ryans cabin. Ryan ran out the back door with his hand on his gun. He met up with the Officers around the back and showed them where he went. Another car rolled up. The Officers came around to where Ryan was with the Officers.

"Where's the Officer that was on duty?" one asked.

"We don't know, we thought he was doing his rounds, but he never came back."

They got Ryan to show them where he was and then told Ryan to go back in the house.

When Ryan got back in, Molly greeted him with a hug. James was indifferent towards him. Carla went right into his arms. "Where's Tara?" he asked.

"She'll be down in a minute," Molly said. They watched the Officers by the dock shinning their lights where he was. One Officer turned his radio on and was saying something into it. The other Officer was now bent over the dock. Next, the other two were then on their knees. They were trying to pull something out of the water.

Ryan watched; he was afraid of that. He quickly warned the others of what they might see. Sure enough, it was a body. They couldn't tell for sure who it was from where they were, but they had a pretty good idea that it was the Officer. It wasn't long and the ambulance came roaring up the driveway. They watched as the paramedics went running gear in hand.

One of the Officers came to the house. He introduced himself and then said he would like to take statements. James piped up right away. "We." he started as he wrapped his arm around Molly. "We just got up, we didn't know anything was going on until Carla here woke us up and told us what was happening."
The Officer turned to Carla and then asked her, "What happened?"

Carla told them she was waiting up for Ryan to get home and she saw some movement out by the dock while she was making a pot of warm milk. The Officer then turned to Ryan and asked him where he was.

"I met my brother in Peterborough for a visit; when I got back, Carla called me and saw me pull in. I came right here and told her to call you immediately." Ryan was watching the paramedics put the body on the gurney in a body bag.

The person was dead. James was doing his best to keep Molly from looking out the window. Ryan asked the Officer if the person was the Officer on duty here. He confirmed it. Then he told Ryan he would give them a full report on what they found tomorrow. His walkie talkie went off, it was his partner calling him outside. He excused himself to join his partner, instructing them to stay inside with doors locked.

Molly put the kettle on. It was funny how every time things got rough, the kettle went on. Molly believed tea would help in any situation.

"We might as well have tea, it doesn't seem like we are going to get much sleep." Everyone sat down at the kitchen table.

"Where's Tara?" I thought she would be up by now," James asked.

Carla jumped up, "I will go see." "No, leave her sleep; she obviously needs it." Molly motioned with her hands for Carla to sit back down. Carla did as she was asked.

So, Ryan, will you tell us what the hurry was to meet your brother?" James asked.

"If that's what you really did," he added under his breath.

"James," Carla snapped.

"That's okay, Carla. I was expecting that response from James," Ryan said in a flippant manner.

"Boys, I hardly believe this is the time to start "Molly interjected, her voice sharp with authority. You could tell from her tone she'd had enough of their bickering. Molly didn't get angry often, but when she did, everyone took notice, even James.

Ryan pulled the folder out of his jacket. "I asked my brother to do some digging for me about the case." Ryan started. "I was going to tell you all about it in the morning." Ryan put the folder back in his jacket. "I don't want to discuss it with the police here, the reason being my bother risked his job to get me this information. So please don't say anything and when they leave, I will tell you all about it." Ryan pleaded.

Molly poured the tea shortly after another cruiser pulled up. These Officers came into the kitchen.
"We don't have good news," one of the Officers began. "The Officers who were here earlier are missing."

"We were called in by the Officers that found the body." He continued. "We have a few more on the way with k-9 units to help search." The Officer continued to talk to Molly and James, letting them know that they were going to stay in the house with them while the rest headed up the search.

Carla spoke to Tara with her mind, "Tara, are you awake?" She asked.

Carla waited for an answer. Finally, Tara answered. Carla could tell that she was sound asleep. She caught her up on all that was going on. Molly could tell that Carla was talking to Tara through he thought by the look on her face. Carla saw Molly watching and smiled at her. "Tara, we could use the portal to find the Officers that are missing."

"Yes, but we would need someone with us. We don't know how powerful this guy is." She said.

"We'll bring Ryan," Carla decided.

"Okay," Tara agreed.

As soon as they could get Ryan's attention without alerting everyone else. Carla excused herself to go stay with Tara. Molly looked at her with a scowl. Carla knew Molly's scowl, and it was asking her what she was up to. Carla winked at Molly. James then said. "I would feel better if Ryan stayed with you up there. Do you mind, Ryan?"

"Not at all," Ryan replied, then followed Carla upstairs. Once inside Taras's room, he closed the door. "What are you girls up to?" Ryan asked.

"We want to use the portal to see if we can find the hooded figure." Tara said," do you think that's smart?" Ryan looked at Carla.

"Didn't you say that he was pretty powerful?" He reminded.

"Yes, that's why you hear in case something should go wrong," Carla assured him.

I have no magic in me; what good would I be?" He said.

"Oh, stop worrying, we'll be fine," Tara said as she started the portal spell.

She created just a window size to see through. They all watched with growing anticipation. The window was showing sheer darkness. Ryan turned the lights out in the room in hopes they could see in the darkness better. As their eyes adjusted, they started to see shapes. "That looks like trees" Carla said.

"A lot of trees," Ryan reiterated.

"Oh wait." He said, "I know this place."

"Yes, me too," Tara agreed. "It's the eagle's nest lookout." They watched as the portal continued to move further into the forest, and then it stopped. Tara made it move so they could see all around that spot. Carla and Tara gasped at what they saw. Ryan grabbed them both. He could hardly believe what they were watching. There in front of them was the hooded figure stringing the Officers up by their necks, and then he slashed both their throats just a little to let the blood trickle out. This would alert the animals to come feast. The three of them stood watching, stunned with fear and distrust. The hooded figure stopped abruptly and then started to look around. "Close the portal, Tara. I think he senses someone watching," Ryan whispered.

Tara quickly closed it up. They all sat down on the bed. "Oh my god, what do we do now?" Carla asked.

"We should notify the Officers," Tara said,

"Yeah, right and what are you going to tell them?" Ryan said.

"You're right. We can't tell them without revealing what we did or having them become suspicious of us. That's right, and not everyone is going to be as accepting of this stuff, witchcraft, like me." Ryan said. His arm was around Carla, and he squeezed her.

"Why is he doing this and what does he want from us anyway?" Tara asked aloud.

Ryan took Tara in his other arm, not knowing what to say. He just tried to comfort her. Carla jumped up to stand, facing Ryan and Tara on the bed.

"I've got it. Let's ask him," Carla said.

"What? Have you lost your mind?" Ryan retorted; he could clearly see she was serious.

"How can you simply open the portal when he leaves and stick a note to the tree that clearly asks why?" Ryan and Tara just stared at her in silence.

"Okay, but if you do that, you're alerting him to the fact you are watching him. That could even make things worse. As you see, he has already escalated to murder where as before it was just threats." Ryan pointed out.

"Who cares?" Carla shot back, her frustration bubbling over. "The way I see it, the more pressure we put on this guy, the quicker he will want to move along with his plan and that's when he's more apt to make a mistake and let me tell you, I will be right there when he does to nail his ass to the wall," Carla said. She was shocked that came out of her mouth.

"Yeah!! Count me in" Tara said, looking at Ryan.

"Okay, okay, I'm in." he said "But it still doesn't answer the question of how e are going to notify the police." Ryan reminded them.

"When we go through, we will see if the Officers still have their radios and if so then I will do my best somehow of using the radio to get them help," Carla said.

"You won't be the one going through, I will. After all, I am the one with the gun and the training." Ryan insisted.

"Okay, but just go through hurry to finish the task and come right back," Carla said.

Tara grabbed a pad of paper and pen and then wrote the note.
"Why are you doing this to our family? What do you want from us?"

Tara was going to sign it but just left it the way it was. Tara handed it to Ryan. Tara handed him a hair clip.

"We don't have a hammer and nails, so use this to clip it to something so he will see it." Ryan shoved the clip into his pocket.

"Okay, open the portal, let's see where he is," Ryan said reluctantly.

The portal opened upon the Officers that were hanging from the tree. It was horrible. It was one thing to see on TV. but it was another thing to see in real life. Tara moved it slowly around; she saw some movement in the bushes, but that could be an animal answering the call fo blood in the air.

"It looks clear, go now and hurry," Carla told Ryan. Just before he stepped through, she handed him a pocket mirror.

"For seeing the portal to get back," Ryan nodded, then went threw. He felt a little disoriented at first but quickly looked around. The men were hanging from the trees, and he couldn't bear to look at them. It seemed no one was around. He quickly grabbed the one Officer's radio and then clipped the note to him. Ryan could hear something rustling in the darkness beyond. He figured it was animals coming to check out the cause of the smell, even Ryan could smell that metallic smell it seemed to permeate the air. He wasn't going to take any chances though, in case it was the hooded figure coming back. Ryan found rocks he then placed the radio between them, with one holding the button down. The red light stayed on the two-way radio, so he covered it with a leaf. Mirror in hand, he turned clockwise until he found the shimmer, then walked into it. Nothing happened. Ryan found himself still in the forest. "Maybe I missed?" he thought. He tried it again, and still nothing. Ryan's cell phone vibrated, it was a text message from Carla. "Tara has gone to get something of yours to put in the portal to see if that will work." Ryan turned on the light on his phone as best he could to read the text. Then, closed the phone. He hid out of sight as best he could. He still heard movement off in the darkness. It sounded louder, as if there were many animals, probably wolves, gathering. Ryan knew he didn't have much time before they decided to take him out to get at the Officers. Right now, he was a threat to them and an obstacle standing in the way of their meal.

His cell vibrated again. He flipped the cover open with his hand over it again to conceal the light. "Try again. Tara found your bathing suit in the laundry room."

Ryan looked through the mirror and found the shimmering. He was just ready to step through when he heard a groaning noise coming from one of the Officers. He was frozen to the spot in fear and disbelief. The Officer that Ryan had noticed earlier wasn't covered in much blood, the one he took the radio from was trying to move. He had lost a lot of blood and was weak but still alive. Ryan went over to see if he could help get him down. He noticed they were both hung up by meat hooks in the back of the neck, so he was hanging by his skull. The Officer that was alive had been hung up by the strap for his bulletproof vest. The hooded figure probably didn't realize that he missed. Ryan tried to unlock him but was unable. The Officer was just too heavy and he was up too high for Ryan. The hooded figure must also be very strong as well as tall. Ryan took out his cell phone he dialed star six seven, then 911. he told the operator he was a hiker and what the scene was he came across. The operator assured that the emergency crews were on their way.

Ryan told him he would stay until he heard them coming. Ryan grabbed the Officer around the waist. Lifted him as best he could to take the pressure off him. He looked up at the Officer; his eyes were swollen shut, he was badly beaten in the face, his nose looked broken beyond repair. Ryan could hear growling noises now coming from the darkness, he knew the wolves were getting restless. It wouldn't be long before they attacked. Ryan was even more threatening to them now as he was trying to save one Officer, but the wolves looked at it as if Ryan was stealing their food. Ryan could hear the sirens but they were still a fair distance away. He would wait as long as he could before he let go of the Officer and left.

"The ambulance is on the way; hang in there," Ryan whispered to the Officer.

The sirens stopped just below the cliff. Ryan heard doors and men talking. "Okay, they're here, I'm going to let go now hang in there, okay?"

Ryan gently let him go with a heavy heart. He knew the wolves had backed off but weren't gone. The sirens made them warry with the sound of the voices as well.

Ryan quickly found the portal and went through. Looking back before he did and saw the flashlights of the Officers and emergency crew coming up the hill.

Carla was watching through a small portal. Just before Ryan came through, she saw the hooded figure behind a tree watching Ryan. Ryan couldn't see him, his back was to him. Carla could hear the sirens approaching; she knew Ryan would be coming through any minute. She and Tara got ready to close the portal. They didn't want to risk the hooded figure getting through. "I don't think it's wise, Ryan comes through, if he does, then the hooded guy will know about your portals, what should we do?" Carla was watching the hooded figure. She saw him turn as if something or someone was coming.

"It must be the emergency unit," she thought; she saw Ryan let the Officer go, and then she saw lights coming up the hill. The hooded figure turned and left. Ryan found the portal with the mirror and was ready to go through it when he remembered the note. He ran back, grabbed the note and hair clip, then ran through the portal.

Tara closed it right after he came through. She looked questioningly at Carla. "The hooded figure was watching you," she told Ryan.

"Yes, but he saw the lights and left, but I can't be sure he didn't see you come through the portal," Carla said.

"I brought the note back with the clip that the plan went awry due to the Officer being alive, plus I thought about it while I was holding the Officer up that the hair clip is not something you want to leave the hooded figure, you know something with your DNA on it," Ryan said scornfully.

Tara and Carla just looked at each other. "Yeah, I guess you're right. I didn't think of that," Carla said.

As far as the hooded figure, seeing the portal, well, we will have to look at that issue later, but I think it's best we head back downstairs for a while and see what's going on down there." Ryan insisted.

"You go ahead. I will be down in a minute," Ryan said as he ushered them out the door.

"What are you doing? Carla asked.

"I'm just putting in a call to Mr. Davies. I'll just be a sec." Carla grabbed him and kissed him hard.

"Wow, what was that for?" he asked delightedly.

"For getting back safely," Carla smiled and left the room.

Ryan stood listening to Mr. Davies's cell phone ring and ring. He wasn't answering his private line. That's when Ryan realized that it was only 3 am, and he would try him at the office when it opened.

Clara met him in the hall just as he was coming down to join them. "The Officers would like to ask you some questions," she said.

"I gather you didn't get a hold of Mr. Davies." She asked, pointing to the watch on his wrist.

Ryan smiled. "No, I forgot it was the middle of the night. I will try him when the office opens up."

The Officers were questioning Ryan in the dining room about his visit and about the case of the hooded figure. Ryan told him about the girl's parent's disappearance and the events leading up to this moment. He insisted that the visit with his brother was impromptu and that they had not seen each other in so long that they decided to meet halfway and spend an hour catching up. The Officers seemed satisfied with Ryan's answers. They joined the rest of them in the kitchen. One Officer got a call and took it in the other room. When he returned to the kitchen, he told them about the Officers being found. The one Officer was alive thanks to a hiker who had spotted them in the forest and called for help. Just then, Officer Thompson came in the back door. He immediately saw the relieved look on Tara's face and smiled. Tara was relieved to see him. She secretly was hoping he wasn't any of the Officers that got hurt. She didn't say anything earlier, but she was trying hard to see if she recognized either of the Officers that were hanging in the forest, but it proved to be too dark. It was all she could do to see Ryan.

Officer Thompson saw Tara and gave her a wink. She blushed. He grinned slightly at the effect he had. He addressed the two Officers who were staying with them in the kitchen, talking to James and Molly. "I'm putting you both on the first shift here, I want you to stay in the dining room or kitchen with minimal lighting and use your flashlights most of the time. We don't want to cost these good people extra hydro." He said.

The Officers nodded, then went to the dining room to take up their post. "Are you okay with this?" Officer Thomspon asked James and Molly.

Molly just nodded. She was awfully quiet. She had a very worried look on her face.

"That's fine; your Officers can use the table lamp in the dining room. If they like," James said.

"That's kind of you, but I'm sure they will be fine." Officer Thompson assured him.

"you folks, try and get some sleep now, we'll finish up outside and see you tomorrow." He said he gave Tara another wink and then left through the kitchen door.

James looked at the girls and Ryan, "Well, Ryan, you can take the guest room, " James said.

"We'll head up to bed now, won't we girls," Molly said. The girls agreed with her and went upstairs.

Ryan was just about to go as well when James said, "Ryan, can you help me make sure the basement latch is locked please?"

"Sure," Ryan said, following James into the basement.

James reached for the string at the bottom of the stairs that once pulled the lights on. "I guess you know I have a few questions." James started.

"Yes, I do, and I am going to show you exactly what I was doing," Ryan said.

"Which is?'

"Well, when Mr. Davies was here, he was acting funny, his behaviour was off. Ryan noticed James was already getting his backup. He knew it wouldn't be easy saying something about Mr. Davies because he was so close to the family, but that is one of the reasons he felt it necessary to make sure Mr. Davies was on the up and up because if he wasn't they wouldn't see it. "I also overheard a conversation he had on his phone that didn't seem to be in your best interest." He continued. "I also felt he was holding back information from me, so I called my brother, who is in the force in Toronto, to do some digging for me." Ryan was interrupted.

"Why couldn't you tell us before why you're so secretive?" James asked, his tone clearly laced with hurt.

"Because if I mentioned that I wasn't sure about Mr. Davies's intentions for the family, I would've been met with resistance. Molly, for sure, wouldn't have believed he was capable of not having your best interests at heart. Plus, I wanted to be certain before making any accusations."

"This is true, I suppose. But you could have come to me," James said.

"Could I?" Ryan replied.

Silence hung between them as they stared at each other. Finally, Ryan broke the stillness.

"Come to the quest room, and I'll show you what I received from my brother," he said.

James agreed, then turned off the light. As they left the basement, just before stepping into the kitchen, Ryan turned to James.

"Don't tell Molly about Mr. Davies yet. I haven't even read the whole report, so we can't jump to any conclusions."

James nodded in agreement. Ryan led the way upstairs.

"Is everything okay in the basement?" one of the Officers asked James.

"Yes, fine. I was just showing the boy my fishing gear. Would love to find some time before summer comes to an end," James said with a smile, miming the motion of casting a line.

The Officers smiled, "Well, good luck. Try to get some sleep."

James thanked them and headed upstairs.

A few minutes later, after telling Molly that he and Ryan were going to look over the case file, James found himself softly knocking on Ryan's door.

Chapter 41

Fear of the unknown

Carla and Tara decided to spend the night in Clara's room. Molly saw the girls were going to be okay and went to her room. She got out her journal from the nightstand and started writing in it about the day's events. Soon, James entered the room to tell Molly he was going to talk to Ryan about his meeting with his brother.

"Don't be too hard on the boy. He's only trying to help," Molly said.

James promised, then kissed her forehead and left her to sleep.

In another room, Tara was quiet as she got dressed for bed. "What's up?" Carla asked.

"Well, I don't know about you, but I'm frightened now that this has turned into murder," Tara admitted.

"Do you think Mom and Dad are still alive?" Carla asked hesitantly.

"I don't… No, I don't want to think like that," Tara replied, shaking her head.

"You're right. I just wish there was some way we could know for sure," Carla said, her voice filled with longing.

Tara hesitated, then added, "You know, earlier I picked up a sense from Ryan, when he tried to phone Mr. Davies, that he wasn't happy with him for some reason. It felt like resentment."

Carla frowned, trying to make sense of it. "What are you thinking?" she asked.

"Well, can we see where he is through the portal?" Carla suggested cautiously.

Tara sighed. "I suppose, if it'll relieve your suspicion. But you know Mr. Davies wouldn't do anything to hurt us. He thinks of us as family," she said firmly.

"Are you stating a fact or trying to convince yourself?" Carla asked.

Tara didn't answer. Instead, she went straight to the grimoire to open the portal.

"Just a small one, to see where he is," Carla said.

Tara nodded in agreement, and together, they opened a portal. Using the only thing they had of Mr. Davies, a paper he had given them, they began scanning.

They quickly determined he wasn't at home in bed. His wife was there, alone in a giant bed. The way she was tucked in made it clear the other side of the bed had never been turned down.

They moved the portal to his office, but he wasn't there either.

"Where could he be?" Carla wondered aloud.

Tara shrugged, then waved her hand across the portal. The scene shifted. They were now looking into a dark room.

Slowly, the image sharpened, and they saw a bed. Two people were in it, but it was too dim to tell if Mr. Davies was one of them. Tara moved the portal around the room to get a better look.

The room was sparse, no windows, a bathroom, a small table, and two chairs. On the table were two plates, likely remnants of the previous night's dinner. Then, the portal revealed the door.

It was closed, but the most disturbing part was the bars, thick, electronic ones. There was no keyhole or card reader on this side to unlock it.

"That's not right," Carla said, her voice uneasy.

Judging by Tara's expression, Carla knew her sister wasn't thinking of Mr. Davies anymore. Tara's thoughts were on their mom and dad.

"Well, at least we know they're alive," Tara said, her voice heavy with a mix of relief and worry.

Chapter 42

Bugs, bugs and more bugs

Tara was awakened the next day by the sound of men's voices coming from the kitchen. She glanced at her alarm clock; it read 11:30 a.m.

"Wow, what a sleep," she thought to herself. With everything going on, she had expected a restless night, but instead, she had slept more soundly than usual.

She got up, dressed, and headed downstairs to see what was happening with the Officers. As she passed her sister's room, she noticed the door was ajar, a sign that Carla was already awake.

When Tara entered the kitchen, she saw two Officers standing by the back door that led to the lake. Molly greeted her immediately with a kiss on the cheek.

"Good morning, sunshine," Molly said, her voice unusually chipper.

Something wasn't right. Tara could feel it in her bones.

"Good morning," both Officers said.

Tara smiled politely and returned the greeting. She then went about making her tea and toast for breakfast, her mind already working to figure out what had shifted in the atmosphere.

"Where is everyone, Molly?" Tara asked.

"Ryan and Carla are at his cabin, looking at the case file. They told me to tell you to head over there when you were up and finished your breakfast." Molly replied.

"Ok, I'll head over there now." She picked up her tea and her plate with the toast on it and was going to walk over there with it in hand.

"Wait," Molly said.

Tara stopped, "What is it, Molly." She asked.

"I just wanted to finish up these sandwiches to take over there. Would you take them for me if I put them on a tray?" Molly asked.

"Sure thing. Where's James?" Tara replied.

"He's over there as well," Molly said, busying herself with bagging the sandwiches.

"Are you coming over too?" Tara asked as Molly passed her the tray.

"No, I don't think so. You go on ahead," Molly said, waving her hand in a shooing motion. "I'll get the door for you, dear."

Molly quickly scooted past her and headed for the door. She reached it well in advance of Tara and had it wide open.

Tara stopped, looking directly into Molly's eyes. "Are you okay?"

"Yes, yes. Now go on. I might come over later. Now go," Molly said, shooing her again. Tara walked over to the cabin and knocked at the door with her foot.

"Come in," Ryan said.

"My hands are full. Could you please get the door for me." She shouted.

Footsteps headed for the door and it was James who opened it for her.

"Thank you, James," Tara said.

"Leave it to Molly to make sure we all have food." James smiled.

"What's going on? Molly is not herself and this is just weird that you, that we are all here but her." Tara queried.

Ryan gestured for her to come sit down beside him at the coffee table and James took the tray of food off her.

"We will catch you up, we didn't want to wake you because you were so sound asleep that Carla couldn't reach you at all." Ryan said as he patted the cushion beside him so she could sit down.

Ryan then caught her up on the events of visiting his brother and the conversation that he and James had late last night.

"James told Molly about it, and she is not very happy about it." Ryan said.

"Yeah, it's like her whole world just did a belly flop," James added.

"Poor Molly," Tara said.

"She will be fine once she gets used to the idea. Anyways, I don't want to dismiss Molly's emotions, but I called Mr. Davies this morning. He is on his way to New York. He says that there is a lead there and that the NYPD called him to come, "Ryan said.

Tara started to get excited about it. Ryan could see the excitement on her face. "Hold on now before you get too excited. I don't believe that he is going to New York," Ryan said. Tara is feeling deflated now.

"I believe he is coming here, he is just trying to throw us off the trail." He said.

"But how does he know what trail we are on anyway?" Ryan pulled up a small wire that was attached to a smashed little microphone looking thing. "This is how. He has been listening in on all our conversations. He has known all along everything we have been doing and saying. Jams and I came to this conclusion last night. So this morning I came here with Jams and we searched in silence, and viola, we found it. We haven't searched the manor yet, but Molly knows about it and she is trying to keep quiet until we find the bugs in the manor," Ryan explained.

"Did you tell the Officers?" Tara asked.

"NO, not yet, see this sphinx person we believe may be working on the inside. A cop, but how far that goes, we have no idea. So we can't even trust the police out here." Ryan said. Giving Tara a look of concern.

"I am sure Officer Williams is not involved," Tara said in the discussion.

"We can't trust anyone, understand?" He sternly looked at Tara.

"Yes, Yes," Disgusted, but Tara knew he was right, "All this over a book, unbelievable." Tara said.

"Yes, exactly, that is why I wanted to know what was in the book, see I don't believe this has anything to do with the book, I also don't believe that your parents ever got on that plane," Ryan said.

"Are you saying this is some elaborate kidnapping for nothing?" Tara paused.

"What am I missing here?" Tara asked.

Ryan then explained that he thinks that it has something to do with the family history. He said that he did some searching and had his brother do a search as well. Ryan explained that he found out that Mr. Davies was born and raised here in Cedar Falls. However, he was still not sure what the connection to the family was. Ryan then said that his brother was looking into the history of the Blackwood family and would go back as far as he could to see what the connection would be if anything.

"Now, there may not be a connection, but I am pretty sure that there is somehow," Ryan said. Tara looked at them all, and James nodded his head in agreement.

Tara was stunned. "I don't understand how you came to this conclusion."

"I spent all night reading the book that your parents wrote, the one that was supposed to be the cause of this whole thing. Mr. Davies said that it was linked to the book because the murder was not solved. But after I had read the book, I realized that the murder was solved. I called my brother and asked him to look into it to see if it actually was solved or if it was creative writing on your parent's end. Well, he called me early this morning and told me that the murder was solved and apparently your parents signed an agreement that they were never to write about the cases unless they were solved."

Tara interrupted him. "We knew that we were always told not to mention anything about any cases that we heard them talking about until they were given the go-ahead to write the book." Tara explained.

"Well, I didn't know that and Mr. Davies used my ignorance against me to lead me to believe it did." Ryan paused for a drink. "When I told James this, he told me about the agreement they had, so this started me thinking that it really couldn't be about the book. James and I discussed it at length last night. That's what made me call my brother this morning." Ryan finished.

Tara sat there for a moment, thinking about what she had just learned. She couldn't believe that Mr. Davies could do something like that.

"So why is it then or rather who is it then, I'm so confused," Tara started.

"Let me help you out," Carla said.

"There has to be something in the house that the hooded figure wants, or the house itself," Carla explained.

"Like what?" Tara asked.

"Wait, are the deeds to the house real?" "Did Mr. Davies give us fake deeds to the house?"

"What about the money that Mom and Dad left in Mr. Davies's care for us? Is that what they want?"

"Is that money real too, or is Mr. Davies footing the bill until we are gone?"

"Hold on there. I know these are all valid questions, and I am ahead of you in all of them." This is why my brother is looking into the history of the house and your family to find out the possible motive." Ryan explained. He gave Tara a smile.

Tara jumped up in surprise and startled all of them. "Poor Molly, does she know all this?" Tara asked.

"Not all of it because we didn't know if the house was bugged," James said.

"She really has her back up about us thinking bad about Mr. Davies, which I knew she would feel this way," Ryan said.

"We have to explain this to her and we have to find the bugs in the house to make sure that she is safe." Tara headed for the door.

"Wait Tara," Carla said.

"We also have to agree on what part of the house to have the bug in. If we remove all the bugs, the listener will know that we are on to them and it may cause them to charge forward with the extermination process," Carla looked around and then corrected "Well, if that is what they want… us dead." Carla bowed her head, embarrassed.

"You always did have the flare for the dramatic." James said as he smiled at Carla.

"Tara is right, though we should go over there and find the bugs," James said.

They all agreed and decided that the only place they should leave a bug was in the sitting room. They aren't in there that often and they should make a point of talking in there about certain plans and things.

They agreed that they were going to have to figure out a plan. "But we are at a stand still right now." Carla said, "We don't know anything until your brother gets back to us." She said to Ryan.

"That is okay I think it has more to do with something in the house than the actual house itself." Ryan said, "That is where you and Tara need to get together and do some witchy work. I'll explain once the house is debugged, come on let's go." Ryan said as he led the way to the door.

When they got to the house, Molly was sitting watching TV and folding laundry from the baskets. Tara and Carla joined her, giving her a helping hand. Molly smiled at the girls.

Tara got up and gave Molly a big hug, "You know we love you tons." She whispered in her ear.

Molly gave her a squeeze back and said, "Of course I do." And smiled at both of them.

Molly then realized that James and Ryan were up to something and asked. "What are James and Ryan doing?"

Carla put her finger to her lips as if to tell her to be quiet, then winked at her and said. "The boys have finally decided to do some fishing today and they are getting stuff ready to go."

Molly caught on right away that they weren't going fishing and went to say something, but Carla hushed her. "isn't that great that they finally have decided to do some fishing?" winking at Molly again.

Molly frowned at her and said kind of angrily, "Yes, I suppose it is." Molly then gestured to the girls as if to say, "What is going on?" Carla leaned in close and whispered in her ear. "As soon as they give us the go ahead, we are going to go to the kitchen and explain everything to you."

Molly replied in a whisper back. "It's not fair that you are leaving me in the dark."

Tara interrupted and asked, "What program are you watching, Molly?" Confused, Molly answered her and said, "It is jeopardy, rerun of course."

They all sat in silence for a while. The laundry was all folded and just needed to be put away. "You girls want to take the basket upstairs for me now? Put your stuff away and just leave the basket with our stuff on our bed and I'll put it away later." Molly said.

"Sure" both girls said as they left to do as they were asked.

James and Ryan came through the house from upstairs. Ryan winked at Carla as he walked past her. They entered the living room and looked around the furniture, behind pictures, in the plants and the lamps. James snapped his fingers and Ryan came over. James was looking at the bookshelf. Sure enough, Ryan could see the bug that was sitting hidden cleverly alongside one of the books, looking like a bookmark. Ryan couldn't help thinking how clever this person was to think about this. It had to be an inside job just seeing where he put the bug. "How did he know they wouldn't notice that on the book?"
 Ryan made the gesture to leave the room and James followed.

As he passed Molly, he blew her a silent kiss. She just frowned at them both. They moved on into the dining area and then into the kitchen. Molly could hear when they went down into the basement. It was quiet in the house, except for the TV. Molly decided she would just sit there until someone decided to come and tell her what the hell was going on and why they were acting so strange and secretive.

She was almost pouting at the fact that they were taking so long. "I should have told the girls to come right back. They could be upstairs to stay for a while now." She thought to herself. "And the boys, how come they are taking so long to get the fishing gear from the basement? Yay, right?" Molly thought.

She sat there waiting and waiting, just as she decided she was going to go see them in the basement and demand an explanation, they came upstairs and saw Molly standing in the kitchen with her arms crossed and one foot tapping the floor, all while scowling at them both.

James looked at Ryan and Ryan nodded to James. "Ok, Molly, you can relax, the coast is clear and we can talk now," James said.

"The coast is clear?" What are you talking about?" she asked annoyed.

Tara and Carla joined them in the kitchen.
"Have a seat. This could take a while, I'll put the kettle on and we can talk over tea." Tara said.

They all sat around the kitchen table and explained everything to Molly. They could see that she was in disbelief. Ryan showed her all the destroyed mikes that were planted in the house. The places they were planted gave Ryan the belief that it was an inside job and that whoever put them there in those precise places had to have known the family really well to know they would not be spotted.

Molly tossed what they all were saying around and was so upset to think all these years, Mr. Davies had ulterior motives. Ryan tried to assure her that maybe he was no more than a pawn in the whole thing, even though he believed differently.

"It's just a waiting game now." Ryan said, "We are just waiting for my brother to get back to us with some information. I have my email connected to my smartphone, so I will know right away when he replies." Ryan assured.

"In the meantime, we need to go about our business as usual and not let on that we know any more than the police are telling us," Carla said Molly agreed.

Chapter 43

Echoes of an Argument

Ryan spent the afternoon on his computer doing some research of his own. Carla and Tara decided that they should catch up on some emails. Little did they know that they had a lot. So many people looking for help on navigating their lives through tarot.

James and Molly decided to spend some quality time together out back by the water to relax for a change. They both took up a book and sat out back in the shade. The August weather was extremely warm this year and even sitting in the shade, you broke out in a sweat. Molly always had lemonade made for them to drink. She was a good wife and James loved her more than anything. He sat there looking out over the lake and thinking of the events that had taken place in such a short time. "How can your world get turned upside down in the blink of an eye?" James was thinking. He started to reminisce about the times they spent up here when the girls were little. Their grandparents were very nice people and treated James and Molly as family. They never had housekeepers or anything to help them with the chores of such a large manor. Their grandfather was always the one who looked after the outdoor chores and the grandmother always looked after the indoor chores. They were amazing people. James was thinking back to one of the many family gatherings that was held up here. Everyone had such a wonderful time.

James smiled as he allowed the pictures of the past to flood his memory, but his smile quickly disappeared as he saw pictures of things that just didn't sit right with him. Back then, he didn't say much but observed a lot. He remembered seeing an argument between the girl's grandmother and their aunt. Molly had told him later that the Aunt was hounding her for something. Molly tried to hear the conversation that they were having, but she only heard a few words.

James perked up, turned to Molly and asked her if she remembered back then when the arguments happened. Molly sat and reflected for a moment. "Yes, that was an awful week, I actually think that was the last time they had seen each other. I believe they parted on bad terms." Molly said.

"Do you remember what the argument was about Between Elsa and Sara the aunt?" James asked.

"Well, let's see, Sara was Elsa's cousin, really, but the girls just called her aunt. Sara was bugging Elsa for something and when I asked Elsa if everything was ok, she said it was nothing to worry about, she said something about Sara not being entitled to anything." Molly said, "Why James?" "Whatever brought this back?" she asked him.

"That's it then; it sounds to me like Sara wanted something from the family, and Elsa wasn't going to give it up." James pondered this for a moment.

"But what would it be? The family never saw them after that," Molly said. "Plus, I think things were not good between them since the fire anyway," Molly remembered.

"I don't know; maybe she just wanted to be compensated for the hospital bills or something," Molly added.
"That may be, but if there were hard feelings, then why did they keep coming back unless…. There had to be something she wanted that kept them coming around for so long." James said.

"Come on, Molly, let's go tell Ryan and see if he can dig up any information for the family on Sara's side. The more I think about it the more I realize we really don't know anything about that side of the family, do we?" Molly agreed.

They left their books on their chairs and went straight to Ryan's cabin.

"Knock, Knock," they knocked on his door.

"Just a sec," they heard Ryan say.

The door was unlatched from the inside, and then it opened. Ryan was surprised to see them both.

"Come in," Ryan gestured for them to enter.

"What brings you by my abode?" he asked.

"Well, Molly and I were just wondering if you happen to know anything about Sara Danes; she was Elsa's cousin," James said.

"I believe her maiden name was Clark," Molly added.

"Let's see if I can find out," Ryan said as he went to the computer and typed it into his system.

"I haven't got a lot to go on as far as the family is concerned as yet. But you may be interested in knowing that Mr. Davies grew up here in this town and attended school with the girl's mother." Ryan continued.

"He apparently was sent away by his mother to a hospital to treat him for schizophrenia, he then came back around the age of 16 and decided he was going to work during the day and do schooling at night. Apparently, the local teacher agreed to teach him separately from the students so he could stay out of class." Ryan paused for a reaction.

"Yes, I think I heard mention of this at some point in time, not the mental issue, just that he grew up here."

"I know that Margaret attended high school with him as well," Molly said.

"Ok," Ryan continued. "He apparently worked out of town and did his best to stay away from all the children in the neighbourhood. His parents even made the teacher sign a legal document stating that she did not know of his where abouts."

"Do you have the teacher's name, maybe we can contact her and see if she remembers anything that might help us?" Molly asked.

"Good question; however, I have looked up this lady and she is nowhere to be found," Ryan stated. "There are no documents or history of her past or his graduation. She apparently resigned and has never been seen since." Ryan added.

"Another dead end," Tara said as she sat down on the window seat. "Officer Thomas Grew up here, and maybe he would know something." She said as she stared out the window.

"Tara? We can't mention this to the police here, I told you we can't trust anyone." Ryan said sympathetically.

Tara just gave a huff and kept looking out the window.

"No word from your brother yet?" Carla queried.

"No, not yet". Ryan continued, "I'll give him until this evening and then I'll call him.

There was silence around the room. "Okay, what about Sarah and that side of the family?" James asked.

Ryan took out a pad of paper and a pen, then handed it to Molly and James, "Write down everything you know about them. Last Name, where they lived, anything you can remember about them and I will look it up and see what I can find."

Tara, still looking out the window, noticed that one of the cruisers sitting out front was leaving. But there was no other cruiser to take its place. The Officers that were patrolling the grounds must still be here because their car is still parked out near the road. She then saw the two Officers come out from around the line of trees. They were headed for their car.

"Hey guys, check this out," Tara said.

Everyone got up and came to the window, "They are all leaving." Do you think this means they caught the hooded figure?"

Ryan concerned, picked up his cell phone right away and dialed the station.

He walked into the kitchen as he was talking to the person on the other end.

"I realize that, but you're leaving us with no protection at all," Carla heard Ryan say.

"I don't think that warrants you to use the entire force of Cedar Falls a few Officers would be able to take care of that, no?"

"Okay, okay," Ryan said and then hung up.
"What is it, Ryan?" Molly asked.

He could see the fear in her eyes.

"It's okay she said they would be back within the hour. However, in the meantime, we are alone and on our own." Ryan said.

"What was the issue that made them leave."? Carla asked.

"Apparently, they had a call to the cemetery, possible homicide," Ryan said.

"And they needed our guys to check this out?" Carla asked.

"That's basically what I asked and she got snippy with me and hung up," Ryan explained.

"What should we do now?" James asked, concerned.

"Well, I think it's best we all just stay together until they get back, you know, safety in numbers," Ryan said.

"Besides, you have some paperwork to do and the girls can just sit there and help you or sit there and look pretty." He said, smirking at them.

Carla got up from sitting on the corner of his desk to go sit with Molly and James, but not before giving Ryan a punch on the shoulder.

Ryan just made a face at her as he rubbed his shoulder. It was all in fun and trying to lighten the mood.

Tara sat down, not moving from the front of the window. It was a bay window with cushions and was quite comfortable.

Ryan went back to his computer to continue his research. The cabin was silent for some time when Carla piped up and said, "Would anyone like a drink? Ryan has popped in the fridge."

Everyone answered, "Yes please."

"Ok, Tara? You want to give me a hand?"

Without saying a word, she got up from her window and followed her to the kitchen.

"Carla, in the lead, turned on her heels the minute they entered the kitchen and looked at Tara straight in the eyes. If Tara wasn't paying attention, she would have walked right into her. They were in the kitchen far enough away from the others when Carla said. "What is up with you?" In a hushed voice.

Tara grabbed her arm and pulled her into the kitchen further. "Don't you feel it?" She asked her sister.

"That horrible foreboding feeling?" Carla looked at her, staring straight into her eyes.
"Yes, I do feel a little gloomy but I was trying to push by it." It's not us; it's around us," Tara stated. Carla was confused now. "What do you mean?" She asked.

Carla replied, "I think you're feeling this way because we have no protection for a little while and your letting your fear get the better of you." No sooner did Carla say that when there was a huge rumble of thunder overhead and a loud crack of lightning that seemed to flash right through the cabin.

Wow, what the heck was that? They went to the kitchen window to look out when they noticed big black clouds overhead, rolling in on top of them really fast. Another boom of thunder rattled everything in the cabin. Then, a bright flash of light. Yet, there was no rain.

"You girls alright in there?" James asked.

"Yeah, we're good," Tara answered.

"A person could die of thirst waiting for you girls."

"Ha, ha, ha," Carla replied sarcastically.

She turned to Tara. If you sense anything and me as well, we will let each other know through our minds, ok? Tara nodded.

They took the drinks out and sat back down where they were "Weather didn't call for a storm today," James noted.

"That's the unpredictability of summer," Molly replied.

Tara and Carla carried the drinks out to the living room. Another loud clash of thunder and lightning made Tara almost drop her tray.

The girls put the drinks down on the coffee table for everyone to get. Tara picked up her glass and was walking back to the window when, all of a sudden, she stopped abruptly and fell to the floor. Her glass went flying across the room, spreading pop and ice everywhere. Carla was the first one to her and as she lifted Tara's head to put it on her knee to check her vitals, Tara's eyes opened, but the eyeballs were rolled back in her head.

She was saying something in a low voice. Carla leaned in to hear her. Everyone was standing in shock around her. James had Molly in an embrace to calm her. Ryan knelt down beside Tara to help.

"She is trying to say something," Carla said, looking panicked at Ryan.

They had trouble making it out as they both had their ear close to Tara's mouth.

Tara stiffened out straight so quickly that Carla let go of her, she slid off her knee and was lying flat on the ground with her whole body as stiff as a board and her eyes still rolled up in her head. Her mouth opened wide, and a voice that was not Tara's came out.

"You and your family will pay for what you did to me. You now know my strength and the lengths to which I will go. I will not stop until you are all broken."

It was as clear as day, it was deep and demon like, not of Tara's voice at all.

They kept staring at Tara, and her body went limp, her eyes closed. Carla checked her out. "She's breathing and her heart rate seems fine," Carla said.

"James, help me get her over to the couch," Ryan asked.

Both men picked her up and put her on the couch. "She can rest here, we'll keep an eye on her." Ryan said, then turned to Carla, "What the hell was that?" he asked as if she would have the answer.

Carla shrugged her shoulders and shook her head. "I have no idea, however in the kitchen, she asked me if I could feel this foreboding feeling, she must have been feeling that presence for a while because she said it started long before the storm," Carla stated.

Ryan was trying to process everything that happened and what Tara had said. Carla could see it in his eyes; he was looking at her but not seeing her as he was thinking.

"That's it, the police were called away on purpose." "Have you noticed that the storm is gone?" "I bet you the police being called away was a false alarm." Ryan was thinking now aloud. "I bet it took everything that the dark figure had to be able to do that and it somehow effects the atmospheric conditions within the area and he didn't want the police to see that because if they called to find out about the storm, I'm thinking they would be told there wasn't one, become alarmed then move in to see what was happening." Ryan continued, not letting anyone get a word in edgewise, "I wouldn't doubt that the figure is near by." He finished. Sat down at his computer and started typing. He was checking the weather network for the county.

“What do you think that meant, what Tara said?” James asked.

Molly just shook her head in worry.

“We have to find out the family history. That is all there is to it.” Ryan piped up from his computer.

“Yes, but fast because I think it is going to escalate and quickly,” Tara said from the couch.

Everyone turned to look at Tara. “Are you ok?” Carla asked. Molly ran to her side, checking her head for a fever.

“I’m ok, but when I was out, I could hear everything that was said but couldn’t move. It was like something had control of my body, a heavy weight sitting on me. I also could see glimpses of what looked either like what has happened in the past or things that are going to happen, I couldn’t make them out clearly, but I have a good sense of it.” Tara said. Tara sat up and noticed the glass on the floor and pop everywhere and pointed at it, “was that my glass?” she asked. “Molly nodded and got up and went to the kitchen to pick up a paper towel. She came back and started cleaning it up, and then Carla took it from her and finished it.

“I think what we need to do is go to the town hall and see if we can find anything out through there, family records etc.” Ryan said.

“Just let me shoot an email to my brother,” he said.

Ryan began typing an email to his brother asking if he would look into the origins and migration of the family. He sent the email off. Turned to Carla and said, “Ok we are off to the town hall and the library.”

“Wait!” Molly pipes up, “What about protection, you can’t leave us here without it.”

Ryan smiled, “the cruisers are back, see?” As he pointed out the window, “They’ve been back for about five minutes now.”

"Wait, I want to come with you," Tara said, racing to put her shoes on.

"No, you are going to stay here. That episode you had may have had some adverse effects on you and I don't want you to jeopardise your health." Ryan insisted.

"Yes, I too think that is best," Molly said as she took Tara's hand in hers.

"Ok, but keep me posted," Tara said as she flopped down onto the couch defeated.

Ryan and Carla left the cabin and James locked up after them.

Chapter 44

Message from Mr. Davies

As Ryan and Carla were headed for the Car an Officer was headed their way.

"Good day," The Officer said to them, "Are you...Ryan Delaney?" The Officer asked as he looked at an envelope he was carrying.

"Yes, that is me," Ryan confirmed.

"This package was sent to the precinct by accident for you." He said, handing him the manila envelope."

"Thank you I will find out who sent it to that address and correct it so that doesn't happen again. Appreciate it, Officer," Ryan nodded.

"No bother, have a great day." The Officer nodded back and headed for his car.

Carla and Ryan get into the car and buckle up. Ryan takes the parcel in his hands, looks at Carla. "Open it," Carla said.

Ryan peeled the adhesive flap back to reveal a letter. He pulled it out and to his surprise, it was sent from Mr. Davies. He shows the cover page to Carla. "Strange he would send it in this manner and address it to the police station as well." Ryan queered.

"The suspense is getting to me, read it out loud," Carla demanded:

They both looked at each other and said at the same time, "That's today." Ryan continued to read:

I will leave the horrific part out for now you have the copy to read it yourself and the pictures along with it. Do not be alarmed, I will be in touch once again. Give my warmest regards to Molly and James and the girls for me, will you?
Regards;
Mr. D.

"Let's read the letter?" Carla asked.

"I think it's best we save that for a bedtime read at this point," Ryan said.

"I am going to lock these documents up in my glove compartment of the car for now and we can read them together tonight by moonlight," Ryan said with a grin and a wink.

Carla Laughed, "Ok sounds good," and gave Ryan a wink in return.

"Now, let's go tell Molly and James," Ryan said.

They both ran out of the car and back into the Cabin.
"What's going on? How come you never left?" James asked, "What were you doing in the car?"

"The Officer handed us an envelope and we were reading it, that's why we came back in. We have some news," Ryan said.

He proceeded to tell them everything they had read, but Ryan chose to leave out the part where they had a copy of the email and pictures.

"So there you have it. I am sure my brother will be able to catch us up on a lot more details and apparently, he is arriving today," Ryan announced.

"Well, I think we would all be safer if we were all under one roof," James announced.

"Ryan, move your things and computer over to the estate and

Molly, you need to make up the two rooms at the back of the hall for Ryan and….?" James trailed off.

"Oh right sorry 'Brian Wood'" Ryan filled in.

"Excellent, Brian, then. Ok, girls, help Ryan move his stuff over to the house and I think it's time we all settled in under one roof," James said, he took Molly's hand and they headed over to the estate.

"Don't dilly dally, be right behind us please," James instructed.

Ryan unplugged his computer, and Tara gathered all the files and papers and put them in a box. Carla packed all his belongings into the suitcase he had and before long, they were working their way over to the house. Carla Helped Ryan set up his computer again after finding him a desk and Tara helped put the rooms together with Molly, they were a bit dusty, seeing how they had not been used in decades. Molly kept up with the cleaning, but with everything going on, she just didn't seem to have as much energy as she had before.

James was making sure all was secure around the house. He past Ryan's room and popped his head in. "Ryan, just had a thought, should we be looking for bugs, could it be possible we are bugged?" James said

"Actually, good thought, let's have a look, shall we?" Ryan said as he joined James.

"Let's make some sandwiches to welcome our company, shall we, ladies?" Molly asked.

"Sound great to me," Tara said. "Me too," Carla said.

They headed down to the kitchen to make the sandwiches. They had sandwiches to feed an army before they knew it. The tea was set up, and Molly put scones in the oven.

"I love tea luncheons," Tara said. "Yes, I agree we need to do this more often," Carla replied while setting the table. She looked out the window which looked over the east lawn to the water. She saw one of the Officers talking to someone who was behind a big pine. She could see that it was a person but couldn't see them well due to the tree, if she didn't know better, it looked as if that person was deliberately standing there to not be seen. Carla called Tara's attention to it, especially when Tara heard her and looked out the window.

"Who do you think it is," Tara said with her mind. She looked at Carla and she just shrugged her shoulders.

"Should we tell Ryan?" Tara asked, "Yes, I will get his attention and let him know. Keep an eye on it to see if you see who it is," Carla asked Tara. She then went to the living room where she heard the men.

"Find anything?" Carla asked.

"No, not yet," James said.

"You know they may not need a device to hear or peak into our house; they are obviously magical, so they may know how to peak in, "Carla Said.

"Actually, we need to do some magic of our own. The mirrors need to be covered, and a magical repel spell needs to be applied to the house. Oh, and Ryan, can you come to see something for me, please? James, can I get you to get that bag of salt you have downstairs, Tara and I will need a lot of that, too." James gave her a salute and Ryan followed her to the kitchen. Tara spoke to Carla in her mind as she was coming to Jason's kitchen with Ryan. "The person just disappeared, and I mean just disappeared." "The Officer walked away and I didn't see anyone else leave the tree?"

"That's weird," Carla said.

"We need to tell Ryan something is up," Tara said.

Ryan saw Carla nod her head. "You're talking to your sister telepathically again, aren't you?" he asked. "Yes, I need to tell you something, but I don't want to alarm Molly or James just yet.' Carla said.

Ryan agreed, "We will figure out a way."

They returned to the kitchen and Carla pointed to the Sandwiches. "I called you for you to see what kind of sandwiches we made, we should have asked you first, but do you think these sandwiches will be ok?" Carla asked.

"Tuna, cucumber and cream cheese, egg salad, looks perfect to me, and they happen to be Brian's favorite as well," Ryan said.

"Excellent," Molly replied pleased. "I wonder what time he is coming, maybe we should cover them for now so the bread doesn't dry out." Molly continued as she went for the Saran wrap.

"Tara, we need to do some magical work on the house. Will you join me upstairs?" Carla asked.

James just came up from the basement with the large bag of salt. "Here you go, put it to good use, whatever you're doing." James handed her the bag.

"What are we doing?" Tara said.

"We are going to magically protect the house from intrusions of the magical and non-magical; I don't know why I didn't think of this before," Carla said.

"You've been reading grandmother's grimoire, haven't you," Tara said.

"Yes, actually, every night, plus the internet has given me some insight into just who we are and what we are capable of doing," Carla said.

The Girls left and went to the attic. "We need to protect the house from psychic attacks and spying. We need to cover the mirrors in foil and we need to protect all reflective surfaces with magic. Then, we need to put salt across the thresholds and window sills of the house. Then we need to put a pentacle on the ceilings and walls, including the halls of the house, so they can not spy by hearing as well." Carla said, "Ok, we have a lot of work to do, so let's get going." Carla said as she handed her candles to light.

"Follow my lead," Carla said.

Tara lit the candles on the altar, Carla found the spell in the grimoire.

"With this candle shining bright, may this our work protect it tonight and always. May no one break the barriers we build; this is our home and our guild. Only those we invite through the door be able to come in, unless evil in their hearts the barriers will not let them pass." This is the spell, my bequest, may it be so!" Carla said it clearly and with great conviction. She then passed the salt around the candle flame, then the foil wrap as well. She then mixed a couple of oils together in a medium sized bottle and passed it around the candle. "Each object is sealed with this magical power times three, may no one try to break it or shame be on thee."

Tara watched in amazement at her sister. "I am borrowing the book to read tonight," she smiled at her sister. Carla winked and nodded.

The two girls started at the attic and worked their way down through the house. They finally ended at the back door of the kitchen. "There all done," Carla said.

"Nope, you forgot about the basement," James said.

The girls sighed and then headed downstairs.
The phone rang, Molly answered, "Hello, yes, I am sorry, a lot on my mind preparing for our guest. It slipped my mind to tell you. Please send him in." Molly hung up.

"He's here, "Molly said

There was a knock at the door. They all went to the door except Ryan, who hung back, after all he was not supposed to have known him, so it would look odd to anyone watching if he greeted him at the door as well.

Once Brian was inside, the girls checked the salt line at the door.

Perfect, not broken. The girls gave each other a high five and joined them in the living room.

"Is the house secure?" Brian asked with a hushed voice.

"Ryan replied we believe so, couldn't find anything. Plus, the girls did a little thing as well to ensure it is secure." Ryan said. Brian just looked at him strangely. "Right, I have to tell you about them and their special talents later after we catch up on your stuff." Ryan said.

Brian then proceeded to thank them for letting him into their home and reassured them that they would be fine with both Delaney brothers around. "Well, it seems that Mr. D. has found out some great information. Apparently, it seems they suspect your parents are being held in a house here just on the outskirts of Cedar Falls owned by the Johnston, who rented it out to a Mr. Pickwood many years ago but didn't move in until two years ago. This Mr. Pickwood seems to have a considerable amount of money and has been becoming very friendly with all the important people within the town. It seems he has a maid who comes to the house every morning and cooks every evening to cook and prepare food. These people were not really forthcoming with information; he must pay them great money to keep quiet.

However, they did say that they prepare a meal for 4 every night. They also said they are uncomfortable while there. He escorted us in and stood watch the whole time, then escorted us out. The maid said the same thing. They figure that he must have something of some value he doesn't want people to take. So, Mr. D asked me to meet him a while back, gave me this information and then asked me to join you on this case. He is in hiding and said he would be in touch with us soon. My position here now is to be the visiting cousin who is enjoying a vacation while working out the estate money that his dad left because, apparently, the girls were left something of value. Brian finished. "Good story, isn't it?"

Well, little bro, where do we start," He asked Ryan

Ryan took his brother around the house and the grounds to allow him to get a feel for the place. Ryan caught him up on everything that had happened so far.

"So, you're saying the girls are..are…witches??" Brian asked, trying to wrap his head around it.

"Yes, the girls are witches, actually from a long line of witches from Salem way back when there were witch hunts," Ryan answered.

Brian didn't say anything for a while. The two brothers walked in silence back to the house and entered through the kitchen entrance. Moly was puttering in the kitchen when Ryan and Brian came through.

"Oh, would you boys like something to drink? I have lemonade!" Molly smiled.
"That sounds lovely." Brian said, "Make that too, please," Ryan asked.
"Where are the girls?" Ryan asked. "They are upstairs looking through their grandma's grimoire for some spells or something.

Chapter 45

Grandmother's Spell

Carla set up the light on the makeshift altar, using an old chest where they had stored all the magical items from their grandmother, including the pieces.

"Okay, Tara, could you look in the pieces for something that would help us? Anything," Carla said desperately.

"No worries, sis," Tara said.

Tara flipped through the pages and noticed some blank ones she hadn't noticed before. She was certain she had gone through the entire book before and never saw these empty pages.

"Are these here for us to continue the book ourselves?" she thought.

She flipped to the back of the book, and there was some writing on the hardcover at the bottom right corner. It was written in runes.

"Good thing I've been studying the runes of old," Tara muttered.

"That which is unseen shall be witnessed here, so mote it be," Carla translated.

As she spoke, the blank pages flipped back to the beginning of the empty section. Tara watched in amazement as the pages began to fill with writing, appearing instantly before her eyes.

"Carla, Carla, check this out!" Tara exclaimed, calling her sister over to witness the phenomenon. She quickly explained what had just happened.

Both sisters stared at the pages in awe, unable to believe what they were seeing.

"Here it is! This is what we've been looking for!" Carla shouted excitedly.

"To reveal that which is missing and to invoke and capture your enemy," Tara read aloud, her voice tinged with wonder.

They both started to read the instructions for the spell when they heard a voice from behind them.

"Yes, my dears, this is what you will need."

They both turned swiftly, and there before them stood their grandmother.

"Grandma!!" they both exclaimed.

"Now, now, my time here is short, but you are growing your powers nicely. I came to help you get a boost in your powers so you can summon this thing and save your parents. Now, chop chop, so little time," Grandma said, directing them back to the book.

They gathered some items they needed, such as shells to cast the circle with the water element, a mason jar, candles, and nine quartz crystals. Tara started setting the shells in a circle, then placed the quartz crystals, two in each quadrant. In the center of the circle was a mason jar with water and three quartz stones, with a mirror on top.

Grandma and Carla were setting up the altar with the book, a wand, and a cauldron with lit charcoal.

"Shall we begin?" Grandma asked, taking each of their hands as they all spoke the spell from the page.

"In this circle of shells, we invoke the energy that plagues this family. Come, be here now."

They repeated it, and on the third repetition, the air became cold, and a draft blew in, rustling their hair.

As they continued to repeat, the air swirled in the circle of shells, making the shells on the floor rattle. The water swished back and forth within the mason jar, and the mirror bounced slightly on the crystal. Then the wind turned to mist, centering itself on the mirror and forming a cyclone that reached tall to the ceiling. Suddenly, everything became still, and the mist fell to the floor with a swish.

Before them stood the hooded figure.

"Now, the second part," Grandma coached. "And don't listen to what it may say. Just continue the spell."

They all started again:

"In this mirror, you are trapped with your reflection held fast. You now become one with the glass. The mirror is as you are. So mote it be!"

They repeated this over and over as the spirit started to shrink into the mirror.

"You cannot contain me, for without me, you will not find who you are looking for," it taunted.

They ignored the figure and kept chanting the spell.

"The Blackwood's are DOOMED!" it yelled.

The girls felt Grandma's grip tighten, encouraging them to continue. The spirit, knowing its demise was near, began to panic, saying anything it could to stop them.

"You will all suffer a fate worse than death if you continue!"

The figure then shape-shifted into the girls' mother, pleading with them to stop.

Grandma squeezed their hands in reassurance, and as hard as it was to see, they trusted her and pressed on. The figure changed back to its dark self as the three of them shouted louder, demanding its confinement.

When the figure was almost fully in the mirror, the attic door flew open. Without thinking, Carla raised her other hand toward the door, and it slammed shut and locked.

Louder and louder, they chanted the spell. The dark one was now just a swirling pool of mist within the mirror.

"The mirror is as you are. So mote it be!"

Grandma let go of their hands.

"Now cover it with the black felt, Tara," Grandma ordered.

Tara quickly covered the mirror with the felt. Then Carla came with a hammer and smashed it to pieces. They swept up every last fragment and placed them in the mason jar of water. The water turned black.

Tara melted the sealing wax and brushed it all around the rim of the jar. Then they put the lid on tightly and sealed the entire lid in a thick coating of wax.

"Grandma, what do we do with this now?" Tara asked.

"We must seal its fate for eternity," Grandma replied. "You must put it in a wooden chest with chains on it, locked. Inside the chest, place heavy rocks. Then take it to the middle of the lake near the dam, where no one can swim, and drop it in. That way, it can never be retrieved."

The girls both nodded their heads in understanding.

"Grandma, I can't believe you are actually here," Tara said.

"We have missed you so much," Carla added.

Grandma looked and smiled at them. "I wish I could stay, but I will always come back to help you out." Grandma took both their hands and gave a loving squeeze.

"I have a task for you both to do until we meet up again. First, get your parents back and stop the man behind these spells before he realizes what just happened," Grandma said. "I will leave the task in the journal for you to read. Once you have your parents safe at home, come read it." She continued, "I have to leave you now. I love you both," she said as she started to disappear right before their eyes.

Both girls just stood, looking into the space where their grandma had just stood.

"Well, I suppose we should get the chest and a chain and some rocks and get ready to put this nasty thing to bed forever," Carla said.

There was knocking on the door and voices yelling from the other side.

"Carla! Tara! Are you all right?"

"Open the door, please!" It sounded like they were all outside the door.

"First, let's just put it in this chest for now for safekeeping, and we will do the rest later tonight," Tara suggested.

"Agreed," Carla said.

They put the mason jar in the trunk, covered it with the black velvet cloth, then closed and locked the trunk.

Carla opened the door, and sure enough, just as she thought, they were all standing at the door.

"What on earth have you girls been doing?" Molly scorned.

"You gave us such a fright," James continued.

Ryan grabbed Carla and Tara so they would be looking at him directly.

"Are you both alright?"

"Yes, yes, we are fine, but man, am I parched," Tara said.

"And I am starving," Carla exclaimed.

"Let's go down to the kitchen, seeing how you are all here, and we will tell you everything that happened with some food and drinks."

Carla and Tara filled them in.

"So that's what happened. Seriously, we were just looking for a protection spell or a finder's spell or something like that, but voila, there was no time to come and tell you or anything. It just all happened so fast," Carla ended their story, then finished her last bite of pie.

"Why were you all up at the door anyway?" Tara asked.

"We were down here having some tea. I was chatting with Ryan and Brian when out of nowhere we could hear wailing, and a wind picked up in the house. Then James came running through the door in a panic, saying we were in for a bad storm and to batten down the hatches. He then asked where you both were, and when I told him, he went tearing upstairs to warn you girls. He opened the door and saw you and your grandmother, then the door slammed shut and locked. He then came and got us. We have been knocking on that door for a while before you opened it. James was just going to go get the axe and break the door down when you girls opened the door," Molly exclaimed.

"Well, thank goodness you trapped that thing. Brian and I will help you with it tonight," Ryan said. "I think we will all get a good night's sleep tonight. Something I don't think we have had in quite a while," Ryan continued.

"Okay, first we need a wooden chest, some rocks, and some chain and a lock," Carla said. "I won't rest until this is put where Grandma instructed us to put it," she said.

"I believe I have just the thing," James said as he promptly got up and went into the cellar.

A few minutes later, he came up with a wooden crate about two feet by one foot, some wood planks, a hammer, and some nails. In the crate was thick dock chain. "This should work, don't you think?" he showed them at the table. "And I believe I have a padlock in the boathouse out back," he said. "But the rocks you will have to get from the beach."

They all laughed with James. Carla and Tara jumped up and gave him a big hug and a kiss on each cheek.

"You're the best," Tara said.

The girls went up and got the jar as James was getting the lock from the boathouse. Brian went to the beach and grabbed two rocks that looked fairly heavy. "These should hold it down pretty good." Brian left them at the back door. Tara took a look and gave her approval.

"Now that this is all set and ready to go, I will finish making supper, and then, and only then, once you have had a full stomach, will you be able to finish this task under the guise of darkness. Muhahaha," Molly said in her vampire voice to be funny.

They all laughed, then left the kitchen to let Molly do her thing.

"Let's go to the boathouse and sit on the dock for a bit," Ryan said.

The four of them went to see James.

"Hey there," James said, holding up a padlock. "I knew I had one," he smiled.

"What are you up to?" he asked.

"We are just going to sit by the water for a bit and relax. Want to join us?" Ryan asked.

"Thanks, but I will go put this padlock with the crate and see if Molly needs a hand," James said as he started back to the house.

Chapter 46

Night to Resolve

"Dinner was lovely, you are an amazing cook," Brian complimented.

Everyone said the same thing after Brian's prompt.

"You just keep outdoing yourself, dear," James said to Molly, giving her a peck on the head.

"I even made a lemon meringue pie for dessert," Molly smiled.

"Oh, I have an idea. When we are all done with this thing tonight, we can come back and have tea and pie as a celebration of being rid of that horror," Tara suggested.

"Great idea!" everyone exclaimed.

"I also don't want to put a damper on things, but I feel that it is imperative that we now start working on getting your parents home safely. Your grandmother did say it should be done before the person behind this realizes what happened, right?" Brian suggested.

"You're absolutely right," Carla said. "And we know exactly how to find them. Come with us," Carla said.

They led Ryan and Brian upstairs to the attic and showed them the grimoire spell to find that which is lost.

"See? This, along with our mirror doorway spell, should allow us to get them back," Carla explained.

"Yes, but we have to get the person behind all this so we can put an end to this torment for good as well," Brian said.

"Oh, and we will. Once our parents are back here, you will get the cue to go and arrest this man. Then we can maybe find out what's behind all this and who he is," Carla said.

"Okay, excellent, let's do it," Ryan said.

He was getting ready as if he were going to war. He looked so pumped and so excited that it made Carla laugh.

"My brother, the peacock," Brian said as he joined in the laughter.

Ryan just scoffed at them and said, "Well fine, make fun, but I was ready to kick some butt."

"Okay, I have an idea then. Why don't we dump this chest in the lake, and then we can do this spell afterward? That will give us a better chance of catching them alone, hopefully," Brian said. "It will prove to be a late night, but maybe—just maybe—we can get this all wrapped up in one night. What do you say?" Brian asked.

They all agreed and went downstairs.

James was in his favorite chair reading the paper, and Molly was in her chair knitting.

"James, can we trouble you to get the boat out so we can do this thing now?" Ryan asked.

James, puzzled, said, "Why so early?"

"It's not that early. The sun is going down sooner now that it's the end of August. By the time we get out there, it will be dusk," Ryan said.

"We have a plan on how to rescue our parents, and we would like to try and wrap this all up neatly tonight," Carla added.

Molly jumped up. "That's fantastic! How can I help?"

"Well, let's get this thing in the water first, then we will have tea and pie while we work out the details," Tara said.

"Perfect! I will have the tea ready and pie cut for your return," Molly said excitedly.

Ryan picked up the box, and Brian brought the rocks.

"Looking at those rocks, I am just hoping it will fit in with the jar. Maybe we would be better off loading it with a bunch of littler rocks," Tara said.

"Maybe. Let's give it a try. If it doesn't work with both, we may be able to use one and then a bunch of smaller rocks," Brian agreed.

James got the boat working while Tara wrapped the jar in a few towels to ensure it didn't break, then added the black velvet cloth and secured it. Brian placed one of the rocks beside the jar.

"You're right. I will get some smaller rocks," Brian said.

"Brian, leave that big rock here. I have an idea," James said.

Brian left the rock and went hunting for smaller ones. Shortly, he returned with a shirt filled with rocks. Tara placed the rocks around the jar, and Ryan gave a trial pickup.

"A few more should make it good and heavy. I'm thinking about the current. It wouldn't be good if the current was able to push it around," Ryan said.

"That's okay. I have an idea for that," James said.

They put the lid on with a hammer and nails. Tara stopped them to count the nails.

"1, 2, 3, 4, 5, 6, 7, 8, 9, 10, 11... there need to be 13 altogether," Tara exclaimed.

"What are you talking about?" Carla asked her.

"Trust me, I will show you later," Tara promised.

James didn't ask; he just added two more nails.

"Perfect," Tara said.

James wrapped the crate with chains. All sides were wrapped like a gift in chains, and the padlock was put in place to secure it. It took Ryan and Brian to help James put it on. Then James took up the slack of chain, which was about two feet long, and wrapped the big rock in it. Again, they padlocked it for security.

Both Ryan and Brian carried it into the boat. James, Tara, and Carla climbed in after them.

James started the boat, and they were off. James didn't want to draw too much attention to themselves, so he went slow at a trolling speed to avoid making too much noise.

When they arrived at the dam, the water was rough. You could feel it pulling the boat.

"Okay, now you have to lower the crate and the chained rock at the same time, keeping the rock away from the crate. We don't want them hitting each other," James said.

Brian heaved the box onto the side of the boat, and Ryan grabbed the rock.

"On the count of three, bro," Ryan said.

"1, 2, 3, lower it down," Ryan counted.

They both lowered their parcel into the water, and they all watched as it flew down to the bottom.

"I hope it doesn't crash," Carla said.

They all watched in anticipation. They could see just a shadow now, and then they saw the shadow of the rock bounce and come to a standstill. They all cheered and high-fived each other.

"Success!" James said. "Let's go have some tea and pie," he added.

James maneuvered the boat around, and they were off back home. The boys helped James put the boat away as the girls ran back up to the house. Molly was cutting the pie, and everything, including the tea, was on the tea cart for the living room.

"Molly, we did it! It's all done," Carla and Tara said.

"Excellent, girls, what a relief off our shoulders," Molly replied.

The boys and James came through just as they were setting it up in the living room.

"We are in here!" Molly cried out.

"That was awesome, good job by everyone," James said.

Everyone had a smile on their faces. Molly gave everyone a piece of pie, and all exclaimed how good it was.

Silence fell over the living room while all were devouring their pie and enjoying it.

"Well, I have to say, so far, being my first day here, it surely has not been dull," Brian broke the silence.

"Oh, that's nothing, wait until you see what comes next," Ryan said.

"Yes, my brother has briefed me on the small fact of you girls being witches. I am still trying to process all that has happened," Brian stated.

"You will get used to it," Ryan reassured him with a pat on the back.

"So, in saying that, let's plan the next task for the evening, shall we?" Ryan asked.

They agreed that they would do a location spell to make sure they could see their parents, then, if that went well, they would do the spell to release them from their binding. And lastly, they would bring them home through the portal.

"Well, that all sounds simple, a bit too simple," Brian said.

"So, let me get this straight: after all that is when you will notify me and I get the police to go arrest him?" Brian said.

"Okay, now just one question: where am I while this is all going on?"

"You will be heading up the arrest party. You will have to show them the evidence," Carla said.

"Wait, aren't they going to be suspicious when there is no one there to rescue? What would they have to go on to arrest this man?" Brian asked.

They all agreed, then Carla and Tara looked at each other, making facial gestures and nodding but saying nothing.

"Girls, speak out loud," Molly said.

"Oh, sorry, didn't realize we were doing that again," Carla said.

Brian looked totally confused.

"Ryan just laughed and said, 'Telepathic as well.'"

"Okay, Carla and I will put a glamour spell on us so they think it is Mom and Dad. Once Brian gets us free and he is arrested, Brian can bring us home where we will change back," Tara said.

"That sounds good, let's do this," Ryan said, pumped like a peacock again.

"I will go notify the police that we have a lead on the kidnapper and to stand by for my word," Brian said.

They all dispersed in separate directions: Brian to the telephone and Ryan and the girls to the attic, Molly and James following behind.

Carla propped the large full-size mirror up against a wall, then Tara set up the grimoire. The girls stood in front of the mirror, and before they knew it, a picture of their parents asleep in a bed appeared. The room was dark, but thankfully, the bright full moon shone in through the windows that were barred up. The window was at the top of the wall, which made them realize they were in a basement. The walls, on closer inspection, proved it, with cinder blocks making up the walls.

"How awful," Carla thought, and Tara, in her thoughts, agreed.

The girls stepped back from the mirror.

"Okay, they are there, let's do this," Tara and Carla started the incantation to bring them home.

"Wait, we should let them know that we are here and what we are doing," Tara said.

"I will go and wake them, tell them what is happening," Tara added.

"I don't like it, what if something happens?" Carla said.

"Then you will all storm the place and rescue us all," Tara said confidently.

"Okay, go, but be quick," Carla demanded.

Tara stepped through the mirror and went to the side of the bed where her mother was sleeping. "Mom, Mom, wake up," Tara whispered. Her mother opened her eyes and was going to scream with delight when Tara covered her mouth. Her father then woke up and saw Tara. As he was going to say something, Tara put her finger to her mouth and gave a "Shhhhhh."

"Listen, I don't have much time," she told them of her plan when her father pulled back the covers to reveal they had chains on their ankles, attached to a large steel piece in the middle of the floor. It looked to be just enough chain to let them move around the room but not long enough to reach the walls at all.

"Okay, this poses a problem, but don't go to sleep. I'm going to work on this, and we are getting you out tonight," Tara said as she slipped back through the portal.

"This is not good, did you see the chains they have on them? Now what do we do?" Tara asked in worry.

Carla went back to the grimoire, flipping pages. "I found something, Tara, come see," Carla called to her sister.

"Yes, this may work," Tara said as she read the incantation. Tara realized it was on the previous page.

"This spell was there all along. These other spells were put there today. We didn't see it because we were focused on the two new spells in the book," Carla realized. "Ok, let's do this. They lit the candle as instructed, then gave it to Ryan to hold to the mirror. They then held hands as they started the incantation.
"Release, release that which binds, release, release that which holds you down. Your tethers are broken, you are free, your tethers are broken, may you now be free, so mote it be!!
Then they blew out the candle that Ryan was holding. They heard a clinking sound, and as they looked through the mirror, they saw their mom and dad take the opened shackles off their ankles.

"Yes, it worked! Okay, now let's do the incantation to get them home." Carla raced to the grimoire. Tara followed, "Be ready, boys, to catch them." Carla said.
"that which is lost come home to thee, that which is lost shall now be free, that which is lost come home to thee, so mote it be!.

The portal lit up, and the next thing they knew, their mother and father flew through the portal onto the floor, where Ryan and Brian caught them.

"Okay, now that you are here, we need to take your place. Ryan, Molly, and James will explain everything." As the girls stood in front of their parents, they uttered a spell. "You are me and I am you, we look the same as you do." They immediately changed to appear as their parents—Carla, her mother, and Tara, her father.

"Ready, sis?" Tara said in a deep voice of her dad.

"Keep the portal open, Ryan," Carla said, then instructed Brian that it was his time now. Brian left, and the girls went through the portal.

"Wow, what a dingy place," Carla thought.

"Let's just sit on the side of the bed and wait for our rescue," Tara said.

They sat on the bed, taking in the room and what it must have been like in this hole. There was a table in the room and a washroom, which consisted of a toilet, sink, towels, and soap. Very prison-like and basic.

Chapter 47

White-Eyed Woman

Brian got in his car and headed for the house just outside of town. He waited there only for a few minutes when the police showed up, four cars, two policemen each. Brian and another Officer went to the front door while the rest of them surrounded the house. Brian knocked, but there was no answer. He knocked again. Still no answer. He peered in the window to the living room—nothing there. The Officer with him radioed the others to look around, as they were not getting an answer at the door. One Officer radioed back and said it looked like the back door was open. Another Officer saw a light go on in one of the bedrooms on the second floor. Brian knocked again really hard. The Officer noticed a doorbell and tried it, but they didn't hear it chime. Still no sound of anyone coming to the door. The Officer at the back radioed back and said he was inside. He and another Officer went in with their flashlights. Brian could see their light coming down the hall toward them. One Officer opened the door for them to come in. The Officer with Brian radioed and told them to come in. He wanted two guarding the back door, two at the front door, and the rest to search the house. Brian and the Officer went to the basement. They flicked on a switch, and as they walked to the bottom of the stairs, they saw a rec room setting.

There was a couch, chairs, and a coffee table on one side, and then, when they looked at the other side, there was a kitchen-like setting. They were both taken aback when they saw what looked like a very old woman sitting in a wheelchair at the table. She wasn't moving. She was just sitting there. Brian went around the table to look at her face. The Officer was ready with his gun to help him in case it was a decoy. Brian motioned that this woman looked as if she was sleeping or dead. He wasn't sure, but her eyes were closed.

The Officer motioned for him to check. "Ma'am, are you okay?" Brian asked. She opened her eyes and stared right at him. Brian flew back out of her gaze; her eyes were all white. His brain and heart were racing. "Is she alive or dead?" he didn't know. She then opened her mouth and let out a spine-chilling scream. Brian and the Officer scrambled to try and get her to stop, finally gagging her with a scarf to muffle the noise. They had to move quickly now.

Brian went looking for the room while the Officer kept his eyes on the lady. He couldn't find a door or opening anywhere. Finally, he thought it could be concealed. He then started looking for a break in the mortar between the bricks. There was a door—he saw it through the portal. "Are we in the right spot?" he wondered. When suddenly, he felt a draft, and sure enough, the wall moved with a push. It took a bit of effort, but he pushed it open to see a small corridor leading to a door. That was the door he remembered in the portal.

Ryan saw that there were a series of locks on the door. He banged on the door and called out to Carla and Tara. They answered him. "You girls wouldn't, by chance, know a spell to open the locks on this door?" he asked, not thinking they would. When the locks on the door just fell off one by one. "Creepy, just creepy," he proclaimed. He opened the door but told them they needed to stay put until they apprehended Mr. Pickwood.

Brian then returned to the Officer. The woman had stopped yelling, finally. "How do we secure her while we go help the others?"

Tie her wheelchair to the table, no better yet, to the fridge. They got a rope and tied her wheelchair to the fridge with the rope going through her wheels and around her so she was restrained and could get out and hurt herself. They were just finished doing that when they heard a gunshot from upstairs. They both took off upstairs to see what happened. They heard and Officer radio for an ambulance, but the Officer was down. "What happened?" they asked when they saw the Officer on the ground. "It's ok I was shot in the shoulder," I'll be fine but he has a gun," the wounded Officer said. "Where is he now" he was asked and he pointed to the room straight ahead. "he somehow is able to go from room to room without coming into the hall." The wounded Officer stated. Brian and the Officer looked at each other. "They must be adjoining rooms," Brian said. The Officer instructed one Officer to take the room to the left of where the shot was fired and the other Officer to take the room to the right of where the shot was fired, and he and Brian would go through the door to the room where the shot was fired. On the count of three, this was all being done with signing to each other without words so they wouldn't inform the perp as to their plan of attack. The Officer then set up his hand and, with his fingers, counted to three. 1, 2, 3, and they all rushed through the doors. Another gunshot went off in the room to the right.

They rushed to the room where they found the Officer pinning down Mr. Pickwood. Brian came over and kicked the gun away from them, as the Officer rolled Mr. Pickwood onto his stomach and then proceeded to put handcuffs on his wrists at his back. The Officer with Brian radioed the rest of them. The Officer guided Mr. Pickwood to the car, and Brian went back downstairs to get the girls, or rather Mr. and Mrs. Black. The ambulance drivers came downstairs to see the old lady. When the girls were clear and out of the basement, they were directed to a car to await the ambulance drivers to check them out. There were two ambulances on the scene. Shortly, one set of drivers brought out a gurney with the old lady on it. They loaded her in the back of the ambulance, and before they shut the doors, she started shouting, "Blackwood's will pay with their lives."

The drivers closed the doors to the ambulance, then got in and drove away. Another ambulance driver was doctoring up the Officer to help stop the bleeding until they could get him to the hospital, where they would have to do surgery to remove the bullet. They then came to the Jasons to give them a check-up. They insisted they come to the hospital for assessment. Mr. and Mrs. Jason refused, but the driver was not taking no for an answer. The unfortunate thing was, the ambulance driver proclaimed, they only had two ambulances on the road this night. They would have to wait until they dropped the Officer off and come back for them. Brian piped in and said, "Listen, they don't live far from here. Let me take them home and you can come and pick them up there." Brian gave the address to the driver, and they agreed. "It shouldn't be long, 20 minutes to a half hour tops," the ambulance driver promised. Mr. and Mrs. Jason (Tara and Carla) agreed, so Brian took them home.

Chapter 48

Homecoming

They were a little way down the road when Brian looked over at Tara/Jason and Carla/Margaret sitting beside him in the passenger seat. No one was talking, but he noticed his passengers nodding their heads. "Are you two doing the telepathy thing again?" he asked. Tara spoke up. "Yes, sorry about that, we were just discussing the room that our parents were in, how lonely it must have been." Carla spoke out from the back seat and asked, "Who was that person they were taking away in the ambulance?"

"I don't know yet. She was an old lady in a wheelchair sitting in the kitchen room you passed on your way out. So creepy," he explained. "Her eyes were all white and she screamed this god-awful scream when we tried to talk to her." Brian shivered with the memory. "I will find out who they were, and between my brother and I, we will come up with the answers to all this," he promised.

They arrived back at the estate. The girls didn't even wait until Brian put the car in park when they bolted from the car to the house. When Brian finally got through the door, they were already back to their usual form and sitting with the family in the living room. He stood in the entranceway watching them have a fantastic reunion when Ryan came over to join him.

"Well, bro, a successful night," he said to Brian.

"Yeah, it was great, but our work is not done yet, brother," Brian proclaimed.

"No, I suppose it's just beginning."

They stood and watched them all, tears, hugs, and laughter all mixed into one. Molly came out from the kitchen and saw the two of them just standing there.

"Come join us for tea," Molly insisted.

"These boys have been our saviors through this," James told the Jasons.

Mrs. Jason got up and hugged them both. "Thank you so much for being here for my family. I want to hear all about it. Come sit, please," she said as she motioned for them to take a chair in the room. Just as they started, the doorbell rang.

"Oh, I forgot the ambulance has come to take you for a check-up at the hospital," Brian said. Mr. Ward got up and answered the door. They could hear him talk to the driver, then the door closed. Mr. Jason came back.

"I insisted we were fine, and that we were not mistreated at all and agreed to come see the doctor on duty tomorrow. Now, where were we?" Mr. Ward said as he sat back down with his wife and girls.

It was a long night of catching up, and around 2:00 am, Ryan suggested that he and his brother move their stuff back to the cabin and see them in the morning. They excused themselves to go fetch their belongings. Molly followed them, grabbing a new set of sheets and pillowcases from the linen closet to change the bed for the Jasons.

"Good night, we will see you in the morning. If you need anything at all, we are just a call away," Ryan assured them.

Ryan and Brian got their things situated and were just heading off to bed when Ryan asked his brother, "What's wrong, you haven't been yourself since you got back." "I can't' seem to get that old lady out of my head, her eyes, so creepy and then when they loaded her into the ambulance, she sat up and looked at us as if she could see us and said the Blackwood's were going to die. Straight out of a horror movie." Brian explained. "Well, you need to get some sleep and put that out of your mind for now, we have a busy day tomorrow finding out what this was all about," Ryan said. "You're right, good night," Brian said as he closed the door to his room.

Chapter 49

Mysterious Old Lady's Warning

Ryan opened his eyes to see the sun peeking in through the curtains. He could hear the sound of the birds chattering away, as if they were praising the sun for its arrival. Ryan glanced at his clock on the wall. 8:34 am, it read. I suppose I should get up and get this day started. I wonder if they are up in the house yet? he questioned. They probably had a later night than me and my brother, he thought.

Ryan got up, got dressed, and went to the kitchen to make some coffee. He opened the door to his room and, in surprise, saw his brother sitting at the desk with his laptop, working away.

"What time were you up this morning, brother?" Ryan asked.

"The coffee is made and you mean, did I sleep? Nope," Brian said. He stopped typing and followed his brother into the kitchen. "But ask me what I found out?" he prompted.

"Okay, what did you find out?" Ryan asked.

"Well, it turns out that this old lady was released by the nursing home so she could go into the custody of her son. There was a lot of legal bickering over whether he could take care of her on his own. But as you can see, he won that battle, and as we saw, he wasn't doing a great job of it. But it turns out this lady is Sarah Wood, Elsa Wood's cousin. So, I'm not sure yet, but Mr. Pickwood is an alias for William Wood."

Brian stopped to let Ryan process what he just heard.

"So, you mean this vendetta is all in the family?" Ryan asked.

"It looks that way," Brian replied.

Brian could see the wheels spinning in Ryan's head. "Okay, bro, your head is going to explode if you don't tell me what's going on.

What are you thinking about?" Brian prodded.

"Where do I begin?" Ryan said.

They took their coffee out to the living area and sat on the couch. Brian just waited patiently. Ryan looked up from his coffee to his brother, Brian.

"Okay, well, I don't know if you know the whole story or not, but that thing the girls trapped in the jar was a magical being of some sort developed by witchcraft, we suppose. It has been watching the girls since they arrived and has gotten bolder and bolder. Its abilities were strange, to say the least." Ryan continued to tell him of the time it took over Tara and spoke through her.

Also, all the other strange happenings with the police Officers, etc. We believe that it wants something from them, an item, but we believe that it also wanted them all dead and out of the picture. How the girls received emails from an unknown IP address, the only info they could get was that one of them came from this town. Then the emails stopped coming. Brian was in awe as Ryan continued, telling him how the girls found out that they were witches from a long line on the Black side of the family.

Molly told them of a memory of when Walter died in a freak accident right here on the property. It was never properly investigated, so it was just written off as an accident. Sarah blamed Walter and then started demanding money from Elsa and Carl to help them survive. Elsa and Carl were helping as best they could to see that they were all right, but Sarah got bitter as the kids grew up and started demanding more and more. This turned into a battle for some time. Even the children, William and Mary, were taking on the bitterness of their mother. Then, one day, the threats stopped—no more letters or phone calls. Elsa and Walter figured that they had finally given up. It turns out, as the years went by, Sarah ended up crippled and in a wheelchair.

Brian stopped him there.

"Yes, my research into the family before I came stated this, and that William was the sole provider for her."

Mary left, and I am still not sure where she is. According to my info here, William put his mother in a nursing home for a few years, visited her every day at the same time, an hour before lights out. He stayed to see her off to bed and then left.

Brian paused. He went over to his notes. "Ah yes, it seems he rented this house around the same time you say all this started to happen."

Brian continued, "Do you think he has powers like the girls?"

"No, I don't think so. I believe it has to be from Sarah. But you saw her," Ryan said, thinking back. "She didn't look capable of taking care of herself, let alone work any magic," Ryan suggested.

"I think maybe we need to question the two of them. I will make a call," Brian said.

Just then, the phone rang.

"Hello?" Ryan answered.

"Good morning, just wanted to let you know breakfast is ready if you would like to join us," Molly stated.

"Sounds lovely, we will be right over," Ryan hung up the phone.

"That was Molly. Breakfast is ready." Brian rubbed his stomach as it growled. They were both hungry.

The two went right over and through the kitchen entrance. Everyone was seated at the table. "Good morning," they were greeted by all. "Have a seat and I'll get you boys a plate," Molly said promptly, getting two plates and cutlery. "Dig in."

Brian couldn't get over the spread, mounds of pancakes and bacon with mounds of scrambled eggs, toasted buns, butter, juice, and jams.

"You have outdone yourself again, Molly," Ryan commented as

he heaped his plate full.

"So, how are you both doing?" Brian asked Margaret and Jason.

"Best night's sleep in what seems forever," Jason replied.

"So, you told us that you were not mistreated, is that true?" Brian prodded.

"Yes, we were given three meals a day, fresh linen daily, and that was it," Jason added.

"How did you get kidnapped? Tell me what happened," Margaret started.

"Well, we were at the airport waiting to board our flight when, over the pager, an announcement came for us to go to the claims area. We thought it strange, but we went."

A woman greeted us there and told us that there was someone who wished to speak with us privately, and it would only take a minute. We were escorted to this office, and that is the last we remember," she finished.

"Yes, the report says that everyone there that day didn't see anything. Everyone was sure you were on that plane. The investigation into the crash of the plane is still ongoing."

"I can tell you what happened. We were kidnapped, treated well, just to end up dead in the end. The kidnapper wanted something and had us on hold to get it. They weren't looking for ransom, they were looking for something else and kept us for their key card, which I don't believe they were able to play out because you caught them," Margaret said.

"Please do not take this the wrong way," Brian started. "If you are psychic, then how do you not know who your kidnappers were?"

Margaret looked at the girls and then looked back at Brian. "Okay, the girls inform me that you know about the witch line, so whoever this was kept a haze over me. I couldn't reach out to the girls, and I couldn't use my abilities to see past the walls that we were trapped in," she explained.

"I am just so happy to be safe and back with my family again," she exclaimed. Jason nodded in compliance.

"So, you have no idea who your kidnappers were?" Brian asked again. Margaret and Jason shook their heads.

"Do you have any suspicions as to who may have wanted you dead?" he asked.

"No, not really, but I am getting the impression you do," Margaret retorted.

Ryan piped in and told them of what they found out. "So, it seems this old family vendetta has risen its ugly head," Ryan commented.

Margaret grabbed Jason's hand, looking sad. "Mom, what's wrong?" Carla asked.

"They are just the pawns in all this. You don't have all the culprits, I'm afraid," Margaret said.

"I'm not understanding. What do you mean?" Ryan asked.

Jason spoke up. "Where's Mary? Did you find her?"

"Actually, our search for her hit a dead end," Brian said.

There was silence at the table. An uncomfortable silence.

"Brian and I just discussed before we came over that we were going to go question them and see what, if any, information we can get from them," Ryan said.

"Why are you so sure they are not the masterminds behind this? You seem pretty confident in it being Mary," Brian asked.

Margaret and Jason just stared into each other's eyes.

"You need to tell them," Jason told Margaret.

Margaret dropped her head. "You see, I didn't think anything of it at the time, but Mary was corresponding with me via email last fall. She was interested in the family history, you know, ancestry, etc. I gave her the info that I knew. It seemed harmless until one email she asked about a family heirloom. It is a wand with writing on it, in an ancient rune text. Well, my reply to her was that I knew nothing of that. She then accused me of lying, and the threats started. At the time, through all the emails, she led me to believe that what happened in the past with her mother and Elsa was just that, the past. But then, when this came about, I realized it hadn't been put in the past. She was very much taking on from where her mother left off."

"The emails became so nasty I blocked her from my email. So this is why I am sure she is behind this. Also, it is the line of the woman who receives gifts, not the males," Margaret explained.

"Also, I believe if you look back through history, you will see that the male line was cursed to be barren of any magical gifts. I don't remember the reason for it, but I remember that they were cursed," she added.

Brian turned to Ryan and said, "Looks like we have our work cut out for us today. Shall we go?"

"Yes, let's get started. Thank you for breakfast, Molly. Delicious as usual. You're a culinary miracle worker," Ryan said.

Molly blushed with the compliment.

"Go on then, get out and get some work done," Molly retorted.

Before exiting the kitchen, Brian turned back and said, "If either of you think of anything else that might be helpful, just call us. See you soon."

Chapter 50

Secrets in the Attic

Molly started the clean-up with the girls' help. Margaret and Jason went into the living room with their breakfast tea.

"Jason, I am worried. I have a feeling that Mary is powerful on her own to pull this off. And if she isn't, she is using magic that is forbidden," Margaret pleaded.

"What makes you say that? Did you have a vision?" Jason asked.

"Yes, but it wasn't clear. My head is still so foggy," she stated. "I fear we are not fully out of danger just yet," Margaret added.

"We should let the girls know. They may be able to help. It seems the fog was just directed at you for some reason and not the girls," Jason said. "Maybe Mary doesn't know about the girls coming into their power," he added.

"Yes, this could work to our advantage," Margaret thought.

They called the girls in to join them and told them what they thought.

"We will help in any way we can," they replied.

"Have you put a spell of protection on the house?" Margaret asked.

The girls nodded.

"Okay, then we need to go to your grandmother's grimoire. We are going to see if we can't do a location spell to find her," Margaret said.

The three of them went upstairs to the attic.

"Wow, it's dusty up here. We are going to have to make this place better for working magic."

"You girls are going to be using this space quite a bit from now on, I am sure," Margaret said. "Firstly, we need to find anything we can, an old photo even, of Mary. So we can have something to go by."

Margaret and the girls started looking through boxes and chests they had never touched yet. Margaret went to the back wall; she had a memory of the wall moving. She placed her hand on it, and the wall slid to the right, revealing a large storage area. There were shelves filled with labeled boxes, shoes, purses, books, and, voila, photo albums.

"Over here, girls," Margaret called. "Let's each take one," she said, pulling a box down from the shelf. The dust was at least an inch thick on the top of the box. Carla took an album and started looking through it.

"Wow, this is awesome," Carla said. "The history in these pages is fantastic." Carla saw a picture of Molly, James, their mother, and a boy standing on the dock.

"Is this William?" Carla asked.

"Yes, that is him," Margaret replied. Another picture she came across showed a man, woman, William, and a baby with Grandpa on the boat.

"This must be Sarah, Walter, Mary, William, and Grandpa," Carla said. Margaret took a look and nodded.

Tara was looking in an album on the floor beside her sister.

"Hey, look at this. There are envelopes with initials on them, sealed with wax." She took them out of the sleeve they were tucked into. The first envelope was labeled with WW, the next EBW, the next WWjr.

"These look like envelopes that are for each of the family

members," Carla said. Margaret examined them. She saw an envelope with her initials and even one for her husband and girls. Molly and James were not included in theirs.

Margaret squished the envelopes gently. They were soft but hard to tell. None of the envelopes were puffy at all, and you would think there was nothing in them. Tara took a couple to look over. The little white envelopes were not white anymore but stained with time to the color of yellow. Some were really aged to the point of almost brown. It reminded her of the time she learned tea staining paper to make it look vintage for a craft she was doing in school.

"Can we open one to see what's inside?" Carla asked.

"I have a better idea. I want you girls to practice your gifts. Look into the envelope with your mind's eye, hold the envelope and concentrate, let yourself see through the paper."

Carla and Tara each took an envelope. They closed their eyes, and within about thirty seconds, they both shouted, "Hair, it's hair inside!"

They looked at their mother's face as it went white.

"Mom? Mom, are you okay?" Carla and Tara asked.

"Oh dear, oh no, this is not good." Margaret took each envelope one at a time and tried to check. "Damn, I'm still foggy. Girls, you have to look into each one, don't open it, and make sure the hair is still there."

Panicked, Margaret passed the envelopes to the girls. They checked each one and found three envelopes empty.

Sarah, William, and Mary's envelopes.

"Actually, look, Mom, your envelope is damaged," Carla said.

Tara took the envelope and compared what she was seeing to the others that were full.

"It seems as though this one, yours, is missing some hair," Tara said.

"That's probably how she is able to stop you from seeing," Carla said.

"The actual name for this ability is the 'Cunning,'" Margaret inserted.

"Yes, this explains a lot. She is able to use the hair to manipulate the people," their mother said as she shook her head. "We need to lock these away. Somewhere with a spell of protection that only the two of you can get to." She said, gathering them together. She grabbed a ribbon and tied them all together. "Not me, though. If she is able to manipulate me, then I can't be trusted. Oh dear, oh dear, this is not good at all."

"We need to tell Ryan and Brian about this right away."

The girls found a chest with a lock but no key. They placed the envelopes in the box, closed the lid, and locked it.

"But there is no key," Tara said.

"That's okay because I am sure somewhere, somehow, we will find or create a spell, or our powers will grow to the point we won't need a key when the time comes if ever, to open this chest."

"But right now, there is a spell for protection in the grimoire," Carla said.

They placed the chest by the wall in the corner, tucked away behind other boxes not of value.

"Mom, we need you to go downstairs and tell Dad, Molly, and James what we have discovered."

Their mother understood and went downstairs. As soon as she left and the door was closed, Carla dragged Tara to the grimoire.

"Okay, in here is a spell to protect that box from anyone but us, and then when that's done, we are going to do that same spell on this book. This book in the wrong hands could cause trouble for us," Carla instructed.

The two girls got to work right away.

Margaret went downstairs and let the girls do their work. She met everyone back downstairs and told them of what they found and the danger that she could be manipulated as well. She warned them to keep an eye on her at all times. She was frightened to what length Mary would go. Until they found this wand and what its purpose was, they couldn't take any chances.

Chapter 51

Sister's Power

Ryan and Brian pulled up in front of the police station. They both got out of the car like they were going to war. Ryan looked at his brother and noticed how serious and stern he looked. He noted his posture and started to laugh. "Now who's the peacock, bro?" Brian realized what he was doing and joined his brother in a chuckle at his own expense as they walked in.

Officer Thomas was at the front desk. He recognized Ryan right away. "Hey, great work in finding the girls' parents," he complimented.

"Thanks, have you met my brother Brian?"

Officer Thomas stood up and shook Brian's hand. "Not in person, but have talked on the phone quite a bit. Nice to finally meet you," he said.

"How are the Jasons doing?" he directed his question to both of them.

"They are doing well, ecstatic to be home with the family again. I think they are going to stay put for a while, which is nice for them," Ryan replied.

"So, what can I help you with today?" Officer Thomas asked.

"Well, we need to question Mr. Pickwood, if it isn't too much trouble," Brian asked. "I called this morning in regards to this," he added.

"Oh yes, of course. I'll have an Officer escort you to his cell," Officer Thomas said. He left, and when he returned, he introduced them to Officer Clark. "He will show you the way," he said.

They followed the Officer through the back office and down a hall to a staircase. They went down the stairs to a locked door. The Officer used his key to let them in.

"It's a small office here, not a lot going on in this small town, so you will find him just two cells over," Officer Clark said.

"There is one other prisoner in there, but he won't bother you. He's sleeping off last night's liquor," the Officer said and closed the door behind him. Sure enough, they saw William lying on a cot.

"William Wood? We need to speak to you," Brian said. The man just remained still, all but one eye opening and closing again.

"We would like to talk to you, and yes, we know who you are," Ryan said.

"You have no idea how relieved I am," he said, still not moving. Ryan wasn't sure if that was sarcasm or truth.

"Why did you kidnap Mr. and Mrs. Jason?" Brian asked.

William just laughed.

"Did I say something funny?" Brian asked.

"I would love to tell you all about it, but..." he stopped there.

"But what?" Ryan prompted.

Then there was nothing. His eyes were closed, and he still didn't move a muscle. They stood for a bit and waited.

"We are still waiting?" Brian said.

Then, all of a sudden, William leaped from his cot and threw himself at the bars.

"Listen and listen well, I don't have much time and probably will not be able to repeat it. It's my sister. She has the power to manipulate me and my mother, and God only knows who else. She has put Mom under some type of curse and is channeling her powers to make her stronger. You know when she is manipulating her though her eyes go white. I think it is a witch thing I don't know its fucking creepy though." William was agitated and rambling on as if he was scared for his life. "She is so dangerous; you need to get her."

"Where is she?" Brian interjected.

"Oh, she is clever. She is hiding right under your nose, and you don't even know it. She can change into anyone she wants to with a glamour," William said. Then he grabbed his head and started tugging on his hair, what he had left of it from balding. He started shouting, "Stop it!" over and over again. He fell to his knees, looked up at them, and said, "Leave now, quickly."

So Brian and Ryan left as they were told. Once back upstairs, they inquired about how long his stay was here at this cell.

"Well, it looks like it will be a month before they actually get room for him in Joyce Ville. Don't know, had something to do with a fire or something and they are overloaded as is," Officer Thomas replied.

"Okay, we will probably be back in a couple of days," Brian said.

"Not surprised your visit was short. He is a little if you ask me," Officer Thomas added.

Ryan and Brian just agreed and left. Ryan's phone started ringing.

"It's Carla," he said, then answered the phone. "Hi, what's up?" he asked. Brian watched him; his face went serious.

"Put her on speaker," he said.

So, Ryan did.

"So, then we found envelopes with initials on them, and when we looked inside, there was hair. All the envelopes were labeled with initials, one for everyone in the family, but the horrifying part is Mary, William, and Sarah were empty. Margaret, Mom, some of the hair was missing, but not empty like the others.”

“Do you know what this means?” she asked, not expecting an answer.

“This means that she is using the hair of these people to manipulate them. She can actually get into their head and make them do and say things.” She was panicked, Ryan could tell. He just let her talk.

“This means Mom could be affected even more than just a foggy brain. What are we going to do?” she paused just long enough for Ryan to tell her what they learned, and it confirms what she said. But the worst part of it all is he said she was using glamour to look like anyone she wanted and that she is pulling—channelling, something like that—magic from her mother to enhance her own.”

Ryan said, and all he heard was a gasp from the other end of the phone.

“Carla, are you okay?” There was a long pause.

“I just thought of something. I am going to go look into it,” Carla said.

“Okay, we are off to see Sarah now. I’ll call you when we are on our way home,” Ryan said.

“Okay, talk then,” Carla replied.

Ryan was worried. Carla went from hysterics to being way too calm. What could she be up to? He didn’t even want to speculate because then his thoughts would scare him.

“Okay, let’s get rolling,” Ryan said as he hopped into the driver’s seat.

They pulled into the nursing home where Sarah was taken.

“I have to say, bro, I am a little nervous about this. I can’t tell you how weird all this is. I come from the city where it’s just crime, not this weird-ass magic shit," Brian exclaimed.

Ryan just laughed and said, "I know what you mean, I truly do." They went to the reception and asked to see Sara Wood. The nurse gave them the directions to her room. "You will need to show ID to the Officers at her door," she said. They nodded and proceeded down the hall to the elevators. The doors opened, and the elevator was empty. Brian pressed the number 4; it was the top floor of the building. The elevator jiggled as it went up slowly, then came to a jolted stop at the 4th floor. The doors opened, and they could only see white barren walls with doors on either side of the hallway. Most elevators are situated in the center of the hall, but this one was at the end. They walked down the hall, looking at each door. Sarah was in 402. This room was on the south side of the building, just before a common area, which had another nurse's station situated right across. Ryan felt this was more like a hospital than a nursing home. Brian couldn't help but notice that there was no one around except them and the two Officers in the hall. No one was in the common room, and the nurse at the station never even looked up. Ryan thought to himself that if he looked at the screen the nurse was staring at, he would probably see her playing computer solitaire.

"Some ID, boys?" the Officer asked. Both Ryan and Brian showed him their badges. The Officer nodded and opened the door. The room was dimly lit, the curtains were open, allowing the sun to shine through to help brighten the room. Sarah was in a wheelchair, sitting facing the outside. She had a nice view of the canal that ran alongside the street.

Ryan went in first. "Hello, Mrs. Wood, my name is Detective Ryan, and this is Detective Brian." Sarah never moved. Brian had a shudder go through his whole body, remembering the last time he saw her. Ryan walked over to her so he could face her. He was shocked to see her eyes were not white but a pale green. He pulled a small chair up beside her and sat down. She turned her head to look at him. She just stared.

"Mrs. Wood? We would like to ask you a few questions, if that's okay?" Ryan asked. Sarah nodded and turned her head to look back out the window. Ryan thought for a minute. "Do I ask her all the questions that I want to know, or do I just go for the punch and ask her where Mary is?" he thought.

"Do you know why your son kidnapped the Jasons?" Sarah just shook her head no.

"Do you know why your son took you from the nursing home to that house?" Sarah just sat staring out the window. Ryan glanced at Brian and shrugged his shoulders. Then Sarah broke the silence.

"Mary told him to."

Yes!!! Ryan thought, a lead into the main question. "Do you know where Mary is?" Sarah turned to look at him, stared straight into his eyes, and said, "No, and you best wish she doesn't know where you are either?" Then she turned and looked back out the window. Ryan couldn't help himself; the words just came crashing out of his mouth.

"Oh, and why is that, Mrs. Wood?" She snapped her head back around to look at him. She looked angry.

"Because she will have her revenge for you too messing everything up."

While Ryan had her attention on him, he quickly asked, "What did we mess up? What was the plan?"

"To rid the world of all the Blackwood's and take what is rightfully ours," she said.

"What is it that is rightfully yours, Mrs. Wood?"

"There are things hidden in the estate that came here with the Blacks many moons ago. They hold great power, that's where they get their wealth," she stated.

"Why does Mary want this?" Ryan asked.

She gave a really angry look at him and said, "It's rightfully hers by blood."

Ryan replied, "But she is a cousin, not the heir in line for any of that."

Still angry, she replied, "They killed her daddy and my husband."

"I heard that it was an unfortunate accident," Ryan said.

Sarah just looked out the window and started to laugh.

"Mrs. Wood, I will look into the records and what you're saying to us today and see what we can come up with. We will keep you informed."

She was silent as she looked out the window. Just as Ryan got up from his chair to leave, she gave a big sigh and said, "Good luck."

Ryan didn't detect any sarcasm in her voice. He believed she meant it.

"You best find it before Mary does, or you will all be sorry," Sarah said.

Ryan sat back down in his chair and asked Sarah one more question. "Do you believe it was an accident?"

Sarah replied without taking her gaze from the window, "I did, but I am too old and tired to bother with it anymore. But not Mary. Just watch out for her, that's all I have to say. Just watch out."

Sarah closed her eyes and tilted her head as if to take a nap. Ryan and Brian left the room.

Ryan thanked the Officers, then gave them their card. "Could you give us a call if she has any visitors or anything weird happens?" The Officer took the card, giving him a look as if saying, "Who the hell are you?" Ryan recognized the look and added, "You can check with your chief; he will be able to vouch for us." The Officers nodded and put the card in his breast pocket.

Ryan and Brian walked back to the elevator and pushed the button. The elevator was taking so long, Brian kept pushing the button. "You know that doesn't make the elevator go any faster," he laughed.

"I know, I just want to get the hell out of this place," Ryan said.

As they were waiting for the elevator, the nurse got up from her station and walked into Sarah's room. The elevator came, and the doors opened. Brian got in.

"Hold the elevator," he said and hurried back to Sarah's room.

"I forgot my keys," he told the Officer. They let him pass. He very quietly opened the door. When he got inside, the nurse turned to him and said, "Get out!" She was not mannerly at all.

"Sorry, I left my keys here on the table." Ryan had them in his hand in his pocket. He concealed them, then reached over to the table with his back to her as if grabbing them. He turned back to her and said, "Sorry to disturb you."

The nurse just glared at him until he left. He quietly closed the door. When he heard Sarah cry out, "No, no more! I don't want to do this anymore. Just leave me alone," he wanted to go help her but instead just looked at the Officer.

"Yeah, she does that every time she is to have her shot," the Officer said.

"What is the shot?" Ryan asked.

The Officer replied, "The nurse says it's a sedative to keep her calm due to her heart condition."

"Oh, I see," Ryan said. He wished the Officers a nice day and hurried back to the elevator.

"That took forever, what did you do?" Brian asked.

"I saw the nurse go into the room, and it's just a hunch, but I have a feeling that Mary is the nurse at Sarah's station," he told her. He explained how rude the nurse was and how she just stared at him until he left. "And her actions while I was in there just added to my suspicions."

Then Sarah cried out something about not wanting to do this anymore. "Was Mary trying to do something to her?" Ryan continued.

The rest of the ride down in the elevator was quiet. They walked to the entrance, and as they came to the desk, Ryan stopped to talk to the nurse.

"Hi there, sorry to bother you, but I'm just curious about this building. You see, we are out of town, and I was just wondering why it is more like a hospital than any nursing home I have seen."

The nurse eagerly replied, "Well, this used to be a hospital until they built the big one just outside of town. You know, more people mean more demand for healthcare, so this building was turned into a nursing home. But then they built a really nice villa for the elderly just down by the lake, just 10 minutes down the road. So, this hospital turned into a... a, how should I say...a home for the aged criminals or crazies." She then grimaced at her own description.

"That's okay, I get it," Ryan said. "It's awfully quiet around the place if that is the kind of people that have residence here."

"Yes, well, thank goodness there are not many here. They will probably be shutting this place down soon due to the cost of it all and not many occupants. But that's pure speculation, you see," she said. Ryan just nodded.

"How long have you worked here?" Ryan asked, noting that she was at least forty to forty-five years of age.

"This year, it will be my fifteenth year," she said proudly.

"And the rest of the staff? Have they been here a long time too?" Ryan continued.

"Yes, most of us are original or shortly after, however, Betty, the one you saw on the fourth floor, she just started today. She got a transfer here, says she wants a quieter life, rather than working in the city with overcrowded homes. She says this way, she can give a lot of care to her patients and get to know them by name, not just a number. I don't rightly know how she did that all those years. I know she will be much happier here," she said.

Ryan was so thankful she was a really nice, chatty lady; he learned quite a bit.

"Well, thank you for the history lesson. I won't take up any more of your time," Ryan said.

"Have a nice day," Brian added. She just smiled back.

They hopped in the car and were ready to leave when Ryan remembered to call Carla.

Chapter 52

Hair's Mystery

Carla hung up the phone to Ryan and went into the living room, where everyone was sitting, talking about the envelopes. Her mother was worried; you could see it on her face. Carla entered and started telling them what Ryan and Brian had found out.

"I have an idea, though. Is it possible that when she emptied out the hair, she ran out of time in order to retrieve all of Mom's hair, so the effects are minimal on Mom?" Carla questioned.

"I don't believe so. This kind of magic just needs one strand, and it will last forever," Margaret replied.

"Then why is she not making it worse for you? Why are you not one of her little puppets?" Carla queried.

"I don't know, but when we put the pieces together so far, she is using some very dark magic. From what you tell me of the dark figure, she was using elemental magic to conjure up a soulless spirit to do her bidding. Then, now we discover that she is using the hair of her family to manipulate them into doing her bidding, not to mention that she is drawing on her mother's own powers to make hers stronger," Margaret explained. She put her head in her hands and just shook her head. She looked at the girls and said, "This is not good. We have to stop her."

"But how?" both Carla and Tara said at the same time.

Just then, Carla's phone rang.

"It's Ryan," she announced.

She answered the phone. "Hi..." That was all she got out when Ryan started to talk. He told her of their visit and the information he found out while he was there.

"Wow, that's creepy," Carla said.

"Yeah, and that's not all. I believe Mary is the nurse on her floor," Ryan added.

"What, you're kidding? Well, that would make sense. This way, she could be close to her mother when she needed her now that she doesn't have her brother," Carla said.

"Okay, we are on our way back. We'll see you in a little while," Ryan said to Carla just before hanging up.

Carla went back into the living area and told them what Ryan said. "They are on their way home now," she added. Molly jumped from her seat and said, "They will be hungry, and so will all of us. I will start lunch."

"I will help you," James said as he rose to follow Molly to the kitchen.

"I have a question. I'm not sure you have thought of it at all or just aren't saying, but why are there envelopes of our hair upstairs?"

"Oh, and one other question, who put them there?" Jason asked.

The girls both looked at their mother for the answer.

Margaret just shrugged her shoulders and looked at them all. "I don't know. I have no clue as to how or who did it."

"Could it have been your mother? And if so, why?" Jason asked.

"Again, I have no idea or any recollection of that at all," Margaret said sincerely.

"Okay, here is another question. Family treasure, secrets, whatever Sarah was talking about, do you know what she is talking about?" Carla asked.

Margaret sat and pondered the question. She was trying really hard to think back to when she was a girl here.

Her brain was still so foggy that she was struggling to remember stuff. "I am trying to remember, but the fog in my head is not clearing," she said with great concern.

"That's okay, Mom, we will figure it out all in good time," Carla said.

"Let's go for a walk on the beach," Jason said to Margaret as he grabbed her hand to pull her up. "A little fresh air and sunshine will do you good."

Margaret agreed. "We will call you when the boys get back and lunch is ready," Carla said.

She then looked at Tara. Tara caught her gaze. "What? What are you thinking? I don't like that look."

Carla got up and headed for the stairs. "Follow me," she commanded Tara. Tara followed her up into the attic. Carla shut and locked the door.

"Did you try to read Mom's mind?" Carla asked.

"No, did you?" Tara replied.

"Yes, as a matter of fact, I did, and as I was trying, that was when she said her head was still foggy," Carla stated.

"And what's your point?"

"At that time, I don't think it was foggy. She was just saying that because she noticed that I was prying or there was something she didn't want to remember," Carla declared.

"I highly doubt Mom would hide anything from us. Did you ever think that maybe Mary is the one blocking her memories?" Tara said.

"Yes, I thought of that too, but I have a gut feeling about this and I am not liking it."

"I just ask that you keep an open mind to the possibility that there is something Mom does not want us to know. Okay?" Carla pleaded.

"Okay, I will," Tara promised.

"Now, if there is a secret in this house, I think it's our duty to find out what it is. After all, there should be no secrets in our home," Carla said.

Tara agreed. "So where should we start?"

"Let's meet up here tonight when everyone's asleep," Carla suggested.

"Agreed."

"Do not tell Mom, though," Carla demanded.

"I understand," Tara said.

"Well, that's our cue. Molly is calling us for dinner," Tara said.

"Okay, let's not keep her waiting," Carla said as she opened the door to the attic.

The girls walked into the kitchen and noticed that everyone was already seated, including Ryan and Brian.

"Where were you girls?" Margaret asked.

"Just upstairs, looking through Grandma's grimoire, hoping for a clue," Carla said as she loaded her plate with potato salad and a hotdog. Tara did the same but remained quiet.

"Were you successful in finding anything?" Jason asked.

The girls both shook their heads.

"No, but we were not up there long," Tara added.

"So, Ryan, you said you thought the nurse was Mary. What do

we do to find out for sure?" Margaret asked.

"I don't know exactly. However, maybe keep meeting with Sarah. Hopefully, she will reveal herself or Sarah will tell us," Ryan said.

"Is there anything you girls can do magically to help reveal this Mary or force her hand in some way?" Brian asked.

"Well, that is why we went to the attic to see if we could find anything that would help," Carla said.

There was silence at the table for a few minutes. The only noise was forks hitting the plates.

"I know!" Tara jumped up from her chair. "If you go back to see Sarah, get something of hers and we can open a small window on her. This way, we can monitor what goes on in the room when this nurse, Mary, is there. We will be able to hear what she says, but she will not be able to see us."

"That's a great idea, especially if we can focus it on a mirror in the room. Mary will never pick up on it," Carla said.

"Yes, there is a dresser in her room with a mirror attached. I will draw you a layout of the room if that will help?" Ryan said.

"Yes, that will help greatly. Now, one of us has to be on alert at all times, watching and listening."

"That's not a problem. Between the four of us, we will be able to do this and not lose too much sleep," Brian assured them.

"That's great news," Margaret said. Jason, Molly, and James agreed.

They started to clear the table, and Margaret started the dishes with Molly. Tara gave Ryan a piece of paper and a pen to draw the layout of the room.

"I think it would be too much to go back today. We will go see her in the morning," Brian said.

"Yes, I agree. If it is Mary, she will get suspicious if we return today," Ryan agreed.

"Has anyone heard from Mr. Davies?" Jason asked.

"No, his last words were that he would be in touch with us as soon as he could and not to try and reach him." Jason nodded, then said, "I find that a bit suspicious of him to just disappear like he did and to have the office not recognize him or anyone that we knew worked there, including you, Ryan."

"I know it is suspicious, and I'm sure we will get to the bottom of all this soon," Ryan said, hoping to console him.

"Good news, though. Margaret got in touch with the publisher. They were delighted to hear from her and want us to get back to work on our book as soon as possible. Now that we know it had nothing to do with what we were working on, we can continue. It will be good to get back to work again," Jason said.

"That's great news, Mom," Carla said, and Tara agreed. Everyone was happy that they could get some normalcy back in their life.

"Yes, your mom and I are going to head home tomorrow. All our stuff is in the office there at home," Jason said.

"Are you sure that is wise? I mean, you are totally protected here," Brian queried.

"I'm sure it will be fine. We are going to have a detective at the house. I have already arranged for it," Jason said. "Plus, we will come up every other weekend to see you all, and I expect to have a daily update on what's occurring here," Jason commanded.

"We know you girls are safe here with Molly and James and you boys, so we feel comfortable about being able to do this," Jason added.

"Okay, but if you need anything, you make sure you call. You're only an hour and a half away," Carla said.

Just then, Ryan's phone rang. "Excuse me, I'll take this in the other room." Carla had one ear on Ryan's conversation and one ear on the conversation taking place in the kitchen, as Brian was asking about the book they were writing.

Margaret piped in and said, "It is not just one book. We are behind on a few books that we have been issued to write. So we have a lot of work to do."

"How's the foggy brain?" Brian asked.

"It comes and goes. I am hoping it doesn't interfere with the writing, but I won't know until I try," Margaret replied.

Ryan came back in. "Brian, we have to go. Apparently, there has been some kind of upheaval at the nursing home. Apparently, Sarah is giving the nurse a hard time, and it is not the nurse from earlier. I asked, and apparently, her shift ended an hour ago," Ryan said.

They both said goodbye and informed the family they would call them to let them know what's up.

"Don't forget to get something of Sarah's, hair, clothing, anything that she has touched, used, or wore," Tara said.

"We will bring something home for you," Brian assured.

Chapter 53

White eyes, screaming

Ryan and Brian arrived at the home. They went to the front desk, and before they could say anything, the nurse said, "Hurry, you need to go upstairs." They took the stairs, this time remembering how slow the elevators were. They could hear the screams growing louder and louder as they climbed. When they reached the fourth floor, Brian recognized that scream—it gave him shivers. They hurried down the hall, and both officers were out of their chairs. They were in the room, trying to help the nurse. Brian and Ryan were shocked by what they saw as they walked in. Sarah was standing and had the nurse around the neck with her arm, lifting her off her feet and holding her close. The officers had their guns drawn and gave Ryan and Brian a look as if to say, *What do we do?* Ryan signaled them to put their guns down.

Sarah was still screaming. Ryan tried to talk to her, but he was sure she couldn't hear him. It was an ear-piercing scream, long and drawn out, just like in a horror movie. Ryan looked Sarah in the eyes and placed his finger on his lips to signal her to be quiet. Sarah stopped screaming, and the noise turned into a moan.

"Sarah? What's going on?" Ryan asked.

Sarah just stared at him.

"Sarah, why are you hurting the nice nurse?" Ryan asked again.

"She's not nice," Sarah replied.

"Why is she not nice?" Ryan pressed.

"She is going to give me a needle," Sarah said.

"Yes, that needle is going to help you relax so you can get some rest and feel better," Ryan said.

Sarah just shook her head.

"Can you let her go so that my partner here, Brian, can have a word with her? Maybe he can see if she can skip this needle today?" Ryan suggested.

Sarah stared at Brian as if to check him out, but her eyes were so piercing it felt like she could see through him.

"Come on, Sarah, let me talk to her. I'll speak with her in the hall so you can relax," Brian assured her.

Sarah then pushed the nurse away so hard that she fell in front of Brian. Brian helped the nurse up and escorted her outside, closing the door behind them. He took her to the lounge near the nurse's station, where they both sat. Brian went to get her a glass of water; she was clearly shaken.

Brian gave her a minute to collect herself before asking, "What happened in there, Ms...?"

"Mrs. Clarke, and I'm not sure. The officers called me because they could hear her moaning. When I went in to see her, she was sitting on the side of her bed with her back facing the door. I asked if she was okay, but she didn't respond. Then, I asked if she wanted any pain meds. She nodded, so I left to get her some. When I returned, she threw the tray of pills and the water cup, grabbed me, and started screaming. I don't know what she was talking about with a needle—yes, she does get one to help her sleep, but that's not until 7 p.m. tonight," Mrs. Clarke explained, taking another sip of water.

"At first, she kept calling for Mary, but I didn't know who Mary was, and there wasn't any point of contact for her on Sarah's file. I know she didn't like that either," Mrs. Clarke added.

"Okay, it may be best if we stick around for a bit. It seems she trusts my partner," Brian said.

"Do you happen to have a report from the person on the shift before you?" Brian asked.

"Yes, Betty left a report from her shift with Sarah. It said she was calm today, and there was no indication of any trouble," Mrs. Clarke replied.

Brian nodded. "Okay, I'm going to go in and see her now. You can go back to your desk, and we'll see if we can calm her down enough to take her meds."

Brian entered the room and saw that Ryan had Sarah back in bed. The officers were standing guard inside the room. "We've got this now if you want to take your posts again," Brian said, smiling at the officers.

One of the officers motioned for him to step outside, and Brian followed. "I know this is going to sound strange, and if you tell anyone, I'll deny it," the officer said.

Brian nodded.

"When we went in, she had the nurse in a chokehold. We tried to talk her into letting go. Her eyes were closed, but when she heard us, she opened them, and they were all white—no pupils. We drew our guns, but she didn't stop. We tried to move closer, and even with her eyes all white, she could see us. It was so creepy! That's when my partner called you. When you came in, her eyes changed back. Weird, right?"

"No, not weird. I experienced the same thing with her when we found her in that basement. The scream and the eyes were exactly the same. And yes, it was very creepy, but don't worry, I won't tell anyone," Brian assured him.

The officer let out a huge sigh of relief. Brian returned to the room.

"So, are you comfortable now, Sarah?" Ryan asked.

"Is there anything I can get you?" Sarah just shook her head. She seemed sleepy, her eyes growing heavy.

"The nurse won't bother you with anything for now, okay?"

Brian assured her.

"We'll sit with you for a while. Would you like that?" Ryan asked.

Sarah nodded, and this time, when her eyes closed, they stayed closed. Ryan got off the bed where he had been sitting beside her. He drew the curtains around her bed to keep the light out. Brian saw a brush on the dresser and grabbed some hair from it. Without a word, he showed it to Ryan, and they were both satisfied. Brian wrapped it in a tissue he had in his pocket and put it away.

They waited a few more minutes and then left when they heard small snoring sounds. They told the officers that Sarah was asleep and went to talk to the nurse.

"So, this needle you have to give her tonight—have you done it before?" Ryan asked Mrs. Clarke.

"Yes, but this will only be the second time I've given it to her."

"Okay, well, if you think there might be an issue, instead of putting yourself in that position, you could give her some Ativan with the doctor's clearance and leave it on her tray to take herself. Hopefully, there won't be any more incidents today," Ryan suggested.

"Good idea. I've put a call into the resident doctor, and when he calls back, I'll ask him. Thank you for your help," Mrs. Clarke said.
"No problem. Don't hesitate to call us," Brian said, handing her their cards.

When they got into the car, they called Carla with the good news that they had retrieved some of Sarah's hair from her brush. Then Brian filled her in on what happened and told her they were on their way back.

"That's fantastic! Okay, see you when you get here," Carla said.

The rest of the day, they all decided to take a break. The weather was great for late August, so they all went for a swim. Molly, being her usual thoughtful self, whipped up some lemonade and brought chips and dip. Even Molly took a break with them, sitting in the water with her glass of lemonade, soaking up the sun. James and Jason sat on the dock, fishing and catching up. Margaret and the girls lay on towels on the beach, while Ryan and Brian swam to the island and back. It had been a long time since they had been able to relax and enjoy the day. They all relished just being in the moment.

Ryan and Brian returned to the beach to find no one had moved. They both laughed. Carla opened her eyes and smiled at them.

"You ladies going to lie there all day, or are we going to play some water volleyball?" Ryan suggested.

Tara jumped up. "I'm in!" she said, grabbing her mom and sisters' hands and pulling them up.

"Okay, okay, we're in too," Margaret said. Margaret yelled to Jason to please set up the net and poles in the water for them and suggested that he and James's join.

"Come on, Molly, we see you sitting there trying to ignore us," Carla said.

And before they knew it, they were all having a blast playing in the shallower water, a game of volleyball with the whole family.

"Okay, I have had enough," Molly said, and Margaret agreed. "We must have played at least six games," she added.

"I think you're right, but look at them. It must be nice to be so young again," Margaret said as she grabbed Molly by the shoulder and drew her close for a sideways hug.

Shortly after, the ladies ended it, and so did James and Jason. They toweled off and joined them on lawn chairs. The sun was getting late in the day when they realized it was almost dinner time.

Molly announced she was going in to find something for dinner.

"Wait, Molly, I have a better idea. Let's all get dressed and take the boat into town and have dinner at the local restaurant," James said.

James, Margaret, and Molly agreed so fast it shocked Jason.

"Alright, let's get ready," James said. He went and told the girls and Ryan and Brian. They packed up the towels and chairs while Jason and James put the net away. Shortly, they were all ready and at the boat, waiting for Jason and Margaret.

When they got to the boat, James gave them each a life preserver to wear, and they were off. James looked around while Jason drove the boat. He was so happy to see everyone talking and laughing and having such a great time without a worry in the world.

Chapter: 54

Doctor's Double

The doctor on residence came up to see the nurse at the 4th floor station of the nursing home. The Officers took notice and was expecting him to want to see Sarah. They could see them talking but couldn't hear what was being said. After a few minutes he was looking at the chart then slammed it down on the desk and started to what looked like give the nurse hell for something. The Officers looked at each other with confusion on their face.

The doctor then left and went down the hall in the other direction, where there was another elevator at the end of the hall. As soon as the doctor was gone, one of the Officers went to the desk. "Are you okay? We saw him yelling at you," he said. She wiped tears from her eyes and said, "Yeah, I am fine, confused. The doctor picked up the chart on Mrs. Wood and said that it says right here to give her Ativan, not a needle, and why am I wasting his time? But I don't see where it says that. Do you?" She handed the Officer the chart. He looked it over and said to the nurse that he didn't see it either. "Right?"

"Is that not weird?" The Officer nodded. "Yeah, there is a lot of weird these days." Just as he said that the phone rang. When the nurse answered it, she signaled for the Officer to stay a moment. "Yes, Doctor, no problem, thank you," she said, hanging up the phone. "Okay, you want to talk weird? That was the doctor on the phone. He said he read my report email and just gave me clearance to give her Tylenol and Ativan and allow her to administer it herself. No needles," she said, confused.

"Wasn't the doctor just here? Was the doctor that was here the same person you spoke with?" the Officer asked.

"Yes, that's weird, right?"

"The number he called from was from his office, which is just a block away," she added.

"Then who was that doctor that came here? Someone obviously isn't the doctor," the Officer said.

"Actually, the doctor that came to see me looks exactly like the doctor that I spoke with. I have known him for years, and I did think that Dr. Campbell, his name, sounded funny but wrote it off as maybe a cold. That was until I spoke with Dr. Campbell on the phone. Now that voice was exactly the one I know," the nurse said.

"Okay, if you will excuse me, I want to inform my partner," the Officer said.

Both Officers agreed to tell Ryan about this. After Ryan hung up the phone at the dinner table, he told them all who it was and what just happened. "I think when we get home, we should put up that window and start watching. I have a feeling she, Mary, just visited as the doctor," Ryan said. They all agreed and finished their dinner, not rushing through it, though they still wanted to enjoy what part of the day they had left.

They arrived back at the estate at six thirty. "I think it would be best to put the portal in the den. It never gets used, is away from the rest of the family space, and it has all the comforts as well," Carla said, and Tara agreed. Tara took the hair from the Kleenex and followed everyone into the den. She set it up just above the TV so anyone could watch both at the same time if they wanted. The only downfall was the volume on the TV would have to be very low or mute to hear conversations through the portal. "Okay, all set."

Brian was bug-eyed; he couldn't believe what he was seeing. "I don't know if I will ever get used to this stuff," he said.

They all just laughed. "You will… trust me," Ryan said. They could see clearly through the Portal Window that was put up. It looked like Sarah was up and watching television. There was no one else in the room for now. Ryan looked at his watch. "The nurse should be coming in soon to give her the Ativan. According to my watch, it's 6:59 PM," he said. Everyone took up a spot in the den to watch what would happen when the nurse came in. A few minutes later, they heard the door to her room open. The nurse walked by the mirror and placed the two little cups on the tray at the end of her bed. "Mrs. Wood, I have left you an Ativan to help you sleep," the nurse said as she backed out of the room. They heard the door close and saw that Sarah never moved.

"So, who's taking the first shift?" Carla asked.

"I will," Tara said. "I need to let my dinner settle; I think I ate too much," she said, rubbing her belly.

"Okay, how about we all have a game of cards?" Carla suggested. Everyone thought that was a good idea and left the room.

"Would you like some company?" Brian asked Tara.

"Don't you want to play cards?" she answered him with a question.

"I don't really feel like it and thought you might like some company," he replied.

"Sure, that would be nice," Tara said. Brian sat in the easy chair. They both were staring at the portal. Sarah never moved, her medicine was still on the tray, and you could hear the TV on in the background.

"It's like watching paint dry, eh?" Tara said.

"You're not kidding," Brian answered.

Shortly, Brian started asking her some questions in regards to the magic and talents that the girls had.

Tara opened up to him, and they sat for quite a while talking and getting to know one another. They could hear the laughter coming from the other room where they were playing cards. Tara was thinking to herself, "Brian is such a sweet guy, despite his rough exterior." Brian was around the same height as Ryan, but you could tell Brian worked out. They really did look like brothers, but Brian had this facial expression that gave you the first impression that he might be angry. He had a permanent scowled brow that gave him this look of being gruff. But really, he was quite nice, and his words were cheerful. And he wasn't half bad to look at either, Tara thought.

Ten o'clock rolled around, and they heard Sarah's door open. "Mrs. Wood, why are you not in bed?" the nurse said. Tara and Brian took notice as they heard this voice. The nurse was the same one they thought was Mary, Brian noticed.

"That is the nurse we were telling you about, we think may be Mary," Brian whispered.

Tara grinned. "Oh, okay, you don't have to whisper. They can't hear you." She smiled at him.

"Oh," he said and just smiled.

They watched the nurse walk over to Sarah and turn the TV off.

She then picked up one of Sarah's arms and directed her to bed. "It's time to sleep now, Mrs. Wood," the nurse said. She picked up the Ativan and the cup, giving it to her. Then they saw the nurse pull out a needle and give it to her in the leg. Sarah threw the cup at the nurse in anger.

"Now, now, that was not nice," the nurse said as she pulled the covers over Sarah. "Have a great sleep, and I will see you in the morning." The nurse left the room.

Brian gave a big yawn. "I think I am going to turn in for a while. I will relieve you of this duty at 1:00 AM," Brian said.

"Okay, have a good sleep," Tara said. Shortly after, everyone came in to say goodnight to Tara as they went to bed. Tara wasn't tired at all and pulled out a book to read, enjoying the peace and quiet.

Tara heard Carla's thoughts. "Hey, sis, I suppose we will have to wait to find this secret, eh?"

"Yeah, but I'm not worried. It must be hidden well. Have a good sleep," Tara replied.

Time flew quickly, and before she knew it, Brian was downstairs, ready to take Tara's place.

"Wow, you look as wide awake as when I left you a few hours ago," Brian commented.

"Yep, mind over matter and a good book," Tara laughed. "There are lots of books to choose from, so help yourself," Tara told Brian.

"Thanks. Hey, anything exciting happen?" he asked.

"No, she has been sleeping soundly," Tara replied.

"Good night, Tara."

"Good night, Brian."

Brian took a look at the bookshelf. "I love autobiographies," he said to himself. Brian noticed a few books on the shelf that were written by Margaret and Jason. He read the back of them and finally picked one to read. He made himself comfortable and checked the portal; all was well, so he dove right into the book.

The house was so quiet and peaceful that he became totally immersed in the book in no time flat. It was an exciting book, so exciting that he could put himself right into the story. There was a noise in the background, but Brian didn't seem to register it. Then, all of a sudden, he popped his head out of the book to look. Sure enough, what he heard was the door to Sarah's room.

It was hard to see, no one had turned the light on, and there was a slight glare from the nightlight over the bed. Brian moved closer to see if that helped. He strained his eyes and turned off the light in the den. That helped a little more for him to see better. Sure enough, it was Nurse Betty. She didn't wake Sarah up; she sat on the bed beside her. Sarah was lying on her back with her arms by her side and the sheets pulled up to her chest.

That is exactly how she had been since she went to bed. "I envy people like that; all I do is toss and turn all night," Brian thought to himself. *Wait, what is she doing? Oh no, I have to call Tara.*

Brian looked at his watch and was shocked that two and a half hours had already passed. Ryan would be coming to relieve him soon. He called his brother.

Groggily, Ryan answered, "Yeah, what's up?" "Bro, wake the girls and get down here," Brian said, panicked. "Okay, give me two," Ryan said.

What do I do if they miss it? Brian thought. Then it hit him. I'll record this on my phone. So, he did. To his surprise, the camera picked up the scene much better.

He could hear Ryan's footsteps as he went to the girls' rooms. He knew they would be tiptoeing to avoid disturbing the rest of the family, but the floor creaked. Then he heard them all start down the stairs.

Slippers were shuffling down the hall to join Jason in the den.

"What's going on?" Carla asked, rubbing her face.

"I don't know; you tell me what she is doing," Brian retorted.

Carla took a hard look, and so did Tara. The girls looked at each other and back at the scene.

"It is like she is pulling something from her," Tara said.

Betty, the nurse, had her hands on either side of Sarah's temples but was not touching her. Between Sarah's temples and Betty's hands was a stream of light, clearly visible, moving in the direction of Betty and coming from Sarah.

"So, it is Mary then," Ryan said.

"Yes, I would say it is," Carla answered.

"So this must be why she keeps her mother sedated—so she is able to retrieve her power. Maybe when Sarah sleeps, she regains the power that was drained from her," Tara speculated.

"Yeah, I don't know much about this. We are really quite new to our gifts as well," Carla added.

"I guess we are up now for a while. I'll put the kettle on," Tara said.

"Can I have coffee, if it's not too much trouble?" Brian asked.

"Me too, please," Ryan added.

"Sure, I'll put a pot of coffee on as well." Tara left the room.

They all watched as the nurse, Betty—aka Mary—left Sarah's room. Ryan and Carla sat on the couch, and Brian settled back in the recliner. No one spoke; they all kept their eyes on Sarah.

They noticed Sarah begin to stir a bit in her bed. She raised an arm to her head and winced while holding her forehead. She then rolled onto her right side, pulled the covers up to her ear, and went back to sleep.

"I'll go give Tara a hand with the tea and coffee," Carla said and left the room.

"Well, what do we do now?" Brian asked.

"We can't arrest her."

"I know. I am at a loss," Ryan agreed.

Tara and Carla returned with the tea trolley. On it were two coffees, two teas, milk, cream, and sugar. They all fixed their cups and sat back, discussing what to do next.

It was clear to them all that they couldn't arrest her. She wasn't linked to the kidnapping; the police believed they had the sole kidnapper. The mother, Sarah, was just an old woman who was forced into guarding the door. They didn't believe she had any real part in this at all but was at the mercy of her son. She uttered the death threats, so she knew what her son was up to, and that's why she was in the nursing home, with two guards.

"There must be a way to stop her, somehow," Tara said. "We have to get her away from her mother."

"I'll put a call in to the station and ask them to do a background check on Betty. Hey, wait—we don't know her last name," Brian said.

"That's right. We weren't told it, and we didn't think to ask," Ryan said in surprise.

"Okay, I'll call the nursing home and see if I can find out," Brian said.

He looked at his watch. It's a little early for that yet, he thought. His watch read 5:40 a.m.

"When the administration office opens at 8:00, I'll give them a call," Brian said aloud.

"Okay, I'm going to go have a shower and get ready for the day," Carla said.

"I'll do the same," Tara added.

The girls both left.

"When they get back downstairs, I'll go up and shower as well," Brian said.

The brothers sat there in silence, watching the dark room with the woman sleeping. Ryan broke the silence.

"I used to dread surveillance duty," he said, remembering a few cases he'd worked on before he started with Mr. Davies.

"Yeah, this part of the job sucks, eh?" Brian agreed. "However, this has its moments, as we all just witnessed." He laughed.

They both agreed there was nothing boring about being at

Blackwood Manor.

"So, off the topic at hand, bro, you didn't tell me you had a thing for Carla?"

Ryan just looked at him. "No, I guess I didn't," he said.

"Well, good for you, bro. They seem like really nice girls and very pretty to boot," Brian stated.

"Yes, that they are," Ryan agreed.

"I hear one of the girls coming down now, I think." Brian got up and looked out the door down the hall.

"Good morning, Mrs. Jason. I hope we didn't wake you?" Brian said.

"No, you didn't. I think the girls' showers did. The pipes are old in this house, and they tend to rattle when the water is running," Margaret said. "Is there more coffee?"

"Yes, I believe Tara made a pot."

Margaret left the room and returned shortly with a cup of coffee in hand. She doctored up her coffee with three sugars and a touch of cream.

"Three sugars? Forgive me for noticing. That is so sweet," Ryan commented.
Margaret laughed and said, "You need it when Tara makes it."

Ryan looked at his cup, still half full, and laughed. He did notice it was a bit strong.

"So, tell me, why are you all up so early?" she asked.

Brian pulled out his phone and said, "I caught it all on video. Here, have a look for yourself."

Brian handed her the phone. She watched it intently, and both

Ryan and Brian were watching her expressions. She was as shocked as they were; her eyes bulged wide open at the part where the nurse was pulling the light from Sarah. She shook her head when the video was over, then turned to look at the woman sleeping in the bed.

Then, back at Ryan, she said, "That is Mary."
"Yes, we gathered that. But what do you think she was doing?" he asked.

Margaret shook her head in disgust rather than confusion. She didn't answer his question but said, "Where on earth did she learn this magic?"

The boys didn't know what to say.

"The stuff she is using is what we call taboo magic, or dark magic. It's all about how you choose to use the gifts you are given, but this…" Margaret trailed off. "This is beyond. Everything she has done is just beyond…" Margaret trailed off again, raising a hand to her head.

"Are you okay?" Ryan asked.

"Yes, I am fine. It's every time I think of this stuff, the fog comes back and it's hard to put two words together about it. Then I get a headache," she said.

"Let me fetch you some Tylenol," Ryan said as he rose to his feet. He was back in a flash. Margaret thought he must have run.

"Here you go, two Tylenol and a glass of water." Ryan handed her the items.

"Thank you, Ryan," Margaret said appreciatively.

The girls' footsteps were heard coming down the stairs and then down the hall. Ryan noticed Margaret's demeanor change immediately; she was chipper, as if she didn't have a pounding headache.

"Good morning, girls," she said as she jumped to her feet to greet them with a morning hug.

"Good morning, Mom," they both said.

"We woke you up with having our showers, didn't we?" Carla asked.

"No worries, girls. I must have been ready to get up. After all, you don't see anyone else up yet," Margaret smiled.

Both Ryan and Brian just looked at each other, and their looks said it all. That's not what they were told five minutes ago.

"Did Brian show you the video?" Tara asked.

"Yes, interesting, isn't it?" Margaret said.

"Maybe when you wake up, you can explain this to us," Tara asked.

"Yes, after breakfast I will do my best," Margaret promised.

"But right now, I think I'm going to go take a shower and get ready for the day as well. I will see you soon," Margaret said as she headed out of the room.

"I'm going to take that cue and go to our cabin to have a shower. I want to look something up on the computer, and I'll get back as soon as I can. Or call me if I'm not back by breakfast," Brian said as he jokingly saluted them all and left.

"Want to bet he goes back to sleep?" Ryan chuckled.

"Well, we are wide awake and ready to take this bitch on," Carla said.

Ryan, shocked by her enthusiasm, said, "Really? And just how are you going to do that?" he asked. Carla just stood there, then looked at Tara. Tara shrugged her shoulders at her, then she looked back at Ryan. "Well, not sure yet, but I just want you to know I am ready." They all had a good laugh. "Tara and I are going to go get some more tea. Would you like some?" Carla asked. "Yes, please. Another cup of coffee would be good. Thanks." Tara grabbed the trolley, and they went to the kitchen.

"What is up with you all of a sudden?" Tara asked Carla. "I have an idea but didn't want to say anything just yet," she said. "Well, what is it then?" Carla filled the kettle, then emptied the trolley. "So, I was thinking that we could make a two-way portal jump through and get her," Carla said.

Tara thought about this for a minute, then shot out multiples of questions. "How do we catch her? What do we do with her when we catch her? How can you be sure she doesn't see us coming?"

Carla stopped loading the dishwasher with the used cups and turned to Tara. "Well, I haven't worked out the details yet," she said.

Tara grabbed new cups, refilled the milk and sugar on the tray, gathered some new spoons for everyone, then went to the fridge to put some fruit in a bowl for anyone who wanted it. She knew she did. Tara's stomach was getting hungry already.

"Let's meet upstairs and we'll talk about it after breakfast," Carla said.

They returned to the room with the tea and fruit. Margaret had rejoined them.

"Tea this time with some fruit to tide us over until breakfast," Tara said. They all helped themselves to some tea and fruit.

"So, Mom, what do you make of what Mary was doing to Sarah?" Carla asked.

"I don't know exactly, that kind of magic is... is..." she looked as if she was struggling to find the word.

"Black magic? Taboo?" Ryan answered.

"Yes, yes, of course, that's it," Margaret said, then started sipping her tea.

"So, what can we do about this, Mom?" Tara inquired.

"About what, dear?" she looked up from her tea with a blank look in her eyes.

"Nothing, it's okay, no big deal," Carla answered as Margaret picked up a magazine and started reading as if there was nothing going on at all. They all looked at each other in astonishment. Carla motioned for everyone to leave the room.

They convened in the hallway.

"What is going on with your mother? It's like she went for a shower and came back with no memory," Brian said.

"Yes, it is odd, and the sooner we get our hands on this Mary and keep her away from Sarah, the better Mom will be," Carla answered.

"All well and good, but it's not like we can arrest her for anything," Ryan shot back.

"And if we can't do that, how do you propose to stop her?" he continued.

Carla and Tara looked at each other, and Tara answered, "Carla has a plan, and as soon as we work out the details after breakfast, we will let you know."

Both Brian and Ryan shrugged their shoulders.

"Okay then, let us know when you can. For now, I am going back in there to continue my shift on watching Sarah," Ryan said and went back into the room.

Brian, Carla, and Tara were still in the hallway talking. Molly came down the stairs all chipper and asked, "Who's hungry?" Ryan could hear them talking in the hall, and Margaret was still reading her magazine, oblivious to what was going on around her. She looked up from her magazine and stared straight at the porthole. Sarah was up and was brushing her hair in the mirror, looking right at them. "Creepy," Ryan thought.

Margaret moved right in front of the porthole to see Sarah. "Guys, you might want to come back in here," Ryan called.

They all came in to find Margaret standing, staring at the reflection of Sarah staring back at them. Sarah put the brush down and leaned closer to the mirror. "I know you're watching, and if she catches you..." Sarah made a gesture with her finger across her throat, as if to say she will slice your throat. Then she walked back to her chair by the window.

Margaret sat down on the chair again, looked at them all, and said, "Strange movie you're watching," as she picked through the magazine rack for another magazine to read.

"Wow, it seems to be getting worse. I think I will go notify Dad about this." Tara went upstairs.

"Okay, maybe we should get that plan in order sooner rather than later. Things don't seem really good right now," Brian said.

"Yes, but we will just be interrupted before breakfast, so it's still better to wait until after. Besides, there is nothing we can do before she comes on the night shift. We don't know where she lives," Ryan said.

"Yes, she must live somewhere. Maybe we can find her in the directory," Brian suggested.

"All we know is she is going under the alias of Betty. We have no idea what she is using for a last name," Ryan interjected.

They all nodded. "Okay, after breakfast, do whatever you have to do to get a plan of action," Ryan agreed.

From upstairs, they could hear Tara calling out. They all took off up the stairs to Jason's room. He was lying in his bed, still asleep—at least that's what it looked like. James came flying in when he heard Tara call out as well.

"What's going on in here?" he asked.

"He's not waking up, I've tried to wake him and he won't wake up," Tara was crying and panicked. Carla came over to her and pulled her away, hugging her tight to calm her. Ryan went right away to check his vitals.

"He's breathing and his pulse is good," he said. "He should be waking up." Ryan tried to wake him again by giving him a little shake and calling his name, but without any success.

"Why is he not waking up?" James said.

"Well, we have a lot to catch you up on that has happened since you went to bed," Ryan said. Brian and him escorted him downstairs to the kitchen where they filled him and Molly in on all that has transpired.

"Where's Margaret?" James asked.

"She's in the den, oblivious to everything," Ryan said. Just then, Margaret walked around the corner.

"Is that breakfast I smell, Molly?" She asked as she entered the kitchen. "You better wake the girls and let them know," she said as she looked at Ryan. James knew then that they were not exaggerating the circumstances of Margaret.

"Right away," Ryan said as he left the kitchen to tell the girls.

"If you'll excuse me while I go wash up for breakfast," Brian excused himself. He met up with Ryan in Tara's room.

"Okay, this is just a bit much," Brian said to Ryan.

"Yes, I agree, this is strange," Ryan replied.

Tara was still upset, and Carla was cradling her until she calmed down.

"Dad's going to be okay, but we need to figure something out to fix this situation. It seems Mary has gotten stronger since she took that energy from Sarah. I feel she has put Dad in a sleep to keep him out of the way. I fear she is getting closer to striking, and we have to get to her before she gets to us. She will lose that power if we can keep her away from Sarah," Carla stated.

"Tara, I need your help. You have to pull it together. I can't do this without you." Tara sat up and wiped her eyes on her arm.

"You're right, it was just so scary," she said through sobs.

"I know, and it is, but it's up to us, you and me. We can do this," Carla assured her as she took Tara's face in her hands to look her straight in the eyes. Tara nodded and went to wipe her face with a cloth in the bathroom.

"There, as good as new," she said as she came back out. Just in time to hear Molly call to them from the kitchen that breakfast was ready. Ryan and Brian caught the girls up about their mother so they wouldn't be shocked.

"Let's not say anything to Mom about this over breakfast," Carla said. "Well, at least if we can help it," she continued.

They sat down at the table, not one person was talking. Margaret seemed to be focused on getting her food on her plate and didn't even notice that her husband was missing. Everyone was so quiet it was creepy.

"It looks like a very nice day outside so far," Molly said, hoping to break the silence.

"Yes, it looks really promising indeed," James said.

Their efforts seemed to fall to the ground. Not one person commented or picked up on their efforts. Carla spoke to Tara through telepathy.

"This is so weird, how does Mom not know where Dad is?" Carla asked.

"Tara, maybe she does know. Maybe she was instructed to put that spell on him." Carla's head snapped around to look at Tara.

Everyone seemed to notice Carla's swift head snap. Margaret looked up from her plate at Carla. She looked angry. Carla actually became frightened that she could hear what she said to Tara.

"What did Tara do?" Margaret asked Carla.

"Do? Do… oh yeah, she kicked me for no reason," Carla said. She didn't know what to say; she couldn't believe that came out of her mouth. She felt as if she was a kid again. Margaret gave Tara a dirty look and then went back to her food.

"That was weird," Tara thought to Carla. "But I think you're right, she probably put the spell on Dad. Oh boy, this is screwed up."

Carla said, "Hurry, finish your meal and let's get this going. I can't live with Mom like this." Carla was shoveling her food in her mouth as fast as possible.

Carla and Tara finished their meal and took their plates to the sink.

"If you would excuse us, we have some work to do, you know, emails and stuff we've neglected to do," Carla said.

Without looking up from her plate, Margaret said, "No problem, you're excused."

Carla looked at the boys and made an 'I will call you' gesture. They both nodded, and the girls left to go upstairs.

They were going straight to the attic when Carla stopped and opened her door and then closed it. Then opened Tara's door and closed it. Tara looked at her funny, then Carla motioned her hands to be silent and keep going. Once inside the attic, Carla quietly opened and closed the door. She locked it behind her.

"I wanted Mom to think we went to our rooms."

Tara nodded and whispered, "Okay, so what are we looking for?"

"I don't know exactly, but we have to find something to trap this woman," Carla said, sitting down on a crate.

"I do," Tara said as she went straight for the Grimoire. She flipped pages frantically, then stopped. "This is it. Right here, this is it."

Carla excitedly joined her. Tara read, "It says here to place this sigil on the floor, then enchant it with rhyme. Then once they are caught, blow this powder into the circle at them. This will freeze them so they can't move. Once that is done, we can bind her up so she can't get away."

Evil witch, vengeful soul

We trap you now from your goal

Through our will and our power

This is your last cruel hour

So Mote it Be

Tara took a picture with her phone of the spell. "It says here to do this with chalk, but wouldn't she be able to see that?" Carla asked.

"Not if we do it in lemon juice, remember our invisible writing as kids?" Tara declared.

"Okay, now we just have to go there and place it on the floor. How do we do that without Sarah noticing?" Carla asked.

"Gees, Carla, do I have to think of everything?" Tara said jokingly. "One of us will spill something on her, and when the nurse comes in to change her, she will shut the curtain and no one will see this being written. Then we will turn her alarm on that she has sitting on the dresser. That will make enough noise to mask your incantation for the sigil. Then we will apologize for the chaos and pretend to leave, slip into the closet by the door to her room, and wait."

"Sounds good, I just hope it works as well as it sounds," Carla answered. "Okay, message the guys and we will be on our way. We will need a rope to tie her with and we will have to make the powder as well. What are the ingredients?" Carla asked.

"It says to grind these ingredients to a powder, then mix with ashes and dirt," Tara said.

- Ashes
- Graveyard dirt or patchouli as a substitute
- Black pepper
- Sage
- Basil
- Yarrow

""Okay, well at least we can get all these ingredients without a problem," Carla said.

"Graveyard dirt collecting is illegal," Tara reminded.

"How you even know this piece of information is beyond me. However, if it is dirt from the outside part of the graveyard, it is technically not grave dirt," Carla said.

"Really?! I think patchouli will work just fine, otherwise it would not be in Grandma's grimoire," Tara said.

"Fine," Carla huffed.

Both Carla and Tara went downstairs to the kitchen. Molly was outside with James, sitting and having tea.

"Where's Mom?" Carla asked.

"I don't know, I'll check the den," Molly said.

Tara went into the den and found the guys sitting there watching the portal like it was an intriguing movie.

"Something interesting is going on in there?" Tara asked.

"Yeah, have a look," Ryan said.

Tara looked at the porthole. Sarah was dancing as if she was dancing with someone. She was in such a pose that you would have sworn there was someone there.

"She's been dancing with nobody for about ten minutes now," Brian said.

"I agree, that's odd, but have either of you seen Mom?" Tara asked.

"No, actually I thought she was still in the kitchen," Ryan said.

"Well, we just have to put together some herbs and we will be ready to go. But I have to find Mom and make sure everything here is okay before we leave," Tara said.

She met up with Carla in the kitchen, where she was gathering all the herbs.

"We are going to need some ashes from the fire pit. I will go collect them and ask Molly where Mom is," Tara said.

Tara walked over to the picnic table where Molly and James were sitting.

"Well, are you done with all your work?" Molly asked.

"Yes, actually all done. Have you seen Mom?" Tara replied.

"She is down at the dock sun tanning," Molly said. She turned to look and realized she was gone. "Oh dear, she was there a minute ago."

James got up right away and started looking around. He looked in the boat shed, then came out and shook his head to notify the girls that she was nowhere around.

"Not good at all, not in her state," Molly answered with concern.

They all split up to look for her outside. Tara went back in the house and went right upstairs to her mom and dad's room. Sure enough, she was lying on the bed with Dad fast asleep. Tara left the room and ran downstairs to tell Molly and James.

"You can't let her out of your sight for anything while we are gone," Tara said.

"Hopefully by tonight this will all be over," she continued.

"Okay, we will do our best," James said.

"I will have Ryan check in with you often to make sure everything is okay. If not, one of them can come and help," Tara said.

James agreed, and Tara went back into the house. Carla was just finishing blending the herbs, including the patchouli from the small apothecary in the pantry.

"Okay, all set. You?" Carla asked.

Tara held up the bag of ash, then poured it into Carla's bag of herbs, grabbed the boys, and left.

They were in the car pulling out of the driveway when Ryan asked, "What do we do with her once we have her tied up?"

Tara thought for a moment and then replied, "Yeah, I guess we will have to create a porthole that we can slip through and take her somewhere."

Carla jumped in, "The abandoned house on the far side of the lake is a great spot."

Tara nodded. "Excellent idea. If we keep her away from Sarah long enough, the power essence will wear off, and she will lose her abilities. She must not have done the ritual and needed her mother's essence to enhance her magic that she knew she had."

Tara had a great concern on her face. "What is it, Tara?" Ryan noticed the change in her expression.

"Well, I just thought we are both gifted like Sarah, so we will have to keep our distance from her so she cannot use the power on us," Tara explained.

Carla nodded. "Not to worry. Us guys will take care of her while you two keep your distance," Ryan said.

"Okay, but we are going to have to risk it initially," Tara said. "We will have no choice."

Ryan replied, "I believe I have duct tape in my toolbox in the trunk. She sucks the power out of you, correct? Well, then bind her from behind and slap some duct tape across her mouth so she can't scream or suck out your energy."

"Yes, yes, excellent idea, good thinking," the girls said in unison.

"Once we have her and the porthole open, we will call you in, then we can all go through," Carla said.

Ryan then realized the Officer guarding Sarah's door would be there and see it. "What about the guard?" he asked.

Carla had a sheepish grin on her face, clearly proud of herself, and said, "I took the liberty of making a powder the other day that will stun someone in their tracks as if they were asleep but look awake. I brought it with me just in case Mary gave us a hard time, but instead, you take it and when we call you in, you can blow it in the guard's face and when he awakes, he won't know what took place."

Carla was so proud of herself, but Tara looked at her with grave concern. "Carla? When did you make this?" Tara asked.

Carla, feeling deflated, answered, "The other day, why? Ok, ok, I will tell you the truth: I made it in case I needed to use it on Mom. She just can't be trusted."

Tara started shaking her head. "Oh, Carla, we know Mom can read our thoughts, and I bet she is still under Mary's control. She found the powder you made and used it on Dad."

Carla quickly grabbed the bottle she kept it in and looked at it. Tara was right. A lot had been used because it was full to the rim and now it was almost empty.

"She gave it to Ryan," and said, "I can't guarantee this is enough."

"Well, let's hope," he replied.

"Let's look at the bright side, now we know what's wrong with your dad," Ryan continued.

Chapter 55

Noon Strike

They reached the facility. Ryan told Brian where the abandoned house was and asked him to drive the car there. It would take him about an hour to get there. Ryan was hoping this was all done well before an hour was up. The girls had all they needed tucked inside their sweaters as they walked into the reception to sign in. The three walked up to see Sarah. Ryan greeted the guard. Tara and Carla said hi and continued into the room while Ryan stood talking to the guard. Weird how Sarah was still dancing, they both thought. Carla went right over to Sarah and broke up the dancing. She could clearly see the woman was exhausted and guided her back to her bed while pulling the curtain closed so she wouldn't notice Tara drawing on the floor.

"Can you put some music on?" Sarah motioned for the radio. Carla immediately turned on the radio sitting on her bedside table. It was tuned into a station that played all the oldies from Sarah's era. Sarah lay back in her bed and started to hum the tune that was playing. Carla peeked around the curtain at Tara, and Tara nodded to say all done. She told Carla mentally that she had done the incantation when Carla put the radio on.

"Okay, let's get into the closet," Carla said back.

Sarah was content at this point, so the two girls slipped into the closet. Tara checked her watch. It was almost noon, and Mary would be coming on shift any minute. Her first stop was always Sarah's room. Tara texted Ryan, which was his cue to go get a coffee and wait around the corner out of sight from Mary.

"Hey, I'm just going to get a coffee. Would you like one?" he asked the guard.

"Yes, please. Two creams, no sugar."

Ryan nodded and left. He grabbed a coffee for the guard and

waited until he saw Mary go into Sarah's room. The wait seemed like forever as he checked his watch. Everything was going better than planned, and this made him extremely nervous. Mary came around the corner, nodded to the guard, and went into Sarah's room. Ryan then quickly gave him the coffee, and as the guard bent his head down to take a sip, Ryan pulled the small bottle out of his pocket, poured the contents into his hand, and waited. Ryan's phone went off as he looked at the phone with the other hand to read the text.

"Done," was what they said.

He blew it into the guard's face, and within seconds, he was just staring ahead like a zombie. Ryan removed the coffee cup from his hand and placed it on the floor. He pushed the guard's eyelids closed to make it look as if he had nodded off. Then he ran into the room. At this point, he saw Mary give him a dirty look from on the floor. Tara had created the porthole, so Ryan grabbed Mary from behind and threw her through, still holding her ropes, with him right behind her. Carla and Tara followed, and Carla turned and closed the porthole right away.

"We made it," Carla said.

"Yes, we did, and a lot easier than we thought it would work," Ryan said. He sat Mary in an old chair that was left behind and tied her to it with the excess rope.

"Do the sigil and incantation again, and I'll push her into it, chair and all. I don't want to take any chances of her being able to squirm her way out," Ryan said.

Tara grabbed the herbs and lemon juice. She drew the sigil, then whispered the incantation. Ryan then pushed Mary, chair and all, into the center. She was squirming in fear as if it was going to hurt her, but once inside the circle, she stopped moving. You could still see the fear in her eyes from over the duct tape.

"Now what? How long is this going to take?" Ryan asked. "I'm not sure, but there is one way to tell, and that's by finding out how Mom is acting," Carla said.

Ryan grabbed his phone and called the house. Molly picked it up. "Hello?" she answered.

"Hey Molly, it's Ryan. How is everything over there?" he asked. Ryan could hear in the background someone banging pots and pans around, and it even sounded like dishes breaking.

"Well, not great at the moment," Molly replied. "Apparently, she didn't like the way I was washing dishes, so she took over and is breaking all the dishes and basically having a temper tantrum. I've tried to stop her, but she just growls at me." Molly said. "It's like she's in her own world and oblivious to everything around her. So, I just left her to destroy the kitchen." Molly continued.

"Where's James?" Ryan asked right away, concerned for Molly's safety.

"He's here with me, keeping an eye on both of us."
"Okay, well, it went well so far, so I'll check in again soon," Ryan said.

They waited around, not talking to each other, just waiting. Tara was watching Mary, and she could tell that she was so angry. She couldn't believe the hate in her eyes. With her mind, she asked Carla,

"Why does she hate us so much? What is the point of it all?"

Carla just shook her head.

Shortly, they heard a car approach. Ryan jumped from his seat to go look.

"It's Brian, he made it." Ryan opened the door to let him in.

"That's a nice drive," he said. "Very secluded."

Brian looked at Mary in the center of the room.

"Wow, I've seen chicks look strung out before, but this tops them all," he said.

"So now what?" he asked.

"We wait for the power to wear off," Ryan answered. "Which should be soon by our guess; it doesn't last long." He hoped. Ryan grabbed his phone to call the house. James answered this time.

"How's it going now, James? Any change?" Ryan asked.

"Yes, now she is sitting on the floor crying, and Molly is consoling her. She is so upset at what she did to the kitchen," James said. "Is this a good sign things are working?" he asked. In the background, he could hear Margaret sobbing, and then he heard someone in the background ask, "What the hell happened to the kitchen?"

Ryan knew right away it was the girls' dad, and he was awake. Ryan gave a thumbs up to the girls, and they both smiled. "Okay, James, I'll let you go and check in with you later?"

"Still be careful," Ryan added.

"Okay, take the duct tape off her mouth," Ryan asked Brian. The girls right away scrambled to the other side of the room where Mary couldn't see them.

"So what do we do with you now, Mary?" Ryan asked, not expecting a reply, and was shocked when one came.

Mary's head flew back, her eyes rolled in her head, but her mouth moved with the sound of another woman's voice. It was crackly, like an old lady's voice.

"Hahahaha, you fools. You have the wrong person. Mary was just my puppet. I am too old to be doing all the things myself, so who better than my own daughter?" The voice cackled with laughter.

Ryan spoke, choosing his words wisely. "So why was she inhaling your essence after you went to sleep?"

"Because she was told to do this. I promised her power, so I gave it to her. This way, I was able to control what she did and thought.

She then controlled Margaret, but it's the husband that was tougher."

She cackled again. "You were watching me, and I was watching you." And continued to cackle.

"So, if we don't release Mary, who will do your bidding for you now?" Ryan asked.

"Don't you worry your handsome head about that. I have another child that loves his mommy more than anything. He is on his way to you right now. You girls should just hand over your powers to me and my children. It's obvious you do not have a clue on how to use them," Sarah said. "Awe, is that a car I hear pulling into the driveway?" Sure enough, Brian looked, and it was a grey car. A man stepped out of the driver's side and a woman on the passenger side.

"Two people? That is not playing fair, Sarah?"

"Hahaha, fair? Who said anything about being fair?"

"Did you know my son?" she asked.

Ryan studied the figure as it got closer, then realized in horror. "Oh boy, it's the guard at the hospital and the nurse at the desk?"

Sarah started to cackle harder than before, Mary's body bouncing all over from the laughter. Ryan grabbed the duct tape and wrapped it around her mouth tight.

"Carla, create a porthole. We have to get out of here."

Carla and Tara created one and then pushed Mary through. As soon as they all got to the other side, the girls closed it, and Carla took her scarf and wrapped it around Mary's eyes. Winking at everyone, she said, "We'll hang out here in the ice cream shop that's closed for the season now."

They all caught on and nodded. They didn't want Mary to be able to show Sarah where they were. She wanted her to think they were at the ice cream shop, but in reality, they were in the attic of the house. Carla said, winking at the rest of them, "Guess it's a good thing we arrived. It sounds like the generator blew. We wouldn't want what they left behind going bad now, would we?"

They all understood and watched Carla leave the room. She came back with a fan and said, "I fixed it, and it should be kicking on any minute now."

Mary was squirming in her seat, and Carla knew what to do. She created the sigil and incantation again and pushed the chair over it. "That's it, I have a great idea," Tara said. She went over to the grimoire and started looking for the spell. She found it and started to write it down. In her mind, she told Carla she needed a few supplies and handed her the list. Carla quietly snuck out of the attic to gather the supplies. She then told the boys via text message what the plan was and to wait for their signal.

Carla came back with the supplies, and they immediately went to work on combining herbs, salt, and ashes from the fire pit. The guys just stood and watched them work. When they were done, Carla opened a portal to see where the guard and nurse were.

"They were inside the house looking around."

"Quickly," Tara said, then opened another porthole on the outside of it for them to walk through. They left it open, then quickly and quietly chanted as they spread the mixture they made around the house.

"With these herbs, I do seal the windows and doors on this property. No one leaves this wooden house unless one is just a mouse. By the powers of the earth and sea, I seal you in, so mote it be."

They finished the incantation and the ring around the house just in time, then they both jumped through the porthole, closing it behind them. Out of breath, they were panting.

"Okay, Ryan, call the police and tell them that two people have a hostage tied up. You were hiking and saw this and called them right away, then hang up without giving them your name."

Ryan did just that. When he hung up, Carla and Tara opened a porthole when the guard and nurse were busy trying the windows in the bedrooms. They couldn't even smash the glass. When the moment was right, they shoved Mary through, then closed it again, leaving a little one to see with.

Soon, the police arrived and knocked on the door. Carla had put the rest of the herbs and salt into an ashtray, waiting for the police to arrive. At that moment, she took a match to the remnants and lit them on fire. This released the curse so the Officers could get in.

The four of them sat and watched as the police cuffed them all and took them away. Mary was released and placed into a police car as well.

Carla said, "It was the only way, and now we have to do something with Sarah. She can't be allowed to control them anymore."

"Okay, I know just the thing." She grabbed her little baggy, and they created a porthole to the nursing home. Once inside the room, Sarah looked panicked; she didn't understand what was happening. Carla created the sigil in marker on the woman's behind, chanted the incantation, and before you knew it, Sarah was catatonic.

"Well, we will have to keep checking in on her from time to time to make sure it didn't wear off, so I think I will take her hair as well." Carla cut a big strand of hair from Sarah's head, placed it in a baggy, and they all left. There were no worries about them—just Mary to deal with next.

After they all got back, they went into the den, and there they opened a window to see Mary. The Officers had taken her to a hospital to have her checked over. As they watched, they noticed that she was catatonic as well. Carla said, "That's not right. As soon as she left, the sigil spell should have broken."

"She is playing them. She is just pretending so that she doesn't have to answer any questions. We will have to keep an eye on her and keep a close watch. As soon as things change, we are going to have to do something about her as well."

Carla agreed, then the girls created a portal back at the cabin on the outside. This time, they were looking for Brian's car. It was tagged, and chains and locks were put on the tires.

"Oh, that's just great. It's all just a matter of time before they come knocking, looking for answers," Ryan said. Ryan started to panic and said he was just going to go to the station and tell them his car was stolen or something; he couldn't think straight.

Tara stopped him. "Yes, this seems like it's going to blow up in our face now too. Man, loose ends, and it's not like we can tell the police the truth. Who's going to believe us when our story is full of magic and supernatural portholes and such?"

"I don't know," Carla said, "but maybe Mom and Grandma will know what to do." Carla said, grabbing Tara's hand and pulling her along. "Come on, let's all go downstairs and let them know we are home," Carla said.

Margaret and Molly were busy tidying up the kitchen along with James and their dad. Tara noticed the energies and was so happy they felt balanced again. No chaos in the air was a nice breather after everything they had gone through. Carla entered the kitchen and said, "Hi, Mom." Molly right away dropped what she was doing and ran to hug the girls.

"I am so glad you girls are okay."

"How are things here?" Ryan asked. James answered and said, "Oh, it's all good here now. Margaret seems to be back to herself, and Dad here is wide awake and full of energy. I guess he needed that little nap." James nudged him. They all laughed, and it was nice to laugh.

"Mom, how are you?" Tara asked.

"I feel like I have been in a very dense fog and trapped there forever, but I'm so glad to be thinking clearly again."

Carla jumped in and said, "I have heard you say that before, and you actually weren't. Are you sure you're okay?"

"Now trust me, girls, I'm fine."

Everyone pitched in to help straighten up the kitchen. After it was all done, Molly sat down and said, "I am not cooking!" Everyone turned and looked at her in shock.

"What's everyone looking at me for?" Molly asked.

"I am exhausted," she continued. They all laughed.

Brian piped up and said, "Not a problem, what do you have in the freezer?"

James replied, "We just bought a whole cow. So, take your pick."

"Well then, you leave dinner up to Ryan and me," Brian said as he started shooing everyone out of the kitchen.

Brian then went down to the freezer and pulled out some steaks. Ryan was upstairs rooting through the fridge for potatoes. Everyone went to the living room to sit and relax. When Carla said, "Mom, can we borrow you for a minute?" Margaret agreed and followed the girls upstairs to the attic.

Carla and Tara filled Margaret in on what happened and who was involved. Margaret just shook her head; she couldn't believe what she was hearing. Tara continued to explain, "Well, we don't know what to do now. We have Sarah in a catatonic state, we have two people being locked away, we don't even know if they understand why they're locked away, then we have Mary who is pretending to be catatonic. We know she's not, and we just don't know what to do. We can't go to the police, and Brian's car was left at the abandoned house. What should we do?"

Margaret sat and thought for a moment, and she said, "You know, I do believe this is something for your grandmother. Maybe she can help."

So the girls prepared the altar, and they all sat together and called in Grandma. After a short while, the candle started to flicker, and right before their eyes, Grandma stood. She reached her arms out right away, trying to touch her daughter, Margaret.

"I was so, so worried about you. I tried so hard to help the girls."

"I know, Mom," Margaret said. "I am okay. I'll be just fine, but we need your help, Mom. We need to ask you a question."

"I know," she says from the other realm. "I know what has happened. You girls did a good job. You girls did probably exactly what I would've done. However, I know there's loose ends and you don't know what to do."

"That's right, Grandma," Carla said. "We didn't think it all through. We're sorry."

"Oh, my goodness, don't say you're sorry for magic. Magic is there to guide us. It's there to help us. It's there to protect us. We can fix this now. Go to my grimoire and turn to page 328," Grandma said.

Tara raced over to the grimoire and looked at page 328, a spell of reversal.

"But Grandma, we don't want to reverse what we've done," Tara said.

"No, no, no, keep reading."

"Oh, a reversal of memory, but who are we supposed to put this memory on? The police and everybody involved?" Tara asked.

"No, just go and put it on the car. Then take the same powder and go to the police station. Rub it on your hands. Shake your hands with the police Officer that is going to help you. Tell the police Officer your car was stolen. He'll fix it for you so that you can get it out of the chains, and then you can drive away. By the time you drive away, they will have forgotten, and it will be erased in the records that the car even existed at that point," Grandma said.

Tara jumped up from her knees, jumping for joy. "Wow, I just knew it, Grandma! You're amazing, you are so amazing!" Grandma smiled. Margaret was so elated to see her mom that she had tears rolling down her cheeks. Grandma looked at her and the girls and said, "I am always here, and now that you know how to reach me, you can call upon me at any time. But I can never stay for long, so good luck, girls. I'll be watching." And Grandma disappeared, and the candle went out.

Tara brought the grimoire right over to the altar, and they all started reading. They prepared the potion of herbs, some oils, and the salts. Once it was all ready, they opened a porthole that opened right beside the car. They rubbed the potion liberally all over the car. Once that was done, they got in the car and drove back right away.

As soon as they got back, they told Ryan what happened. Ryan felt a great sense of relief, then said, "OK, first we eat dinner. You girls have been gone for far too long, and dinner was ready half an hour ago, so let's eat." Everybody pitched in, getting plates, cutlery, condiments, and napkins to put on the table. They couldn't wait; they were starving. They missed lunch and missed out on a lot of food today, but it had been a very busy day.

They're all sitting down, and the boys bring in steak, filet mignon, fried mushrooms and onions, baked potatoes, and tomatoes sliced up on a dish. They couldn't wait to dig in. Each one of them just sat there and ate and ate and ate, enjoying their food so much that it was silent for the first five minutes of their meals.

"OK," Ryan says, "So tell me again, what am I to do?"

"Well, let me tell you. We spoke with Grandma, who showed us exactly what you are supposed to do. You have to take this stuff that we have, and you have to rub it on your hand. Then you shake hands with the Officer you're talking to about getting the chains removed on your car, that it was stolen. They must've taken it out of the parking lot at the nursing home, and you just didn't report it because you were worried about us or something to that effect. It doesn't matter what you say to the police Officer, you're going to shake his hand, and this will seal the spell. He will forget the instructions on how to remove it, and then once you've removed the chains, you can return the chains. That car will be erased from their memory and the records."

Ryan was amazed. His eyes were as wide as anything. "Are you serious? Wow, this is awesome. OK, I never believed in magic. I've always thought that was just fairy tales and hocus-pocus Disney stuff, but I am actually amazed at how much you girls could actually do. By the way, that grimoire had better be under a protection spell. You do not want it to get into the wrong hands," Ryan stated.

Both Carla and Tara snapped their necks around and looked at each other straight in the eyes with this uh-oh look on their faces. They excused themselves from the table, ran upstairs to the attic, and immediately put it under a protection spell. Ryan was right, Carla thought; this could not land in anybody's hands. They immediately came back and sat down at the table again.

Molly said, "Well, when Ryan and Brian said that they were going to cook dinner, I thought it would be nice to have a good dessert after their marvelous dinner, so I took this special dessert I made for a special occasion, and today is that day."

Molly excused herself, went downstairs, and came back upstairs with a homemade tiramisu cake. Tara's mouth started to water. "We will have dessert and tea when Ryan comes back from clearing up the car mess. Then we can all relax a bit," Molly insisted.

"You're absolutely right." Carla gave him the potion and a kiss, then Ryan grabbed his keys, and Brian followed him out. "We will make it as quick as possible so we can all have that delicious cake," Ryan promised.

Once at the police station, everything went smoothly. The Officer handed him the keys for the lock. Ryan and Brian were driving when Ryan said, "Brian? I don't know if you thought of this or not, but what about Mr. Davies?"

Brian replied, "Yes, I did think of that and was going to talk to you later when we got back to the cabin for the night. I am concerned after seeing everything that has happened and how and what is actually possible, is Mr. Davies really Mr. Davies? Or did he end up being a victim of Mary's?"

"Yes, we need these answers and soon," Ryan agreed. "Let's work on this without the girls. Let's let them enjoy this bit of bliss they are feeling."

Ryan said. They arrived at the cabin and went right to work with taking the chains off the car. Brian threw them in the trunk.

"OK, I will meet you back at the house," Brian said to Ryan.
They pulled into the driveway at 8:00 pm, one right behind the other, then raced inside as not to keep everybody waiting to have dessert any longer.

Molly had everything ready and had put the kettle on when she heard the cars pull up. They all had a big piece and a cup of tea, then spent the rest of the evening around the fire outside, having tea, beer, chips, and a few laughs.

The next morning, Ryan awoke with the sun peeking through the shutters. He looked at his watch; it read 6:59. He got up and dressed, then went to the kitchen to put the coffee on. He noticed it was already on and brewed. Ryan poured himself a cup and went into the living room where he found Brian on the computer.

"Good morning, sleepyhead," Brian joked.

"Good morning," Ryan replied. "What are you doing?" and when did you get up?" Ryan asked.

"I have been up for some time now. I had trouble sleeping, thinking about Mr. Davies. After we went to bed, I got up and emailed him, hoping for a reply that all is fine," Brian said.

"And what? Did you get a reply?" Ryan asked curiously.

"Yes, I did get a reply but not the one I was looking for. It says that I must have the wrong email address, that there is no one here by that name, and this is a residence, not a company," Brian explained.

"I googled the company, and there is nothing coming up for that company," Brian said, then continued, "I knew it was early, so I knew if I called the company number that we have, I would get a recording stating the name. No such luck, it was a business alright, but it's a bank, not a lawyer's office."

"Wow, it's like the company and the person I worked for never existed," Ryan pondered.

"I think we are going to have to ask Margaret and Jason about this. Didn't you say he was a long-time family friend and he was the one who notified the girls, Molly and James, about their parents being missing and setting them up properly here?" Brian asked.

"Yes, that's right. We will have to mention it after breakfast. In the meantime, let's see if we can find an address on this Mr. Davies," Ryan suggested.

"Why don't we get the girls to see if they can peek in on him if they can find him first? If that doesn't work, I will call in a favor at the station," Brian suggested.

"Good idea," Ryan agreed. "All this thinking first thing in the morning has made me hungry. Let's go to the house and get some breakfast." They grabbed their coats and left. The autumn air had started to have a chill in it now, especially in the mornings.

They got to the house to find Molly to be the only one awake. Molly poured them a cup of coffee and herself one, then joined them at the kitchen table. "Sleep well?" she asked.

"Yes, we did. How about you? I notice you didn't sleep in like the rest of them," Ryan asked.

"I never sleep in. I have always been an early bird," Molly smiled. "What can I get you for breakfast?" she asked, then gave them a list of options. "There's bacon and eggs, toast and home fries, which are prepared already, but if you don't want that, I can make you toasted English muffins or bagels." Both Ryan and Brian opted for the big breakfast. Molly grabbed two plates and filled them for them.

They were just finishing up when Margaret, James, and Jason came in. "Good morning," Margaret stated.

Molly got them all a cup of coffee and Margaret a tea. "You boys are up early?" Margaret queried.

"Yes, it promises to be a good day today," was all Brian said.

"Chilly outside?" Margaret asked. They both nodded.

"Okay then, I will have my tea right here," she said with a smile. James and Jason joined at the table with their coffees and a plate full of food.

"By the way, Margaret, Ryan and I would like to talk to you and Jason when you've had time to wake up a bit," Ryan asked. "If that's okay?"

"Yes, absolutely!" Margaret said. Jason had a mouth full, so he just nodded.

"Is there something wrong?" she couldn't help asking.

"Not wrong per se, just a loose end," Ryan answered.

"Molly gasped. "No, don't worry, I don't believe we are in any danger from this, but Brian and I would like to be absolutely sure," Ryan tried to calm the room.

"Do the girls know?" Jason asked as he finished up his breakfast and wiped his mouth with his napkin.

"No, we haven't said anything at all. You're the first we wanted to speak with," Ryan explained.

"Molly, can you fill up my coffee, please?" Jason asked her. Molly went right for the pot, then filled his cup and placed it back on the heater.

"Is this a private matter for just my wife and I, or can we speak openly?" Jason asked.

"No, no, not private. It's just you both would have the best knowledge of the matter," Brian explained.

"Okay then, let's have it. What's on your mind?" Jason prompted.

"Well, the loose end is Mr. Davies. We have not heard from him. The number you call for his office is not a lawyer's office anymore. His email address apparently is a private residence with no one by that name. So we were wondering your history with this Mr. Davies," Ryan told them.

Margaret thought about it for a minute and then said, "Well, when we got our first book deal, we wanted to hire a lawyer to protect us from royalty problems and legal stuff that could come up. We were given his name by our publisher who took on the book. We would have to meet him every time a book got published for paperwork pertaining to that book, so he said, and we didn't question him because we were green and put our full trust in him, knowing what he was talking about," Margaret stated.

"Well, come to think of it now, in hindsight, he did overstay a lot of his welcome many times, having dinner at our place or popping in and bringing wine and stuff. He just became close to us, not exactly sure how it happened, and he was the one who told us about how to look out for the girls' future, and we just went along with what he said. You know, now I get the feeling we were being set up," Jason said with great concern on his face as he reached out and grabbed Margaret's hand.

"Ryan, I am inclined to think that Jason is right. It wasn't long after you signed the will and deeds to this place before you went missing, is it?" Brian asked.

"Well, yes and no. We did a will with him when they were about 14, and then we did the little things in between, but not long after we signed the last paperwork about our money and stuff, we were kidnapped," Margaret said.

"Just as I thought, and from what I have heard here, these people, Sarah and Mary, have been planning this for many years, so they have all the patience in the world to put something like this in motion," Brian said. "Well, if there is anything else you can think of, let us know, but in the meantime, we will try and get to the bottom of this."

"Just one last thing, how come you never came back here after your mother died?" Ryan asked.

Margaret sat and pondered for a moment before answering as she looked around the kitchen. "To be honest, it just didn't feel welcoming anymore," she said sadly. "Not like it used to. We tried to come up a couple of times, and it just didn't feel right. We would plan on staying for a weekend, but we would always pack up and leave after one night here," she said. Jason looked at her and nodded his head in agreement.

"And now, how does it feel?" Brian asked.

"It feels like home again," Margaret said with a smile. But what she wasn't saying was how she felt a dark presence over the house. It was unsettling to her because she didn't know what it was, and she noticed it the first time she came back after the passing of her mother, Elsa. She remembered how comfortable, warm, and welcoming it always was. In the beginning, she thought it was due to the absence of her mother, but it never changed, and even though the whole family is here, it still feels off. She didn't want to worry anyone right now, but knew she would get to the bottom of it soon, and knowing the girls were really coming along with their power, she knew she would have lots of help. But for now, she will keep it to herself.

"Okay, well, Ryan and I are headed out today to do some digging. We will be back later this evening," Molly piped up. "Dinner is at six, and it's a full-course Roast Beef dinner." Ryan and Brian laughed. "Okay, we will be home for dinner."

When the boys left, Margaret went to wake the girls. Both she and Jason agreed they needed to know about this. After breakfast, the girls said they were going to check on Mary and the rest to make sure all was the same. Margaret stopped them and asked them to sit for a minute. She and Jason told them about their conversations with Ryan and Brian.

"I wondered why we didn't hear anything more on Mr. Davies, and to be quite honest, I think we were all a little preoccupied," Carla said.

"Hey, we haven't looked in on him in a while. Why don't we see if we can find him?" Tara asked. Margaret agreed.

"I just love watching you girls do Grandma's magic. You were born with these gifts, and Grandma knew it."

Tara used the paper that Mr. Davies gave them. She hoped it was a strong enough resonance of his energy still on it to be able to locate him. She held the paper in one hand and opened the portal with the other. It started off as small as a quarter and then grew. She stopped it when it was about the size of a dinner plate. They all stood and tried to make out where they were. Tara opened it a bit wider, and they could see a graveyard. Carla got the chills, remembering the emails that started this whole thing. People were walking slowly in a procession, and then there was a coffin with six people carrying it. They tried to look for Mr. Davies or his wife. She would be the one dressed in black. There were people playing music with instruments as they walked. Then they saw them lower the casket onto the elevator over the grave. The priest or minister started the funeral ritual, quoting from the Bible. They were listening intently to hear the name of the deceased. "The Lord is waiting to receive Danielle Gerome Davies with an open heart."

Carla looked at her mom to see her reaction, she looked sad. As much of a mystery that he was he must have a special place in the family. Tara Closed the portal. "Well I suppose that answers our questions?"

Chapter 56

Davies' Legacy

"Where are we headed to first?" Brian asked Ryan.

"Well, I figured we would go visit the police station, you know, have a chit-chat with the Officers in regards to the case and perhaps close the file on what's been happening," Ryan replied.

They walked through the front door of the police station, and a familiar face was sitting at the desk. Officer Thompson had his head down and was so absorbed in what he was reading that he didn't even hear the front doors. Brian and Ryan stood there waiting for the Officer to look up. Brian got tired of waiting and tapped the desk.

"Oh, I am so sorry, I was just reading something and believe that you may be interested in this as well, so you came at the perfect time," he said. He showed Ryan and Brian the notice.

"To whom it may concern;
Due to an unfortunate accident, Mr. Davies died Sept 12. I have sent a package along to be delivered to the family at Blackwood Manor as per his final request.

It is imperative that these parcels do not get opened by anyone except the family members that own the deed to the manor."

"I was looking at the parcels that came with it and was just wondering what could possibly be so important?" He paused. "Well, also it is strange how it is signed. If you notice, it says 'sincerely' and then a symbol."

"I was trying to look up the symbol but no luck. What do you guys think?"

Brian and Ryan looked at it. "No, can't say I have ever seen this before," Ryan answered.

"Well, no matter," Officer Thompson said. "I was going to have them dropped at the house, but seeing how you're here, you can take it for me."

"It would be our pleasure," Brian said.

"Can you take the stuff to the car, and I'll clear up this paperwork?" Ryan said.

Brian gathered the stuff up, put it in the car, and waited by the car for Ryan.

Shortly, Ryan came out with papers in hand. "Well, it's all signed off on and everything is clear," Ryan said. "I have to tell you, what a relief it is to finally put an end to this."

"Absolutely," Brian agreed.

Ryan called the house to see if anyone needed anything before they came back. "We'll have to go to the city maybe tomorrow. It can wait, and I am curious about these parcels and the symbol for a signature as well." Brian nodded his head, and away they went back to the manor. Molly assured Ryan that she had everything and there was no need to stop.

They pulled into the driveway 20 minutes later. Carla and Tara were sitting on the porch swing. They each grabbed the boxes and parcels along with the letter. The girls were curious as to why they were back so soon but glad they were.

"What's all this?" Carla asked.

"Well, that's what we would like to know too," Brian stated and handed her the letter.

"So odd," Tara said. They followed the guys into the house, and shortly everyone gathered in the living room. Tara looked at her mom.

"What? It is clearly meant for you girls," Margaret said. "Open it."

They ripped into the box. It was a fair-sized box, not all that heavy though. Inside the box was a lot of packing material. Molly saw that and ran to get a garbage bag. "Here, put it in here, not all over the floor," she said. Ryan took it from her and opened it so it was easier to put the stuff into the bag. Once all the packing was removed, they saw a small lockbox, reinforced with metal bands around it and locked with an old-fashioned padlock.

"Wow, this is really creepy," Tara said.

"No kidding. Is there something that bad they don't want it to get out?" Carla said.

"No, it's probably so not everyone can get in."

"You girls and your imagination," Margaret laughed.

"But we don't have a key," Carla said.

Tara started ripping into the parcels; there were three of them. One parcel was files and papers. Tara handed it to her father. The other parcel was full of envelopes; they all had a symbol on it. Tara took one, and Carla took another. One envelope contained a small journal and some smaller notebooks. The other one contained more of the same, but there was a smaller envelope inside, like a bank envelope for bills. In that envelope was an old skeleton key.

"This must be the key," Tara said. She tried it, and sure enough, it unlocked. There was a silence like no other as she lifted the lid open. Inside the box, there was a piece of rawhide clearly wrapping an object. Tara gave a shiver as she reached for it.

"It's heavy!" she said. She laid the parcel in her lap and unwrapped the item. It was a wand, about 7" long and about 1" thick and round. The tip was carved to a point, and there were engravings all over it. Symbols that they didn't fully understand. There were stones, colored green, yellow, purple, inlaid into the shaft of the wand as well. It was very busy with everything on it, and on the other end was a larger stone, a big bright red one, inlaid in the top. You could tell it was really old.

There was a smaller leather-wrapped object as well. Inside the wrapping was a small copper bowl with rubies, it looked like, inlaid all around the bowl. The inside of the bowl had all these different symbols carved in it.

"What is all this? What does it all mean?" Carla asked.

"I think I know," her father said. There is a letter here from Mr. Davies. It says"
"Dear Margaret, Jason, Carla, Tara, Molly, and James,

If you are reading this letter, then it is a sad day indeed. These things were given to me by your grandmother. The wand itself is something that needs to be kept and protected from getting into anyone's hands but Carla and Tara. It was Grandma's last wish. The booklets explain what the items are. She was desperate to make sure they didn't fall into the wrong hands. I have had them locked up, but once I realized what was going on, I transferred it to one of my other homes. I closed up my business and went silent for your protection. I knew my buddy Ryan would figure it out for me.

Girls, I know you think I abandoned you, but let me tell you that is so far from the truth. I was following your grandmother's wishes. Yes, and to answer your next question, I know all about your powers and the powers of your grandmother and her family. Within a couple of weeks, you will be receiving a parcel with a lot of information in it as to your heritage and bloodline. I have known your grandmother for many years, and it is through her wishes that I get to know your family and help your parents out to protect you two girls. See, you are a prodigy of a special bloodline, and your birth was predicted. I wish I was around to be able to tell you the story myself; however, sadly, I am not.

Everything that you have and will receive will explain everything, and don't forget to tell your grandmother all about it. I know you can. Well, I will say my goodbyes now, and I wish you all the best of luck from here on in.

All my love,
Davies."

There was not a dry eye in the room. "Wow, I had no idea," Margaret said, stunned. "Neither did I. It's so sad. I'm going to miss him. He was such a nice man," Molly said.

Chapter 57

Blessed Be

Molly made an early dinner, an easy one so they could all look through the stuff. Tara put the wand and bowl back in the box and locked it back up to keep it safe until they knew more about it. The papers and journals were about everything since the day Mr. Davies was given the wand. He made a daily journal for many years on the happenings and conversations with Grandma. They found it amazing that all the notes and everything were dated way back before he met Margaret and Jason. How can that be? He was only in his 40s. This didn't make sense, Carla was thinking, but didn't say anything. She didn't want another mystery—not yet. She just wanted a break for a while. She made a mental note to herself to take that up later and figure it out then.

They didn't realize the time when they were almost done reading and talking about the papers and journal entries. Everyone went to bed around 11 p.m. They all had a great night's sleep. A few days later, a couple of parcels arrived by Purolator.

"Well, it looks like a few more late nights are to be had," Molly thought as she picked them up off the porch after signing for them. The time was 8:30 a.m. Molly put the parcels down at the front door, grabbed a cup of tea, and went to the sunroom to read the paper. She thought, All is silent. I'll let them all sleep in today.

She made an entry into her journal she carried in her apron pocket. Everyone thought it was recipes she was writing down or reading because that's what she told everyone, that's what it was.

"Today is a great fall-feeling day; the sun is shining, the birds are chirping, and everyone is fast asleep. No more witches with bad tempers on the loose, and Grandma is really happy her family is safe. Grandma said it was soon time to make the big reveal; I could hardly wait. They will be surprised and bewildered but I do hope they take it well. I love them all so much and so does James. But until I hear from her again, for when I do, a new chapter begins. I Bid you fair well, dear journal. Keep my secrets safe. Blessed Be! Your beloved

Molina

End

About The Author

Tina Cooke has been crafting stories since childhood, drawing from a vivid imagination that flourished as an only child. With a lifelong passion for storytelling, Tina continues to weave captivating tales that blend reality with the fantastical. Inspired by real-life events and her own creative twists, she brings readers into worlds where the ordinary meets the extraordinary. Her writing invites you to explore the unknown, always with a touch of mystery and magic.